FOUL SHOT

FOUL SHOT

D.L. COLEMAN

Foul Shot
Copyright © 2017 by D.L. Coleman

All rights reserved. No part of this book may be used or reproduced in any manner whatsoever including Internet usage, without written permission of the author.

DISCLAIMER: This story is a work of fiction by the author, as are the characters portrayed. Any resemblance to anyone living or deceased, or to any events or other stories, real or imagined, is purely coincidental.

Book design by Maureen Cutajar
www.gopublished.com

This story is dedicated to those who bother to read it, especially those who bother to pay for it and read it. Without them all the whole thing is pointless.

ACKNOWLEDGMENTS

My gratitude to my daughter, Eugena Coleman, my prime proof reader and all-round computer person, without whose help and patience I could not do much in this life, except maybe get out of bed in the morning, because in a wired world I'm a maverick and a misfit who belongs in another time and place. Also, to Detective Ricky Mattocks of the Sampson County, North Carolina, Sheriff's Department in Clinton, who years ago, when I started to the finish of this story, was helpful with details regarding the state crime lab and medical examiner's office, most of which I haven't used but needed to know just the same. He's forgotten all that by now, I'm sure, but I haven't, and I thank him.

1

She just had to go, her killer figured of this young woman. Sure, it was sad, even tragic—and certainly unfair—but it would serve a higher good for the stronger person, also a survivor of sorts.

So who was to say it was all *that* unfair?

And it was looking easier than planned, here in the darkness, in the middle of no-damn-where, it seemed, at this construction site. Make it look at least like somebody, some derelict, surprised her when she couldn't resist coming out alone in the rain at this hour, to take a look at this wonderful real estate opportunity to invest in with all this new money she was falling into these days.

She didn't know she was about to die, so she unlocked the door so her killer could get in with her wearing a floppy hat and raincoat, the pistol in hand but hidden from view.

"I can't see a thing," she told her killer. "We should've waited till morning. Don't you think?" She said it as she looked away to the left, into the darkness, exposing the back of her head, which her killer chose at that moment as the point of opportunity, lifting the pistol and squeezing off a single round into her skull, behind the right ear. The noise was deafening, even painful in the car—should have learned more about that—not that anyone else would hear it. And the smoke was gagging, too, but a small price to pay.

The killer got out and walked the few feet to the car in front, where it had been parked after leading the victim here, and got out the gas can, came back and poured it inside, all over the seats and floorboard. Sprinkled some on the woman's clothes, too, then lit it with the lighter, closed the door and walked back to the first car, put the gas can back in. Then U-turned out of there, slowly, making sure the victim wasn't still moving.

She wasn't.

A plume of smoke rose into the air, muted by the rain. It would be morning, maybe later, before the construction crews would be back in here and saw anything.

Done. Problem solved.

2

"You know, Ames, I'm happy you called, really. And you know that. But this crap's from left field somewhere, even for me. All the people in the world, why me? Cops'll have this bonehead in the can in two days, most. You have to know that. But you call me with this bullshit and have me cussing like a brat in his twenties."

Of course this was the first call I'd gotten from her in two years, so maybe that was what bothered me.

"Wray, please, just do it for me. If you'd just known this girl."

"I don't give a rat's ass about the girl, Ames. Sorry for the bluntness. No disrespect intended to the deceased, but I didn't know her. Nice people are killed all the time and there's nothing I can do about it. It's the world we live in, just another piece of news. Besides, I'm really busy now."

"But the police won't solve it in two days, if at all. It's why I called you."

"Oh, like I can and the cops can't. So how do you know they won't?"

"Because the unknown in this thing is too big. The reason why. There is none."

"Some folks don't need a reason to kill others."

"Will you quit the bullshit and do it for me, Wray, please? Just this once," she said.

There you go, an idiot and his weakness. The way she asks for something. Brought back memories of how we were before and how two years ago she got up from the bed we shared, got dressed, and left for the new job out of state, her smell still all over me, leaving my life as quickly as she'd entered it. Not a dump job on me, exactly. It was a great opportunity and I was happy for her. But still.

"You're not listening," I said. "I'm trying to get the boat house converted over to my living quarters before fall."

"That's four months away, and you've been doing it for years."

"It takes that long, I'm a jackleg."

"Listen to you. You sound like one of those characters in a mystery novel, you know it, the part up front when the sarcastic, reluctant detective has to be begged, then dragged kicking and screaming into the case, before finally dazzling the world with his crime-solving brilliance."

"You have a slick way with words and a good sense of humor. Why you're the hot-shot news reporter and I'm not."

"So you'll do it?"

I let out a deep breath and couldn't believe myself. Correction, couldn't stand myself. "Okay, I'll go down there and consider it. No promises. I don't like it, I leave. You understand?"

"Thank you, Wray. You won't regret it."

"I already do."

3

According to preliminary reports, she died from a single gunshot wound behind the right ear. And because of who she was it was all over the news for two days now, and running. Her body, only barely burned, was found soon after death in her car, which smoldered at a deserted construction site in the wee hours of this rainy July morning, an attempt by one or more killers unknown to destroy the crime scene. To the police, her ex-fiance, with a tough guy reputation and evidence all over him like a glue trap, would be the obvious and only suspect. Case closed, one would think.

But one might be wrong, because things are not always the way they first seem.

The victim was Toni Jean Semieux, a twenty-two-year-old superstar athlete with her whole brilliant life in front of her, until someone had just stolen it.

Normally, and by choice, as a private investigator who does not like to be called a private investigator, and one who does not advertise, I would never be involved in a high profile case, especially one related to another dumb, spoiled, rich jock, for whom I have never had any sympathy. I prefer to approach the case, not the case approach me. But my former girlfriend, Morgan Dalton, called and insisted I consider this one and come down because it was different, even though it had to look just as open-and-shut to her as me, and probably would be before I got there. And when Morgan asked something of a man, most any man, and particularly *this* man, she usually got it. She was a stunning-looking woman and, at forty-two, was kept on air to hold the ratings for the local cable affiliate TV station where she worked as a reporter and relief anchor, when many her age would have been behind the camera or doing public programming by then, or out the door.

So without a whole lot of arm-twisting—okay, with joy in my heart—I put down the wine-over-ice I had just poured, got up from my chair on the pier in front of my house in Hampton, Virginia, and turned my back on the view of the busy Hampton Roads harbor, where the James River and the Chesapeake Bay meet the Atlantic Ocean, and packed my bags for the three-hundred-mile trip to Wilmington, North Carolina, if for nothing more than to make an old friend and lover happy in some way.

Okay, a little something in it for me, too.

Though she had said business only, I would be staying with her, a personal thing. That set off little bells way back in my mind. But Ames, as I called her by her middle name, at first teasingly when we met—something she did not like but tolerated from me only—was predictable only in her relentlessness to do what she set her mind to. If you were to bet on any other aspect of her personality, you could lose money. I'd discovered that the hard way, like I said. Just like that. *Wake up, it ain't you*, I'd walked around thinking for a week, then got over it. Never had long-term luck with women, anyway. My first wife left me, claimed I loved the Marine Corps more than her and my daughter, which was not true but surely must have looked like it. And my second wife, whom I loved more than life itself, died before her time, so I never expected much. Don't suppose they did, either.

I arrived at Ames' place in Wrightsville Beach in the Wilmington area at one-thirty a.m.

She was barefoot, hair down, in a short, blue terry cloth bathrobe trimmed in white, a way I always found her especially sexy.

"My, my," I said, my hand against the doorjamb. "I am an evil and lost soul with a need for salvation, and I have come to the temple to be saved by the High Priestess of *Love*."

"And you're still full of it." She laughed and threw her arms around me and squeezed hard. "Wray Larrick, you piece of driftwood." She kissed me on the neck, grabbed my hand and pulled me inside.

"Nice nautical metaphor."

"Come in. Come."

I set down my two travel bags.

The motif was simple. Real beachy. Stripes, florals, pastels, boats, gulls, shells.

"Nice place for a struggling reporter." I walked into the living room. "Excuse me, I mean *correspondent*."

"I got a break on the rent from a co-worker whose family owns it." She was going behind the counter to the kitchen. "I'll fix some coffee. I keep it around for company. You still drink the filth, don't you?"

"Of course."

We small-talked a while and it was all I could do to keep my eyes under control. There was a certain tenseness in her, which brought up the little bells again.

She opened the balcony doors and we sat opposite one another, with the warm breeze blowing in off the water, and she sipped tea.

I asked her about the Semieux girl who was murdered, what she was like, and she told me about her, where she was from and how she got to this point.

"Oh, Wray, she was such a sweet and beautiful girl. God, what a horrible thing. Of all the people for this to happen to. Why do the good always have to be the ones?"

"What about suspects? The boyfriend the only one?"

"So far, from what they tell us. John Steinmark is her ex. She didn't have a current."

"But she was seeing him."

"Off and on. They went together three years. Met in college. He went to school in western Pennsylvania. She broke off with him for good, supposedly, a few months ago. They fought too much. He crowded her. He was trying to get back with her."

"And she didn't want to, so he killed her. Case closed."

"I doubt it. I don't think he did. I know John. Not intimately, but he's no killer."

"The police will be glad to hear that."

"He loved her."

"Give me a break. Graveyards are full of well-loved women. What about him? What's he do?"

"You've never heard of John Steinmark, the football player? You know, for an old jock you're out of touch."

"They lost me with artificial turf. And a couple years ago you didn't know the shape of a basketball. So don't lecture me, just tell me."

"Let's don't argue." She took a sip of tea and reached into a pile of press photographs on the coffee table and extracted one, a picture of the victim and Steinmark, and handed it to me. "He's a linebacker with the Cougars expansion team in Charlotte."

"So they're in camp now, not that far away, and he could have killed her."

"Not exactly. He's in camp, but he rented a place here at the beach to be close to T.J.—Toni Jean. He was in town when she was killed. Sleeping, he says."

"Looks bad for him. Where was she killed?"

"Her body was found in her car on a dirt road leading into New French Fort subdivision. It's an upscale place being built down at Snow's Cut, where the bridge crosses over the inland waterway to Carolina Beach at Federal Point. Nobody lives there yet. Dark road."

"Was she robbed? Molested or anything?"

"Not sure. I heard nothing was taken. Not positive, though."

"I'd like to see the place."

"I'll show you in the morning, after we meet with Carol and Jacqui."

"*We* meet? I'd like to see it now."

"Now? In the dark? It's two-fifteen."

"She was killed in the dark, wasn't she? I'd like to see it in the dark. I can look again in the morning."

She caught the *I*. "So you can see in the dark now."

"There's a moon out tonight."

"Sounds like a song from the fifties to me."

"Cute. My car has lights. I just want to get a feel for the place. It's not closed off, is it?"

"No, but the sheriff and the state police aren't talking, either."

"Who's asking them? Cops don't give out information, they collect it."

"But I do know from John," she said, "that the police might think the mud on his tires and floor mats is the same as that on the road were the car was found. They're examining it."

"Then they don't think it's a robbery or whatever. That looks very bad for him."

"And there's a gasoline spill in the back of his Jeep. And the car was set fire with gasoline, supposedly." She was getting up now and dressing at the closet near the front door.

"All this Steinmark told you?"

"Yes."

"Doesn't he have a lawyer to tell him to keep his mouth shut?" What was this, Keystone Cops? "Jeeze, I'm going home, Ames. This is crazy."

"No, no, you can't. Look, take the money, hang around. We need you. Be patient, damn it."

There was the *we* again.

"If there was mud on his tires, were there tracks?"

"I don't know. It rained all afternoon and night and there were no clear tracks when I did my report there. John said he didn't take the car anywhere, that there shouldn't have been mud on his tires. And on the wheels and up under the car."

"Right, somebody's framing him with mud pies. We'll call in a framing specialist."

"You know, Wray, your sarcasm is a bit annoying."

I thought about that. "You're right, I'm sorry. I'm tired. Maybe I should just wait till morning."

"Great thought." She stopped short of zipping up her parka. "Can I get undressed now?"

"Can I watch?"

"The shower's down the hall. I'm sure you can find your way."

"Just sniff for water, like a camel?"

"Right. Your room is in the back, on the left, across from mine." She pointed like a school marm.

I picked up my bags and headed for the hall.

"Good night," she said, and I could tell she was relieved.

4

I showered and dried off, but knew I couldn't sleep, so I wrapped a towel around me and went into the kitchen and got out some ice cubes. This woman had wine running out her ears. No wonder I was crazy about her. I poured myself a vin rose.

It was the photographs bothering me. I had not looked at them all that closely, just the ones she'd handed me. I went to the coffee table and sat on the sofa, turned on the lamp and began looking over them. Most were eight-by-tens, in color, pictures, both candid and staged, of Toni Jean Semieux, the murdered woman, and her teammates and others in action shots and on tour. Promos and the like, some formal, some informal, behind-the-scenes, scenes of crowds.

There was a DVD disk labeled "T.J. Semieux/Shorts/Bio." I put it in the player, without sound, and turned off the lamp. At first I watched, casually, leaning back and sipping the wine. As things moved into her collegiate days, I was slowly moving to the edge of my seat, putting down the glass. I was impressed, struck by the increasing, even awesome display of talent and physical presence of the central figure and soon-to-be victim. I was transfixed by the kaleidoscope of this girl's unparalleled career chronicling her rise from obscurity to the national scene. The video was a collection of excerpts from numerous sources, some obviously amateurish, others highly professional. The games, the crowds, the flashes going off.

The awards, the horseplay, the track and field events and talk show appearances slipped in, as well, and even the visits to orphanages and children's hospitals and women's centers. The ceremony of induction into Phi Beta Kappa. Throughout the video I watched her abilities manifested and her personage grow. But the one thing that impressed me most was the permanent, consistent sense of simplicity I saw; her shy and gentle smile, her warm and giving response to those around her, the sense of humanity that seemed to radiate from her, almost god-like in its innocence, void of any hint of selfishness or egocentricity. That must have been what the fuss was all about, from what I had been hearing in the media, as little as I had paid attention to it. I could understand now how she could be held in such high esteem by those who knew her and by fans of the game of basketball, especially young girls looking for someone to worship.

But there seemed to be something else about all this, about the videos, that kept ringing the little bells. I was just too tired to think about it.

I took my drink to the balcony and looked out at the ocean, while drinking. Shortly, Ames came out.

"I couldn't sleep, either," she said.

"Maybe you have a hard time sleeping alone."

"I do alright."

"Have a boyfriend now?"

"It's not important."

"You mean it's none of my business. Is it someone special?"

"No."

"Great, I can be bumped by someone who's not special."

"I don't have time for complications right now."

"Is that what it is, complicated?"

"It's not you, it's me. It's just not a good time for me. I don't want the involvement and all that goes with it. Maybe later."

"Understood." I switched the subject. "Why in hell do you want me here, Ames?"

"The *Storms* team owners don't want to be seen sitting idly by while no one has been arrested."

"A PR thing."

"Yes, mostly."

"Why me?"

"Because I recommended you, and they're friends of mine. I started following this team last year, Wray, when they came here to prepare for getting this new league started. I know these people. True, they want to hire you for PR reasons, but I want you here because I don't think John Steinmark killed T.J. If they hire someone else, they might take the money and let the police railroad him. With you he might have a chance, especially if we work together."

"There goes the *we* again. You know I work alone."

"Take the case. I need your help here."

"For you it's all about the story, I suppose."

"That's part of it. I get exclusivity with the *Storms*."

"And other reporters, especially sports people, envy the hell out of you."

"Yes, they do."

"I don't blame them, Ames." But there was more to it than that. I studied her face in the moonlight a long moment, and she felt the look. "So how's it going at work?"

She considered it. "Is it that obvious?"

"To me it is."

"I'll be gone in a month. Terminated."

"Why?"

"Replaced with a twenty-five-year-old blond who makes me look like an ugly duckling. That's why."

"Nobody could make you look like that. I thought you were hot stuff with these people."

"Hot today, gone tomorrow, Wray. This is a take-no-prisoners business."

"So what now?"

"I'm looking. I know a few people."

"If you need to hole up somewhere a while, you can stay with me if you want. Separate beds is fine. Or you can stay with the folks. You know that."

"Thanks, but I'll be okay. I've got savings."

"Just the same, give it some thought. You don't need to call, just show up."

"I'm going to bed. Good night." She went inside, cutting off the conversation.

5

I was up at six. I exercised and took a short run on the beach, then swam in the breaking waves for the exhilaration of it. I did not like going a day without some kind of stressful workout. If I missed two days in a row, I felt sick. It was an addiction, but I was fit and felt as good and energetic as when I was a kid. There were the little hurts, of course, for someone my age, accumulated with time, the foot problem from track in high school still here, the pinched nerve in the neck from diving into a pool, the rotator cuff damage from judo practice when younger, the shoulder pain sometimes, caused by the hit I took in an ambush outside Danang, the cause of my early medical retirement from the Marine Corps. But I was lucky and thankful to be alive when a lot of others were not, so no complaints. Every day alive in the world was a gift and a reason to celebrate, far as I was concerned, and the only detraction from it were some of the sorry bastards we had to share it with. So the workouts were like a gift from heaven.

Walking back to the condo, I could see Ames beyond the dune, doing her own daily ritual. Nothing too hard, I would sometimes tease her, just something a little harder than eating right. But whatever it was, it worked because she was gorgeous and nimble, and I missed sharing that physical dimension with her. I also felt it might not ever happen again, even sleeping in the same house again.

She had not even asked if I were seeing anyone, was not showing the interest. I was almost always seeing someone. And that was a dead giveaway with its own special kind of disappointment.

I went to the steps from the outside and stood on the balcony, toweling off, while she worked out.

"Tell me about Carol and Jacqui before I meet them," I said.

She thought for a moment. "Well, Carol's the one you'll be meeting first. She's the boss of bosses. Carol Phillips Gambrell."

"Sounds melodramatic. She the owner?"

"There are others, but she controls it. Thirty-five, looks twenty-five. Petite. Short blond hair, big blue eyes. Very rich. I could shoot her." She caught herself. "Sorry. I didn't mean that.

"Anyway, she's originally from Asheville, a farm girl. She went to Duke, then did graduate work at Harvard—MBA—where she met her husband, the youngest son of the Gambrell textile family. You've heard of them."

"This is beginning to look like a celebrity crime story. You have to be famous to be involved here?"

"They were married eight years," she went on, ignoring my comment. "Two children who live with her, mostly. At a certain point, she became suspicious of him and had him followed. She caught him sleeping around, which was easy to do with him, and divorced him. Big settlement, mucho millions. Moved back home and invested in the franchise. A sweet person. Very savvy about business. Don't be fooled by the sweetness, she stings like a hornet."

"But why basketball? Was she an athlete?"

"No. She got involved the same way everyone else did. Jacqui went after her the way she goes after everything she wants. You'll meet her, too."

"They didn't know one another before?"

"No. Jacqui read about her in the paper, went to her door and introduced herself and told her what she wanted, literally. She was already a well-known coach. They became friends and that started the ball rolling."

"This Jacqui is a real tiger, I see."

"That's an understatement. She's the most dynamic person I've ever met in my life."

"Next to me."

"Of course, in your world.

"You know," she said, "she went after T.J. in the ninth grade and never let up. Visited her two or three times a year in Louisiana. Sent cards, Christmas gifts, called her hours at a time. Wooed her parents. The kid never knew it, but once Jacqui locked her into her sights, she never had a chance of going anywhere to college but Ivy Ridge University. And it was the best thing for her. Nobody, no coach, would've taken the kind of personal interest in her as Jacqui did. She was her surrogate mother.

"Did you know her own mother tried to kill her and her younger brother when T.J. was nine? Alcoholic dope head stabbed them and set fire to the house with them in it. Brother died. T.J. was pulled out by a passerby, adopted by a good family, the Fortiers. Jacqui worshipped that girl like she was her own child. They were close. She's close to all her players. They're not just ballplayers. That's how she built the championship dynasty at Ivy Ridge, and that's why there's a new pro league and she's part of it."

"She married?"

"Divorced, no children." She got up, catching her breath. "When Jacqui wants something, it's already done. It's just a matter of paperwork."

"What's she like, personally?"

"Like all winners or highly successful people in a highly visible and competitive field, a little bit of a tyrant, a whole lot of heart. I guess you could say she's kind of the Vince Lombardi of women's sports, very demanding, a bit brusque perhaps, and doesn't take no for an answer." She hesitated a moment. "I suppose if you really had to describe her by a single outstanding feature of her personality, it'd be the fact she cannot stand to lose. It's devastating to her. I mean, it really affects her. Losing T.J. is crushing. She's deeply wounded, like a mother crocodile. I almost feel sorry for the s.o.b. who killed her, when he's caught." She reached for her towel.

"And you're going to stay here and help us it the hunt. Right?"

"Where were these people when she was killed? Gambrell and Jacqui?"

"Carol was in Charlotte, the home office. Jacqui was home here, laid up with menstrual cramps. She gets them sometimes. It's the only thing I've seen that can knock her down, in fact, which is unusual for an athlete. A medical problem of some kind, I think. But she doesn't play and train now, so she gets them occasionally."

"Does she get them often? The bad cramps?"

"That's an odd question. What difference does it make? Just occasionally, I think."

"Well, you know these people, I don't."

"All I know is she had cramping that night. She was getting ill in the afternoon when I was with her."

"Does anyone stand to gain anything with the girl's death?"

She looked offended. "The *girl*? You mean T.J. Nobody. Everybody loses."

"So the kid had no enemies, no jealous teammates, according to what you told me last night, no stalkers anyone knows of. Only a jilted boyfriend who could crush her head like a melon if he wanted."

"I guess that's right. You say it so harshly."

"Were any of T.J.s relatives in town?"

"No. And everybody on the team is accounted for that night. The police have been all over the place. They still are."

"Forget about the crime scene for now. Let's get cleaned up and go see these people. You shower first."

I sat down in the padded chair and picked up the morning paper as she started inside. I caught her by surprise in a way I kidded her sometimes. "Where were you when she was killed?" I looked across the top of the paper, not smiling.

"Smart-ass." She didn't look back.

I grinned big.

6

I followed Ames out of the beach. We crossed the canal lined with boats and restaurants, took Oleander Drive, a stretch of strip malls, shopping and entertainment centers and more restaurants, to the *Carolina Storms*' temporary office. It was eight-thirty, cloudless, the sun already midday hot, and vacationers were taking control of the streets. I blended right in with them, driving my GMC SUV and dressed casually in topsiders, white stone-washed khaki slacks and navy blue golf shirt, which was somewhat a misrepresentation because I never played golf. I just liked the shirts.

"No use making an impression," Ames said before we left. "They might think you're serious." She had dressed more for work, herself, in slacks and blouse, as she was due on camera at a moment's notice, with the help of Bernie, her shooter, cameraman.

Across from the university campus on College Road, we took New Center Drive to the Regency office complex, a cluster of two-story, glass-wrapped buildings. As we entered the parking lot, we saw a crowd in front and Bernie recording the scene. He was a husky man with a short, dark beard and wore a floral print Hawaiian shirt.

It was Carol Phillips Gambrell. She was trying to get to work, while addressing a gaggle of demanding reporters and fans.

"You reporters are always the first to know," she was saying to them. "Why don't you tell me."

"There must be something you can tell us, Ms. Gambrell," someone said.

"I can tell you what the police told me, and at the present that's nothing. You know as much as I do. Now, if you'll excuse me."

"What about the reward?" another said. "There's talk of you putting up one."

"See what I mean?"

I approached the scene with Ames and noticed how calm and unthreatened Carol Gambrell was trapped against the building with microphones almost touching her face, with hardly any breathing room. She seemed poised and confident, though not necessarily enjoying the attention, a classy-looking lady, like a royal, posture perfect with eyes all on and all over her. She wore tinted glasses and a pinstripe business ensemble that must have cost as much as the annual budget of the local school system. My initial assessment was as generous as Ames', but I could see, too, she had bypassed any farm I could have imagined on her way to power and fortune in her field. I would bet, too, she never drove a tractor or slopped a hog in her life. People who could afford a Duke and Harvard education usually did not have to do those things. And I would bet that, before this, she had never had a job in her life, even at a copy machine.

"Since you brought it up," Carol Gambrell said to them, "I was going to make an announcement at this afternoon's press conference, but I'll do it now. The owners of *Carolina Storms* Basketball, Incorporated, are offering a reward of two hundred-fifty thousand dollars for information leading to the arrest and indictment of any one or more persons responsible for the death of Toni Jean Semieux."

That excited the crowd.

Ames introduced me to Bernie, who kept the camera rolling.

"Glad to meet you, Wray. She told me about you."

"All lies."

"I know, you can't trust a damn thing she says."

"Hear anything this morning?" Ames said to Bernie.

"Only that it's not looking good for Steinmark. Guys around the courthouse think he's going to be arrested any time now, probably today."

"Stick around. We'll work county-city after I finish here in a few minutes."

"I'll be right here, babe." He nodded toward Carol Gambrell. "You need to talk to her about gaining some weight. This woman's anemic. She doesn't even have a shadow. Why don't you take her a big bag of sausage biscuits and a bucket of gravy. She'll love you for it."

"Now you know why I don't eat lunch with you."

"I'd give up grits for you, babe."

"That's a lie," she said over her shoulder as she went through the door into the lobby. "You'd give up your country before you'd give up grits."

"You caught me lying again. I hate it when you do that."

Ames and I were in the elevator when Carol Gambrell finally broke loose and took the adjacent one, arriving on the second floor at the same time. We met in the hall.

"Good morning." Carol Gambrell took off her glasses. "Give me a minute." She gave me a quick once-over, as if maybe I had not had a chance to change clothes from last night or something. She went into the suite ahead of us and disappeared.

Could not understand it. Here we were in a beach resort town, in the middle of summer, and she looks at me like I'm nuts for being casually dressed. Not a good sign.

Ames introduced me to several of the office staff, including Ethel Palmer, the office manager, and showed me around. The walls were loaded with team paraphernalia; logo, pennants, photos and such, and life-size posters of the team players in action poses, including in the center that of Toni Jean Semieux dribbling a basketball full speed at the camera. I stopped to gaze.

Shortly, Carol Gambrell appeared from her office with a business smile. "You must be Mr. Larrick." She extended a hand.

"Guilty as charged. We just met in the hall. You forget already?"

"Wray, Carol Gambrell," Ames said, jumping in.

"My pleasure," Carol said. "Morgan speaks highly of you."

"She spoke highly of you, as well. A couple more people and we can form our own club and call it the Highly Spoken Of."

Ames cringed.

"Yes, well. Come into my office, Mr. Larrick. We'll let Morgan recruit members out here."

"Morgan, I'd like to meet with Mr. Larrick in private, if it's okay. But I'd like to see you as soon as we're finished, if you're going to be around." She went back into her office.

"Fine by me." Ames tugged at my arm. "Don't go in there with a chip on your shoulder."

"Me? A chip?"

The office was not at all that large, but it was not a broom closet, either, and had the best corner view. No expense had been spared in furnishing it in leathers, woods, marble, and other appointments. Not bad for temporary digs.

"Have a seat." Carol sat behind her desk in a black, tufted highback, looking like a canary in the lap of a gorilla, something one might see in a slick magazine ad rather than in a corporate suite.

She offered me coffee from the silver set on the table behind her, but I declined.

She took a sip from her cup. "Just so we understand this meeting. I'm the president of the *Storms* and we're looking for an investigator to help us in the murder investigation of T.J. Semieux. You were highly recommended by Morgan, whose opinion we trust, and you're here to discuss this possible arrangement. Is this correct?"

"Yes." I was surprised by the continued formal tone.

"Morgan told me you're the best at what you do."

"I'm pretty good in real estate, on a small scale." She wanted to roll her eyes, I could tell.

"I mean the investigation part."

"I know. Thank you, but she's being kind."

"She told me the two of you were close and lived together a while."

"That's right."

"And that you're just friends now, not still romantic."

"Yes."

"Well, we love Morgan here. She's a good and loyal friend. And you might have guessed, if she hasn't told you, we have a special working relationship with her."

"I think she mentioned it."

"It's true, we prefer her over other reporters. She's been with us from day one last year, never a bad rap, always fair, gave us coverage when we needed it. And we need that more than anything, especially now. So we're biased. She gets first crack at anything leaving this office for the time being.

"But please understand, too, Mr. Larrick," she said, leaning forward a bit for accent, "nothing leaves this office, unless I say so. We have our own public relations department."

I was now wondering what was so important about a basketball team operation that one would want a "first crack" at it.

"Accordingly," she continued, "should we offer you the job and you accept it, your loyalties and findings are to me and only me. Like I said, we love Morgan, but she's still a reporter. She doesn't need to know everything. That has to be held in perspective."

"I've always been a pretty good perspective holder," I said, taking another jab at her presumptuousness. "And I was going to tell you, anyway, that if you wanted her tailing me on this, I wouldn't be interested. And that has to be help in perspective."

Another almost eye roll.

"I'm glad we agree on that," she said. "Now tell me, she said you were a little different in the way you operate, which I won't argue with one bit. But what does that mean?"

"It means I'm not a private investigator in the usual sense. I have a license because I like to get paid when I can, and the tax people insist on it. But I don't follow people around and wait for them to come out of motel rooms. I don't do undercover work, skip-traces or credit cases, or chase deadbeat dads. In other words, I don't do snitch work. I'm more of an analyst of sorts, a researcher—something that started as a personal thing years ago—and generally don't get involved until a case is old, usually as a last resort because a grieving relative wants justice or closure, or because I'm aware of a case that's particularly interesting. So I don't work all the time."

"I see." She was still listening.

"I don't work so much in the conventional way police do. I don't have their resources. I rely on a criminal, if it's a criminal case, leaving a trail or giving a clue in his behavior, the way he does or doesn't do thing, et cetera, and it's for me to see it, which usually means the guilty party, or parties, are in the environment somewhere. Sometimes it works, sometimes it doesn't."

"So you were never a policeman?"

"No, not exactly. I was a CID—Criminal Investigation Division—clerk for a while earlier in my career in the Marine Corps. And briefly before I retired, I was with the NCIS people. But that's the extent of my experience in any formal sense."

"Well, you must be doing something right. Morgan tells me you're quite successful."

"Ames stretches it a bit. Most of my success, if you can call it that, is with the few small investments I make and disability retirement from the Corps. So I make a living, but I'm not Columbo."

"Ames?"

"Morgan. Ames is her middle name. She wouldn't like it if you called her that."

"I'll keep it in mind. You don't look disabled to me."

"I'm not. I argued with them for months and lost."

"What are your terms?" She picked up her pen.

"When I get paid, it's a thousand dollars a day." Her pen was now going back down. "That includes any running around expenses. If it's something extraneous, like travel, lab work, whatever, I bill you for it. I report to you once a day, usually, if you wish, in person or by phone or fax, whichever works best. If I can get somebody to show me how a fax machine works. I haven't used one yet. It just sounds good. But I don't take orders or direction. Nobody tells me what to do.

"I'll never ask for anything illegal, but I might get close to the edge. If I ask you for something, I expect to get it without a hassle because there's a reason for it. If my efforts result in the arrest and conviction, or conviction in absentia, of any person, or the determination by authorities of the guilt of a person who subsequently is deceased and, therefore, not tried, I get a twenty-five-thousand-dollar bonus, due on the day of conviction, or on the day of determination of guilt. If, in such a case, one is tried but not convicted, for whatever reason, I get a ten-thousand-dollar consolation bonus for bringing him that far. The two hundred-fifty grand you just offered outside, to the whole world, is included. I get that, too."

"You're an expensive man." She frowned and looked at me with something akin to contempt.

"Not nearly as expensive as a professional athlete. And what I do isn't a game."

"Nobody buys tickets to see you work, either."

"They will if I get lucky before the cops do, which isn't likely, so your money's probably safe. But I wouldn't charge them a fifty or a hundred bucks a ticket, or more, either.

"Listen." I moved forward in my own seat. "I'm not a social worker. Their office is downtown. If you can put up a quarter million dollars for information from some creep turning in his brother-in-law, you can pay me to work, without bitching. And I'll expect the quarter million if I pull it off."

She was about to protest, but I cut her off.

"Less anything paid to me at that point."

"Oh, like that's a great deal for me." She shifted in her chair. "You're abrasive."

"And you're awfully young. But I don't question your ability to run your own business, or stand in the way of your making a killing. No pun intended."

She studied me, her eyes darting around, trying to settle somewhere. "Alright, I'm offering you the job. Do you want it?"

"Yes."

She picked up her pen and made a note on her pad. "Morgan said you were a loveable smart-ass. I wouldn't know about the "loveable."

"She's the sweetest thing."

She gave a little smirk and handed me her card. "My numbers are here. Call me anytime, anywhere. I don't care what it takes or what it costs."

"Now you say that."

"Please."

"Thank you. What, if anything, have the police told you, or what do you know about the murder, so far?"

"I know nothing, except they suspect John Steinmark, her ex-fiance. They haven't told me anything, except that she was killed by a gun, a thirty-two, someone said. I think. And that there does not appear to have been any drugs or alcohol in her system, which I already could have told them about her. But they're still examining her body, I assume, since they still have her at the state medical examiner's office in Jacksonville. Otherwise, what's in the press is all I know."

"Do you have any ideas on it? Any speculation?"

"Not a thing. I'm at a loss."

"You have your own alibi, I suppose."

"Me? Yes."

"What is it?"

She looked at me as if I had a nerve asking.

"I was in Charlotte at a charity benefit." I was still waiting. "With about three hundred people, including the mayor and city council." I was still waiting. "And the police chief and district attorney, and about four judges, forty police officers and the attorney-general and lieutenant governor."

"So you can vouch for them. Think they can vouch for you?" I gave a little grin.

Her tongue was now squarely in her cheek.

"Were you in any way involved in the death of Ms. Semieux?" I was staring at her like one would a specimen, and not smiling.

"Absolutely not. Do you expect me to pay you for this?"

"Whatever it takes, whatever it costs. I'm just doing my job."

"By doing a job on me?"

"How much insurance is involved?"

She let out a breath of air. "Twenty five million." She hesitated. "About one-tenth of what we stood to earn from her over the course of her contract. And that's privileged information at this time. The police already know. It's not unusual."

"If the league survives that long, you mean. Don't get me wrong. I'm not trying to be a hard case, but everybody's a suspect. I rattle cages because I can't arrest anybody, or haul them in for questioning."

She seemed appeased somewhat but just as insistent. "And I want you to know that when I pay someone a thousand a day plus bonuses his motivation is suspect, too, until he proves himself, Mr. Larrick. And I expect that to be soon."

"Thank you. Feel confident in knowing the moment I feel useless, I'll quit. Until then, keep in mind that you called me, I didn't call you."

"You have a strange way if engaging people, Mr. Larrick. Maybe I'll just *re*call you."

"Go ahead. But I'm already on this case, and I'm going to stay on it. I can work for you and report to you, or I can work for myself and tell you nothing and owe you no loyalty, and you can get someone else."

She gritted her teeth, then stood up. "You have carte blanche inside this club, Mr. Larrick. I'll instruct my staff to cooperate with you. But please try not to rattle my players and coaches too much, as you've tried to rattle me, for whatever reason. They have enough to worry about, without dealing with the Grand Inquisitor."

"I'll try." I rose from my seat.

"Morgan's right, you are different. And your sense of humor is confusing, if not frightening."

"Where can I find your coach, Van Autt?"

"Across College Road, at the university, a couple blocks down. At the gym in the back, behind the coliseum, which is front and center of campus.

"Thanks, I can find it." I started for the door.

"Mr. Larrick." She was more pleading now, less commanding or business-like. "Please take this case seriously and help us find this no-good son of a bitch. If you'd known that girl, you'd know how I feel. How we all feel."

"Well, if the cops don't get him first—and I feel they probably will—I'll sure do what I can." I smiled. "If you'll just quit calling me 'Mr. Larrick.'"

She returned the smile, disingenuous. "Deal."

7

"How'd it go?" Ames said, when I came out of Carol's office.

"Fine. I'm hired."

"Great. You didn't wise off, did you?"

"Just a little bit."

"Why do you always do that? Treat people that way?"

"Only certain people when they need it. And she needed it."

"Where're you going?" She followed after me.

"To work. Where else?"

"Where will you be?"

"I don't know."

"Then why leave? You'll just get lost."

"Funny."

"Let's meet for lunch."

"You don't eat lunch."

"We don't actually have to eat. Call me on my cell. We'll swap notes. Okay? We really do need to work together on this as much as possible, Wray. We can help one another here."

I stopped in the hall. "How come you didn't jump on that story while ago, when Carol announced the reward?"

"That? I recorded that earlier. It's running now. I told you I have exclusivity here, in case you haven't noticed."

"Your fellow reporters must really love you."

"So what? Screw 'em."

"I'll call, okay. You get anything, you let me know."

"You've got the key," she said, referring to her place. "We'll talk tonight, if not before."

Carol Phillips Gambrell was a liar, I was thinking. Probably not by nature. By nature she seemed a very decent individual. That was my read on her anyway. And very appealing, an attractive, intelligent woman. But in this instance she was lying. I had gone into her office like a casual tourist who hadn't had his morning coffee, had been rude, unprofessional, in fact, and insulting, promised her nothing in the way of performance and charged her twice the going rate for it, and she hired me anyway. But I'd needed to know.

Me. She hired *me*. Not someone else, just *me*.

Those little bells again. You'd think it was Christmas.

So that was two of them now, Ames and the team owner, who wanted only me on the case, ostensibly, because they did not want anyone else. Apparently, Ames was suppose to have some kind of influence over me, they must have figured, which might be important if something or other might occur. In other words, a control thing, as I had already suspected. They wanted a chump. Now I would go see the coach—the other big shot—and, assuming she was part of whatever it was, she would want me to be a chump as well. Maybe I would just hang out a big shingle saying, "Wray Larrick, Private Chump for Hire. It'll Cost You, but I'm a real Dummy."

Bernie was still out front with the other press people who were camped out for whoever or whatever might come by related to the case. I chatted with him, to get to know him a little. He was about forty-five, a jovial, energetic person, seemingly intelligent, and very animated when not shooting. He had been an Army photo journalist, he said, and had freelanced since, which, in my language, meant lancing for free. He met Ames when he got the assignment to go on the *Storms'* European promotional tour. Since returning, she was doing her own filming and using him only when on camera herself.

Hopefully, she might help him get on permanently with the station here, or at another of their locations. If only he knew.

"What about Van Autt?" I said. "What do you know about her?"

"Nice looking, built well. Every man's dream, every man's nightmare. A real brassy bitch. Don't tell her I said that."

"Can't wait."

"Don't get me wrong, she's smart, a winner. And very intelligent. On the other hand, she'll steamroll over your ass and leave you in the dust like there's no tomorrow, to get what she wants. Of course, I only noticed that. I wasn't lucky enough to learn it firsthand, you understand." He grinned big.

"I'll wear a football uniform."

"Physical presence, that's what it is. Proactive lover type. Again, an assumption. She's the kind of woman you're thinking about when you're already making love to the woman of your dreams."

"Damn. Ain't nobody that hot. You'd make a great PR guy."

"I'm available."

"It must drive you nuts working around these women."

"Personally, I can't take my eyes off her when I'm around her. Not so much the looks as it is the other thing. It's kind of like you're in the jungle and there's just you and this one fascinating beast, and you're afraid to fall asleep or relax, you know. But you don't want to leave. It's always her world and you're just a nervous visitor. Yeah, that's it. That's her."

"I'm scared to death already. I'm going home. Let Marlin Perkins handle this."

We thought that was funny, invoking the name of a famous wildlife expert.

"He's already dead," Bernie said.

"That'll teach him. Got to be on a safari to meet her." More laughter.

"You're crazy, Bernie. You know it? Let's have a drink sometime."

"Anytime. I'm around." He handed me his card.

"Was Semieux everything they say she was?"

"Kid was a fantastic ballplayer, buddyro, tell you that. Knocked the crowds off their feet. Sweet kid, too. No telling how far she could've gone. That's what grabs me about the whole thing."

"You get to know her well?"

"Well, not too, you know. Of course, I was there, on the tour, took some pictures. Got to know them all a little. But I think she was the same with everybody, except Jacqui. Always seemed to have a little something she was holding back inside her. I tried to capture it in my stills. You know, the great photographer, but it didn't work. Film's my thing. Just couldn't do it. Of course, it was understandable, you know, her childhood and everything. She was good at covering up the pain, I think."

"She have any problems with anybody?"

"Grief, no, never to my knowledge. Everybody was nuts about her. You know, that kid gave up almost all her signing bonus to start a foundation to help abused and orphaned kids and start a woman's shelter."

"I didn't know that. Who's her manager or agent?"

"The only one she had, to my knowledge, according to Morgan, was Jacqui. Jacqui handled everything for her. But I think she was in the process of turning her business affairs over to a regular sports agent, you know, because it was getting to be too much for both of them. Jacqui's got plenty enough to do, anyway. Something like that. Who am I, just a camera, hired help. Nice tour, though, had a ball."

"When was the last time you saw her?"

"T.J.? I dropped in the gym last week to say hello to everybody and watch them work out. Just staying in touch. I live here."

"Know anything about Steinmark?"

"A little, not much. Only that he plays football, a bad-ass. Went with T.J. I never met him, just saw him once."

"What's your view of Morgan? Between you and me?"

"I call her 'the morgue' sometimes because she's so deadly serious about work. I like to have a good time, myself, when I work. You must've been nuts to let her go."

"Actually, it wasn't my decision."

"That's one big comprende. She's a real independent-minded lady. You could have tied her up and put her in a closet, maybe."

"Can I ask you something? I'm asking everybody. Where were you when the murder took place?"

"In Raleigh, at a press association meeting. Morgan called me there to come back and shoot for her. I flew down I-40. Hell, yeah, I'll shoot for her."

"Listen, a hypothetical. Say the police already know who killed Semieux—and they might at that—and they aren't saying who it is. But you know they're about to arrest somebody. You go down to the station to cover it. Who do you really expect to see there when they bring him in, if anybody? Gut feeling?"

"Steinmark."

"Why? You never knew him."

"But I know his record. The guy's been arrested a half dozen times since high school for hurting people. A real violent type, I hear. Steroid freak."

"But you really think he might have done it? Guy like that wouldn't need a gun."

"No, but a guy like that knows what gasoline will do. He was a chemical engineering major in college, they say. And there was a gas spill in her car, I hear."

"Chemical engineering majors aren't the only ones who know that gasoline will burn something. So he's violent and no dummy."

"Deadly combination, buddyro. And T.J. had been smelling a gasoline odor in her car for days."

I had not heard that his car had a gas odor, too, like Semieux's own vehicle. "He'd have to be awfully dumb, though, to burn that car and leave a gas spill stinking up his own car.

"Thanks, Bernie. Be talking to you. The first drink is on me."

8

Wilmington is one of those towns that probably was overlooked by most of the world for much of its history. A quaint, sleepy port with long, beautiful beaches and a smattering of ancient magnolia and Spanish moss, a winding river vista ideal for painters and water colorists. It is a smaller version of Charleston or Savannah, but with modern conveniences. People find it by mistake, fall in love with it, and don't go home. Kind of like Williamsburg, Virginia, They sell off their possessions and give up lucrative careers and take drastic cuts, even leave marriages and become unemployed, just to be there. It does that to one. It is the great treasure of the east coast only recently discovered. Traffic is heavy but it moves. The pace is casual but you get there, the atmosphere friendly, if not disarming. The economy reasonable but rising rapidly. And nobody is leaving.

The threat to this suburban-like paradise—there is no larger city near it—is the simple charm, evolving popularity, and the omen of death by word of mouth. And on the flip side, the fact it lies smack in the middle of the great Atlantic hurricane corridor. Storms getting this far north go to it like a magnet. The great hurricanes of legend have paid visits here and left their marks. The waters can be treacherous. The river region, itself, is called the Cape Fear. So it was understandable and fitting, when the new women's professional basketball system started, that the Carolina franchise, in Charlotte, would want to practice here until its arena was built. And adopting the name *Storms* would reflect a readily identifiable force to be reckoned with on a regular and periodic basis.

And the person most responsible for the formation of not just the team but the league, from germinal dream to reality, was Jacqueline Van Autt, the *Storm of Storms* herself, team coach and vice-president, as Ames had informed me. According to fans and others who follow these things, I was supposed to be flattered and shaking in my knees at the prospect of meeting this woman in person. But because I did not follow these things, nor worship athletes, her name was only vague and recently familiar. I was hoping she would not be the third person in a row looking for a fool, and help me get started on the case. If she was, I'd seriously have to question my intelligence and how the world perceived me. Because the fault likely would have to reside somewhere in my own deficiencies, and not just in their perceptions.

I turned off busy College Road onto the campus of the university and immediately into another world, almost like a Twilight Zone effect but not spooky. It is sprawling in its own way—looks bigger than it is and growing—pristine acres of tall long leaf pines forming a canopy over dignified and unpretentious brick colonial buildings symmetrically arranged and stretching out un-crowded and uncluttered. And quiet. Very quiet with but a few summer semester students about. Wait till night, I was thinking.

I went to the gym, where the team was practicing.

The woman clearly in charge could only be Jacqui Van Autt, pointing, yelling commands, and people on the court reacting quickly to her every gesture. And she was as attractive as Bernie had promised. Or warned. Not in the typical beauty queen way, but the other way, the one that evokes carnal images in a man's mind. It is always a treat for a man to look at an attractive woman. And when she is in motion it is even more special. And I looked. She was about five-nine or so, I guessed, well-proportioned, tanned and athletically toned, strong. I looked for the masculine edge, the hormonal imbalance one tended to automatically expect in a female super jock or coach, but it wasn't there. Good. But she wasn't dainty either. She was in shorts and pullover and there wasn't a thing that reminded me of any of my buddies. Her dark hair was pulled back in a ponytail and a whistle hung from a cord around her neck. It occurred to me that a woman like this could hurt a man's feelings.

I noticed the uniformed security guard, a hefty man with a mustache, who was also busy looking, except he seemed unable to make up his mind which woman he liked best. An obvious and funny sight. Some guys are just hogs.

The guard saw me and immediately approached. I explained who I was. He seemed a friendly sort.

"Yeah, they called from the office about you." He gave his name as Ken Enright. "Anything I can do, just let me know."

"You work for them all the time?"

"My company assigns one or more of us to them while they're in town. But not permanent, no. Not full-time."

"Exactly what is your assignment?"

"To be here when they start arriving for practice and keep people away from them and out of the gym. And stay here till they've all left. To keep people away from them when they leave."

"Just here? You don't go anywhere with them?"

"Well, if there's a function or something where they all go together on a bus, maybe. I went to Myrtle Beach last week. Three of us did, a promo trip."

"But these kids are rich, some of them," he said. "They drive their own cars most places, or fly. It's not like hauling around a bunch of high schoolers. These girls ride first class. You see all those expensive wheels in the parking lot? They don't belong to me and the janitorial staff."

"When was the last time you saw T.J. Semieux?"

"The night she died. Hours before. Right outside where her and coach Van Autt were leaving, after practice."

"They left together?"

"No, they came out together. We were out in the parking lot. I was out there first to make sure nobody was around to bother them.

Nobody was, not a soul. Usually, there's people out there trying to take pictures or get autographs or something. But the coast was clear. It was raining off and on, must've been. They walked out together and talked a minute or two. I talked with them some. And they got in their own cars.

"If the kid had listened to her coach she'd still be alive now," he said.

"Why's that?"

"Like I told the detectives, when they came out the coach was telling her not to get in the car, but to call the dealer and have them pick it up and leave a loaner, or whatever it took. She was suppose to be taking it to a dealer, I think. But not to get in it because of the gas leak. She even asked me to come over and smell the leak and help convince the kid not to drive it."

"Did you smell it?"

"Yeah, there was a gas smell, alright."

"Did you see where the gas was coming from?"

"No."

"See any gas on the ground under the car?"

"No, too much water from the rain. And I didn't get down on the ground to look under it."

"Did she drive it away from here?"

"Yes, she did. The coach said if she felt she had to drive it, at least have somebody go with her later on and take it to the dealer's, but not go alone. But the kid went anyway."

"Wonder why the coach couldn't have given her a ride to the dealer's then?" I was thinking out loud.

"She said she wasn't feeling good, had to go to bed. Said she didn't have the time to drive to the opposite side of town to the dealer's. But she could drop her off at one of the other players' places, or she could come home with her, the coach."

"Do they ever use the other gym, the one up front?"

"Sure. Sometimes, but they mostly stay back here in the old gym."

"Let me ask you something. Just between us. I won't say a thing, so speak freely. Let's say the police know who killed her and they've arrested somebody, and they're offering a million-dollar reward to the first person to guess correctly who it is. What's your guess? Who is it?"

Enright thought about it a second. "Heck, I don't know, some nut case, I guess. Unless it's the boyfriend. They suspect him, I hear. But I'll take the million bucks anyway, if I can get there first."

"Where were you when she was killed?"

The friendliness dropped from his face. "Well, now, since I don't know exactly what time she was killed, only approximate, I couldn't really answer that. Could I? But I was helping my neighbor and his brother with their race car most of that night, after I got off."

"I believe you. I just have to ask."

The whistle blew on court and the practice stopped.

"They're finished," Enright said. "I'll tell her you're here, but you'll have to wait a couple minutes. This reporter over here is scheduled to interview her first. It's only suppose to take a minute or two. Poor guy's been chasing her a week. You don't mind waiting your turn, do you?" He was enjoying doing the asking.

I walked to a bench on the side and sat and waited. I watched the team managers gather up the equipment and begin leaving. Then it came to me. The smell of the gym, the echo sounds of walking on the hardwood floor, balls and doors and things banging around. The kind of noise that scares a kid to death when he hears it on his first visit inside one of these places where his manhood is challenged, his ego threatened by the violence of bullies and the fear of facing himself. The same noise which, with time and rising confidence, becomes as sweet as a mother's lullaby, in a place that becomes womb-like in its comfort, a place one never wanted to leave, and a place one could never go back to. It now dawned on me, and impressed me, that I was in the midst of some of the finest athletes in the world, and that everyone but I had known this. And for a moment I felt, as a kid might feel, awe-struck around larger-than-life stars.

I studied each one of the players as she left, trying to guess who might be the fastest, who probably the best jumper, best shooter, by their body types and movements. I listened for the names I might identify later, should I hear them on TV or bantered around. After all, I had been a jock all my life, organized and later unorganized, a track and football man, even making the Redskins as a receiver between tours in the Corps, though I had been cut early. And I still practiced martial arts, so I knew what it was like to work and sweat and sacrifice quietly and unnoticed for something you love. I knew I was in the presence of sports goddesses just being born who were very much being noticed, some of whose names were becoming household words already. I could get a lot of mileage out of this with the folks around the coffee shop back home.

I noticed, too, all the players wore little teddy bear patches on their uniforms, a good luck symbol, as Ames had told me, the toy bear T.J. Semieux's baby brother, Buddy, carried around before his death by arson at the hands of his mother. That brought me out of my little dream state, just as Van Autt left the interview and walked over to me.

"So you're Wray Larrick?" She smiled and extended her hand.

"Don't blame my parents. It was an accident." I shook her hand.

"I'm Jacqui Van Autt. Morgan's told me about you. I'm glad you're here." She waved a finger. "She warned me about your sense of humor. I feel like I know you already."

"Don't judge prematurely, you might come to hate me."

"I'm sure you're not that bad. Come on, we can go to my office, where we can talk."

She led me into the lobby and around the side hallway to a small, cozy if not cluttered and temporary place for use when at the gym. Her official, more formal digs were back at the Regency, next to Carol Gambrell's, she said.

We small-talked a minute. She wiped the sweat from her face and blew at a sprig of hair on her forehead. She was amiable enough, but I was looking for that Nazi Bernie had warned me about. Frankly, her strength came across warmly. We were instantly comfortable with one another, so it seemed, and easy to get on a first-name basis.

"Jacqui, let's talk about this thing a little bit and see if I can get oriented and find a place to start here.

"And, please, tell all your players, since I'll be talking to them, they don't have to worry about me. I work for the *Storms*, so I'm not a cop. I can't arrest anyone. I just do research, you might say. I probe around, and some of the things I say or ask might seem bazaar, or weird. It's just the way I approach things."

"Yes, Morgan told me you have a peculiar way of working."

"Am I correct in what I hear, that Ms. Semieux had no enemies, no stalkers, to anyone's knowledge, no conflicts with anyone, past or present?"

"That's right. Nothing that would have caused something like this."

"Would she have been vulnerable to a stranger getting into her car, or having her car door unlocked?"

"Absolutely not. T.J. was extremely cautious that way. That's what's so odd about it. Unless someone was at the dealer's and surprised her when she pulled up to drop off the car."

"She didn't drop off the car when you two left here. Did she? Actually, she went home or somewhere, intending to drop it off later but never did. She might've gotten to the dealer's, but she never dropped it off."

"Yes, that's right. Obviously, I didn't talk to her after she left here. I feel so guilty. If I'd just called one of the other girls or coaches to go with her, or gone myself, no matter how I felt, this wouldn't have happened."

"Maybe. Don't kick yourself. There was a mistake made somewhere. Obviously, it wasn't yours. Ms. Semieux was careless somehow or other. Or completely surprised by someone for some reason other than robbery."

"That doesn't make me feel any better."

"I understand. Do you think there's the slightest chance she had an alternative lifestyle or secret association with anyone or anything?"

Jacqui was already moving her head no. "No way. That girl was under my personal watch the moment she came to Ivy Ridge four years ago, except when she was home with her family. Impossible.

She couldn't keep anything from me. She wouldn't want to. Toni Jean was like my own daughter."

"What's your best idea of who might have done it?"

"Well, it's not John Steinmark, if that's what you're thinking. That's for sure. I'd never believe that."

"Everyone so far seems to think maybe it is."

"I know. I think they're wrong. I know John. And I can tell you right now that Toni Jean never would have gone with him in the first place if I hadn't approved of him."

"That's a lot of influence."

"That's why my girls perform well and don't get into trouble." She caught herself. "Well, they never have before. And they won't again.

"I know John's past," she said. "I know he's been violent. But he's never been accused of hitting a woman. It's always been other men he's had scrapes with. He never touched Toni Jean. Ask anyone. If he had, he'd have been the one hurt because I would've hurt him myself. Or any man who lays a hand on one of my girls."

"So from the time you left here that night, around six-thirty or seven, until she was killed at about eleven or twelve midnight, as I understand it from Morgan, that's anywhere from four to five hours she was supposedly alone."

"I guess so."

"And you were home. Right?"

"When it happened, yes. I was there the whole night."

"I suppose the police, the sheriff, asked you about all this."

"Oh, yes. I told them I was home then, in bed. And that my car was in my parking place, until I got the call about, well—."

"Yes. Yes, of course." I cut her off, as I could see the pain in her face. "If you don't mind, what was it you were ill from?"

Her eyelids flew up. It must have seemed an odd question, and I already knew what the answer was suppose to be.

"PMS. Premenstrual pain. Cramps. I have them sometimes, now that I'm not a player and don't train regularly."

"Sure." I waved it away as if sorry for even asking.

I shifted in my seat, uneasy, trying to find a way. "Look, this is a little odd. In fact, it's very odd, and I admit it. But sometimes the dumbest questions come to me at the worst possible times for no apparent reason. But later on they usually make sense in some way, even if it's something unimportant." She was canting her head quizzically. "So I'm going to ask you this dumb question and we can both wonder why. Okay?"

"Sure."

I leaned toward her. "You say you get these menstrual pains bad sometimes. Not all the time but sometimes." She was nodding cautiously. "Is your menstrual cycle regular? I mean, it's at the same time you expect each month?"

Her eyes squinted. "That is an odd question."

"I told you. I feel like an idiot. But the reason will come to me later, I'm sure. Jeeze, I hope it does, so I can run and tell you." I leaned back in the chair.

"Now I know what Morgan meant when she said you were different. Yes, my period is like clockwork, even if it isn't a long one."

"It's always good to follow up one stupid question with another one. This gives the person asking the stupid questions time to look for a rock to crawl under for asking the first one, or in this case a rug, since we're indoors."

"I can't wait."

"The women on your team, the players and coaches. I mean, to the extent you would know it, are they all regular with their cycles, as well? I mean, have any trouble or anything?"

Her left eye squinted but the brow lifted. Never a good sign.

"No, I don't think they have any trouble along these lines. The players anyway. Not sure about the coaches."

"I can understand your knowing about the players because it might affect their performances in some way, maybe."

"That's right, when and if it does."

"Okay, end of stupid question time. I guess what I'm trying to do is find something that can be common to all or most of you on the team. I don't know, a virus, a condition or something that might impact one's judgment differently, something that might have caused Ms. Semieux to make a bad decision where others might not. Something. Anything. I'm reaching."

"Like a man. Yes, that's—Yes, that's reaching. But I understand, Wray. Just keep reaching, you'll grab something, I'm sure." She blew at a sprig of hair again.

I could not help the urge to laugh, and she could not help appreciating it.

"Sorry, I didn't mean for it to sound like that."

"Actually, you're kind of charming, in a weird way," she said.

"Thank you. I'm usually threatened after such questions."

"I can't imagine why."

"Is there anything at all you'd like to say, any guess you might have, a hunch or whatever about this thing?"

"I'm completely stunned by it. I haven't had time to think about who or what or why. I'm blindsided. I've got so much to do for this season coming up. I haven't even had time to grieve properly, something else I feel guilty about. It must look selfish of us. We're dribbling a ball and she's still lying in the morgue. I don't sleep well."

"And you don't think it's Steinmark?"

She hesitated as if unsure this time. "I don't like to think that. I just don't see it. I know it looks bad for him. And I suppose it's possible. But—No. No, it can't be him."

"Look, you knew this girl better than anyone in the world, except maybe her parents. In fact, you were with her more than her family the last four years. You watched her grow. She didn't make a move without you, as I understand it. She loved you. And I know you loved her. She was special to you. So if there was anything, ever how miniscule, about her behavior, her condition, her anything, you would've noticed it if no one else did. So think about it. Something. Anything."

"Wray, I'm sorry. I—I just don't know what to say. I'm no psychic. I can't tell what nut case might be out there doing this." Her eyes were narrowing.

"I'm sorry. I don't mean to be pushy."

"No, it's okay. Maybe I should just break down and let it all out and scream and kick and curse until it stops hurting." She took a deep breath and let it out. "But, unfortunately, I don't have that luxury right now. Maybe after the season. I'm too busy to weep and be human now. The game goes on. This is big business, not rec league. I'm expected to function, regardless."

"How did you feel about Ames—Morgan, I mean—recommending somebody like me for the job, as opposed to someone local, or a big agency, a regular private investigator?"

"You're not a regular investigator? I thought you were. I agreed wholeheartedly with it. And so did Carol. As a reporter, Morgan's had experience with investigators before. We haven't, at least not in a criminal sense. So when we decided to hire someone, she insisted it be you. And I hope we're right. And I hope you're an investigator. You are, aren't you? Don't tell me you're a truck driver."

"Hardly."

"Good."

"I appreciate your confidence. You have a lot of confidence in Morgan, too. Don't you?"

"Yes, I do. She's very rare for a reporter. She's honest and trustworthy. That's more than I can say for a lot of them."

"How do you feel about her wanting to work on this thing with me?"

"I know Carol will tell you to keep her out of it, if that's what you mean. And I'm not going to say anything to contradict that. Not officially anyway. But Morgan knows everybody here, she knows the league. Some bastard killed Toni Jean, and let's just say it would be a shame to waste Morgan's input, or anyone's, when they might be able to help. As long as nothing goes out to the public without Carol Gambrell's approval. You make that mistake and you'll both be out of here."

"Roger." I got up and went to the window and looked out and spoke over my shoulder. "I understand Ms. Semieux put up most of her signing bonus to form a charitable foundation."

"Yes, that's true, three million dollars."

"Who manages it?"

She hesitated, her eyes locked on me. "Right now I and Maurice Fortier, her father," she said, cautiously. "And her priest, and a lawyer friend of her family in Louisiana make up the board. But I'm getting out of it. It's just too much to handle."

"Her family have any insurance on her you know of?"

"I don't know. If so, I'm sure it's not much. Maybe enough to, well—. You know, if you're thinking anyone in her family had something to do with this, forget it. Those people aren't like that. They're the salt of the earth. Please don't bother them with this."

"That's what I hear. Did any of them come up?"

"Maurice and the boys came up immediately. Poor souls. They were destroyed. But they were told they didn't know when the body would be released, so they went back. I can just see them now, especially Maurice, worrying himself sick, eating his guts out." She looked hard at me. "Don't let anyone here think you're even insinuating a member of her family had anything to do with her murder, especially me. Leave them out of it. They're very special people, and sensitive. They've got enough to worry about. They're like my own family and I don't want them hurt in any way."

"Oh, no." I turned back toward her. "It's nothing like that. I'm not going to bother them." I smiled at her. "Not if it means having to deal with you about it."

"And don't humor me. I don't need it."

"Whatever you say."

"And I'd like to be kept informed of your progress, if that's okay."

"You must know I was hired by Carol Gambrell with the proviso I report strictly to her alone. You might want to ask her about it first. Have her call me."

"And you must know that if I turn a blind eye to Morgan's working with you against Carol's wishes, I expect something in return. At least a little respect."

"You asking me or telling me? I'm working alone."

"I'm telling you that you are here in the first place because of me, not Carol, and you can be gone because of me. Carol's the boss, but don't ever fool yourself about what I can or cannot do around here."

"And don't ever think I'd be gone because you might want me to be. I covered that with Carol.

"What's in it for me to violate a trust with my employer to appease you?"

She rose from her chair. "I'm your employer, too. Look, this is driving me nuts. I can't just sit back and be out of the loop. I loved Toni Jean like my own child, for God's sake. Give me a break, will you. I want that bastard who killed her more than anyone. *Me. I* do. *I* want him. What the hell do you care, or anyone else for that matter? Nobody cares like I do."

"I know you do. You're vice-president and a board member. You'll have to be informed. But it'll have to be by Carol. The way you people run this office is your business. Keep it to yourselves, I don't give a damn.

"Look," I said, "we just met and we're already arguing. It's unnatural. Maybe I just affect people that way. So I'm sorry. I promise to be civil if you do."

"We can do that another time, Wray. I have things to do now, if you don't mind. This meeting is over." She opened the door for me. "It's been very nice meeting you. I think."

I started for the door and stopped close to her face. I could smell her sweat, feel her body heat. I stared into her eyes. "And I think we ought to talk again real soon. I'll do whatever I can for you if it doesn't compromise my loyalty to whoever writes the checks." I gave a little smirk. Couldn't help it.

"Well, while you're thinking about checks, think about this one: I'm adding a hundred thousand dollars of my own money to the quarter million already offered as a reward."

"I'm sorry I have that affect on people. I think that's very interesting. Awfully noble of you."

"Well, oh mighty one for whom the checks toll. Then get your ass out there and find the killer." She slammed the door in my face.

I checked to see if my nose was still there.

Bernie was right. I turned from the door, mumbling. "That's a tough woman. Ain't going to fall asleep around her."

A few steps away I heard the door open.

"Wray, I'm sorry. Please forgive me." She approached me. "This is all more than I can handle. Please don't tell Morgan how badly I just treated you. I'm so sorry. She'd never forgive me."

"It's okay. I can take a beating sometimes. It's not your fault."

She places her hand on my forearm and squeezed firmly. "Let's do talk again. Maybe we can have a drink. Tonight, if you can."

"I think that would be a good idea."

"Anytime after nine." She gave me her number and address. "And I'll talk with everyone to set it up so you can interview them as you wish. Maybe starting tomorrow."

Or starting when I say so.

I sat in my car in the parking lot thinking about this weird meeting that just transpired between us. There were three of them now who were madly in love with my detection abilities. Only two of them wanted Ames sticking close to me, Ames and Jacqui. So it seemed the three of them knew something together, but only two of them knew something else. And I did not know any of it. What a mess.

Whatever it was they were holding among themselves, they weren't giving it up. Maybe it was important to the case and maybe it was not. Maybe it was just a smoke screen for still another thing. They had to know I was not dumb enough to wonder, but they were stonewalling anyway. I did not want to confront them right away with it, whatever it was. Sometimes you learned more if you kept quiet and waited, like a dummy. But I would have to keep Ames close, keep her at bay and still use her, if I could pull it off. She was no dummy, herself. But there was a picture now forming in my mind, ever how hazy, and at least I had a place to start. If they thought I asked the oddest questions, they hadn't heard anything yet. I would ask Ames the next one.

9

I turned left out of the campus and headed south on College Road through heavy traffic and cramped, over-developed roadsides of restaurants, spot malls, shops, offices, and more restaurants. I dialed Ames.

"I'm out front, at the sheriff's office," she said. "Where are you?"

"I just crossed Oleander heading for Snow's Cut. Can you meet me at New French Fort?"

"It'll take at least thirty minutes. I have a quick spot to do on air first."

"Anything happening there?"

"They're still pulling people in like crazy down here. Anybody with a violent record, looks like. Lawyers Row around the courthouse is loaded, no parking places. And just found out the soil on Steinmark's wheels and floor mats matches that on the road to New French Fort. Apparently, they've known that from day one. They just brought him in for questioning again."

"Who'd you say his lawyer was?"

"I didn't, but it's Loomis Sullivan. The best criminal lawyer in the area, they say."

There was something familiar in the name. "How about asking Mr. Loomis Sullivan, a turnip at law, if I can talk with Steinmark sometime today, assuming he's available. Can you do that?"

(47)

"I'll ask him for you. This mean we're working together, no holding back?"

"I guess so." Or I guess not. "Just don't make it obvious. If Carol finds out, I'll be canned."

"I'm on the air for a live update in two minutes. Bernie's staying here. I'll have him talk to Sullivan when he comes out, or I'll call his office if I have to. See you there, but I can't stay long. I've got to get back."

I took the last left, just before Snow's Cut, the entrance to the Intra-coastal Waterway leading over into Carolina Beach, and pulled into the dirt road to New French Fort, where the body was found. I was not aware the French were ever up this far in any appreciable way, or that there was an old French fort, but here was a new one. Just another tacky name by some real estate developer to make potential buyers feel they'll be living somewhere apart, but not out of sight, from the rest of the world with their imagined wealth and pretending they have always been that way. This would be the kind of place where parents named their children after soap opera characters. The curbs were already installed and ran for a hundred yards before homes appeared under construction. Pines and myrtle, magnolia and honeysuckle, palmetto and moss lined the roadsides and lots and blended with the scent of the ocean. People were going to pay big to live here. Always thinking real estate.

I got out of the car, walked around and waited for Ames.

The murder scene had been cleared. I asked a passing plumber where it had been. Any remains of it were gone forever, but he had seen the spot, at least, and was not a forensic expert anyway. With woods set back on either side, this must have been one of the darkest places on earth that night in the rain. No way one could come here by mistake. One could barely come here on purpose under those conditions. This was the kind of place, too, jacklegs came to steal building materials and equipment, or teenagers came to have sex. I used to go to the graveyard myself to make out, when I was a kid. Safest place in the world.

Perhaps Semieux had been scouting the property, maybe considering buying a lot or something, or was meeting someone here, and was surprised by one or more thieves who killed her.

It was forty-five minutes before Ames arrived.

"Sorry it took so long." She got out of the car. "Tell me, what do you think, so far."

"I think it's both a very exciting and scary feeling being in an environment of beautiful, powerful and wealthy women, none of whom seem to need me."

She liked that. "Not so comfortable when you're not in charge, is it?"

"It's like being a kid in a candy store with no money."

"Just like you."

"Did you see this spot before?"

She pointed. "Yes, I did my report from just over there, but I couldn't get close enough until the car had been taken away. They wouldn't let anyone near it."

"How'd they know she was out here?"

"Somebody saw the flames from the road and called nine-one-one on a cell phone. Unidentified."

"You haven't seen the car up close then?"

"No. Like I said, it was roped off when I got here. And then they towed it away later, before daylight, and impounded it. It's still impounded."

"You think maybe Bernie can find anything on it? I mean, this is his hometown, isn't it? He ought to know somebody."

She stared at me, something on her mind.

"What?" I said. "What is it?"

"Don't you think we need to discuss what kind of working relationship we have here, before you start issuing requests like I was your personal aid or something? I mean, I have a job, at least for the time being, thank you."

"Hey, I'm just trying to make use of whatever resources we both have, that's all. Don't get so sensitive on me."

"Oh, don't complain, just do what I'm told. Sure, anything you say, boss."

"You're the one who wants to work with *me*. I didn't ask for your help. I'm risking my job by doing it and you know it. What did you expect to contribute to the effort, besides your shadow following me around for the story?"

"Like hell, follow you."

"Then let's cooperate."

"We share everything. And that includes legwork. You ask me for something, I ask you for something."

"Terrific." I was unable to hold it any longer. "Let's start with you telling me why the three of you want me so badly for this job. And don't tell me it's because I'm such a damn genius."

"What? I recommended you. I told you. Aren't you at least a little appreciative I did this? This is a big case, Wray, and I had the presence of mind to think of you first. I put my reputation for judgment behind you, so don't make me look bad."

"How bad will it look if I go to Carol and tell her you and Jacqui are having you to stick to me like a rash?"

"Don't do that."

"So you three are conning me by keeping a secret of some kind, and you and Jacqui are conning Carol by keeping this from her. What a brilliant arrangement. Did you really think I was dumb enough not to notice?

"Sorry," I said. "You want to play hardball with me? The buck stops here. You either tell me what's going on, or I'll turn you in to Carol and work this case for myself and tell nobody anything but the police."

"There's nothing, I swear."

"You're lying."

"If there's anyone keeping anything from you—and not that there is—then it's something unrelated to this case and, therefore, none of your business."

She turned to the side, uneasy.

"I'm waiting," I said.

She did not move.

"Fine, I'm leaving." I was bluffing. "Maybe I'll get something done on m own." I started for the car.

"Please."

I stopped and looked back. "Say again."

"Damn you. What do you want me to do, crawl? You want to cut something out of me? You want me to betray a trust to my friends so you can know every damn thing about their personal lives? No, I won't do it."

"You're way too close to these people, Ames. They're suppose to be a story to you, not a family."

"You're right about that. One reason I'm being let go, the unpardonable sin of getting too personal with my source.

"So what are you going to do, gloat?" she said. "Go ahead, gloat. Say you expected me to fall flat on my face, that I deserve it for leaving you. That I really don't pack the gear, as you would say. That it was inevitable I'd be washed up before ever getting dirty."

"Actually, it hadn't occurred to me to say that at all."

"What do we do from here, Wray?"

"What we do is you tell me what you're hiding from me."

"What there is or isn't being kept from you, as I've said, would have nothing to do with this case or story. What I might or might not have, I might have promised friends and sources I wouldn't reveal. And I won't break a promise, even if it means losing everything. What kind of journalist would I be then? Who would want me? I wouldn't break a promise to you, and I certainly won't break one to them. So you'll have to make up your mind without it."

"I don't think your career goals hinge on whether or not we work together. I'm not that valuable to you. I just think it's part of your walking on two sides of a fence and hiding your little secret, trying to satisfy yourself and your friends, too. No wonder you're in trouble.

"But I don't need mind games, either. So I'll tell you what I'll do. We'll consider it a level playing field from here on if you like. You keep your little secrets, I'll keep mine. You don't ask me any whys and I don't ask you any. But if I ask for help, I expect to get it. Remember, you're claiming to need me. I don't need you at all. Not trying to be nasty, but that's the way it is."

"And everything you find that would go to the media comes to me first, exclusively, before any other media. It's my story."

"Assuming you've helped me. After Carol gets it."

"Carol. Of course. Okay, deal."

"Frankly," I said, "I think the police will wrap this thing up today or tomorrow and we'll both be finished. Sorry, I don't mean to use the word *finished* around you." Trying for a little humor.

She stared like she was looking right through me. "I think you're crazy. I've always thought you were crazy."

"When you get back, do this for me: get me an appointment with Steinmark and his attorney, if you can. Even if he's in jail. Tell his lawyer, for what it's worth, I don't think Steinmark is guilty, and anything I might find that might help him I'll let him have. It won't cost him a cent. But I'll expect him to talk to me. Free private eye service. He should like that."

"So you don't think he did it either?"

"I don't know anything now. I'm just scrounging. I haven't met him. Also, do you know if anyone associated with the *Storms* has looked at this place or considered buying into it?"

"Not that I know of. But I don't know everybody's personal business."

"I think we just finished arguing about that. Was there a guard on duty here the night of the murder?"

"No. That I know of. No guard."

"Okay, fine. Now, what about Enright, the guard at the gym? What do you know about him?"

"Very little. He's just a guard. He's polite, does his job, I guess. Just guards, that's all." She shrugged.

"And looks at women like a cat looks at a cage full of parakeets."

"Well, yeah, I guess you could say so. And you don't?"

"Strictly business. I just got here. My eyes haven't adjusted."

"Yeah, right."

"Ask Bernie if he can find anything on him. Be careful, though, this is still a small town. He might be his cousin."

"Ain't that small. You have an awfully suspicious mind."

"That's why I do this and you do reporting."

"Oh, excuse me, of the lower realm."

"You know what I mean. Listen, there's something else I've got to have from you. This is very important to me. And don't ask any questions, just do it for me. Okay?"

"I'm not having sex with you, Wray."

"*Sex*? Who in hell said anything about sex? Who's mind is in the candy store now? Are you suddenly happy or something? Because I don't get it."

"No, it's nothing."

"Alright, here's what I want. I want to know when the *Storms* team players—just the players—have their monthly periods."

She looked at me. "You are nuts. I knew it."

"I want to know, to the woman, if she is regular, or has her period and when it is, how long it lasts. Except Jacqui. I've already asked Jacqui. Don't mention it to her. I don't want her to know." Fat chance.

"You asked Jacqui that?"

"I sure did."

"My god. How did she react?"

"The way you're reacting now. Look, you can tell them anything. Tell them you're helping some old nutty professor gather data for a study of some kind, menstrual cycles of athletes, whatever."

"I can't go to those women and ask those kinds of questions."

"And you think I can? They'll understand. They're a bunch of brainy people who thrive on that kind of stuff, because they've spent their entire lives in school. They'll run around waving their arms in the air, saying, 'A study! A study! Oh, my gracious, a study! Everybody listen up! Rattle your Phi Beta Kappa keys! All together now!'"

"You're insane. Why do you need this?"

"No whys, remember. How long have these women been with Jacqui?"

"Most of them since they got out of college last year and the recent year. A couple have been around a few years with other teams and leagues. They've been practicing, playing exhibition games, then touring recently."

"So they've been a close group, I guess, even live together?"

"Yes, most of them room together in twos and threes."

"Good."

"I know you're not implying Jacqui had anything to do with this."

"I'm not implying anything. If she finds out, and she probably will, tell her to see me. It has nothing to do with her." Or it does.

"Can't I at least inquire as to the nature of this, so I'm not destroyed or arrested as a pervert in doing it?"

"You must know what I'm doing."

"Are you trying to draw a correlation between Jacqui's and her players' periods?"

"Yes."

"I've got to get back."

"Where is Steinmark's place?"

"He rented a house at Wrightsville Beach, a duplex on the water side. Turn right across the second bridge onto Waynick Boulevard, then take a sharp left at the end, and a right again." She gave me the number.

"And Jacqui lives close by?"

"Yes. Why?"

"I've got a meeting with her tonight at her place."

"Oh, really? Fast work."

"Yes, but not that kind."

"Just across the canal at the first bridge, where we came out this morning, except on the other side of the park. The post office is on the right. Just beyond it some high rise condos set back. There."

"Call me about Steinmark," I said. "I'll see you tonight if you're going to be in."

She opened the car door and stopped and looked back.

"Wray." She paused. "I know it's uncomfortable for us right now. But I want you to know, no matter what it is I might be holding back or keeping from you, I would never do anything that would harm you in any way, nor allow anyone else to. I hope you know that."

I had never seen Ames desperate before, nor talk in riddles. Being fired from her job must have been like old home week for her, the insecurity of it. She had always been so strong and aggressive, so confident, perhaps running scared and hiding it well, but never doubtful. But it had not been an easy life for either. Her father had left her and her mother high and dry to struggle on their own. An early, childish marriage to a man who later became a drunk and abused her ended when she beat him senseless while he slept, then left and divorced him. And though we had given ourselves to one another passionately for two years, explored together every cell of our bodies, exchanged thoughts on a metaphysical plane, and promised to always be friends when the chips were down, no matter what, there always seemed to be this little shield around her heart allowing one to enter but never touch the very center. My instinct was to reach out and grab and hug her, but I knew I should not. I looked at her without responding. Let her live with it awhile, I figured. Me, too.

She got into her car and left.

I sat in my car and called Carol Gambrell and asked for permission to rummage through the desks in her offices.

Carol explained that it might pose a problem with the staff, what with the personal, private effects, the implication of mistrust, infringement of rights, et cetera, not to mention the hard feelings it could cause and the resulting affect on morale. But it was just a cursory look I wanted only after everyone had gone home. And I insisted she accompany me. After all, the police must have done the same thing. If they had not, they would soon if this thing was not shut down first.

She thought about it a moment, then relented. "Okay, but you leave everything the way you find it. And only that which appears to be related to your purpose. No messes. And that doesn't include my office. That's off limits."

"Of course. And your office at the gym, too. I'd like to see that, as well. I don't want anyone but you feeling left out or embarrassed by being scrutinized. Just trying to cover all the bases but yours, be almost thorough." I could just see her tapping her pencil on the desk and biting her lip. "I'm sure, with the money you're paying me, you want me to be thorough."

"Yes. Oh, yes. I do want you to be thorough. Be here at seven."

10

It was quarter to two and I found a karate dojo on Market Street—Route 17. The street ran north to south through the center of the city and clear down to and across the Cape Fear River through the old downtown area. The dojo was a place Bernie told me about that practiced my style. I went in and showed my card and practiced an hour and a half as the guest of the owner-instructor, or sensei, an amiable enough young man who beat the living hell out of me. Not sure I could've beaten him over twenty years earlier, in my prime. His name was Aaron Sepp. He was short and powerfully built, bald, with a mustache, and bore layers of scar tissue and combat marks on his arms and legs from years of learning the hard way. I was sure he tried to teach it all to me in this one visit.

After the workout, I showered—goody, most dojos don't have showers—and dressed to leave.

"Aaron, let me ask you something." I stopped at the desk. "Since you're from around here, do you know a guy named Ken Enright?"

"Who doesn't? How do you know him?"

"He's a security guard for the *Carolina Storms*."

"The fox guarding the chicken coup. I didn't know that. Or the fox guarding the foxes, whichever. I'm not surprised."

"Why?"

"You kidding? Kenny Enright? You always find him where the girls are. And he's not usually welcomed. Don't trust him with your daughter. What made you ask about him?"

I explained my connection.

"I went to high school with him," Aaron said. "In fact, he worked out here a few years back. Pretty good student and athlete. But I think I hurt his feelings. He kept hitting on the female students. I told him he'd have to stop or go elsewhere. So he never came back."

"What about him? What's he like?"

"He's a gun freak. Guns, knives, explosives. Classic case. Tried to get into the Wilmington P.D. and sheriff's department years ago. Turned him down flat."

"Think he'd hurt anybody?"

"Not without a license. Put a badge on him and he'd wipe out that village Hillary Clinton said it takes to raise a child. He needs approval, especially from women.

"Kenny's not that bad. He just wants to be everybody's hero. He could have been a good athlete in high school, but wouldn't play football. We used to tease him about it, said it was because he might miss cheerleading practice. Always pawing at the girls, but never seemed to have a girlfriend. Actually, I kind of felt sorry for him."

"What about Bernie Woods? Know him?"

"Not personally, only when I see him. Think he works for the TV station, a cameraman or something."

"Thanks a lot. If I have a chance, I'll stop by again if you'll promise not to beat the crap out of me next time."

"Anytime. And I'll show you a block I've developed that'll protect that shoulder in a fight."

"Now you tell me. I just had a fight. Hope I'll never need it."

"Since you're working with them, think you can get me a couple good seats to the opener? My wife and daughter are basketball nuts. Wife played in high school. I'll pay money for them. Only reason I ask is because I hear they're already sold out for the first couple games."

"Probably can. No charge. I'll see what I can do."

"My daughter worshipped that T.J. Semieux girl. Got her autograph one day at the mall. Posters all over her room. Damn shame. Cried her eyes out when it happened that day. My daughter is handicapped. Wheel chair. She can't play well, but she loves the game."

"I'll bring the tickets by."

"Great. They'll even let me eat at the table with them again."

"Oh," he said, "not that it means anything, but you never know—and don't get me wrong, I'm not trying to hurt Kenny or anything—but the word was he couldn't get on with the police or sheriff mainly because he had a pornography problem. Started in the service, I hear."

"That certainly adds a dimension of depth to his character."

"Yeah, but it won't get him a date, I bet."

I went to my car and called Ames.

"I've been trying to get you most of the hour," she said. "John will talk with you if you make it quick. He's at his place now, but he's leaving for Charlotte, so hurry."

"So they haven't charged him yet. I knew it."

"They could still charge him, though. But his lawyer, Sullivan, seems pretty confident they don't have a case.

"Bernie's trying to get something on the car," she said. "The sheriff's people won't tell us a thing, but he's still trying. And, oh yeah, I got an ear full about Ken Enright. Some character. Bernie actually knows him. Not as a friend, but enough to now he probably shouldn't be guarding the female gender."

"The fox guarding the coup."

"How did you know?"

"I'm working, too, you know. And Bernie hasn't mentioned before that he knows Enright?"

"No, he hasn't. He said the times he's been around the team other guards have been working. He didn't know Enright worked for them."

"Why else would he wear a uniform and show up?"

"Hell, I don't know, Wray. Ask him."

"Have you mentioned this to Jacqui or Carol?"

"No, not yet."

"Don't. They'll fire him and we need to keep him on the job, close by, to watch him."

"Alright, fine."

"I'm on my way to Steinmark's." I broke off.

I crossed the canal into the beach, passing Jacqui's condo, noticing its proximity to Steinmark's place, about a mile by car. Or foot. Nothing like closeness. Everybody wants to live at the beach.

Just before reaching Steinmark's, my car phone rang. It was my father, back home. I put it on speaker. One of the few electronic things these days I know how to do, though I didn't install it.

Harry Larrick's leathery voice crackled. "Williams called from the zoning office. You've got three days before they physically remove you from the pier, at your cost, and condemn it. Either that or you disconnect the plumbing and electric and remove any fixtures or items constituting—I'm reading here—or contributing to a permanent residence or facility, or any kind of living quarters. And he cites the code. And he says he'll cite you personally again."

"Oh, jezze, not now. Did you tell him I was out of town, working?"

"He said he didn't care. In fact, he said he was glad, it would make it easier. He won't have to bring the bulldog with him to jump up and bite your ass off when you got in the way. He said they're trained to attack wise-asses, but if you wanted to be here, it would be a good time to try it out."

"See if you can get me an extension. Call Jeff." I was referring to my younger brother, an attorney.

"Jeff can't save you, Wray. You're on borrowed time that just ran out. You're encroaching on the waterway, trying to extend your home into the creek. They're not going to give you a variance, son. You've got to realize you can't beat city hall. You broke the law, really, when you put that plumbing and stuff in there without a permit. Keep messing with these people and they'll make you tear down the boat house and the pier too."

"Damn."

"The zoning board meets next week and Williams wants to have this resolved before he meets with city council, so they don't start looking at him funny. Everybody knows you're on that pier, and everybody wants you to hell off."

"Stall them if you can. I'll think of something."

"You better think of a way to get that stuff moved when they put it on shore. I'm too old to be messing with such stuff as that."

"Get the Lewis brothers to move it, if it comes to it. I'll pay them when I get home."

"You mean brother, singular. Lloyd's already in jail for moving other people's stuff illegally."

"Can't say he's not career-oriented. Damn."

"I'll take care of it. Don't worry yourself, though it might not be what you want. You just be careful down there. You hear me?"

"I'm fine. How's mom?"

"She's in heaven. She's out with her co-conspirators making sure nobody forgets who they are and where they came from. U.D.C, D.A.R. X.Y.Z. Hell, I don't know, one of them

"Anyway," Harry said, "I saw Morgan on the news today reporting on that dead girl. Tell her we said hello. And she knows where we live. You really screwed up royally when you let her go."

"So I hear. Talk with you later. Got to go. Thanks."

John Steinmark was staying on the top level of a very large beach house facing the ocean, about three-and-a-half-million dollars worth of view. It was a cramped neighborhood, like everybody had to be there at once, but very clean and neat, the homes well-kept, boundaries respected, and every square inch worth a gold mine. A very high-rent community. Rent because most could not afford to own here.

When Steinmark answered the door in shorts and no shirt, I knew I was looking at a linebacker. Six-three, two-sixty easy, a small waist, massive torso, the kind that bench presses six hundred pounds, and a neck wider than his head, with enough scar tissue to suggest there might be a truck graveyard out there somewhere. Other than that, he seemed clean-cut—well, he had on Sperry topsiders—with a friendly voice, and a little haggard from it all.

He invited me in.

"You're a friend of Ms. Dalton's," Steinmark said. "Can I get you something?"

We sat at the dining table with a view of the beach through the large windows.

"We go back a while. No, thanks."

"Classy lady. Nice person. My lawyer, Loomis Sullivan, couldn't be here. He said it's okay to talk to you. I've got nothing to hide. Long as it's private, like you said, no press. Except Ms. Dalton."

"Ms. Dalton has nothing to do with what we discuss here."

"What'd you want to see me about?"

"Well, if I can, I'd like to see what I can do to help. I don't think you have anything to hide, either. Of course, I don't know you. And, on the surface, I don't think you did it. Right now, from what I see, the only evidence the authorities have points to you, sloppy as it is. So I know it has to look bad. If they don't find somebody else real quick, you're it. Cops hate not having somebody to burn, and when they're desperate, they're not picky. So it's going to pay for you have all the friends you can get on this. Unless you know something I don't know."

Steinmark rubbed his hands across his head, pitiful, like a child. "Yeah, jeeze, I know.

"What do you want from me?" he said. He was already bored with the thought of going over it one more time.

"When was the last time you saw Ms. Semieux alive?"

"Two days before she died. But we talked on the phone the day before."

"You got any ideas about it, yourself?"

"Me? No, none. Like I told the police, all of them, I wouldn't know where to start. I just know I loved her and couldn't have done it. Wouldn't have done it. I'd just like to get my hands on whoever did."

"What about the mud on your wheels and floor mats? Under the car? The Gas? Everything says your car was there."

(61)

"Like I told them, I didn't drive the damn car that night. I don't know how it got there, if it did. Or how the gas can got in the trash out back."

"Your gas can was found?"

"Not mine. I don't have a gas can. I don't know whose it is."

"They say anything about the gas can?"

"Only that it's in the lab. The S.B.I lab in Garner, up by Raleigh."

"Anyone have access to your car?"

"No, T.J. was the only one."

"She had your car key?"

"Yes. She had it from before, when we were still going together. I just forgot to get it back, and she forgot to give it to me, I guess, not that it mattered. They found it on her key ring."

"What did they tell you about her car?"

"Nothing. My lawyer's trying to get a report on it."

"Where'd you tell them you were when she died?"

"I was here. I went out and took a walk on the beach a while, just before dark. Some neighbors saw me. Then I came back and watched TV and went to sleep."

I did not doubt that. Half the beach was on his floor. I could feel the grit under my shoes. Stealing sand, maybe, but not killing somebody.

"Was it raining the time you were on the beach?"

"Yes, a little."

"Make any long distance calls?"

"No. Didn't make any calls."

"When were you suppose to see Ms. Semieux again?"

"We were suppose to meet for lunch the next day, to talk things over. The day she was, uh—." His words trailed off.

"But she wasn't going back with you, was she?"

Steinmark did not like that. "She's not here to say, is she?"

"Did the two of you ever plan to marry? I mean, make actual plans?"

"If you're asking if we had insurance on one another—or me on her—the answer is no. And neither of us owned a gun. And I never hit her. I've been asked that and accused of it a million times."

"Jacqui Van Autt ever accuse you of it?"

"Who? Jacqui? No, never did accuse me."

"Ever ask you if you ever hit her? Not once?"

He was thinking now. "No, never asked me. Looked at me hard a couple times after T.J. and I would have a fight, but never accused me."

"Any other women in your life?"

"No. I won't say I haven't been out with anyone else since we broke up, but nothing serious. And she didn't date anyone either."

"You know that?"

"Yes."

"Any homosexual women on the *Storms* team, to your knowledge?"

"Kris Caldwell is the only one I know of, but she doesn't hide it. And she's in a committed relationship with her live-in girlfriend. And T.J. wasn't funny, if that's what you're getting at."

"How come your lawyer isn't here? Why does he let you talk to people?"

"He had a prior commitment, a client on death row in Raleigh. He'll be back tomorrow. I don't have anything to hide, like I said. And he's cooperating with the police on my behalf. To a point anyway."

I was wondering how you did something like that.

"Do you think Ms. Semieux was killed for a specific reason of some kind?"

"I don't see what the reason would be. No."

"So you rented this place down here and ran back and forth from Charlotte, just so you could be near Ms. Semieux and try to get her back?"

"That's right, I did."

"I don't want to sound too nosey, but were the two of you intimate, physically, since your initial breakup?"

Steinmark's head dropped briefly and he hesitated answering, then said, "Not since March."

"You like Jacqui Van Autt?"

He shrugged. "I guess. She's alright. Never had any problem with her."

"She like you?"

"I don't know. She never hassled me about going with T.J."

"You see her often?"

"No. I saw her after T.J. died, just for a few minutes."

"Where?"

"She called me here the next morning, then came by. Maybe she doesn't hate me. I don't know. We did a crying jag together."

"What about this house? You giving it up?"

"Might as well keep it a while, in case I have to come back here. I'm sure I will."

"You were All-America your last two years in college. Weren't you?"

"Yeah."

"What kind of grades you make?"

"A in my major, B overall."

"How'd you go in the draft?"

"Second round."

"What kind of contract you have with the *Cougars*?"

"Three years, one-point-one million a year, with performance escalation clause. Eight hundred thousand signing bonus."

"Who's your agent?"

"Long Run Associates, Charlotte. Jay Davenport."

"What's your future look like?"

Steinmark hesitated again, studying my face. "What do you mean?"

"Football. When this is all over."

"Oh. Barring any injuries, I expect to be around a long time and get a Super Bowl ring. Then business investments."

I asked him nonchalantly, not looking at him, "What burns your ass up more than anything else in this life?"

He looked at me like it was a stupid question, but a quick-rising anger pulsated in the blood vessels of his neck. "The fire that burned up T.J." He was up from the chair and slipping on his shirt and slacks now and looking in the mirror on the wall by the table, more at trying to control himself.

I waited for the blood to subside, then asked, "What else burns you up, I mean? Has to be more than that one thing. Life is not that easy."

The blood vessels reappeared. He stared over at me through the mirror. "My father working thirty-five years in the coal mines, then the steel mills, in the stinkingest job there was, only to lose everything because he got too sick to do it anymore. So he stays in bed and fights for breath and suffers every waking minute of his life. And I make a fortune playing games. And people paying two hundred bucks for a cheap seat to see guys like me play every Sunday, then bitching because they're asked once or twice a year to help elderly and sick people get through the day, or die with a little dignity by making a stinking donation to a charity, or pay a few extra pennies in taxes. That's going to be hard to take when the season starts. That burns my ass up." He looked away, suppressing the tears trying to well up in his eyes.

"Yeah, it's a scary world."

I was now looking at the portrait of Steinmark and Semieux atop the TV.

"When did things start falling apart for you and T.J.?" I said, sounding more personal now.

"Last January."

"What caused it, if anything?"

"Me. She said I was crowding her and she was right. I should have had my ass kicked."

I was wondering who might be able to do that.

"I understand she broke it off for good, just before leaving on the European tour. And you rented this place then, so you could be here when she got back. Is that right?"

"That's what I said."

"You were a chemical engineering major?"

"Yeah."

"How did Ms. Semieux—T.J.—react when she got back from Europe and found you here?"

Steinmark was going into the kitchen for a can of soda. He returned and sat down with it.

"Well, actually, I expected a big fight, her to tell me to get lost, mad as hell. But she wasn't mad. Actually, she was kind of glad to see me, like she was relieved. We went out to dinner the first night and talked. Had a nice time. I really believed she wanted to be with me more.

"She had something else on her mind, though" he said. "Business problem back home with her family or something in Louisiana. The foundation, I think. Anyway, she went home the next day for a few days vacation and to straighten things out."

"Did she?"

"Apparently so. I called her there from Charlotte. She said everything was fine and looked forward to getting back and getting started. She had the Olympics to do. She was really excited about it."

"She loved her parents."

"Yeah, they were close."

"You meet them?"

"Yeah, once, when they were up for a game at Ivy Ridge and I was there too. They're nice people. But they don't say much. Not to me anyway. I don't think they cared for me. T.J. never said. Those people down there are kind of funny, real clannish, I think."

"She discuss her business interests with you?"

"No, and I didn't ask. Jacqui handled all that."

"I've got to ask you something else personal. Not about you, but about T.J., since the two of you had once planned on marriage, been real close and all. Don't take it the wrong way. If you know it, could you tell me if she was having her monthly menstrual period when she died?"

"No, I don't think so."

"You know when she generally had her period, of course."

"Yeah, it was in the middle of the month, best I remember. What's that got to do with anything?"

"She ever have any female problems? Irregular periods?"

He was thinking I was an idiot, I was certain.

"No, I don't think so. Sometimes she said her period was a little shorter than usual, do to training and diet. But it was regular, I think."

Steinmark got up. "Look, I've got to get going, Mr. Larrick."

"I won't hold you up any longer. I appreciate your talking to me. If I need to see you, I'll contact your lawyer.

"You know," I said, straggling to the door, "mud on your wheels and floor mats, under your car, the gas spill in your car, the can in your trash, you say. That looks awfully bad on you. You either did it or you didn't. If you didn't, somebody is going to a lot of trouble to make it look like you did. Consider this: what if you were standing before a judge and jury right now on the charge of murdering Ms. Semieux." I moved her name from the personal. "Which is a real likelihood, you know. The charge, I mean. And you were given one chance to save yourself. If you give a good answer, you go free. A bad one, you go to jail in a six-by-nine, or you die. But somebody has to pay.

"So the judge looks down at you and says he thinks you were framed, but the evidence says otherwise. So unless you can give the court some reason, or some person who might have been involved, whether they're ever tried or not, you take the fall. The jury is watching. They'd like to let you go. Last chance. What do you tell them? Who could it possibly be, in your wildest imagination?" I shrugged. "And what could be the reason, no matter how far out? Who? Why? And I won't tell anybody."

I stared into his eyes and they darted around, as if processing the possibilities, then stopped darting, as if hitting on something.

"I don't know," he said. "I don't have any idea."

But I think he did not like the idea of my maybe reading into his thoughts.

"Well, you're a bright boy, John, if I can call you that. If you don't know what you think, nobody does. If you think of anything, run it by me if you don't mind. I'm on your side."

We shook hands and I went to my car.

He was lying. He might or might not be a killer, I was thinking, but he's definitely lying or hiding something.

11

There were nine individual offices in the *Storms* regional headquarters suite. Most were cubicles, with the exception being Carol Gambrell's and Jacqui Van Autt's offices, and one or two more. I didn't look that closely. I really didn't care about that side of College Road.

Carol Gambrell was clearly uneasy about it. "I want you to know this cuts against everything I believe in. So make it as quick as possible and only superficial, as I agreed to. Even the police didn't ask for this much intrusion."

"They will. And I'll be quick. I'm not approaching this like a policeman. I'm only looking for anything that might jump up and bite me."

"Get too nosey and that'll be me."

"Okay, bite me. Just a joke."

I couldn't help noticing her perfect white teeth. Maybe trying to spot the incisors.

We started down one side of the rectangular island. She handed me the keys as we went from one desk or module to another. I didn't bother with most drawers. The calendars, the notepads, the doodling, the obvious out-of-place writings and scribbling were what interested me. Besides, there was but one office that concerned me anyway, since I could not get into Carol's.

We made the loop and finished back up front.

"I won't do this again," she said, noticeably relieved.

"Just one more and I'll be through." I was referring to Jacqui's office over in the gym, on campus.

"Look." She extracted the key from the ring. "I don't have time for that. I've got a meeting to make." She held out the keys only to Jacqui's office, desk and file cabinets. "I'm going to trust you with these. I want them back immediately after you finish, which shouldn't be long. Drop them off in an envelope with the security guard at the Eastwood Road entrance to my home near the beach. You know where it is? I'll be downtown at the Hilton, in the dining room, until about nine-thirty or so, in case you need me."

"Maybe when this is all over, when we have time."

She rolled her eyes.

"I'll be passing through the gate. Make sure these keys are there. And don't make copies."

"Oh, one more favor," I said.

"What *is* it?"

"I need four home tickets for the first two openers, down front and center, floor level, preferably close to the team. They're for some special friends of mine. They're the best fans you've got. Can you do it?"

"Yes, or close to it. I'll leave them here at Ethel's desk tomorrow."

"And videos. Do you have any videos here of the team I can take with me to look at? Games, practices, anything?"

She went to a shelf and quickly selected several at random.

"Let's go." She reached for the door.

"Just one more thing. I almost forgot."

"What is it *now*?"

"I need the address and phone number of Ms. Semieux's parents in Louisiana."

Carol Gambrell stopped dead still, suddenly not so much in a hurry. "For what?"

"Because they're her parents. The girl's been murdered. I'm talking to everybody."

"Can it wait till later, when I'm home? About eleven-thirty. I'll need your report anyway."

"That'll be fine, long as I have it by tomorrow morning."

I left her with that thought as a seed and wondered how long it would take to go through the lines to Ames and Jacqui.

Only the janitor was there when I got to the gymnasium. I explained that I was with the team and asked when he locked up. Ten I was told.

I went into Jacqui's office and began looking around. Neat but very busy woman, I could see. Lots of stuff for a satellite office. I looked over at the computer, then looked away. No use looking there, I figured. You have to know how to turn one on first. When I got home, I was thinking—if I still had a home after the zoning office finished with me—I'd call my daughter and have her come over with a hammer and teach me how to operate a computer. For now I would have to rely on the old hand-eye approach.

I settled into the chair and began picking over things. I flipped through the desk calendar first. There was a page missing—April—so I extracted the page representing May, which might bear impressions, and kept it. I opened the drawers and took my time with the files, pads and notebooks. Maybe the computer age had not completely taken over the world. Somebody else writes in long hand too. It occurred to me it was an unusual amount of material for a temporary sub-office, but it was not mine, so what did I know. Her office back at the Regency was almost sterile by comparison. It appeared Jacqui was like a pack rat and wanted everything at her fingertips wherever she was and she would beat the living horse shit out of it if it wasn't, not unusual for a control-conscious personality, I supposed.

There was a steno pad lodged against the side of the lower drawer I was into. I opened it and leafed through. Names, initials, and telephone numbers, some numbers marked, with others written below them. Like bidding figures, maybe something like commodities traders might jot down on their crooked little pads. Not unusual, either, for a professional coach. Maybe.

I turned on the photocopy machine. There was hope for me yet. I copied pages in the steno pad, as well as the desk calendar pad with the scribbling for later reading. There wasn't time to go over it here.

I locked the desk, turned off the copier like a proud papa, and gathered up the papers. Just as I turned to leave, the door opened and Ken Enright, the security guard, in uniform, stood in the doorway, surprised to see me.

"Oh, it's you," Enright said. "I didn't know." He turned to leave.

"What's up?" I said.

Enright stopped. "Nothing. I was, uh, just passing by on my way home. Just thought I'd stop in, see if everything was okay."

"I see. You on duty now?"

"Here? No, I'm off from another site."

"You normally do this? Come by here, I mean?"

"Well, a couple times I have. It's no trouble, Coach Van Autt's here late, usually, by herself. I stop in and talk with her a little bit, make sure she gets to her car okay."

"What made you think she was here tonight?"

"When I swung through the parking lot, I thought I saw the light on through the front doors."

"But her car is not out there, is it?"

Enright did not like being caught off guard, literally or figuratively. "No, it's not."

"Then what made you come inside?"

"Just to check, if that's alright with you."

"Sure."

"I guess I'll be going."

"I met an old friend of yours today." He stopped. "Aaron Sepp. You know him, of course."

Enright looked like his heart might descend into his stomach.

"Yeah, I know him. Sure."

Sure." In my eyes I let the implication of it absorb a moment. I began pacing the room, and he wasn't moving to leave, slowing down the tempo of the conversation, a quite threatening tactic at times, like a big cat stalking its prey, but not desperate, not in a hurry, not really hungry. "Yeah, you two go back a long way. Aaron's an interesting guy. Really knows his stuff."

"Yeah, he's a super karate instructor. Really knows is stuff."

"He knows a hell of a lot more than that." I looked dead at him. "You know, he teaches self-defense to the police and sheriff folks."

"Yeah, I know."

"Guy could pick up a lot of information like that." I was not looking at him now. "Of course he could pass along some too."

"Sure, he'd be in a perfect position to do it." He was hanging on my every word.

I let an uneasy silence loom for a moment, until he could stand it no longer.

"So what are you trying to say? Just spit it out."

I knew I had him. I also knew that if you put a guy in a corner you had to leave him a way out. I approached him, standing just outside his personal space.

"What I'm saying is there's been a brutal murder here. And nobody's been arrested for it. If it means anything to you, I wasn't really looking hard at you. But you've got to admit a guy like you, your background, your interests, your position, snooping around here at a time and place you're not supposed to be. That looks awfully bad. If I were to mention it to certain parties, you might come under a lot of suspicion, a lot of heat real fast. You understand that." Truth likely was he would have been a suspect, since they all knew him downtown, and probably had an alibi or wouldn't be employed here now.

Enright understood, was nearly paralyzed by the thought. I knew he must have been one of the first persons questioned by authorities. And he did not need any further possible complications.

"So I'm going to do you a big, fat favor." I threw him a bone. "I'm not going to say anything about seeing you here tonight, and you don't say anything to a soul, either, including, and especially, to coach Van Autt. I hear that and you'll be downtown. But only on one condition."

He was listening.

"Aaron said you were dedicated, basically a good man. That's a good quality. That part interests me. And I need help, so I'll expect you to help me on this case if I need your services. Of course I'll pay the going rate, if that's acceptable. You have a phone number I can use, I assume."

"Yeah, right." He was cautious but thinking fast. "Whatever I can do."

"I'll put you on a retainer. Six hundred a week plus, starting now. Strictly undercover. Keep it quiet."

"You serious?"

"As a heart attack."

"Okay, sure. Just call me when you need me. But I can't quit my job here."

"Don't expect or want you to. Here is where I might be needing you." I handed him my card. "Whatever you do, though, stay away from the *Storms* people and facilities, except when you're working for your company, or on assignment for me, none of this crap like tonight. We don't need anybody wondering about us."

"Alright, no problem." He was still a little cautious, like waiting for a hammer of some kind to drop on this sick joke.

"I'll be in touch. When you see me around, don't be obvious. I don't want anyone knowing we're connected." I took out a couple hundred-dollar bills and handed them to him. "Here's an advance to work on. I'll have you sign for it later. Tax people, you know."

Enright looked at the windfall that just fell in his lap and realized I must be on the level. "I'll do whatever I can to help."

"Thank you. It's good to have somebody local who knows his way around."

"No problem. I could get used to this."

"And you might have to earn it."

"Still no problem. When's payday, usually? Not trying to be greedy, but you know."

"I'll let you know more later."

"Okay by me."

"Thank you," I said. "I'll be in touch."

Enright closed the door behind him, like he'd just won a door prize.

I let out a breath of relief. Now if he would just keep his mouth shut.

12

I dropped off Carol's keys, but not before having the unauthorized copies made just in case, and drove to Jacqui's place. It was a quiet complex, no tourists, just retired or semi-retired folks who were friendly but minded their own business, apparently, because their presence wasn't evident. Her place faced the park and town hall complex across the street and overlooked two roads forked off leading into the beach a half mile further along and across the second, flat, bridge.

"It's ideal." She was looser, more receptive now. "Not on the sand but close. Right smack in the middle of what I want and far enough away from anything I don't."

"And the price was right, I'll bet."

"No, it was outrageous." She almost laughed. "Let me fix you a drink."

"I guess a red wine on ice, if you have it, would be okay. Since it's dark outside now. I never take my Swill Brothers out in the daylight, by the way, too risky. Light is wine's enemy, you know."

"A connoisseur." She was enjoying the humor with me.

"No, just a wine head."

"Rose it is."

She handed me the glass and sat on the adjacent sofa. I was in the matching floral chair, coffee table out front.

The motif was casual but expensive, a lot of original art stuff, and I guessed nobody in the complex had spent as much on décor. A lot of windows, light. Some people could enjoy the money, but others couldn't hide it.

"Wray." She reached over and touched my arm. "I'm really sorry about blowing up at you today. Please forgive me."

"If it were a problem I wouldn't be drinking with you. Forget it. If people owed me a drink every time I upset them, there wouldn't be enough booze in this town."

We chatted a while about nothing in particular, the beach, how she liked it here. She would keep the condo, since she was in Charlotte anyway. It would be a convenient and close getaway.

She was immaculate in crème slacks, with sandals and a blue shell, and hair swept back in a way that lit up her raw beauty and teased a man's deepest visual fantasies. It was intended to be that way, I knew. But it also seemed she had a big sign hanging around her neck visible to only to the unqualified reading, *Look all you want, but you'll never have me.*

"I've told everybody at the gym to expect you tomorrow. They'll give you as much time as you need."

"I find it better if people are in the privacy of their own homes. They think and remember better, actually."

"Makes sense. And they act better, too. Ask me what you want. I promise to be nicer."

"I understand Ms. Semieux—T.J., I have to get used to that—was upset about something to do with her foundation plans right before she died."

"Um, yes." She swallowed and nodded, seemingly dismissing it as trivial. "Right after we got back off tour. She was a little upset but not for long. She was considering some investment idea someone had approached her about, some kind of real estate thing, motel, I think, in New York or New Jersey. And I strongly advised against it. And rightfully so. After all, we didn't know these people. At least I didn't, and I don't think she did either. In fact, I know she didn't."

I was still listening.

"Anyway, she was pumped up about how much profit could be generated for the foundation, how the thing could grow into a chain, et cetera, and I prevailed. I convinced her it was safer to deal with people she knew and could trust, like her father and her priest, who are on the board with me, as well as a friend of her father's who's a lawyer."

"You know who these people were? Their names or anything?" I reached for a pen clipped on the placket of my shirt.

"No, I can't even remember that. That was the scary part of it. No one knew them or enough about them. These girls get all kinds of nutty propositions coming at them every day. You can imagine."

"That I understand." I clipped my pen back onto my shirt.

"That's why I'm getting away from giving advice to anybody. It's too much to handle. I'll run the team and let the business agents handle the rest."

"Do you handle business for anyone else?"

"No. I've advised a number of girls over the short time they've been with me, like a parent would a child, but I haven't been involved with it directly. But this is the first time, this past year, women in the sport have made this kind of money, too. T.J. was the first for whom I took an active role, because we were so close and she was so vulnerable, and the foundation is such a good cause.

"T.J. had a lot of insecurities, Wray. In spite of the incredible progress she'd made since childhood. You're familiar with that by now, I suppose. It's no secret. She's been dissected and written about probably as much as any woman athlete in the last twenty years, in fact, some say even more. I don't know.

"What I was trying to do was to wean her away from me, in a sense. She depended on me too much. She really did need to start wading in the water alone. Besides, the foundation was in Louisiana. They're all there and I'm here. It's just too much to fool with.

"But, God, I loved that girl so much. I miss her terribly." She was rubbing her forearm gently and fighting back what might have been tears trying to run, easier now with the alcohol. "That's why it's so important for me to take some part in this thing, to do something, anything I can to help. At least to know what's going on. It's the thought of that somebody still out there that bothers me. Someone else could get hurt, too.

"Excuse me. I'm not normally a crier. If you know my reputation, you know that."

"I understand. But don't worry about this guy killing anyone else. It won't happen."

"Wish I could believe that."

"Well." I sipped from my glass. "If he kills again, who's he going to frame then?"

"Oh, I see. Yes, John. Do you really think John is being framed?"

"The flip side is do you really think he did it."

"Of course, I see. No, I still don't think he did it. But it's looking very bad for him. Isn't it?"

"Yeah, it sure is."

"And that's a shame. He doesn't deserve it."

We talked a bit longer over another drink, about T.J., the team, the league, as well as other matters unrelated to the game or the murder. She was a very intelligent and well-informed woman, in addition to possessing the kind of looks that can make slaves and fools of some men. But she had, too, I sensed, an equally prominent ego which seemed a common thread holding all her together and giving her identity. No man would ever have this woman totally to himself, nor take away from her without paying two-fold. I felt that very strongly. Very smooth, very polished, but a take-no-prisoners lady indeed. And I wondered if one of such a motivating drive, an unrelenting focus which she seemed to have, might be genuinely warm or, perhaps, just be a sociopath with all the right moves. Exciting to think about trading ideas with her on the higher levels, or of spending countless nights in her bed, but as Bernie had insinuated—and I had discovered earlier—don't make the mistake of falling asleep around her. What made me think this again was the conflicting feeling I got when she touched my forearm. Each time, instead of the warm, disarming sexual suggestion a man might get from a woman like this touching him gently, I felt a coldness like a freezer burn. Just something there.

That was my read on her anyway. Either I was right, or I was dead wrong and she was a bleeding-heart social worker. I had been wrong before.

I checked my watch and got up to leave.

"Can I tell everyone to expect you to start calling on them?" she said. We were at the door now.

"Day after tomorrow, yes. I think I need to get up to Charlotte to see Steinmark again."

"Oops. You told me something. I'm surprised you haven't bothered the players yet. I'm afraid you might hurt their feelings. They loved T.J., too, and they're eager to help."

"I'm sure the police have bothered them enough for a while. But I'll get around to it.

"Look," I added, "about what I said today concerning my loyalty to Carol and all first. That's still true. But I know where you're coming from in wanting to know what's going on. So I'm willing to take a risk. I'll keep you informed, myself, as long as you don't get me in trouble with her."

"Oh, no, no problem." She waved it away. "Your loyalty is to Carol. I wouldn't have it any other way. After all, I am vice-president and a board member. Ordinarily, I'd fire you myself," she said, tapping my chest lightly. "But I appreciate you knowing the anguish this is causing me. Please keep me informed. There won't be any problems. I promise."

"I figure you know the organization better than anyone. I'll need you as long as I'm here, so it only makes sense to cooperate. If it's okay, I'd like to get with you when I get back, if you're not that busy. This time drinks are on me."

"From Charlotte? Sure."

"No, I'm going down to Louisiana first."

"Oh. Yes, please. Just call."

"And, Wray? Thank you. This really means more to me than you know."

I shrugged it off. It was nothing.

And it would stay that way.

I called Carol Gambrell and gave her a rundown on my activities. No findings the first day. I intentionally skipped asking her for the Fortiers' address and phone number in Louisiana so she would wonder about it. And she did not offer it.

I dialed the Fortiers, having gotten the number from the last caller assistance service on the planet, a recording, since there weren't any real, live operators any more. Real spooky, high-tech detective work. I often wondered if I looked as dumb as I sometimes felt. Had Ames told these people that about me? I asked Maurice Fortier if it would be okay to fly down and talk to him, explaining who I was and what I was doing. I asked him not to acknowledge to anyone that I had called or was coming. It's better to keep some folks confused by being contradictory about what you say and do. The *Storms* people, I mean. He agreed.

13

I let myself into Ames' apartment. The sliding glass doors were open to the sound and smell of the ocean and beach.

Ames was at her computer station in the corner of the living room, apparently having just gotten in herself.

"I see you found your way back." She was not looking up. "How'd your day go?"

"I could be Jack the Ripper." I put down the disks and papers and the bag of groceries. "And you're asking me how my day went."

"He died years ago and he doesn't have a day."

"Okay, his great-grand nephew. Okay?"

"You forget I lived with you. I know how you sound coming in a door."

"I'm a marked man."

"No, you're a wise-ass." She glanced over at the bag I was emptying at the counter. "Great choice of wines. I see the quick stop was still open. How many rednecks you have to bribe to get it?"

"Just say something about the guys who make this shit and see what happens."

"So how's it going so far?"

"I'm beat. And I know who the killer is." I began slipping off my shirt.

She stopped abruptly and turned in her chair. "Oh?"

"Yeah. But I can't say. The killer asked me not to tell anybody and I promised I wouldn't. And I won't break my word, not for you, not for anybody. If I did, what kind of investigator would I be? Who would trust me?"

Her eyebrow rose. "Smart-ass son of a bitch." She turned back to the keyboard. "I didn't ask for that."

"Let me take a shower and we can talk." I headed down the hall.

"Please do, you damn grouch."

Minutes later I returned in slacks, shirtless and shoeless. The salt breeze was coming in and felt good.

Ames was in shorts and shell, on the floor, doing a combination of stretching and strength exercises.

I watched her, her fluid, graceful moves, lithe, nimble body contorting, sweating, struggling to stay young, and succeeding.

I passed through to the kitchen. "Sorry. I feel better now."

"Well, I know the world's a better place then."

I poured the wine.

"Your confidence level seems a little higher today," I said. "What happened?" I walked around the counter and stood at the edge of the living room.

"Is it that obvious? Carol offered me a job today."

Why did that not surprise me.

"Oh, yeah? Great. Doing what?"

"Public relations. Consolidating a number of PR jobs into one. A new position created for me. Responsibility for the overall image of the organization."

"You going to take it?"

She stopped exercising a second to consider the answer. "I don't know, it's a nice package. More than I've ever made, in fact, when you figure in the benefits."

"But you're a reporter."

"I know I don't eat much, but reporters get hungry too." She resumed exercising. "Anyway, I've got until this thing is over to decide. A couple weeks maybe." Like she knew how long it would take.

"It's a big mistake."

She looked up as if offended.

"Why? Why do you say that?"

"Sports is not your field, Ames. You're a fish out of water. You wouldn't last six months and you'd quit. You'd be a front, not a reporter. That's why you're in a mess now. Your own words. You're already working for them. You're just not getting paid."

"I beg your damn pardon." She stopped moving and glared at me.

"It's true and you know it. You were hired by your network because of your background in print journalism and, yes, your looks, too. But your employer made the bonehead mistake—and you let them get away with it—of taking you out of your area of expertise—public affairs—and miscasting you in an area you knew nothing about, dealing with people you wouldn't be caught dead with under other circumstances. And look where it's gotten you, too close to your source, helping them hide their little secrets, in the middle of a murder case at that, and getting fired for it. Hell, you should be covering the senatorial race now, not some damn basketball game. No disrespect intended, of course, for the deceased, like I say."

She jumped up, angry and hurt.

"I'll have you to know that T.J. Semieux is one of the biggest human interest stories to happen in decades, Wray. And I'm right here doing it, and I believe in it."

"That's only because she was killed. Without her death, it's just another success story, entertainment."

"Whatever makes it real." She was dripping sweat and breathing deeply.

"You know it's true."

"I know I have to take a shower. If you'll excuse me." She went down the hall. The hall was getting a workout too.

"You're too good for this crap. Take charge and get your life back."

She disappeared into the bathroom.

Well, I figured, if we were still together this would be dog house time.

I put one of Carol's disks into the player and sat on the sofa and began looking over the papers I had lifted from Jacqui's office, especially the notebook and calendar, and alternately viewed the video and drank the wine.

I was thinking maybe I should leave. I had no business here. She was lying to me, conning me. Obviously, she did not want to be involved with me again in a romantic way. She was just a desperate soul looking for God knows what and finding only trouble and failure. Maybe high-level failure, but failure nonetheless. And though I knew she was not capable of murder, nor of knowingly being a part of anything near it, she was still part of a nasty cover up of some kind related to it for these people. I was sure of it. She was eating from their table. The food was getting better and she was getting in deeper and using me to sustain her involvement, very much like an addict affects everyone around her.

I was considering all this, of just picking up my stuff and walking out, when the TV screen with the videos caught my attention. Footage of a news conference after a big win in the national championship tournament for Ivy Ridge the previous season, just months ago; the microphones, flashes popping, people, players and coaches crowding around, trophy lifted high overhead, confetti and streamers snowing down. As much like a political victory announcement as a sports win.

"Whoa, wait a minute. What's this?"

I scrutinized the scene, the people in it and their actions and mannerisms, their body language; T.J., her teammates and coaches, the press and fans, security, and the general hoopla from one shot, one scene to another. And T.J. Semieux, not with a happy demeanor, but with a sullen, worried look, not like all those around her. Alternately, I flipped through the papers in front of me. And the closer I studied the video on the screen, the more critically I examined the papers and their scribbling, looking for something, anything to jump out and tell me why T.J. was not reacting like the others. I inserted one video, then another into the player, flipping back and forth the same videos of past and recent games, each time making mental notes of my observations.

I was completely absorbed with this when distracted moments later by Ames coming back into the room looking more than a little bit ready for bed. She was never the type to wear curlers, always looked inviting, but now, when she should not be so, I sensed a hint of allure from her, a subtle scent of perfume I was particularly fond of, hair combed just a little too shiny, and the short, blue terry cloth bathrobe against her tanned legs that drove me nuts. Why, too, did this not surprise me? After all, it was her job in this lying little triangle to keep close watch on me and now, ostensibly, to keep me from going to Louisiana. It would be the only way I would get lucky, if I could call it luck.

"Peace?" She stopped just inside the living room.

I clicked off the video player.

She went into the kitchen for a drink.

"It always puzzled me, Wray, how we, at our age, could disagree so much. Life is too short. We should be more mellow."

"People get mellow only when contented or brain-dead. Besides, we never disagreed that much."

"Well, we know we aren't contented either."

She brought around the wine, hers more expensive, and sat in the chair and put her head back.

"What's it all about, Wray?" She was staring up at the ceiling. "Where are our lives really going?"

"Wherever it is, apparently it's not the same place. So why don't we talk shop before we fall asleep. I've got to get up early and get to Charlotte."

"Of course, nothing like business to cap off a hard day at work."

She got up and handed me a sheet of paper from her computer station. "Menstrual cycles. Fifteen of them. And they all think I'm crazy, thanks to you."

"Crazy only by proxy." I was pleased. I looked them over. "You get it, of course, what I'm doing here."

"I'm not sure."

"What'd Bernie pick up? Anything?"

"Well, Enright, the security guard, is clean, as far as having a record goes. Never convicted of anything. Everybody downtown seems to know he's weird, but he's never been arrested. Questioned but never arrested."

"Questioned for what, exactly?"

"Peeping Tom kind of stuff, lurking."

"Great. I guess that qualified him for security, inasmuch as he has to know how to keep his eyes on things."

"Long as it's focused on something exciting."

"I know, I've heard about him. He's worth watching. But like I said, don't say anything to the team people about him yet, if you haven't. If they fire him, we won't know where he is."

"I haven't said anything."

"What about the car?"

"Bernie knows the brother of a mechanic who works at the county garage where the car is impounded. The car, according to this guy, never had a fuel leak problem they could find. It was burned mostly on the inside, and not that bad. Not burned under the hood or under the car itself. The gas tank never caught fire and it was nearly empty."

"If the car didn't have a fuel leak of some kind, how was it Semieux smelled it the week before she died?"

"You asking me? How would I know?"

"Of course, it doesn't mean there wasn't one."

"You didn't want to tell me that, did you?"

"Makes sense with the gas can found at Steinmark's place, the gas smell in Semieux's car before the murder, and the mud on Steinmark's wheels and floor mats, which shouldn't have been there. Sloppy attempt at a frame-up, if that's what it is."

"And she never showed up at the dealer's to pick up the loaner," she said. "I checked it out myself, went there. They have their own security guard at night. The police have already dismissed him as a suspect. He's an older man, sixty-eight, with one lung. Can't walk across the street without giving out of breath. In fact, he stays inside all night. He can see the whole place from his desk in the showroom and from the back, in the shop, which is under the same roof. The place is lit up, only a few tire kickers and dreamers at night looking at cars when the salespeople can't bother them. Her loaner was parked right smack in front of his desk, just outside, in front of the window. She never showed up."

"Obviously, since she was found in her own car."

"Well, she might otherwise have shown up and left with someone. But he said she didn't."

"That's good to hear. Good work."

"What's so good about it?" she said.

"It cuts out another link in her chain of movements that night."

"Now, what can you tell me?"

I thought about that while taking a swallow from my glass.

"I've afraid you've been more productive than I have today, Ames. I got a prospect mailing list from the realtor for New French Fort. Some guy named Randall. Like squeezing blood out of a rock at first. The guy is sick about the murder taking place on his site. Can't blame him, you can see his sign all over the world now. But I convinced him the sooner he could eliminate his agents and associates from suspicion the better it would be, so he bought it."

"Well, you got that much. Any interesting names on it?"

"How would I know any of them? Maybe you'd like to take a look, yourself."

"And how would I know any of them?"

She dismissed it too quickly to suit me.

"Just do me a favor and look it over. Maybe somebody from the team is on it."

"Do I have to now?"

"Yes, in keeping in the spirit of our teamwork."

She scanned the list quickly, a computer printout of over six hundred names on twenty-five sheets, and I looked at her, watching her face closely.

"You're a fast reader, Ames."

"It's alphabetical, Wray. No." She put it down. "Not a soul."

I slid the list back into the envelope.

She went out onto the balcony. "I want to take a walk on the beach. Will you go with me? I'd feel safer."

I did not answer at first.

"Well?"

"Let me get my sandals."

We crossed the dune on the footbridge and walked northward at the water's edge. The sky was now overcast, with little moonlight getting through. The surf was barely visible and only a smattering of light from the houses and condos and the Holiday Inn along North Lumina, all behind the dune, lit the way. We spoke little at first. I knew she was uneasy with it, wrestling with her conscience, looking for both a way in and a way out of seducing me, assuming I was right.

She stopped, arms crossed, and faced the ocean and let the foam wash over her feet. Her perfume, the salt air, the smell of sand and lotions, her hair, intoxicating to the senses, mixed and wafted in the air around me.

"What time are you getting back tomorrow?" She looked out into the dark of the ocean.

"I don't know."

"You're lying. You're not going to Charlotte. You're going to Louisiana. You know I knew that."

"Yes, I did."

"I don't suppose it would do any good to ask you not to go, to leave the Fortiers out of it."

"No, it wouldn't. And I suppose that means you'll lose everything here."

"Probably." We resumed walking. "But if you think I'm going to tell you anything, you're wrong. You can go there and find anything you want, until hell freezes over, but you won't hear it from me. I have nothing left but my word, and I'm not giving it up."

"You've already made that clear and I'm no longer asking you to. But you need to find wherever it is in this world you belong, Ames, and go there, because you're a lost soul here."

She turned and faced me. "So damned smug, aren't you? So righteous. What the hell kind of risks do you take in this life? Living in that little world of yours on that, that damn pier, out on the water, away from everybody, everything, except when it suits you. People paying you money to live and work in your little buildings. Exercising, reading, studying weird-ass shit, academic crap. How dangerous. How awfully risky, Wray. Why, you're liable to be killed falling off your bank account or strangle on some dissertation."

"You want to borrow some money, Ames? You've got a funny way of asking for a loan."

"I don't want a damn thing from you. Everything's a damn joke with you. I can't stand it."

"I took my risks years ago and it cost the hell out of me." She knew what I was referring to. My marriage to my first wife, my career in the Marine Corps. "And I live on that pier alone. And I can't stand *that*. So it's not all that rosy."

"And I suppose you're celibate these days. So lonely. That you're not seeing what's-her-name—Sandra—your sweet, loyal little bird-dogging real estate friend who fills in between serious people."

"Sandra's a good and decent friend, yes, but she's not you."

"I'm not me either." She turned and headed back alone.

I watched her disappear into the darkness, then continued until I reached the inlet marking the end of the island, taking my time. The beach was beautiful at night, even in anger.

Wray Larrick, master of relationships.

I got back to the parking lot and dialed Ken Enright and apologized for calling so late. I asked him if he had a couple people he could trust to work with him about two days, while I went out of town. Sure, he told me.

"Good. I want you to keep a twenty-four-hour-a-day surveillance of John Steinmark's place at Wrightsville Beach. You know where it is. Anybody who gets anywhere near it, the police, the garbage man, anybody, whether they enter the place or not, I want to know. Descriptions, makes and license plates of vehicles, times, the works. Even Steinmark if he shows up. But don't interfere, don't go on the property yourself. Stay away from it and just watch. I'll call you when I get back. If anything happens, you have my number."

I went back into Ames' apartment and closed and locked the sliding doors behind me. Now was as good a time as any to pack up and leave, get another place. I went back to the bedroom to get my stuff. As I threw the travel bags on the bed and began stuffing them, Ames spoke from her room across the hall behind me, and a dim light came on there.

"Wray?" Her voice was soft now, even tender.

I turned to see her lying on her side in the dimness of the nightlight, head propped up on her hand, her long, sleek, nude body facing me, her hair falling over her face, the stiff nipples of her firm breasts pointed at me. I swear, right at me. She held out her hand.

"Please. Just us tonight," she said. "No harsh words, no problems. No tomorrows and no strings. Just us."

I walked over and leaned on the doorway. God help me. "I admire your skills in diplomacy, but maybe I'd better leave."

"No, please don't. Not this way, not angry."

I looked down at her shrewd smile with a hint of my own deviousness. She knew my button. And I think it was pointing at her.

"Think I've got a shot at Secretary of State?" she said.

"This is America, babe. Be what you want to be. You've got my vote."

I went to her. I was not yet, in all my shortcomings, a complete idiot.

14

When the plane landed at Louis Armstrong International Airport in Kenner, outside New Orleans, and the cabin doors opened, hot, humid air the weight of lead rushed in to claim those aboard. Those acclimated to it casually walked off, while the few unaccustomed moved slowly and seemed stunned by it, like they had been betrayed, one or two even fainting.

I was used to the heat and humidity. Even in coastal Virginia in summer, sweat ran from the pores like syrup. But this was a different heat. This was a tropical kind of heat that hung over and consumed everything and burned you like a woolen blanket in a steamy-hot kitchen. Ironically, I liked it. I had never been in Louisiana, though I had been in the tropics, and it would be a challenge to my lungs not experienced in years. Maybe, time permitting, I would get in a quick workout while here.

I checked out my rental, a dark green Ford Explorer, and left the airport and drove southwest to the Fortiers' home in Thibodaux.

The Fortiers lived in an immaculate, quiet neighborhood with people who evidently worked as hard on their property as they did on their jobs. The house was set back about a hundred feet from the street. It was a sprawling brick contemporary with large windows, on about one-and-a-half acres of lush green lawn, trimmed hedges, and flowers. Moss hung to the ground like stalactites from the trees on the borders of the lot.

I pulled into the wide, concrete driveway and stopped just short of the carport.

Maurice Fortier, dressed casually and wearing slippers, came out the side door under the carport to greet me with a congenial if tired smile. He was a wiry man whose muscles seemed to have worked hard and were still capable. We chatted a moment there, then went inside where I met Edna, whose smile was a little more forced, whose pain was more visible.

Edna would fix us some ice tea.

Maurice took me through the kitchen and dining room to the living room, a long, large space with an open stone fireplace and picture window offering a serene view of the backyard with pond and bird baths and gazebo and outbuilding. There was a covered patio and, at the rear of the lot, a patch of woods separating them from the next street over. The house was furnished with a blend of traditional and contemporary décor, and there were many family photos about, including a fair number of their just-murdered adopted daughter.

Before retiring, Maurice explained, he had been a maintenance superintendent on oil rigs for his company, mostly offshore. After Toni Jean joined the family, he had gotten transferred to the refinery onshore and taken a step down and a pay cut to be home where he could help more with her. They—he, Edna and the boys—had seen the story in the media when it happened. They had heard more about her through their church, the little girl whose mother tried to kill her, killed her brother, the one people felt sorry for but were afraid to, or couldn't, take in.

After she entered college, Maurice had gone back to his old position, until retiring last year. Just when things were going so well for the family, especially for Toni Jean, this had to happen. It seemed unfair, so cruel. His faith was shaken. For the first time in his life, he said, he questioned God's wisdom, His motive, even His true identity. He was hurt and bitter and wanted vengeance. He wanted somebody to pay.

"I never liked him," Maurice said of Steinmark. "I knew when I met him he was wrong for Toni Jean. He was a spoiled brat, a bully. I know the type. I tried to tell her, but I didn't want to interfere too much. I should've interfered more." He was near tears.

"He killed a lot more than my little girl. She was more than just another girl. Not another story in the news. She was—was—." He got up.

"Come here. I'll show you what I mean. Out here, in the back."

He led me out into the backyard to what appeared to be a shop or storage building about thirty-by-forty feet, perhaps even an elaborate playhouse with scalloped wood trim accented in colors.

We went inside and Maurice switched on the lights.

"I started building this when she was a junior in high school."

"Good grief." I was impressed.

It was nothing less than a museum of her athletic and academic accomplishments, planned and meticulously laid out, resembling as much a shrine to a goddess as a collection of memorabilia for an athlete-scholar; trophies, short and tall, plaques, ribbons, medals, banners and pennants, mementos and photographs, including many later ones of Toni Jean with celebrities and public leaders, all arranged in groups and categories representing her performances and honors from the earliest to the latest. A banner stretching overhead proclaiming Ivy Ridge the *National Champions* and T.J. *Athlete of the Year*. Lighting was installed to focus on and highlight the collection, giving it the effect of a treasure chest of shiny crystal and precious metals. It was like a timeline, a gallery marking the progression of her rise from obscurity to national, and to a degree, world prominence.

Maurice put on his glasses.

"Here's where it all started." He pointed and stepped closer to it. Gently, he picked up a small blue ribbon displayed in a box frame. "The seventh grade."

"I'll never forget the day she won this," he said. "A field day at school. The look on her face. It was the most beautiful sight I'd ever seen in my life. Still is. Liked to knocked me down in the driveway with it when I came home from work. You could see her whole life, her whole attitude just change from that point on. Amazing what a little thing like this can do for a child. I knew right then she was going to make it. Nothing could stop her after that." He put it back and took off his glasses.

We slowly began walking around the room, Maurice pointing out a number of items as we went. I was looking at the pictures now more than anything, especially the most recent ones. I was highly impressed by the symbols of greatness, had never seen anything quite like it up close. This certainly dwarfed my cigar box half full of stuff back home. But it was T.J. and those around her who most interested me now, particularly the last few weeks of her life. But I could tell, too, this was all there was left for Maurice and his family, this and the memories of T.J. And I could not help but feel moved by their sorrow. I could see moisture glistening in Maurice's eyes and felt we should go back inside.

The ice tea was on the coffee table and we sat across from one another. Edna, short and plump, almost listless, joined us for about five minutes, saying little until the doorbell rang and agitated her. The press was hounding them. But, fortunately, these were some friends calling on her.

After introducing her guests to me, Edna excused herself and went back into the kitchen with them.

"Do you know where the place is, where she lived when she was a child? Where the house was burned?" I said.

Yes, he knew. He tended the grave, Buddy's, a couple times a year, to keep it from being overgrown. I asked him if he could tell me how to get there. I assured him I was not some self-proclaimed psychic looking for vibes, but that I had come this far and might as well go back in her life as far as I could while here.

"You'd never find it. And nobody would tell you. I'll take you there."

I drove southward from Thibodaux, deeper into the bayou toward the gulf.

Southern Louisiana is at the far end of the moss belt, as I call it, a band that stretches from Wilmington, North Carolina, along the southern Atlantic seaboard and gulf states clear into southeast Texas, growing thicker through the deep South, where moss hangs from trees like witches' hair, a place of occasional tree-canopied back roads, thick, murky swamps and miles of pristine glades and wildlife, of vast stretches of sugar cane fields and tin-roof buildings. It is still a region qualified to call itself God's Country because, in spite of humanity and the oil industry blotting the countryside, there remain vestiges and vistas of prehistoric landscape, of rich, dark foliage and rising steam affecting an eerie, exciting feeling of being at the precipice of a mysterious and unexplored world in which one might expect to see giant raptors flying and dinosaurs feeding.

I brought up the subject of the foundation, as we drove, and Maurice's eyes lit up.

"Oh, that's going to be something," he said. "The things we'll be able to do for so many kids. And mothers."

They had just bought the land, he explained. The groundbreaking was scheduled for March. Individuals and corporations had pledged support from the start and it would be an overwhelming success. Abused and neglected children, children no one else wanted, abused women with nowhere to go at all, to the extent they could absorb them, would have a refuge on campus, a place where they could feel love and warmth and compassion and belonging, where they could heal, until ready to enter life again on a level playing field. He would take me to the site in Thibodaux on the way back and show me. It would be a prototype, hopefully, for others to copy, God willing.

"She was upset about something to do with it," I said.

"Not about the foundation, itself, about where the money was going. Jacqui trusted the wrong person and could have lost everything."

"How so?"

"It was April, when Toni Jean was signing with the *Storms*. She kept a half million dollars of her signing bonus, after taxes, and put the three million in a non-profit foundation. This was the seed money to get the land and get things going. She was going to pump money into it from her income every year, if she was lucky and kept playing."

"April, you say? I thought it was June, when she got back off tour."

"No, that was when we got the money back."

"I see. I'm lost."

"This was before the rest of us were on board, me and Paul Bonham, a friend of mine who's a lawyer, and father Connelly. Jacqui handled everything. She knew this investment advisor up in Philadelphia, been knowing him for years from her days at Ivy Ridge. Dennis White was his name, she said. She had him to manage the money, to invest it so it would grow. He was a lawyer, too, knew a lot of people with money, and he could get others to donate.

"Everything was okay until Toni Jean asked Jacqui to get her a statement, a report on where everything was going. Of course, this Dennis White fellow didn't have the money very long, but he already told Jacqui about all the great things he had lined up, so Toni Jean just wanted to see. After all, it was her money.

"Anyway," Maurice continued, "it was like he was dragging his feet. And when he finally sent them a statement, it was so general it didn't give any details. She called me and told me she wasn't very comfortable with the way things were going, that she'd feel better if everything were closer to home.

"I was talking to Paul Bonham about it at church the next Sunday. I've been knowing him all my life. He used to be attorney-general here in Louisiana and, before that, the district attorney in the parish. He's got offices here and Baton Rouge and New Orleans and knows more about this kind of stuff. And he said it didn't sound right to him, and said if it was okay with me and Toni Jean, he'd have it checked out, and I said fine."

"And he checked it out?"

"Oh, yeah, he checked it out. He came over that Wednesday night and we had a talk. Then, together, we called Toni Jean. Jacqui was out of town somewhere and we couldn't talk to her. We told Toni Jean to see Jacqui as soon as she could and have her contact Paul when she got back, that this Dennis White guy was not as forthright as he should be, they shouldn't be dealing with him, and she wanted her money back.

"Well, she called the next night and told me that Jacqui got mad as hell when she told her, saying she trusted Dennis White, she knew he was honest and responsible, and we had a nerve suggesting he was not when we didn't know beans about him and she did. He was a respected attorney with a successful practice, legally and financially, and so forth and so forth."

"So what happened?"

"Nothing for a while. Paul told me it might be tricky business, didn't offer any details and I didn't ask, but he would keep trying to see what he could do. That's when the team started the tour."

Maybe the worry over this accounted for Semieux's unhappy demeanor in some of the tapes and photos, I was thinking, since the problem had begun before leaving on tour.

"So," I said, "this was right after she got back." This, according to Steinmark, was when she was feeling better about things.

"Yes. She was upset about it the whole time she was gone. Every time she'd bring it up to Jacqui, Jacqui would tell her not to worry, she was handling everything, that her money was going to be fine.

"When they got back from Europe, they went to North Carolina, to Wilmington, to the training camp for two days, then she came home for a long weekend. But when she got here, she told me the first day they were back in Wilmington a man came to the gym where they practice, to see Jacqui in her office. A husky, rough-looking man in a suit.

"Toni Jean was about to go into the office. She couldn't tell exactly what they were saying, but she knew it wasn't good. She got a look at him when he left. When she went in the office, Jacqui was crying and shaking like a leaf. Scared flat to death."

"Who was the guy?"

"Jacqui wouldn't tell her. But Toni Jean got the license plate number off the car when he was leaving. It was a rental car, she thought. Just in case they had to call security, which Jacqui didn't want."

"Did they? Call security?"

"No, Jacqui told her it was a personal matter, an old aunt who died or something, not to say anything about it to anybody, including us."

"What'd she do with the license plate number? Or did she say?"

"Nothing. She wrote it down on Jacqui's desk somewhere, she said."

"Think the guy had anything to do with her getting her money back?"

Maurice grinned. "I don't know. I just know that Toni Jean said he had a south Louisiana accent. And a few days later, right before she went back to Wilmington, Paul called and told us he had her money back, in New Orleans. And he brought the paper work over."

"Unbelievable." I was amazed.

"Up here on the right." Maurice pointed.

It was a sparsely-populated area of stick houses with tin roofs, shanties, an occasional mansion or two for the local gentry, a country store with a gas pump, a brick or wood rancher or two, flickering images of past and present shown on a screen of roadside foliage thinning out as we went deeper into the countryside. The road went about six miles, then turned left onto a dirt road and went another mile along a strip of land bordering a swamp.

"Right here, on the right, that little clearing, there."

We pulled in and got out. It was five p.m.

15

So this was Gator Bite, as it was referred to, I was told. I could understand it. More like Mosquito Bite. The immediate area was deserted, no houses or people in sight, just remnants of what used to be a home place of some kind now overgrown with four-foot-tall weeds. We walked along the path about fifty yards, to where the charred remains of the house were located, an almost-clearing of what remained of debris.

"Careful of snakes," Maurice said.

"How about gators? Isn't that the 'Bite' part of this place?"

"Every now and then you'll see one up here sunning itself, but they usually stay closer to the water than this. We bother them more than they bother us."

We stopped where the front yard used to be, if a place like this could have designated yards. Off to the side, about twenty yards away, was the reasonably well-kept gravesite of Buddy Semieux, the only thing out here with special attention to make it stand out.

"I need to get back down here and do some more cleaning."

I stared at the remains of the house and imagined it whole in the dark of night and the screams of children begging for their lives, the flames bright orange against the night, growing larger and consuming it, and the shadowy figure of the witch-like mother creeping away, leaving her children to burn.

"This is all Semieux and Terraneau and Garneau land out here, "Maurice said. Some Touviers. Toni Jean's mother, Nadine, was a Terraneau, herself. Never knew her, of course. Some of her distant folks still live a couple miles up the road, there. Max, her great uncle, helps me keep the place from being completely run over with weeds. They're nice people, her folks, what's left of them. But none of them were able to do much for a child way out here, so they couldn't take care of Toni Jean. In fact, Max and his wife offered to, but the state said no. Too old, I guess."

We walked over to Buddy's grave.

"So this is the little fellow here the foundation's named after," I said.

"Yep, this is him."

"It's incomprehensible."

"They say before she got on drugs, Nadine was as sweet and innocent as Toni Jean was."

"Will she be buried here?"

"Yeah. Yeah, she'd want to be out here with Buddy. It's their land. We might have them moved on the campus, in Thibodaux, when it's finished, probably. Maybe sooner."

I began walking around the clearing, while Maurice checked over the property. I spotted something small and man-made sticking out of the ground. I bent down and scraped around it with my fingers and pried it loose from the soil. A plastic toy truck. How about that. I showed it to Maurice.

"That's funny. As many times as I've been here, I've never seen this before." He took it and placed it on the grave.

"Who owns this place, now that she and her brother are gone?"

"Well, Edna and I do, technically. It'll be the foundation's."

"How long before the oil companies get in here?"

"Tomorrow, if they have their way, but it'll be over my dead body."

"How much land is it?"

"Seven hundred fifty acres."

"Seven hundred fifty acres? You can put a couple oil refineries on seven hundred fifty acres. Can't you? I'm no expert."

"You can preserve a lot of land and wildlife, too. This is not money-making land, except for oil."

"Sounds strange coming from an oil man."

"I know. The oil business has been good to us. But it doesn't stop me from thinking right."

"Has anybody tried to buy it from Toni Jean, or you and Edna now?"

"Oh, yeah." He chewed on a weed. "But it ain't for sale."

"Anybody you know?"

Maurice hesitated, perhaps a little alarmed at the tone of the question. "Doesn't make any difference, they know it's not for sale. Not now, not any time. And when Edna and I are gone, Mark and Jeff aren't selling, either. God, I hope they don't."

"Has Paul Bonham ever shown an interest in it?" I was treading closer.

Maurice sucked on his weed and spat, taking his time answering. "Paul Bonham is an old friend of mine." That drew the line and shut down the subject.

I let it sink in, unable to think of a way to get around it without offending him, if I hadn't already.

"Well, I've got a nine o'clock flight to make in New Orleans."

We returned to the car.

"Let me ask you," I said. "If Steinmark turns out not to be the one who ki—not responsible for Toni Jean, who would be your next guess, if anybody?"

"He's the one."

We got in and drove away.

"But what if he's not?"

"Probably some hoodlum, some common criminal looking for somebody to hurt. Or maybe it's Dennis White. But I know in my heart it's Steinmark."

"You don't think it could be anybody with the *Storms*?"

"No, I don't think so. Of course, these days you think you know the world and you don't."

"How do you like Jacqui personally?"

"Jacqui's okay. Pushy as hell, but that's how she got where she is, I guess. She was great for Toni Jean. Best decision she ever made, going to Ivy Ridge with Jacqui. Not much for business, though. Needs to stick to coaching. We love her like family."

"She came down here a lot, didn't she?"

"Frequently. Stayed with us many times."

"Think she could kill anybody?"

Maurice gave a surprised look, then answered. "No, but she could chew your leg off and make you wish you were dead. Tough gal."

Maurice took me for a quick look at the site for the campus. We walked around the grounds and he was animated in his detailed description of the plans, excited as a child, himself, and near tears standing in the open field, reminded that Toni Jean would not be here to share in the joy of it all, her own dream.

We pulled into the driveway at Maurice's and got out and shook hands. I thanked him for his help and hospitality. I appreciated the invitation for supper and the chance to meet the boys, but would not be able to stay, under the circumstances, as I was sure there would not be much eating going on. Perhaps I would come to the funeral. Yes, I would.

Edna came out and called to Maurice.

"Just a moment." He went to her and they spoke. He patted her on the shoulder and hugged her. She went back into the house. He walked back down the driveway to my car.

"The state medical examiner in Jacksonville, North Carolina, just called the funeral home here. They're sending Toni Jean's remains back on a plane tomorrow."

"Sorry. I know it won't be much coming from me, but for what it's worth, I know everyone was right when they said you did good by her."

Maurice nodded, unable to speak, and I shook his hand. Then he caught his breath and made a sweeping gesture with his arm at his home behind him, and spoke haltingly.

"See this? This is all we have in the world of value to call our own. The rest belongs to the foundation. But I'll sell the whole damn ball of wax, every damn thing I have, to get that no-good son of a bitch that killed my little girl, John Steinmark or no John Steinmark."

I nodded back and said I would do what I could to help and it would not cost him a penny. Then I left him standing in the driveway grieving in a way no one could but a parent who had lost a child this way.

On the way out, I picked up my cell phone and dialed my daughter's number back home in Virginia and chatted a moment. I do not, by habit, talk on a cell phone while driving, but just felt the urge to do so this one time.

At the airport I called Enright, who was off duty from his regular job and was watching Steinmark's place on my behalf. No one had been there but Steinmark's lawyer and the police, which could be expected.

"I want you to do something," I said to Enright, holding a photocopy of Jacqui's desk pad in my hand. "Go out to the airport right now and check the rental car companies for this license plate number and date." I called them out to him. "I need to know who rented the car, the name and address, anything you can get from them. Tell them that you have to have it, that there was an accident or whatever. I'll call you in about three or four hours."

My workout in the steamy heat would have to wait.

16

After a couple stops, the flight landed in Philadelphia at 1:15 a.m.

I checked into the airport hotel and took a shower. Afterward, I switched on the news to watch a repeat of Ames' nightly report concerning the murder being looped on the network. She certainly was getting some air time out of this.

I called Enright, who told me the car was rented the day in question by a man named Carmine Philyaw, from New Orleans. No other information on him. Not surprising. I did not think the rental car agent would actually give out even that much information. Laxity on his part, but I would take it. Maybe Enright was smoother than he appeared, which might be good or bad.

I opened the newspaper I had picked up in the lobby and went through it until I found the column of the well-known reporter-columnist I thought might be able to help me. If anyone knew what went on in this town, outside the police, it would be this guy. After all, newspaper people were in the business of gathering and disseminating information and, sometimes, if you gave them something they would give you something. And this man would have it all to give, if he were willing to talk to me. Cops and public officials did not do that. And neither did the people I was interested in. They are the last people you ask about themselves, especially if the implication is negative. In this case it was Dennis White I wanted to know about.

I turned up the TV to better hear Ames's report.

"...I'm here, outside the coroner's office in New Hanover County, where Dr. Melvin Conway just announced minutes ago that the state was releasing the remains of the body of basketball superstar Toni Jean Semieux from the medical examiner's lab in Jacksonville, for transport tomorrow to her parents' care near Thibodaux, Louisiana, where funeral arrangements have not been finalized.

"Dr. Conway would not comment on the autopsy report, which was turned over by medical examiners to police and the district attorney here. This information could be released to the public in a matter of days, we're told, but isn't expected to include much more than is already known, that she died from a gunshot wound to the head and that the murderer, or murderers, burned her car in an attempt to conceal the act.

"Ms. Semieux's former fiance, professional football player John Steinmark of the *Carolina Cougars*, who, at the time, is the only person of interest in the case, has yet to be arrested or charged. Steinmark was questioned extensively on two occasions since the murder and released both times. He is currently in camp with the *Cougars* in Charlotte and is expected to return to Wilmington, probably tomorrow, for more questioning.

"A *Cougars* spokesperson says Steinmark is busy with the team and unavailable for comment. His attorney, Loomis Sullivan, of Wilmington, who I spoke with earlier today, says he'll meet with the press tomorrow morning to discuss his client's situation, though it's not expected he'll have much to add.

"*Storms* president Carol Phillips Grambrell confirmed today she had hired the services of a private investigator to help in the case, but would not disclose the name. Reportedly, he is out of state pursuing leads in the case…"

I was sitting on the edge of the bed. Christ's sake, tell the world, why don't you.

"And that's where the story is now," Ames said. "We'll be standing by to inform you of any further developments as they occur. Until then, in Wilmington, North Carolina, live for Channel Eight, I'm Morgan Dalton."

I called the newspaper and asked for the news room. Nobody else would be there at night but the printers and carriers, and maybe one reporter doing the graveyard watch.

A young man answered.

"I don't suppose Gil Russo is in," I said.

"Won't be until tomorrow. Can I help you?"

"I'd like to get a message to him as soon as possible. It's important."

"What is it?"

"He covers crime and the courts, doesn't he?"

"Yes."

"My name is Wray Larrick. Wray with a W. He doesn't know me. I'm staying here at the hotel next to the airport." I gave him the name and number. "Tell him I'm calling about a private investigation matter I'm involved with, and a name of one of your local attorneys came up. I don't expect him to crawl out of bed, but I'd like to see him as early in the morning as possible, if I can."

"Can I tell him the attorney's name?"

"Not really. I'll let him tell you if he wants. But only if he calls to find out who it is and what he's done, which won't be any later than the first flight out for me."

"Will do."

I thanked him and hung up, then dialed Carol Gambrell.

"Why do you call me at this hour, and where are you?"

"You said anytime, anywhere."

"And you said a report every day. And it's tomorrow and you're late."

"I've been on a plane, on my way back."

"From Louisiana?"

"Yes."

"And?"

"And what?"

"What did you accomplish? Anything?"

I could sense her rising in the bed at the other end in anticipation.

"I know about the three-million-dollar investment that was called off. So what's the big deal with that?"

"And you don't say a word about it to anyone. You understand that, Wray? Absolutely not a word. Not now, not ever. I'm trusting you. *Paying* you and trusting you."

"I won't. I work for you. Don't worry." I could hear some relief in her movement. "Is there anything you'd like to tell me about it?"

"Me tell you? No, what should there be to tell?"

"Well, you were keeping it a big secret from me until now."

"It has nothing to do with this case. Where are you?"

"In Atlanta, changing planes." Lie, lie.

"And you'll be back early in the morning."

"By mid-day anyway."

"I'll see you right away in my office when you get back."

"I'll do that if you tell Ames not to mention my name on the air. I can't work effectively when everybody knows who I am before I get to them."

"I'll take care of that." She hung up. Some people let you know how important they are by the way they do it.

I switched off the light and lay down to sleep.

The phone rang minutes later as I was falling off. A sleepy, gravelly voice spoke to me.

"This Mr. Larrick? Gil Russo here. You left a message for me."

"Yes. It could've waited, but since you took the trouble I'll get right to it. I'm a private investigator from down south representing an anonymous client about to do business with some people, one an attorney here, and my employer wants him checked out. I thought maybe you could help me."

"Why me? Why not the bar association or Better Business Bureau? Or the consumer affairs people?"

"I'm checking with them, as well, but they don't give out the kind of information I'm looking for, and they're not open at this hour."

"Neither am I, usually."

D.L. COLEMAN

"But you called, though, didn't you?"
"Okay. Who's the lawyer?"
"I'd rather discuss it in person. How about in the morning?"
"It's already frigging morning. I'll be busy."
"Fair enough. Tell you what I'll do. I'll give you the lawyer's name now and you tell me what you can about him, if anything. If I'm satisfied with what I hear, and you want to know the other name, you meet me in person to get it."

"So there's another name. This is getting confusing." There was a moment of silence. "Okay, throw the bone."

"Dennis White."

There was another silent moment.

"You going to be up long?"

"Not long. You know what frigging time it is?"

Russo chuckled, then coughed hard.

"I'll meet you there, in the lobby, in forty-five minutes. Have some I.D. with you. I don't walk into blind alleys." He hung up. People like to hang up.

I met him in the lobby as requested. He was in his late fifties, overweight, and looked much older than in his photo at the head of his column. He was dressed casually, wore flip flops, and his gut hung over his belt. He looked like one of those homeless nomads seen around flea markets. He smoked a cigar and had a hacking cough from it. He seemed a man who was battling illness and was on the verge of either winning or losing. His breathing was labored, his demeanor crusty, but he seemed amiable enough. He scrutinized my I.D.

We went directly to my room.

"So what made you call me?" He was tired from the ride up the elevator. He turned his chair backward and faced me.

"I don't know anybody here. I get your column at home, thought I'd come here. So what about Dennis White?"

"So why don't you level with me first."

"Meaning what?"

"You're here on the Semieux murder case. Right?"

"You're fast as lightening."

"It's have to be dead not to know that."

"Small world. I'd have made a hell of a spy."

"Like I said, I don't walk into blind alleys. Your cell phone area code puts you from Virginia, caller I.D., an out-of-state investigator. Your flight originated from New Orleans, the Semieux girl's home area. And your original flight from Wilmington, North Carolina, where the murder occurred. I was watching the murder update on the news earlier. The reporter's a looker, by the way. I just connected the dots."

"I'll tell her you said so. And she's looking for a job, if you know anybody."

"I'll ask around. A face like that couldn't hurt anybody. And you think Dennis White has something to do with the killing of this girl?"

"I don't know. That's why I here asking."

"How does his name figure into it?"

"I can't say."

"Okay." Russo was more serious now. "I'll tell you about Dennis White, you give me the other name. Fair enough?"

I nodded in agreement.

He coughed hard and long again. "Dennis White is a very successful lawyer and investment consultant who has a low-key but lucrative practice representing some very important people, among others, in business and tax matters. That's not a secret. He lives well and anybody around here who is anybody knows him.

"On the flip side," he said further, "what few of us know for sure, and even others only suspect, Dennis White has a darker side to his practice representing organized crime. He launders dirty money for, let us say, certain unnamed characters, and makes it clean by blending it with legitimate money. Some of his others clients don't know this. Some do and don't care. He's slick and the law hasn't been able to touch him. Not yet anyway.

"But he's not a killer. Some of the people he deals with would kill you in a second, but not Dennis. And he wouldn't have anybody killed. He's not made like that."

"You know him personally?"

"Oh, yeah, very well. As an acquaintance, not a friend. I don't socialize with him, except lunch a couple times. But I don't see how that could figure into the death of the Semieux girl. Unless, of course, you could shed some light on it for me."

"Afraid not."

"So what's the other name?"

"Carmine Philyaw," I said.

Russo'e eyes squinted and he blew out a puff of smoke and coughed. "New Orleans, where you just came from."

"That's right. I think *you're* the godfather around here."

Russo chuckled and coughed again. He stood up.

"Look, Larrick, you've got me interested. We can help one another here. I'd like to know about the connection between Dennis White and Carmine Philyaw and the Semieux murder. And you need to know something about Carmine Philyaw, if I'm correct."

"I can guess at it."

"And there's something about Dennis White you don't already know. Something that, from where I'm sitting, will blow your socks off. 'cause I don't think you already know it."

I got up and paced slowly. "I have a confidential agreement with my employer."

"And a deal with the pretty face, I'll bet."

"Yes."

"Figured as much. Had to be. Her last job was in Virginia, same town you're from."

"Yes." I was amazed at the speed of his work.

"Figures. I understand. No sweat, I can appreciate that. I'm willing to wait until after she breaks any initial story before mentioning a word of it. That's a promise. I work on my own publishing schedule, and I don't break my word. Ask anybody. I've been in this business thirty seven years. I didn't get this far by being a liar and breaking my word. It's all I have, that and a good set of ears. She can have the meat. I'll gnaw on the bone for years to come, if it's worth it." He coughed. "Or months."

I paced and thought about it, but I couldn't stand it and he knew it. "Okay, tell me about Philyaw."

"As you probably guessed, he's a gangster. The New Orleans mob. Muscle. Enforcer. Big time scary guy, a guy who'll hurt you. How do you know him?"

"I don't. He paid a visit to Jacqui Van Autt, the *Carolina Storms* coach. Scared her half to death. Not long before T.J. Semieux was murdered."

He stopped puffing his cigar and stared at me, listening.

I did not want to tell him, as I had said, but I needed this man's help. I told him about the three million dollars of Semieux's signing bonus money and how it looked like it got recovered, not mentioning the Fortiers or Paul Bonham, not the foundation, referring to them only as certain parties. I was also careful not to insinuate Dennis White actually murdered anyone. I did not need that complication, as I was just trying to fit all the pieces together, what I had anyway, and find other pieces to go with them. And as I paced and explained all this to Russo and glanced at him repeatedly, I sense from that he might be ahead of me.

"So what does all this look like to you?" I said.

"Sounds to me like some home boys from New Orleans were possibly taking food out of the mouths of the Philly boys. But the original deal was between Van Autt and White. There's no way you can know if the mob guys even knew about it, much less assume they had their hands on Semieux's money. If they didn't have it, they couldn't have lost it. And they damn sure wouldn't have given it back if they did have it, just because the girl asked for it."

"And there's no way to find out for sure?"

"Not unless one or more of the New Orleans or Philly boys gets hurt, Philyaw or somebody higher. That'd be your tip-off. You take from them, somebody pays.

"But I'll tell you one thing, the mob people didn't kill the girl. It's not their style. She wouldn't figure in it at all. It's the money that counts. It wasn't even a professional job. They'd kill Dennis White, maybe, but never the girl."

"That I understand. Now blow my socks off with something about Dennis White, like you promised."

Russo smiled and blew out a puff of smoke. "You ready for this? Jacqui Van Autt and Dennis White are first cousins."

My eyebrows went up.

"Oh yeah, that's right. Their fathers were brothers, Fred and Tony DiLuca, low-end soldiers with the Philly mob in the sixties and seventies. They were executed together in seventy-three, their bodies found in the trunk of a car, case unsolved. Serious family problems, Dennis's mother with depression, Jacqui's a drug addict, so Dino and Jacqueline, as they were called then, were raised by an aunt and uncle in the Midwest under their name, Van Autt. Dennis changed his to White when he started college, apparently thinking ahead, severing any connection with the DiLucas, the taint of the mob. But as they say, you can take the kid out of the 'hood, but."

"Those sons of bitches." I wondered if the cops knew this. No wonder they kept it a secret, Ames, Jacqui and Carol. So damned concerned about their image. And they needed a moron who wouldn't find out but would help them look good while being stupid. Find the killer if you want, but don't you dare find anything else, dummy.

Was there something burned into my forehead?

We talked a little longer and I slowly cooled down. I thanked Russo for his help. He certainly had done more for me than I had for him. We agreed to talk further by phone as the case progressed, assuming it did.

I couldn't sleep, too restless. I checked out and caught the early plane.

17

It was mid-morning when I got back to North Carolina and Ames' apartment at Wrightsville Beach. I was beat, not having slept since early the previous morning, and I did not like going without sleep. It was bad for health, it disrupted my regimen and made me moody. I dropped my bag and envelope and plopped down at her computer station to use her phone, since my cell battery was weak. I dialed Ken Enright.

"I'm back," I told Enright. "Where are you?"

"Here at the gym. They're practicing now. But don't worry, I have somebody at Steinmark's. How goes it with you?"

"Okay. How about your end?"

"Nothing much, just the police going in a couple times and a few tourists gawking at the place. He's coming back here tonight, I hear."

"Great. Stay in touch."

"Will do."

I changed into my trunks and went down to the water for a swim. I felt better then, revitalized, still tired but looser. Afterward, I went back and toweled off on the balcony. When I entered through the sliding doors, Ames was coming in the front.

"I see you made your way back." She avoided my eyes. "When did you get in?" She put down her gear and went into the kitchen to wash her hands.

D.L. COLEMAN

I stood in the middle of the living room with the towel around my neck, water still dripping off me.

"Dennis White," I said. "That's when."

She hesitated, without eye contact. "So?"

"So you could have saved us all a lot of time and expense."

"It couldn't have saved *me* anything. Besides, you were told it had nothing to do with this case. But, no, you had to go trollop half way around the country to see for yourself. So don't get bitchy with me, Wray, darling, please."

"Nothing to do with the case? You put a three-million-dollar raw steak in a shark's mouth and yank it out before it gets a bite and you think he's not going to be upset? Who in hell are you people to presume there could be no connection with that and T.J.'s death? These are gangsters we're talking about here, Ames. What the hell's wrong with you?"

"Gangsters? What damn gangsters? Just Dennis White." She put down the hand towel and came around the counter to me. "And just as soon as Jacqui was informed, she got the money back. Presto. Case closed about the money.

"You think they're stupid, Wray? Carol and Jacqui? They can't afford any of their people dealing with characters like him, or anybody finding out they did. If it got out, it would ruin them. There's too much at stake here for them. The money, the league, the whole concept would be jeopardized. T.J. wasn't killed by any mobsters. You said as much, yourself." She turned back to the kitchen.

"I was implored not to discuss it and I didn't," she said. "I've gotten some exclusive reportage out of it. I've worked all year on the story of this league, along with everything else I report on. True, I wish T.J. hadn't been killed, but she was, and money can't buy this kind of exclusivity. So you're damned right I played along."

"Jacqui got the money back?" I said. "Jacqui got nothing back. Don't feed me that crap. You know the deal. Why in hell didn't you tell me Jacqui and Dennis White are cousins?"

Ames froze, then turned back, shocked.

"What?"

I told her what Gil Russo told me.

"That's important information, Ames. You can't keep something like that to yourself in a case like this. Have you told the police this? Maybe they don't know."

She stood there, momentarily paralyzed.

"I—I didn't know this, that they were related, I mean."

"You're either still lying like hell and conning me, or you're also being conned, or both."

She reached for the sofa and sat down, clearly stunned.

I could tell she was genuinely surprised and hurt at being left out of the loop by Jacqui, maybe Carol, too. She looked pitiful, but I was not finished.

"I'm surprised at you, Ames, a person of your intelligence and experience, your background dealing with lying-ass politicians and the like, and you can't even remotely sense the presence of a phony, a liar in your midst. I find that hard to believe."

"I didn't know, Wray. I swear to God, I didn't know. Where did you get this?"

"The same place you might have found it if you'd looked. You've been shadowing these people for a year, even traveling with them. You're the one who discovered White. Now you tell me you don't even have a clue of the connection?"

"I didn't know they were related, or anything about their family, and that's the truth." She buried her face in her hands. "Oh, God, how did this happen? How did I miss this?"

"Tell me about it. White changed his name when he moved away to college and law school, so he could blend in with the woodwork when he got back. Jacqui's never been associated with the mob, of course. She's supposedly afraid of all that, but she's greatly influenced by White. They're like brother and sister more than cousins. Frankly, I can't imagine anyone influencing her. Dennis White must be an awfully strong character.

"Carol and Jacqui didn't want a regular investigator," I said. "Hell, he might find something. They wanted a chump. 'Yeah, that's it, Morgan. Would you happen to know a chump? Somebody who's stupid, somebody you don't mind sacrificing so we can look like we really give a damn about finding T.J.'s killer and, at the same time, hide our little secret so we don't ruin our image by showing the world how bumbling and corrupt and tied to hoodlums we are?'"

"Where did you learn this? I want to know." She got up and went to the balcony, gripping the rail hard, and looked out at the ocean, not seeing it.

"Carol and Jacqui told you to do whatever it took to stop me from seeing the Fortiers."

"That had nothing to do with the other night," she said of our sexual tryst. "Don't you dare accuse me of that."

"Maybe." But I really believed her. She had been as much a chump herself.

I stood in the doorway behind her.

"Gil Russo, in Philadelphia, is who I talked to."

"Gil Russo? The columnist? You went to Philadelphia to see him?"

"It's his backyard, his beat. Dennis White lives there. Why wouldn't I see him?"

"You see Dennis White?" she said over her shoulder.

"No, Ames, I didn't. Why don't you just tell me everything you know so we don't run into this problem again."

"That's it. There's nothing else to tell. I swear. When I found out about Dennis White's sometimes shady associations, I told Jacqui and she immediately went to him and told him she was withdrawing T.J.'s account. That's what she said. He couldn't afford the negative exposure any more than she or the team could. That's when she told Carol and me."

"Were you present when she told Carol?"

"No, I wasn't."

"And she didn't, I'll bet. Jacqui got a visit from a thug with the New Orleans mob. That's what happened. He threatened her, and T.J. saw it. And Jacqui went to White with it, her cousin, you know.

That's when the money came back, and quick. And that wasn't until they got back off tour, as you must know.

"You know Maurice and Edna Fortier," I said. "They never mentioned the name of their lawyer friend who's on the board of the foundation?"

"Not by name. Jacqui told me their friend, who is a lawyer, would be handling the Buddy Semieux Foundation business with them. But she never mentioned his name. It wasn't important to me. Why? Should it be?"

"More important than you think. He's a heavy duty guy down there. He's the one who got the money back faster than Fedex."

"How?"

"This lawyer friend of theirs went to the enforcer to get the money back."

"Does this mean the New Orleans mob people have her money now, like switching banks or something?"

"No, I don't think it's a game of musical money bags with the mob. I just think this friend of theirs was doing them a favor, that it's a matter of local pride. From what I felt down there, these people are crazy as hell about T.J. Semieux and madder than hell about her murder. I think the lawyer friend went to the edge and asked a favor from the other side, and the other side gladly granted it. Maybe a quid pro quo of some kind nobody will ever know about. A guy like this friend of theirs, believe me, is a guy who can pull a lot of strings around Louisiana.

"According to Russo," I continued, "when Jacqui was coach and athletic director at Ivy Ridge, white was trying to use her influence there to gain access to the school's investment accounts and leading supporters, all those millions of dollars of alumnae contributions and trust funds. But it didn't work. She wouldn't hear it. She didn't have that kind of clout. But when she made the switch to the pros, it was a different ball game. She was a founder, a key player with a lot of authority and influence. Jacqui says something, everybody jumps. And all those millions in contracts and bonuses and naïve young women in need of guidance. So Dennis White, Esquire, had a whole

D.L. COLEMAN

new frontier to reap, with the willing help of his secret little cousin. And that's the way it's going to be, unless it's stopped.

"Personally, I don't give a damn about their millions. That's their problem. I'm looking for a killer here and all I've gotten is a smokescreen, and you've been a part of it."

"I wonder if Carol really knows all of this," she said.

"I just know that everybody around here knows more than I do. But if she doesn't, she will soon as I get cleaned up and get there."

"I'm truly sorry for my part in all this, Wray. Please forgive me and believe me."

"I'll sleep on it."

"Damn." She brushed by me and went outside. "Damn. Damn. Damn. That lying bitch." She grabbed her bag and started for the door.

"Whoa. Where you going?"

"You want to see Jacqui, you can see what's left of her."

"Hold it. No, no, come back. Don't do that. Not yet."

"Why the hell shouldn't I?"

"You'll get arrested, for openers, and lose everything."

"What the hell else is there to lose, Wray? She used me, she used both of us. Worst of all, she had *me* to use *you*. Damn her. Damn both of them." She went out the door and ran down and jumped into her car.

I stood at the top of the steps and yelled down to her. "Don't do it. I need time. I need you. I need your help."

Her tires squealed as she left the lot.

"You'll get a ticket. Slow down. You'll kill a tourist. You damn hardhead. Jeeze."

I closed the door and went to the shower. Afterward, I slipped on light slacks, a golf shirt and topsiders. When I went into the living room, a subdued Ames was on the balcony again, looking out, pensive. I stepped out and leaned on the railing next to her.

"I cooled off at the end of the street," she said. "Damn traffic. Can't get anywhere."

"How did you discover White was a crook with the mob?"

(118)

"I had no idea he was with those people. I didn't know until you just told me. He came to Ivy Ridge to see Jacqui. I was staying with her at the time, doing the feature series that ran just before the national championship playoffs. She introduced him as an acquaintance, an investment consultant and tax law specialist who was opening a new agency to take on professional athletes. He seemed very uncomfortable around me. I sensed he didn't like the press. I mentioned it to Jacqui, she said it was just his nature. But I thought I sensed something else.

"I mean," Ames said, "why would a sports or business agent be afraid of a reporter? It's part of their business, dealing with the press, the public. Anyway, Jacqui said she was considering referring him to handle investments for some of the players she was signing onto the team in the draft that was set up for the league. So I talked with my boss later and we figured it would be a good idea to do a segment on this end of the game, sports agents and what they do, that kind of thing. Especially with all this new money being thrown around. Gobs of money. I called White first, among others, for an interview, and he turned me down flat.

"Red flags," she said. "I called a reporter I know who checked him out as best she could. Some people liked him, she said, some lost their shirts with him, like dumping money in a black hole in space. Had a few rough characters for clients, too. I told Jacqui and she told Carol, supposedly, and that was it. Or so I thought."

"When was that?"

"April sometime, right after T.J.'s signing."

"Did you tell T.J. yourself?"

"Yes."

"Which was when?"

"Late April, just before the tour started in May. I figured she already knew. Apparently, she didn't. But I didn't know at the time she hadn't known. I figured Jacqui had told her. T.J. must have been pissed.

"So," she said, "Jacqui knew all along White was crooked and turned over T.J.'s money anyway. How could she?"

"Keep it the family, right or wrong." I could see the huger for revenge growing in her look.

"Ames, I'm the only one here who hasn't lied to you and conned you, except for Bernie, I guess."

"I know, Wray. Please don't gloat."

"You've got to play hardball with these people for your own sake. They're not your friends. They're in a big business with a lot at stake, and the most you are to them as a journalist is a potential public relations blunder. Your being offered the PR job by Carol is no more than a cooptation for neutralizing you. They'll use anybody or anything to succeed. It's understandable, women's basketball has never been a big money maker, but it's dog-eat-dog and you've been bitten."

"I know that, too, Wray, and please don't preach."

"You'll have a hell of a story to tell when you break it."

I could see the killing fields in her eyes. Then her head jerked.

"What do you mean, *when*?"

"Not a word of this, until I say so. Please."

"Are you crazy? Sit on this? You must be nuts. What about Russo?"

"He won't run it until you break it. He promised. But he won't wait forever either."

"Why wouldn't he break it?"

"It's part of our deal. I keep him informed of anything I learn about the case and he holds it a while, at least until you break the initial story."

"Why would he agree to that?"

"Couple reasons. One, he's sick. Emphysema. He hasn't got much time and there's nothing else to prove, he's said it all. So it's not important at this time in his life to be first."

"That's too bad, I'm sorry. He's a brilliant investigative reporter."

"Second, I told him of your situation, being forced out and looking for a job. He thinks you're beautiful and have the look to make it work. But he knows you're not cut out for sports. Your ignorance of things athletic comes across strongly with people who know sports, he says."

"He said that about me? Gil Russo did?"

"He meant well by it."

"Gil Russo said I have the look to make it? Well, that's a consolation, I guess, considering how important he is in the business. Maybe there is hope after failure."

I leaned on the rail with her. "Failure? When were you ever a failure?"

"You're right, I admit it. This is the wrong beat for me. I'm not taking their job. They can go to hell."

"And I'll drive them to the airport when they go. But you didn't fail, you were given an assignment and you did what you could. There will be a great story out of it, no matter how this ends up. So quit brooding."

"I have a right, Wray, I hurt. I've been used, betrayed by people I've cared about, people I've trusted."

"I'll get us a drink." I went to the kitchen. Drink. Good excuse to drink something. Tired as hell, hadn't slept, but it's the middle of the day and I am drinking already. Like a damn soap opera, let's all get dressed up, grab a drink, and bitch at one another. Must be the fatigue.

I returned with the glasses and stood next to her. There had never been any serious friction between us. Our relationship to this point, and to the point we now had one, had been passionate, intense and gratifying, then non-existent, but always respectful and never volatile. I was thinking more about that than the case and the fighting it was presenting, about how maybe I had lost her forever, after all, how maybe through the present minefield of mistrust, I might have bridged the gap back to her, especially in light of the return of this explosive and god-unexplainable sex imprinted in me by her, like something cosmic and gravitational branding my chest with a sizzling, smoking "Nobody fucks you like I do." How right you are. How promising.

Yeah, must have been the fatigue.

She broke the momentary silence, her gaze a light-year away.

"Wray, why did you never tell me about your sister? Why did you never trust me with it?"

It caught me by surprise. She was referring to the thing that happened when I was twelve, when I turned my back on my five-year-old sister, who I was watching at the time, for two minutes and she disappeared off the face of the earth, never to be found. The experience had done more to define and alter the course of my life than anything, more than war and losing twelve dead and wounded in an ambush, or losing the love of my life to cancer. I looked into my half-full glass. "I have to meet with Carol. She's expecting me and I'm late. We can talk about it another time, if you like."

"It's okay." She touched my shoulder gently.

I went back to the bedroom to dress for my meeting with Carol Gambrell. When I came back through the living room toward the door, Ames called out from the balcony, where she was now leaning back on the rail, looking at me. "Where are you going?" It was a commanding, lustful look.

"I'm late." I strapped on my watch. I could feel her pull but truly wanted to keep my mind on business. I was exhausted and needed to account for myself and the money I was charging, before crashing.

"You can do that later. You can do me first." She walked inside and pulled me to her.

"You're making it awfully hard for me to do my job."

"I'm making it awfully hard anyway." She pulled at my shirt and began kissing my chest, my shoulders.

"I am a man of steel." I was already melting down. I was especially excitable when sleep-deprived.

"We'll see." She slid down and pulled at my belt, kissing her way.

"You know," I said, "I think what you're about to do is still considered a felony in this state."

"So read me my rights. Just don't try to stop me." Fleeting kisses.

"'course, I don't think they really enforce it that strictly."

"Um-hmm."

"I think they might have changed it to a misdemeanor."

"Mmmmm."

"In fact, I think they look the other way."

"Ummmh. Ummmh."

Oh, god. I was a goner. Might as well help her.

I stripped and picked her up and held her close to my chest, kissing her deeply, her legs clammed around my waist. I carried her down the hallway, scraping, bumping against the walls, passionately thrusting the whole way. I almost broke out laughing. "I wonder what a spaceship full of alien tourists would think if they could see us now." Kiss. Break. "Probably say, 'Oh, we've seen this before. It's a rodeo.'"

"Wray, shut up."

I put her on the bed. The dynamics were fierce. She was more animated now than ever before, not just passionate but aggressive, more taking than sharing. No pauses to savor it, no interludes to hold things, just a desperation, an insatiable hunger I found distracting, almost violent, even painful. Strip mining, I thought, scorch and burn. I had experienced this once years before, in my twenties, a one-nighter with a young woman whose fiance was in service and overseas . She had been loyal until she could stand it no longer and took it out on me. It was then I learned women could be rough, too, especially when it was impersonal, did not mean anything.

When it was over with Ames, we lay silently stuck to the sweaty sheets catching our breath. There was no cuddling. She did not look into my eyes this time, and I thought maybe she had confused me with someone else. This had never happened before. This was not our routine, modus operandi, not the way we treated one another. I felt more like I had been in a dog fight. She had not just made love to me, or with me, or even just had sex with me. She had just screwed me over. And I had not liked it.

So much for any bridge I might have imagined between us.

18

"You're late." Carol Gambrell looked up from some papers on her desk as I entered her office carrying a plastic grocery bag full of videos and papers.

"You have an awfully fine watch." I took the chair in front of her desk and set the bag on the floor beside me.

Carol's appearance perked up my sleepy eyes. She wore solid purple dress slacks, white blouse, and her golden hair was pulled back in a bun with a matching purple bow. So daintily perfect, an elfin-like creature. She looked like a garden I might want to fall asleep in. Nobody ever looked better in clothes, best I can remember, every subtle line and curve evocative. But I was also temporarily spent, thanks to Ames, so the observation was purely intellectual. Sure.

"Sorry I'm late. I really mean that. I got tied up." In a manner of speaking.

"I know. I called Morgan." A touch of sarcasm.

"So you know she's doing her part then."

"Can it, will you. Just tell me what you've been doing."

"First of all, I'm asking you to say nothing to anyone—I mean *no* one—about what I'm about to discuss with you. Is that okay?"

She put down her pen.

"I hire *you* and pay *you* and you ask *me* for confidentiality?"

(124)

"Hear me out first and I'm sure you'll agree with me. You're not going to want to have this get out."

"Look," I said, "there are some things I don't want to tell even you right now, to be perfectly honest with you. I don't know who I can trust around here. You understand that, of course. But you're the boss, so I'm going to let you hold it and see what you think. But make no mistake about it, no matter what you think, Carol, I'm staying on this case, with or without your blessing or support. Like I mentioned before, you understand that, too."

"What about Morgan?"

"She doesn't know what I'm about to discuss with you." I was lying, at least partially, if there was such a thing.

Carol leaned back in the lap of the gorilla, prepared to leap and bite if she did not like what she heard. Or peck. "I'm listening."

"You're not going to like it."

"I'm not going to hear it if you don't tell me."

I got up and turned from her desk and started to pace slowly. I did not want to do it, but I had to tell her something. After all, she was paying the bills. But I was uncomfortable with it, and I was tired and irritable, my resistance low, and it—she—might blow up in my face and fire me on the spot and I would not have the advantage of being on the inside any longer. Besides, fifteen hundred a day was not exactly the soup kitchen at the homeless shelter.

"I don't have any hard evidence, but so far everything I've run into leads right back to Jacqui being involved somehow."

She looked at me and waited for the punch line to this sick joke.

"Oh, yeah. I think so," I said.

"You're crazy. That's outrageous." She was insulted.

"Is it? Let me run it by you and you tell me what you think."

"I think that would be a good idea to see where you get crap like this."

"First of all, you hired me, which was the dumbest thing you could've done."

"It's looking like it."

"The police will notice that with interest, you can bet. Hired me so I wouldn't find anything, because in this kind of murder, from all appearances, some common street thug, some crack head—and that has to be the initial perception of what happened—kills his victim and, in true crack-head fashion, does something stupid like tries to make a bullet in the head look like a fire, cover the evidence, you know, and sloppily at that. Until, of course, the evidence—gas can, et cetera—is found all over John Steinmark, like he was a traveling junk dealer. But crack heads don't carry around gas cans, either. Doesn't make sense, so you hired me to what, find a crack head? Nothing PR about that, just dumb. Nothing personal. I know you meant well.

"I'd like to know who was first," I said, "with the idea to hire a private investigator, the seed, I mean. Where did the idea actually emanate from?" I held up my hand quickly. "Don't say it—Jacqui, not you." I could tell by her expression it was true. I knew that already.

"And that makes her guilty of murder? I hope you're going somewhere recognizable with this."

"Second, I know about Dennis White."

"Of course, you saw the Fortiers. We know about the incident with Dennis White, which will *remain private*, of course, so cut to the chase, will you."

"You don't know everything about him, I don't believe. But we'll get to that later. First, I want you to see something." I picked up the plastic grocery bag and took out the videos and went to the large-screen TV set on the far wall, between the door and the window. I inserted the first disk and set it where I wanted it.

"I want you to watch and tell me what you see. I think this must be some of Bernie's work," I said. "I'm not sure, the ones you gave me the other day, bits and pieces."

I kept the audio off. It was joy at the podium after their first game victory on the European tour, Scandinavia somewhere. Oslo, maybe, not a huge crowd but a respectable showing; smiles, laughter, sweat, flashes exploding, each player, in turn, commenting into the mic, mugging for the press. I let it run a bit, then pushed the pause button. "Notice anything?"

"No, not a thing."

I ran it back and started over. "I want you to watch this again, very closely."

On tape, Jacqui Van Autt speaks first into the mic, her sweaty, jubilant players surrounding her. She then steps back and makes way for T.J. Semieux, the star player and team captain, at the podium. T.J. speaks, then hands the mic to another teammate, then steps back to her right, to the edge of the group. Jacqui moves over to her, puts her arm around her shoulder, still smiling out at the crowd. T.J., just for an instant, drops her own smile and, without looking, eases away from Jacqui and moves to the far side of the group, away from her.

I paused the disk again. "See that?" I pointed to the screen, touching it. "See how Jacqui gravitates to T.J. and T.J. runs from her?"

"*Runs* from her? Where do you get that from? I don't see any run—."

I put up my hand again to stop her.

"*Fourteen times*." I stabbed my finger at the screen. "Fourteen times over the period of the tour, in every city they played, every single time Jacqui got near her like this she moved away. Jacqui was chasing her and she was running from her. But don't take my word for it, just watch and see what you think. We'll do it quickly."

I fast-forwarded to each incident so she could see as I pointed them out, having to insert several more disks to complete the run.

"That's peculiar," I said when finished. "Two people who had the greatest admiration and respect for one another, in fact, loved one another like mother and daughter, no question about it. And in every aspect of their lives, public and private, apparently, that's the way it is and everybody knows it. *Except* right here, right there on the screen, subtle, but right out in the open for the world to see, if anybody's looking. One of them chasing, the other rejecting and running."

"And your explanation?" She was impatient.

"Well, it's not Dennis White and the money, if that's what you think. That would have been handled very quickly by Jacqui. Sure, T.J. would've been upset about it, at least concerned, but Jacqui would've handled it and alleviated any fears. Jacqui handles everything and nobody questions her. She would've given T.J. her explanation, her assurance that all was okay, and that would've been it." I took out the last disk and help it up. "But in no case would there have likely been a prolonged, negative and repulsive reaction like this by T.J. toward Jacqui. *Unless* there was something a lot bigger going on that no one else knows about. At least I don't know. I don't know about what you folks might know. I'm not privy to that.

"And by the way, you don't think there's anything sexual here, do you?" I said.

"Of course not."

"You certain? I keep asking everybody."

"I know my people. No, there isn't."

"Great, I'll take your word for it."

"And that's it?"

I walked back to the chair, put the video disks back into the bag and sat down.

"Jacqui lied to me about Dennis White and the money," I said. "I don't know if it's because she thought I was dumb as hell and couldn't ever wonder about it, or she just didn't give a damn about what I might think or find, or both. That's the kind of careless thinking that might have someone hanging gas cans all over John Steinmark."

Carol might not have known about the second gas can, the one Steinmark told me the police found at his place, because it had not been reported in the media, at least to my knowledge, but she was piqued by my assertion.

"Lied to you how?" She moved forward in her seat.

"She never mentioned Dennis White or the possibility of losing the three million dollars. According to her, no money ever passed to anyone. She casually passed it off as an approach from parties unknown with a proposition she advised against and was rejected. I mean, that's a brazen omission, a flat-out lie." I threw up my hands.

"Of course Ames was covering me, you know, to make sure I didn't make a wrong turn down Bright Boy Boulevard and find something. I suppose one might expect Jacqui to lie about such a thing. Who would want to admit such a blunder. But I'm working a case *she* wanted me on, and I resent it."

"You know we don't want that to get out."

"Not before I found out on my own, I didn't. Even when I told you I was headed for Louisiana, where you knew I'd likely learn it, you still didn't give it up."

"From that I suppose you're now insinuating Jacqui and I both are murderers."

"Not yet. If I find anything implicating you, you'll be the second to know. Cops will be the first." I wasn't about to let her out-smart-ass me. That was my field.

"I'm not here bitching at you, just reporting," I said.

"And I'm still listening for something meaningful from all this."

I pulled a couple sheets of paper from the bag and spread them on her desk. "If you don't mind. This is not hard science, but this is a matrix, I guess you could call it, actually a calendar representing the pattern of menstrual cycles of your team players, and how those cycles relate to one another in time and, most interestingly, how they relate to Jacqui's."

"This is what you and Morgan were asking the team about."

"Yes, but she doesn't know the reason for it." I was still lying. "When did you know it?"

"Minutes after she asked one of my assistant coaches."

"And Jacqui knows, too, I guess."

"Oh, yes."

"Loyal troops." Damn. Now Jacqui would confront me with it and kill the rapport I wanted to develop with her. A bad person to be sneaking around on, but I had to know it would happen.

"So what does it mean?" She asked it as if I might be mentally unstable.

"I think she's lying about her monthly period."

Her eyes eased wide open.

"Oh, really. How horrible. And exactly why does one do that? I can't wait to hear this."

I had the feeling she might be touching the button under her desk to summon the white coats. I even caught myself glancing at her hands.

"In any close-knit group of fertile women," I said, "where there's a dominant member, the alpha female, the menstrual cycles over time tend to coincide with the cycle of the dominant member, much like those of daughters to mothers. "

Carol was now fully back in her seat, fingers of one hand lightly tapping the armrest, jaw starting a downward movement. I could see in her eyes a series of thousand-dollar bills, my fee, going into the garbage.

"A few years ago," I continued, "there was a study done at one of the universities up in the Midwest—I can't remember which at the moment—dealing with this phenomenon. What they did was, the researchers, they observed a group of young women from different places, with monthly periods at different times, who didn't know one another, as they entered the same college as freshmen. Or we can call them freshwomen, if you really like. They lived in the same area, same quarters, so that their relationship to one another was physically close. Space-wise, I mean. And by the end of the first semester, even, the monthly cycles were converging noticeably, and by the end of the *second* semester the monthly periods were almost perfectly aligned with that of the known dominant female in the group. And the experiment was replicated, I understand, with similar results. I think that's amazing. Don't you?"

"Oh, I think that's amazing, alright. But I think you should get to the point, Wray."

"Now I know that athletes in training don't always have periods, or aren't necessarily regular, but these women seem to be fairly regular, at least in respect to when they're having their cycles. It's right here. According to the data, if we can call my little thing here data, it's the same time each month. But to whom are they converging? You would think Jacqui. She's definitely the dominant member, the alpha. In fact, she darn well is, but according to her, her period is two weeks away from all the other members. She claimed to be in bed with menstrual cramps the night when T.J. Semieux was murdered. How convenient. And all those players meeting with their periods at this one point for Jacqui, and she doesn't show up. Is this science selectively true only for the players and not the coach? I don't think so. Even Steinmark said T.J.'s period was at the same time, which I found coincided with the others on the team. Very observant guy. And even if none of the women, including Jacqui, has a monthly period, because of training, et cetera, then why lie and say you do? This period business doesn't mean a thing, except that she's lying for some reason. I think it means she's lying about what she might have been doing that night."

"Even if your little science project is well founded, even if she was lying, it doesn't mean she has done anything illegal. Menstrual cycles are not dependable anyway, especially as you age."

"No, of course not. Even if she is a flat-out liar, by itself it is nothing. And included with a number of other odd-seeming circumstantial things, it's still nothing, legally."

"Then it remains that way. I don't want to be a party to any scurrilous accusations. I don't believe for one instant Jacqui would be guilty of anything like this. It's an irrational concept. Besides, there is no motive, whatsoever. And there won't be for Jacqui to have harmed T.J. in any way."

"Other than the insurance thing, you mean, which should pay double for murder, by the way. But if she did it, it's out there somewhere and will be found, eventually.

"But you know, too," I said, "whatever we come up with, no matter how lame it might seem, it'll have to be turned over to authorities soon, especially in a case like this. It's the cops' call, not ours."

Carol jolted and blurted out. "No." Then she caught herself. "I mean, you don't say anything to anyone. I'll talk to my lawyers first if it comes to it. There's too much risk of things leaking out, too much at stake here. I don't want anyone pointing fingers at Jacqui. Nothing good can come of it."

"I know. And if it turns out I'm wrong in my hunch, nobody will have to know if they don't find out themselves. But I'm going to tell you something, too." I put my hands on her desk and leaned over it. "Whoever killed her had a reason to make it look like Steinmark did it, unless, of course, by some stroke of stupidity he actually did. And I'll never believe that. With the evidence all over him, he'd be in jail now, and he's not. But that surely narrows the field to a few potential suspects. Doesn't it? And a crack head is not one of them. That's the biggest mistake the killer made. Never should have tried to frame Steinmark, unless he, or she, wanted to bag both of them for some reason. Should have just killed her and walked away. Now the hounds smell blood and it's just a matter of time. Dumb move, but most murderers are dumb anyway."

"You said there was something else about Dennis White."

I moved back from her desk and sat down and studied her face for a sign of guilt or deception, but did not see any.

"Well?" she said.

But I had that little habit of drawing things out on occasion, which tended to drive people nuts, along with a host of other things I did that drove them nuts.

"What do you know about Dennis White?" I said.

"Little. Only what Jacqui told me, about her stopping T.J. from doing business with him, about getting back the money."

"She never told you she and Dennis White were first cousins?" That locked her head into full attention. "That they were raised together after their fathers, who were brothers and mobsters, were executed?" Her pupils exploded open to take in the light. "That he, himself, is mob-connected? That she brought him to Ivy Ridge for the express purpose of turning over both university and players' money to his care for investment? Until, I'm told, she got cold feet and broke it off because certain parties were on to it? That she didn't get back a damn thing, that it was a friend of T.J.'s family, a fellow down there who asked other mob people to do it for him? She didn't tell you that? Of course not. If she did, you'd know about it. Wouldn't you?"

Carol was temporarily speechless. Her face went into her hands, fingers gently rubbing her temples.

I was feeling a little cheap now about the way I was breaking it to her. The woman looked like her heart had just been broken, embarrassed and hurt.

"How do you know this?" she said.

"Maurice Fortier gave me their side of it. Gil Russo, the crime columnist—you've heard f him, I'm sure—Philadelphia? He gave me the background on Jacqui and Dennis White. I called you from Philadelphia, not Atlanta. Sorry for the curve, but I have to hold my cards a little close sometimes."

"Damn." She got up and went to the window, her hands wrenching. "This is very disturbing, to hear something like this."

I could only feel at least a bit sorry for her. Here was a young, intelligent, beautiful woman, a vibrant and successful person who had opened herself, offered her trust, not to mention her purse and no small fortune, to a woman with whom she had forged a close personal and professional relationship, with whom she had probably already accomplished more in the way of opportunities for women athletes than anyone ever had, only to be standing on the precipice of their shared dream come true and feeling the ominous rumbling beneath her threatening it all. She seemed the kind of person who, despite the silver spoon hanging from her very beautiful mouth, and the fact she was raised in a no-work zone, did not deserve this kind of luck. A dead-on case of Murphy's Law. But I was not hired to weep at her misfortunes either. I was hired, no matter her, or their, intent, to dig up bad news on some damn body, no matter who.

Carol spoke back over her shoulder, dejected. "This is all horrible stuff to hear, Wray, but how does it relate to T.J.'s death? Do you feel you're getting anywhere concrete with this? Maybe it's just a case of an unrelated closet skeleton falling out on the living room floor, something best kept in the closet."

"Nice metaphor, but I don't think so. Have the police been back around here to anyone in the last day or so?"

"No, and they haven't told us anything either."

"They're not going to tell you much of anything. But we can't keep stuff like this from them but for so long. There are legal implications, as I've said. And the moment we find a motive, we've got to turn it over."

She returned to her desk. "Don't say anything, I told you. Let me worry about that." She sat back down.

She seemed to wrestle with her conscience, but in a businesslike manner I should automatically accept. "I do owe you an apology," she said. "We all do. True, you were hired strictly as a public relations decision. What else were we expected to do, sit around? Hell, no. We—I didn't think you'd find anything because I didn't think there was anything to be found. How could there be? And I still don't think any of our people are involved, regardless of Jacqui's background or relation to Dennis White. She wouldn't have broached the idea of hiring any investigator if she were guilty.

In fact, it's been bothering me, this whole business of hiring you, or anyone, to do what the police are suppose to do. On close examination, you're right, it doesn't make sense. It looks presumptuous, maybe cheap and pathetic even. God, I hope not. I am truly sorry for bringing you in under such circumstances. I hope you'll forgive me." And she expected me to.

"Of course. Does this mean I'm fired?" An image of the homeless shelter soup kitchen I referred to earlier flashed in my mind, not that I was poor. But nobody likes to be abandoned, even us wise-asses.

"Oh, no. Not at all," she said. "I want you to keep working, if you will, and find what you can. If we stop now it'll look even worse, look like quitters. I don't want to forget the important thing here, that we need to do everything in our power to help get the no-good low life who killed Toni Jean, no matter what kind of bones we drag up or whose they are. At least now you're here for the right reason. Even though you're a strange one, indeed."

"I always was. Is there anything else?"

"Yes, there is." She spoke with a hint of pleading but more as a mandate, as if I were being given marching orders. "Wray, everything we're doing here, this team, this league, this whole endeavor could very well pivot, for good or bad, on how this case is resolved and on what kind of information gets to the public. Those beasts out there in the press would have a field day. I can't tell you how crucial it is that there be no inkling of impropriety finding its way out. The vultures are perched and waiting for us to fall flat on our faces. A pro league like this has never succeeded on a large scale. This was no easy task getting this far. The investment was extraordinary, the planning and negotiations, all of it. These women need and deserve this opportunity in sports. Toni Jean was doing, we're all still doing, for women's basketball what Ham and Chastain and the others did for soccer, what Jones did for track and field, even more, a quantum more. All they, or any of them, need is a venue. You must see on the videos how they're received when they perform at the highest levels. These women can sell tickets. This is it, this is their shot, and it could be the only one for a long time. We can't fail. That's why it's important that, one, nothing gets out of here, except through me. And that means be careful around Morgan. And, two, we do everything we can to find Toni Jean's killer and that it not be one of us. *Most important* it not be one of us. So, yes, I do want you to keep digging up bones. I just want you to bring them to me and on a regular basis. I don't want to have to call you, like I said before."

"I dig up the bones and you bury them. With all this dog business going on, maybe I'll pick up a couple cans of Alpo and do lunch." It was fatigue, of course, but she was in no mood for it.

"If there's nothing else." She leaned back in her chair, dismissing me.

"There is. I need to get something off my chest and you need to hear it."

She gave a thoughtful but cautious look, then nodded okay. She was ready for whatever bullshit I might have.

"You're right," I said. "You shouldn't have brought me down here for the reason you did without telling me. It was a con. It was dishonest. But I'm an adult and I smelled a rat and I came anyway, so I have to accept part of the blame. You've apologized and I accept it, and I'm getting paid well, so that's life.

"But what really disturbs me about the whole business are a couple of things. First, I have a reputation, too, not a rich and famous one like you folks, of course, but mine is just as important to me as yours is to you. And being duped and made to look like a clown won't help it if it gets out. Second, Ames was involved with you and your little PR ruse. I particularly resent that because, from my perspective, in the time she and I have known one another, until now, until becoming involved with you people, she'd never lied to me about anything, much less used me unfairly. And now, of all things, for your benefit, not hers. That pisses me off. Something between us that might have been ain't no more. And that saddens me. I'm not saying my loss is your fault, I'm just saying her hanging around with you people hasn't helped her or me a damn bit, so I don't figure I owe you a whole lot.

"I know you're doing something worthwhile here with this league, and for what it's worth coming from me, I wish you all the luck in the world. But I'm looking for a cold-blooded killer here, one who I believe might be a part of your organization. The scent of the killer bitch is all around me and I can smell it. And I don't need the people who're paying me to find her, or him, lying to me and hiding something from me. I'm not the police, I don't have their protection. People don't fear me, I'm a lone wolf. I get too close to a killer and I can get hurt. It's important not to be handicapped or endangered by my employer, of all people.

"Once," I said, "I and a number of other men walked into an ambush. I was hit and put out of the Marine Corps I loved so much. It changed my life and my family's life. But worse than that, twelve others were killed and wounded and maimed. You might imagine the fallout from that. And it was all because of some prick who was wearing our uniform and was suppose to be one of us, but who didn't have our best interest in mind. But mostly it was the information, the knowledge he had that we didn't have and what he did with it.

"So you'll have to forgive me if I seem not to give a rat's ass about the precariousness of your league, nor of the reputation of your esteemed coach, that it all might seem somehow secondary or even irrelevant to me. I don't want anything getting out either, but for my reasons, not yours.

"Jacqui has something to do with that girl's death. I feel it very strongly. I'm going to focus on her. If that makes you uncomfortable, you should cut me loose now. But I'm not giving up. And if I bring you something the police should have and you don't turn it over, I will. Now I'm sorry if that hurts your feelings, but if I'm sticking around you'll have to live with it. And this crap better not happen again." I rose from the chair with the plastic grocery bag of disks and papers, looking like a hobo.

"And I'd like it if you didn't say anything about this little talk to Jacqui. Just be quiet and let me do my job. If she's innocent, you won't have anything to worry about."

Carol was part contrite, part incensed at being rebuked. Her perfect white complexion was crimson.

"You've made your point, Wray. Accepted and duly noted."

"Long as we understand one another. I'll call you tomorrow. Promise."

I stopped at the door.

"Oh, yeah, there's something else," I said.

"What?" Her voice had a snap to it.

"I'd like to have a complete itemized copy of your phone records, all offices, cells, everything incurred by this organization from January One through today. I don't have the authority to get it. The phone companies' billing offices will fax them to you. I'd like to have them tomorrow. That's okay, I assume."

"Yes. Would you like to tell me why?"

"No, I wouldn't, but, yes, I will. I might want to see the numbers. Until then." I pulled the door shut behind me.

"Sure, brilliant," I heard her say as it closed. And I knew if her neck had been long enough she would have stretched out and bitten my ass off right through the door.

19

Out in the office I stopped to tie a knot in the plastic bag and was wondering why I did not choose something better for carrying around these disks and papers, and how goofy and amateurish it must look. What would a lawyer or policeman look like going into a courtroom with something like this? *"Well, your honor, let me see what I have in my little bag here." Crinkle, crinkle.*

Next to me on the wall was the giant portrait of T.J. Semieux charging the camera with the dribbling basketball. I stared at it, understanding better now, since I had met her parents and knew more about her, why she was so magnetic. Energy. Energy and life. Ravenously hungry life at a desperate full speed running from the darkness like a hot ball of light illuminating and warming indelibly those around her in her profound if ephemeral path.

And maybe scorching at least one of them in route.

"Everybody does that, until they get used to seeing it." Ethel Palmer had come back up from the rear of the office. There was a spring in her walk and she was smiling approvingly.

I had met her just briefly my first day when Ames introduced us, just before the initial meeting with Carol. She was the office manager and special assistant—fancy term for secretary—to Carol Gambrell. She was near or at a very young sixty, extremely attractive and, despite any skills she might have, the kind of woman who in her earlier years would have been hired to pretty up the place or be the boss's girlfriend. And she was no slouch now, with her own perfect white teeth. Amazing. Still a nice figure in slacks and form-fitting blouse, with black, gray-streaked hair cut short and black frame glasses over a pretty nose that looked like it belonged on a nineteen-year-old.

I knew a girl like that in the tenth grade, Mary Jane Hathaway, pretty as a picture. I had just gotten my driver's license and took her to the drive-in on a rainy Friday night to a movie guaranteed to bore her, even if she could have seen it, and tried to talk her into the back seat as an alternative and a way of apologizing, but she would not buy it. I had even given her the old line about the high probability of nuclear war coming soon, that she might miss her chance, something on the news about the Russians coming Tuesday. She said she would wait until late Monday night to make up her mind. Every time I saw a pretty woman with a nose like that I thought of Mary Jane.

"I can see why," I said.

"She was the sweetest thing. Best player to come along since Lieberman and Donovan. Heard of them?" She stood next to me, hands in her pockets.

"Yeah, Old Dominion. Late seventies, early eighties, I believe."

"How's your investigation going, Mr. Larrick?"

"Call me Wray. It's going. Where to I'm not sure. How long have you worked for the *Storms*?"

"Since Carol decided to found the league."

"So you don't live in Wilmington?"

"Oh, no, Charlotte. Just temporary here."

"You don't have a Carolina accent. I hear Great Lakes."

"Chicago. You are perceptive. I didn't think it was all that noticeable. People back home think I sound southern. Been here thirty-two years."

"You can run, but you can't hide. Must be straddling the Mason-Dixon, but you look good doing it."

"Thank you. My husband took a job with Phillips Agri-Machine. He was a metallurgist before he retired."

"Phillips, as in Carol Phillips Gambrell?"

"Her father."

"So much for the farm girl thing."

"If you can call forty-two thousand acres of crop land with six hundred-twenty hands in five states and a manufacturing plant with eight hundred employees and worldwide distribution farm girl, that's her."

"Figures. Think she could kill anybody?"

"Whoa." Ethel put her splayed hand on her chest as if about to choke. "Boy, you are direct."

I thought that was funny.

"Just asking, not accusing. I don't think she killed anybody either, but I also don't know her like you do. Cancel the question."

"Glad you qualified that, but no, she couldn't. And I've known her all her life, practically."

"What'd you do, Ethel, before this?"

"Worked for the City of Charlotte for thirty years. Retired two years ago. City Manager's office."

"Larry Graham."

"Yes, he was my boss the last twenty years. You know of him?"

"He was our city manager in Hampton, before going to Charlotte."

"Yes, that's right, he sure was. Your loss, our gain. Small world."

"Down here anyway. You know what they say, us rebs know one another because we're all related."

She grinned wide. "You said it, I didn't."

"Do you eat grits?"

"Not yet."

I laughed at that. I liked Ethel Palmer. She seemed like a nice sort.

I looked back at the portrait of T.J. Semieux, my eyes moving all around, and dropped the funny stuff.

"Let me ask you something, Ethel, if I can. Don't be alarmed. Just between the two of us."

"You're not going to ask me if I could kill anyone, are you? Because I haven't."

"No, no, I'm not. But let me ask you this." My eyes were still on the portrait. "Do you think Jacqui Van Autt could kill this young lady?" I looked over at her.

There was a slight delay in her response—surprised again—but without the sense of being startled this time.

"Oh. Oh, oh, no, I don't think so. Jacqui, she—No. No, she couldn't. No, I'm sure. What peculiar questions."

"I'm a peculiar guy."

"So I hear. Not that I mean—."

"No, that's okay. I admit it." I waved it away. "Did the police talk to you?"

"Yes, they did, all of us."

"Individually?"

"Yes, for a few minutes each."

"Did they ask you about Jacqui?"

"They asked me about everybody. They asked us all the same things."

"Did they seem to express an interest in anyone in particular?"

"No, they didn't. I think they were just looking to see if she—T.J.—had a problem with anybody."

"Did she?"

"No, unless you consider that ex-boyfriend of hers. I think they'd had problems, broken up or something."

"Ever heard the name Dennis White?"

"No. Who's he? Should I?"

"I'll tell you later. Do you know Steinmark?"

"Never met him. Saw him a couple times is all, from a distance, but not to speak to him."

"What do you think might have happened?"

"About what? T.J.? I think somebody tried to rob her."

"Then put the evidence all over Steinmark?"

"Oh, I see what you mean. I haven't given it a lot of thought as to who or why."

"If the police told you that you knew the person who did it, who do you think they'd be talking about?"

"That would have to be the boyfriend, from what I hear, John Steinmark. She didn't date anyone else. And like you said, the evidence."

"Cops say no, who would be your second guess?"

"Nobody. Just someone trying to rob her. Maybe the gas can and mud have nothing to do with it."

"I think a woman killed her."

"I'm not surprised you'd say that, considering you just asked me about Carol and Jacqui doing it." She was looking around, self-conscious, though we were out of earshot of others in the office.

"If the police told you one of them, Carol or Jacqui, killed her, which one would you pick?"

"What? Wray, I have loyalties here. I can't answer these kinds of questions. I'd say neither of them anyway."

"Understood. I would pick Jacqui."

"Well, you'd be wrong."

"Why?"

"Because she's not the type to kill anybody. Especially somebody like this sweet thing here she worshipped." She gazed up at the portrait. "What a waste and a damn crying-ass shame."

"That's what everybody seems to think. About Jacqui, I mean."

"They know her better than you. Besides, she was here working that night."

My head snapped around. It was all I could do to contain my anger. Jacqui had told me she was home.

"What? She was *here*?"

"Yes."

"You *saw* her?"

"Yes."

"What time was that?"

"Ten-thirty, quarter-to-eleven."

"Quarter-to-eleven, latest?"

"Yes."

"But the murder took place later than that." I was careful not to sound too accusatory. "Plenty of time to get to New French Fort."

"Well, she didn't look like she was going anywhere, if you're implying anything."

"No? You were working too?"

"No, I stopped in to get something from my desk. My daughter Lila and her husband, Bryan, were down a couple days, staying with me at my apartment near the beach. We had dinner and a couple drinks at a place on the canal at Wrightsville, then came back here so I could pick up some folders I needed to go over for one of Carol's meetings the next day."

"Was anyone with her?"

"She was alone. It's not unusual. In fact, she didn't see me and I didn't want to bother her. Just got my stuff and left. I'm certain she didn't know I was here."

"What was she doing that she didn't notice you?"

"Watching videos in her office. The door was halfway open and her back was turned."

"What was she watching?"

Ethel did not respond immediately and I looked at her for it.

"You really do suspect her, don't you?"

"Didn't the police ask you the same things?"

"Not exactly. They wanted to know where everybody was, of course. I just told them my own whereabouts for the evening, including dropping by here, and they seemed to be satisfied with it. But not you, right?"

"Well, I'm not the cops either. What was the video about?"

"Game videos of some kind, I think. Scouting video or something."

"Not the *Storms*?"

"No, I think it was a college team, best I remember. Tell you the truth, I don't know a lot about basketball, Wray, just hear some of the talk and names around, like Lieberman and Donovan. Never met a one of them or saw a game. But they weren't our people on the video I saw when I was here. And that was no more than one minute. She could've been looking at any team."

"So that's what she was doing, sitting there alone with her back to the door watching a video and not noticing you come and go?"

"Right. It's not unusual. She was focused on the screen."

"If you saw the same video again, could you recognize it?"

"I doubt it. I didn't pay attention to it."

"Who was on the video? White women? Black women? Red uniforms? Green? Anything you can remember of it? Any players you recognize?"

"Not really. I just know they weren't ours. Is it suppose to be important?"

"No way to tell."

"Because I mentioned it to the police, anyhow, about stopping by here."

"To Carol, too?"

"No."

"Does Jacqui know you mentioned it to the police?"

"I don't see how she could know."

"You know if Carol knew if she was here?"

"Have no idea."

I certainly hoped not. I had just gone through that with her, that withholding information business. And I looked over at her office door and visualized kicking it off its hinges.

"Has anyone asked you not to talk to me or tell me anything?"

"Lord, no, of course not. Why would they? On the contrary, I was told by Carol to help you in any way I can."

"Thank you. And I'll take you up on that now by asking you what you think about something. And it won't go anywhere, so speak freely. Is that okay?"

"Sure, go ahead." Ethel took another quick around.

"Have you ever known Jacqui to lie about anything? Anything, big or small?"

"No, I've never known her to in the time I've known her."

"Well, she sure lied to me."

"Really?"

"Yeah. She said she went straight home after practice, around seven, and stayed the night T.J. was killed, didn't go anywhere. I'll bet she told the police the same thing. And she was actually right here part of the time, according to you. So she was up and about and not in bed just prior to the murder."

"Oh, I see." She was cautious not to tread further.

"That's odd. I mean, it's her idea to hire me but she flat-out lies to me about where she was just before the murder. At a time when she was supposed to be ill and uncomfortable, in pain, so much so that she had to go home after practice, too ill to even drop off T.J. at the car dealer. Don't know if you knew about that. But she's right here only hours later."

"Maybe she felt better then."

"No. If she did, she wouldn't have to lie to me about it. Would she?"

"No," I said, "the season hasn't even started yet and we have a coach who's suppose to be in bed but who's up and about and down here alone and lying about it, looking at what seems to be potential recruits, somebody to maybe take the place of somebody else who's going to be dead a couple hours later. Looking for talent, maybe, when she already has the talent and is preparing for the first season, which is still months away. Maybe she's got a crystal ball or something. Does that seem a little odd to you? Don't answer that yet.

"Let me ask you this," I continued. "What time did you get home after you left here that night, Ethel?"

"Me?" She was caught a little off guard. "Must've been eleven, eleven-0-five. Why?"

"Did the police ask you that?"

"No, they didn't, not specifically."

"They'll get around to it, if this isn't solved quickly enough."

"Why? Why do you say that?"

"Did you go out alone after you got home?"

"No, I certainly did not."

"I'm just asking the kind of questions the police will ask."

"What makes you think they should ask me anything? I've already told them everything I know, which is nothing."

"No, just bear with me, you'll see. I'm just trying to help you here. What did you do after you got home?"

"Worked on the folders until about one, then went to bed."

"And your daughter and her husband, of course, were up with you."

"No, they went to bed soon as we got in."

"Eleven or eleven-0-five."

"Yes, ten after or so."

"So you have no alibi from that time until when?"

"Now, see here, Wray. What are you trying to do here? You're not insinuating—."

"No, no, of course not. Heck, who would suspect you of anything wrong? You're just the office manager. No, what I'm trying to say is, from a detective's perspective, police or otherwise, I have to consider you're the only person in the world, so far, who claims to have seen Jacqui here that night. You told the police that, you told me that. And I appreciate you sharing it with me, because not everyone around here is being that cooperative.

"Now, assuming Jacqui had told everyone she was home the whole time that night, and we have to assume that because she wouldn't tell the police one thing and me another—it wouldn't make sense—and no one else in the world can corroborate what you say about her being here. And given that nobody, but *nobody*, including you, would believe Jacqui capable of harming T.J.—I mean, that wouldn't make sense, I agree—what are we left with when there's no clear suspect or motive?"

"The boyfriend, Steinmark," she said.

"No, it's way past the time he'd be in jail if the police thought he was it."

"A robber."

"No, the police don't think that." Taking license, since I didn't really know what the police thought, and didn't care. "No, the police are hounds. They go with the scent of the blood. They look for the smallest thing, a place to start.

"Tell me, did your daughter and son-in-law see Jacqui's car here that night?"

"No, they don't know her car. There are several cars in the lot overnight, usually. I didn't notice it, myself. Doesn't mean it wasn't there."

"Sure, makes sense. But if she didn't want anyone to know where she was, she could've parked her car somewhere else. The diner across the street. She could've parked there, maybe. And no security guard, I'm told."

"Correct," Ethel said.

"And she has a special parking place here, though. I saw it."

"Yes."

"Well, that leaves the two of you, with one of you saying she was here and one of you saying she wasn't. And one of you with a vested interest in T.J. remaining alive and healthy and productive playing basketball, and one of you who doesn't. I don't mean that in a bad way, of course."

"Let's get this straight, Wray. Are you saying that *I* could become a suspect?"

"Now look who's perceptive. Somebody's always a suspect in a murder case. Otherwise, the police can't work. It wouldn't mean you did it, and I'm sure they'd feel the same way, eventually. But I'm bound by law to report anything relevant to a felony that's known to have been committed, as in this case, and that means I have to tell them what you told me about seeing Jacqui here."

"You said this conversation wouldn't go anywhere."

"I'll hold it as long as I can, but sooner or later they'll haul me in for questioning simply because I'm investigating this thing, then I'll be just as obligated as you to be forthright. It's Jacqui I might be suspicious of. But what do I know? I won't tell anyone but the police and Carol, of course. But you've got to know that the media is all over this thing, and if the police keep coming back to talk to somebody, specially one or more persons in particular, the implication, well." I let it trail off, leaving it to her imagination.

"Do yourself a favor," I said, "ask Jacqui if she was here that night. See what she says. Don't tell her you saw her or that you were even here. If she tells the truth, fine, she probably told the police the same thing and lied only to me, for whatever reason, and that's my problem. But if she lies, you're likely going to become a suspect, because the police are going to start looking at the two of you and wondering who is lying about her being here and for what reason. Personally, I think she'll lie to you."

I let that sink in a moment, see what it does to her loyalties. Then I thanked her and left, knowing she would fly directly to the others, especially Carol Gambrell, and probably Jacqui, too, and immediately build a wall of self-preservation, not that it was necessary. The woman did not kill a soul, but I had made her feel awfully insecure.

Just an office grenade. Drop it in and walk away, it explodes into chaos, maybe shakes something loose.

20

It was twelve forty-five a.m. when I woke up in Ames' apartment at the beach. I could hear from down the hallway from the bed what seemed like the talking-scratching sound of a CB radio in the distance. Must be coming from somewhere else, I figured. After briefly cleaning up with a shave and a breath killer—maybe a perfume-loaded cherry bomb down the throat would do it—I put on my running clothes and went up front.

Ames was sitting at her computer station fidgeting with a scanner placed next to it and barely noticed me going around the counter to the kitchen for water, easing my way into full consciousness.

"Oh, hi." She turned, then switched off the scanner.

"What was that about?"

"Just trying to get used to it. I've never operated one before."

"Why now?"

"Hopefully, so I'll never be last to know something. A reporter for the paper suggested I get it, so I bought it today. She has one in her car and one at home and work. You know, I was one of the last of the media to know about T.J. the night she was, well—by the time I got there the scene was already roped off and the story was flying out."

"She's already dead. You're not going to get the word again. And you're not a police reporter."

"Well, excuse me, but I bought it anyway without your informed recommendation or approval. Maybe I'll listen to truckers."

"If you could pick up some of the old shows, the sitcoms, I could see it. Otherwise, I don't see the point." After saying it, I realized I was out of line. "Sorry. Really."

"If you're going to wake up criticizing, go back to sleep." She turned back to her desk and some papers on it, mostly to avoid me.

"No, no, I'm sorry, forgive me. Beat me to death with a baseball bat."

She turned in her chair and studied me a moment.

"If you'll forgive me, too. Of course, I'll take you up on the baseball bat offer."

I put down the glass and walked around and sat on the stool next to her.

"For what?" But I suspected I knew.

She took my hand, rubbing my forearm. "You know for what."

I knew she meant our most recent sexual episode earlier in the afternoon and my disappointment with it, something she had to know without my having to say it.

"No apologies necessary," I said, "just one of those things. Sex is a most forceful communicator, Ames. The message was inherent in the communiqué. You already knew it, I only suspected it. Now I know it.

"There are worse ways to get bad news," I said. But I couldn't think of any. "Besides, it was all my fault. You called me down here for a business reason, Ames, not a personal one. First thing I did when I got here was try to make it personal. I should've listened to you. After all, we haven't had a relationship since you left home, so I guess I was just hoping for too much. If I were still thirty, it might bother me. At my age I roll with it. But I will tell you this: seeing you get away from these damn people and back where you belong is going to make it a whole lot easier."

"For me, too, if I can find a job."

"You will. When you get back on your turf the doors will fly open. I know it."

She kissed me gently.

"You're so sweet, Wray. I'll always feel close to you."

"Long as we're not in the same town I can deal with it. Don't worry, I'm not going to cry my eyeballs out and become a celibate monk."

She laughed.

"No, I don't think so. If there's no sex in heaven, you'll go to hell for sure."

"My plot's bought and paid for, and I'm taking air conditioning."

"So." I switched the subject. "You pick up anything downtown? Have I missed anything?"

"No, but I saw Carol in her office this evening. T.J.'s funeral is day after tomorrow, and she said to tell you you're welcome to fly down with the team. She'll ask you herself."

"You blow up at her?"

"No, of course not. Jacqui's the real bitch here. But I'm not going to work for her either. I'll starve first."

"Smart woman."

"Great, smart woman. I'll starve."

"You know what I mean."

"Oh, and Loomis Sullivan's office called and left a message here for you after you left. Don't you have your cell phone or answering service on?"

"Sometimes, but I don't know how to do the answering message thing."

"He'll talk to you in his office in the morning at eleven-fifteen or so, if you want, after court."

"Great. And Jacqui? You see her?"

"Oh, yeah. And it was everything I could do to keep myself from strangling the bitch. Wray, I don't know how long I can hold this, pretending all is okay. She's going to notice sooner or later something is wrong and say something, and I'm going to explode on her."

"Don't. Whatever you do, don't blow up. You've seen her only once since this afternoon. Right? Hang on. She's never said anything to you about nosing around with the menstrual business, has she?"

"Well, she knows."

"I know she does." I sat in the floor and started the warm-up exercises, stretching, loosening up.

"For how long?"

"You act cold around her and she's going to know you and I are colluding on something. I'm the one who's supposed to be used and pissed off about it, not you. You're supposed to be one of them. Just keep right on being her friend and confidant. Let me be the smart-ass son of a bitch I usually am, and tell her nothing."

Ames got down on the floor and began her own warm-up. "Point well made, if I can manage my part. I know you can do yours as a smart-ass son of a bitch."

"You don't have to agree with me on that so quickly."

After a minute or so, I hesitated, to break the rhythm.

"I hate working out with a woman."

"Why do you say that?" She was puffing.

"A woman thinks she always has to fall right in and synchronize her breathing with a man's, like it's a damn Olympic team sport or something. I feel like somebody is following in step on my heels. I can't stand synchronized breathing. It's the worst form of conformity, completely void of even a trace of individuality, like you were scared to death to breathe on your own. And it sucks."

She stopped a second and stared at me, about to tell me where to get off, but it clicked inside her and she burst out laughing.

"Oh, my god, you didn't say that."

I studied her laugh, then realized how imbecilic and childish it sounded and laughed along with her.

"Don't ever tell anybody I said that." I was pleading, and struggling to catch my breath. "I'll deny it."

After a few pushups, I said, "Enough for now. I'm working out with the weights at the dojo later, anyway." I got up and went to the kitchen. "Vino time. Light up some ice cubes. Want one?"

"Sure, I'll drink it in a minute, when I'm finished."

"We don't need to be on the floor at the same time doing this." I reached for the glasses. "If that busload of alien tourists happens by here again and sees us, they'll think, "'Gee, these creatures sure have a funny way of screwing one another.'"

"You're insane."

"With portfolio. Or is it Fort Polio?"

I sat on the sofa and sipped as Ames finished her routine. How much to tell or trust her and how little to, I was thinking. But she might be aware of some things I was not, in fact, should be, so what could it hurt. We had already as much as settled our differences and matters of turf, even drawn proverbial lines in the sand and blocked out our relationship in this whole business, in a manner of speaking, as well as having defined our personal one.

At least she seemed to know now who her real friends were and were not and was responding accordingly. As long as she kept her mouth shut, her very beautiful, wonderful, succulent mouth at that, and did not jump the story too soon, I did not care.

"I want you to do something for me," I said. I turned a note pad and pen toward her on the coffee table and she stopped exercising. "Write here what I tell you. Letters or numerals where called for, short form."

"Sure," She picked up the pen, blowing hair from the corner of her mouth, seeming not to mind at all.

"L.T. dash one point five. Right. F dash three point 0," and she wrote again. "Great. Now just one more. Point seven five plus three zero asterisk five C.M. Good, thanks.

"Now," I said, "I want you to look at something for me." I went to the counter and got the plastic grocery bag and brought it back to the coffee table, extracted some papers and spread them out. "I copied these in Jacqui's office the other day from her notebooks and desk calendar pad."

"Oh, god, Mr. Analysis escapes from Happy Acres again. Grab the nets." She got up and fetched her drink from the counter and sat next to me on the sofa.

"Some notes and stuff from her desk and drawers."

"Oh, so you did get in her drawers. And she had these in there?"

"You going into comedy or something?"

She gave a little snort to hold in the laugh.

"The first thing I noticed," I said, "was how some things are written in what seems to be her regular style, cursive, from everything I've seen of hers, so far. Easily recognizable as hers. Seems to always write in cursive style. Even numerals like these." I pointed to a couple examples. "A cursive-like style and you can tell they're hers. But others, both numerals *and* letters, are written in block-like fashion, indistinguishable from most anyone else's handwriting style, neutral, like these, like they were written specifically so no one could identify the writer."

"Maybe they were written that way for clarity."

"What, half the notation clear and the other half not? I don't think so. Besides, her handwriting is perfectly clear in cursive." I pointed to other examples.

"But notice, too," I continued, "right here where both letters, initials or something, are in cursive, but the numerals accompanying them are in square block, yet they obviously were of the same message or notation written at the same time by the same person, with the same pencil, her writing. Either a person usually writes in one style or another, but not two styles, especially in one short message or entry.

"Like you did here," I said. I pointed to the samples she just did for me. "Everything I dictated to you, you wrote in one style, just as I would, or most anyone else in the world would. In my case, I have to handprint everything because my penmanship stinks, but you would know it was mine. But she didn't in these particular examples and *only* in these, at least from what was in her desk. Take away her cursive and cursive-like entries and you'd never be able to tell who wrote the block-written entries. I think that's very odd. I wonder what that could mean?"

"You're asking me? Ask her."

"Not yet."

"Maybe," Ames said, "and that's just in case there's something Freudian going on here, those things written in her regular hand are things she might be expected to write about, not be concerned with, but that the entries in block form are somehow alien to the cursive entries, don't belong with them. And she, sub-consciously or something, whatever, separates herself from the block part so as not to be identified or associated with it or reminded of it, of its impropriety or something. Listen to me, I'm sounding as batty as you."

"You mean, or like, if someone else saw the message it might infer she might not have written the bad part."

"Yeah, maybe. I guess. Or maybe she doesn't want to be reminded, herself, that she wrote it."

"If the block part is suppose to be bad, as opposed to good or neither. You know," I said, "you're starting to think like me. That's exactly what I was coming to. You're right with me."

"God, I hope not. We'll need two rooms at Happy Acres."

"It's okay, we can room next to one another and drool together. Just don't do it in synch with me."

"Well, now that you've thoroughly dissected and complicated something as simple and innocent as someone's personal notes and writing style, just what are you going to make of it all?" She got up to get a sweat towel from the kitchen cabinet drawer, sipping her wine.

"I don't know. But there are some other notes here, too. And one might assume if one person writes all these entries and notations in one place, her office, and she's involved in but one business, and that's basketball, and the entries seem similarly written, that is with similar incongruities, cursive, block, one might assume they're all related to one aspect of the basketball business or subject somehow. Frankly, I don't know if that's going to help simplify things or just confuse me."

"I pick confuse." She came back over. "And I think if someone has the audacity to doodle her fragmented private thoughts down on paper, she ought to be lined up against the wall and shot as a free-thinking traitor."

"You're a great help."

"Of course, I'm serious about the *shot* part. I don't like the bitch."

"Just since today anyway. Until this afternoon, you two were buxom buddies. That's what's so strange about you women, you hate one another too easily. Too cut and dry, black and white. No gray areas."

"Screw a bunch of gray areas. What other notes?"

I moved around some papers on the table. "Well, we have here some phone numbers."

"Yeh. Reh-Rah, phone numbers."

I set the pen down and took a sip of wine. This was not the time to work, especially for her.

"How long has it been since you watered your head?" I said.

"Early sign of mental illness, I'm afraid. Stress, strain. Maybe I need to shower and go to bed."

"Good idea. Me, too. I need the sleep."

"Yes, someone who doesn't have to work for a living, who dabbles in other people's criminal problems for fun and profit, needs all the sleep he can get." A little silly giggle with a sharp edge to it. "Just a joke."

"You're right. I think you're on the verge of space discovery. See you in the morning, if you're here." I got up and went back to the bedroom, careful to gather up and take my crinkly bag of papers with me.

When Ames was asleep, I took my cell phone and dialed the numbers from Jacqui's notes. Southeast Technical University. Old Dominion University. University of Connecticut. North Carolina State University. University of North Carolina-Chapel Hill. Ivy Ridge University. Stanford. Duke. Tennessee. Louisiana Tech. All recorded answers this time of night. Top women's basketball schools. I knew that much, as unversed as I was in the sport. If, for whatever reason, Jacqui was going to kill her protégé, the top player in the world, it is highly likely she would turn to these schools for a replacement. A little early recruiting maybe, or just a wish list? No crime to dream or plan for the future. And no way to tell for sure whether the numbers were written before or after the murder, even though the entries made on the calendar were all made on pages representing months preceding the murder. Kind of dumb to do something like that and leave it lying around. And even if they were written before the murder, I would bet no phone calls would show up on the phone bills I asked Carol Gambrell to get for me. Jacqui would not want a record of that if she should not have been calling those places, in light of the fact the new league had recruiting rules. That would be dumber still for someone like Jacqui, especially as one of the numbers, that of Southeast Tech, had with it what looked like an extension number.

When I dialed the number and punched the extension, a young female voice on the answering machine asked the caller to leave a message.

I hung up. I would call again tomorrow and try to see just who it was.

21

Ames was asleep when I got up at sunrise and did two miles hard on the beach and cooled off with a swim. When I got back to the apartment to clean up, she was gone, had left a note for me to *please* call her if I came across anything interesting, just *anything*. She would be around the courthouse and the *Storms'* office. Please call by lunch, even if you haven't a thing. *Love*.

It was good to see her sense of the hunt was still alive and well, her sniffing, even begging for information. I was certain she was going to make it past this horrible period, was glad to see it, and that made me feel good, even if the *"love"* message was figurative. You always want the best for people you care about. I just was not going to tell her everything and let her, in her desperation to survive, jump the story too soon. She knew me well enough to know I was holding something back and would not dare go with it without the whole package and maybe lose it to some other reporter and look like a rookie.

I stopped by Aaron Sepp's dojo on Market Street to work out with the weights and give Aaron the *Storms* game tickets I promised, including autographed pictures of the team players and coaches I finagled, as well, from Carol Gambrell, which made Aaron very happy.

"You know what kind of hero this is going to make me when I get home?" Aaron said. "I might even get to sleep inside a while."

After showering, I left, rejecting for now the offer to learn the great block he promised to teach me for protecting my bum shoulder.

"I'll have to pass on charm school today, Aaron." The last thing I needed after already doing two workouts was to get my ass kicked around Market Street by this guy. How would that help my shoulder? I asked him about Steinmark's attorney, Loomis Sullivan, since they were both locals.

Loomis James "Loo" Sulivan Jr.'s office was in the historic overlay district downtown, in an area once a middle class residential neighborhood overlooking the Cape Fear River, the city's economic center now in revival after decades of neglect. Rather than set up shop in the low-key steel, glass and brick bank and office buildings popping up around the city-county government zone, he had chosen, apparently because he could afford it, to go a couple blocks the other way, closer to the water in the now artsy-commercial residential area on the riverbank, with his own private building, a renovated, rustic old mansion of three stories, a huge wrap-around porch and gables, two paralegals, two assistant trial attorneys, a private courtyard and beautifully landscaped gardens with enough oxygen-producing plant life to supply the local hospitals. This place would be a great gift shop, or a quaint restaurant, I was thinking as I entered. The real estate thing again.

It was not surprising Steinmark would have secured Sullivan's services. For one, he could afford it. And, two, reputedly, Sullivan was the top criminal attorney down east, the eastern quadrant of the state, that is. And including criminal and civil cases together, according to the trial lawyers association, he enjoyed one of the best won-lost records of any trial lawyer in the whole southeast U.S., setting him apart from the typical courthouse rats who over-populate every legal community and compete for the limited but dependable number of low-paying repeat drunk drivers, dope heads, and wife beaters. A man who had made a lot of money in an area of law in which most attorneys game enough to try it starve to death. And it had not come easy for a share cropper's son who went to college on an athletic scholarship and a C average and worked the fields in the summers with his family, as I had been told.

When I walked into his office, I was struck by his size, his physical presence. He was an imposing man of about six-six, rangy, a huge bone structure, bald on top. He was turned sideways in his chair, behind his desk, one foot propped up on a drawer pulled out for the purpose. His large feet reminded me of some of the ships I had sailed on while in the Corps. His tie was loose, expensive shirt wrinkled. He had a small spare tire—I call them doughnuts—around his waist, looked like he had not shot hoops in twenty years, was pale, his face freckled and ears large. When he dies, I was thinking, it will likely be from the force of gravity that kills him.

As I shook his hand across the large mahogany desk, I was thinking, too, maybe turnip was an unfair choice of words to describe him, as I had done earlier.

Sullivan was popping into his mouth and savoring a steady stream of Jujyfruits.

I nodded to the right wall, where all the lawyer crap was hanging.

"East Carolina." I sat down across from him. "You were a defensive tackle."

"That's right. And offensive. You don't look old enough to remember that. Somebody must've told you." His accent and demeanor was strictly country, a giant Andy Griffith.

"I've been around a while, longer than I look. You had to have played against my cousin, Tucker McGuire. Fullback at V.M.I., fifty-nine, sixty."

"Remember playing them every year. Don't recall the name."

"His head still hurts, though."

"Tell him I'm sorry if I had anything to do with it. Otherwise, the statute of limitations has run out."

We both thought that was funny.

We kicked around the names of a few people we each had known or come across, people Sullivan played ball with, guys who had played at East Carolina where numerous Tidewater, Virginia, athletes and non-athletes matriculated, and a school that supplied both states with a steady supply of teachers and coaches.

"Here," Sullivan slid over the Jujyfruits. "Have some. You're drooling."

"I'll warn you, I haven't had these things since I was a teenager at the movies. Haven't seen them anywhere. I'll eat them all."

"I have an inside source—SuperMart—and I'm not going to run out." He reached in a drawer and produced four large boxes in his massive hand. "They say you can't take anything with you when you leave this world, but I'm taking two boxes of these, whether they like it or not, or I'm not going."

"And if you run out, you're coming back."

"Damn right. What can I do for you, Mr. Larrick?"

"You've probably already done it by allowing Steinmark to talk to me without you present."

"Why not? He has nothing to hide. He's innocent. The more people know him, the more they'll believe it."

"Why do you think he's innocent?"

"Because he's my client, for one. Two, I've been working with criminals for forty years. I know one when I meet him, and he's no criminal, certainly not a murderer."

"I believe it. Are there any other suspects you know of?"

"There's a suspect, alright, just not one we can identify. Whoever is framing him, that's the damn suspect. You couldn't shed any light on that now could you?"

"Not at the moment, the light part anyway." I knew I could not just walk in the man's office, plop down and eat his Jujyfruits and take up his time, like an idiot wondering in off the streets, without saying something at least. "But I do have a suspect." See how that grabbed him.

It got his attention.

"You do? Who is it?"

"I can't say right now, it'll screw things up. But I do think I'm on to someone who was involved in the killing of T.J. Semieux, and it's not your client." I wondered how long it would be before my suspicions of Jacqui reached Sullivan, if they had not already.

"Well, that's damn good news because nobody else seems to. You a magician or something?"

Sullivan's chewing speed slowed down a notch, though he did not want to show it—just remain cool, casual, like it's no big deal—his attention locked in like radar, I could see.

Now I would have to follow up with a disappointment, like slapping his face on one side, then another.

"I can't say at the time why I make this statement, not even to my employer yet, but I am acquiring a body of circumstantial evidence. And it seems every time I walk around a corner, I bump into something else implicating this person. Sooner or later it'll be something concrete, unless it's all over before I find it."

"I'd like to know who it is and what you've got. Have you talked to the police about it yet?"

"No. And I promise that if you say anything to them or the press about it, I'll deny I said it, and none of you will get a thing from me. And neither will my employer, and you can take your chances without my help."

Sullivan must have thought that a strange attitude but did not say it, except with body language. "Maybe that's what you ought to do then."

"I will soon enough, I'll have to."

"Detective Sergeant Thomas, New Hanover County Sheriff, is doing the investigation, he and Captain Bobby Crile, Chief of Detectives. Ed Serrano, S.B.I., is also in on it. I'm sure either one of them would be glad to hear from you. I know damn good and well John and I would."

"What about you? Anything you can give me?"

Sullivan nodded no, but it seemed more a cautious no than a genuine sign of ignorance or a refusal to yield anything. Certainly, he had his own private investigator and would not feel the need to cooperate with me, unless advantageous to himself. But there was no doubt I had his full attention, and his interest was piqued, a sure sign the cops had not focused on anyone, so far. If they had, Sullivan would know about it. A guy like him knows everything in his environment. And in that case, he would be blowing me off like a piker.

This was going to be a cat and mouse thing if one of us did not put a stop to it. I had given up something, maybe not much more than speculation, as far as he might see it, but something, and I did not want to leave without receiving something in return. I had plenty of time, myself, but it was eleven-forty and a busy, schedule-laden attorney like Sullivan , now sneaking a look at his watch, was hearing the approaching sound of the lunch bell and would soon end the meeting for sure. Most people do not miss any meals, whether they ought to or not. Not that Sullivan looked over-fed. It just showed where his mind was, and I needed to get it somewhere else.

"Steinmark doesn't seem to have a real alibi," I said.

"Nor a motive to kill."

"That seems to be the lesser opinion. Ms. Semieux broke up with him and he has a documented history of assaults—I know, I know—." I put up a hand. "Like I said, I don't buy it either."

Sullivan plopped another Jujyfruit into his mouth and gave a sly grin.

"What about you, Wray, you find a motive? I mean, you've got a suspect, you say."

"Not yet, I'm afraid." I noted the familiar reference, being called by my first name. "You have a client on death row, I understand." I threw that out to see what reaction I would get.

He sensed it for what it was.

"Every criminal attorney worth a crap has a client on death row, in a state with a death penalty. Otherwise, why would a person accused or convicted of a capital offense come to him in the first place?

"Look," he said, "you're implying I'm playing fast and loose with my client's life. Well, I'm not. Anybody like John suspected of a serious crime who has no solid alibi, even if there is no clear-cut motive—and there isn't—needs all the friends he can get. And that means getting out and meeting people. Shit, I'd book him on 60 Minutes if I could get them. He's a good kid, he didn't hurt anybody. The better people know him, the less likely he is to be convicted, if charged at all, and that's highly probable. The police like him, they think he's great, but the D.A, doesn't give a damn. He'll burn him in a minute. There's going to be a grand jury and you can bet on it. And I don't want him bound over for trial without him riding into court on a sympathy train. Yes, in case you're wondering, and I'm sure you're a guy who's wondering, the reason I agreed to see you today is to see if I could find a way to use your influence with your reporter buddy, Morgan Dalton, the TV girl, get some quality air time. You two are very close, I hear. So sue me."

"Maybe in small claims. She's the one who called here for me."

"I wasn't here. When I tried to reach her later, she didn't return my call. Can you help us with this?"

"I'll talk to her."

"Somebody ought to. She knows John personally but she reports the story like he's some stranger, never met him, just another criminal. It's not right, she knows better."

"I'm not certain what she knows. I just know she's under a lot of pressure right now for her own reasons. And there's the thing of objectivity, not showing partially. But I'll talk to her, it's worth it. Like I say, I'm trying to help here."

"Damn right it's worth it. Hell of a time to de-personalize somebody you know personally. How much more objective can you be than to be open and tell what you know about somebody? The more personal the better, seems to me. John's an open book. I just want people to see it. There's a jury pool out there that needs to know him before they meet him, before his life is in their hands."

"You've got a point. Have the police told you anything you can share with me?"

"He hasn't been charged yet, so they don't have to tell me anything."

"That's not really what I asked you. You've been practicing law around here forty years, you say, so you have to know what's going on. How else would you know the cops love him?"

Sullivan grinned, tongue-in-cheek, as if surprised at old Wray for noticing and calling him on it. "What are you doing for lunch?" he said.

"Eating all your Jujyfruits, so far."

"The hell you say." He called out the open door to his secretary. "Shirley."

"It's not long distance out here, Loo," she yelled back. "It's a local call."

"She's been with me twenty years. Talks to me any way she pleases." Then to Shirley again, "How soon after lunch is my next appointment?"

She came into his office, a cherubic-looking woman of forty-something in a gray business suit, quick of step, no-nonsense and glasses reflecting light so bright you could not see her eyes. She reminded me of a principal who had caught me in the hallway and scared me to death when I was five and had sneaked into the neighborhood grade school to see my older cousin, Rudy, Tucker's brother, just to shoot the bull with him. But Shirley's voice was gentler, more civilized and heavily southern. "One-thirty, Jarrell, civil. Re-scheduled from last month. Remember?" She acknowledged me with a nod.

"Okay, that's good. You've met Mr. Larrick here, of course."

"Yes, I'm the one who introduced him to you. I work right out front, Loo, right where people come in the door. In fact, it's my job, among other things, to welcome them. That's where I met Mr. Larrick." She dipped her glasses and gave me a wink.

"See what I mean," he said, and stood up. "Wray and I—Mr. Larrick—are going to lunch. I'll be back by one-fifteen. Did you know this guy's a Jujyfruit commando?"

"You mean there's another one?"

"Eat every one of them if you don't watch him. That's why I'm taking him to lunch, get him away from my stash." He took his suit coat from the rack and opened the French doors behind his desk, leading out the back way.

"Ought to be a twelve-step program somewhere for folks like y'all." She gave me another wink.

"You or Judy, whoever's going to be here, tell Gary and Tracy, if they call, I'm not eating at the club today, I'm eating outside, so they can call me on my cell if they want. Tell them to stay in Raleigh another night. I'll be up in the morning." So he was a bit uneasy with phone gadgets too.

We went out back through the garden and Sullivan loosed his tie more and threw the suit coat into the back seat of his Lincoln, and we got in and headed the block or so toward the federal courthouse.

"Your death row case?" I was speculating on his mention of Raleigh, and maybe getting a little nosey too.

"Yeah, afraid so. Got a guy named Grady Millett in Central Prison scheduled for execution in two weeks. First degree murder. Rape, mutilation, what all. Hasn't got a prayer. Don't repeat that, I'll deny it.

"The governor's a good man, but he's been in office almost sixteen years, total, and he's never stopped an execution. Not one, not even for a woman. He's leaving office in a few months, so we're fighting for time until a new governor goes in, probably the current attorney-general, try for life without. Hard line guy, too, but maybe not intractable, so we play with the courts. And I don't want to see John in this situation. And I'll be damned if I'll let it happen. No sir-ee."

We parked across the street from the side door of the courthouse, a huge granite and concrete building at the bottom of the hill facing the Cape Fear River. We could have walked.

Directly in front of the courthouse was an almost-park, a tiny arbor of trees with a scattering of picnic tables and benches where people strolled the riverfront, ate lunch and lolled in the shade. We bought hot dogs and soft drinks from a young woman who operated her vending cart on the corner, then found a table. Adjacent us was a small Coast Guard station with two cutters tied up, beyond that the Hilton Hotel, and the WW II battleship U.S.S. North Carolina floated in a swampy creek across the narrow river. A multi-deck paddle wheeler for tourists was nearby.

"I didn't bring you here because it's a cheap lunch," Sullivan said.

"Not at all. It's kind of nice here. Haven't had hot dogs in a while. Don't suppose two will give me colon cancer."

"If they do, you better find a bubble to live in."

We sat opposite one another, elbows propped on the table in eating positions. A mild breeze stirred in the trees and helped relieve the effect of the ninety-degree heat and the stifling humidity. Like old home week to me.

"So why here?" I was glancing around.

Sullivan finished a bite and wiped his mouth.

"Tell you the truth, I come here occasionally when I've got a lot on my mind, when I'm worried."

"How do I figure into that?"

Sullivan did not respond to that, just ate and looked around.

"I used to come down here when I first started out working for somebody else," he said. "Not because of the peace and beauty, although it is, but because I was broke and couldn't afford to eat in restaurants every day like a lot of the rest of them. I'd bring a bag lunch. People think because you're a tall lawyer and people defer to you—and they do—you don't have lunch money problems. Reminds me of where I came from, who I am. Person needs that every now and then, good for the soul. Most of the people I work with come from the same place. They just couldn't get out for one reason or another."

"Some of them maybe. The rest of them, the predators, I mean, can go in a meat grinder, far as I'm concerned."

"Popular sentiment."

The image of my baby sister being snatched up and taken away by a person or persons unknown, who have never paid the price for the crime, popped into my mind.

Sullivan finished one of the hot dogs and wadded up the wrapper, then threw it over my head to the trash barrel about twenty feet away.

"I looked behind me to see it. "Three-pointer," I said. "You're good. Duke material."

"Cussing me already. Duke, hell. Carolina all the way. Where I went to law school. Still got it. Can't hide talent."

There was a silent moment or two before he spoke. "You and your lady friend, Dalton, have been asking around the *Storms* people about when they have their periods. Is that related to the case, or is it just something you two get off on together?" He gave the tilting hand gesture suggesting perversion, and grinned. A friendly jab, trying to hit a nerve, shake something loose maybe.

I grinned back at him. "Tall people aren't suppose to have a sense of humor, either, because the blood flow to the brain takes too long for them to get it. But I see you're the exception. Or you've been to comedy school."

"Forget I said it. Not sure I want to know the answer."

His way of letting me know he does not miss much. I wondered if he might know, too, of my suspicions regarding Jacqui Van Autt.

"I asked you out here because I needed a little more time with you to see if my initial hunch about trusting you was right, before confiding in you. I think it was," he said.

"Like I said, I'm on your side."

He nodded toward the river and looked around.

"Let's take a walk, if you don't mind."

We put a foot up on the seawall and leaned on a knee, looking out at the activity on the river.

The tide was ebbing and the river surface was calm and smooth as glass. I put on my sunglasses to block the reflection of the midday sun off the water.

"If you hadn't contacted me I would've gotten in touch with you sooner or later," Sullivan said. "I had you checked out because I like to know who I'm dealing with. No offense."

"Not at all."

"Your last case was a real piece of work. Who would ever guess somebody could see a recording of a man kneeling at an altar in a church and spot something that would help close a case that was driving the police nuts for months. Man with that kind of perception is scary."

"And sometimes I don't get it when everybody else does, and that's scary. So it's not like it's a special gift."

"Don't be modest with me, your ego is as big as mine. No, so far, including the state and local police, and my own investigator and you, you're the only one claiming to have a suspect other than John Steinmark. That's good news to me. Not detailed enough, but good enough for now if that's the way you want it. Don't suppose you have a motive to go with it."

"Not yet I don't."

There was a pause in Sullivan's response.

"And?" I said.

"I want to share something with you. It might help you on your side of things and help me, too. But it could also backfire and burn both our asses if not handled right. But you have to promise me this conversation never happened, until or unless I say so, or you're subpoenaed."

"Eventually, I'll have to talk to the police. I'm not giving up my license or going to jail."

"You haven't heard me yet. I'm not asking you to. I'm stuck between a rock and a hard place here, Wray. There's something I need to find, but it's something I don't need the police to find first."

"You can give me a try on speculation, but don't put me in a corner because I won't stay there."

"I need help here and I can't go to anyone local."

"Okay, you've baited me. What is it?" My curiosity would have driven me nuts anyway.

"Toni Jean Semieux was killed with a thirty-two. You know that. Well, John owns a thirty-two. Or did. A Beretta, unofficially, that is. And nobody knows that except him and me, and now you. And I would prefer, in fact, insist it stay that way."

"Ho-ly jeeze. Why did I have to ask? You sure the police don't know?"

"I'd know if they did, believe me."

"If they find it, don't they have to tell you?"

"Eventually. It's part of discovery. They'd be more than happy to tell me."

"So where is the gun?"

"Probably in the middle of this damn river somewhere." He nodded at it.

"So what's the problem here on your part? What do you want to accomplish?"

"I'd like to find the gun if it's around, but I don't think so, and or the person who might have it and hope it's the same person you suspect of the murder. That would be a nice package."

"Why is the gun missing?"

"It was stolen. He kept it in the glove compartment of his vehicle, never took it out. In fact, it's never been fired, according to him, not even test-fired. He bought it new, still in the box, off a friend back home in Pennsylvania when he was in college, a guy who deals in guns without a license.

"John travels on the road a lot from Charlotte to home, to here, back and forth, et cetera. He kept it for protection."

"Does he have a concealed permit?"

"No."

"Any other firearms or weapons?"

"No, just a hunting knife back home in PA."

"Why do you think he told you?"

"Because he's innocent and scared to death and I'm his lawyer."

"That'll put a nail in his coffin."

"There's a good chance the gun wasn't even used in the murder. That would be nice to know for sure. Last time he saw it was a week before the murder. Could've been taken by anybody with access to his vehicle, any two-bit thief, but almost certainly by whoever's framing him. Bet my damn life on it, too coincidental."

Oh, yes, how well I know, I was thinking.

"So the police don't know he owned a gun?"

"No. He would've told them he had it. It wasn't like he took it out and played with it all the time, like it was his pecker. When he was first asked about owning one he said no, without thinking, and was afraid to change his story when he remembered. That's why he confided in me for advice."

"Okay, let's say a miracle happens and you find the gun before the police do. What then?"

"I have it tested, privately, and compare the results with the police report of the slug found in the girl's head, and the shell casing in the car, which I'll be getting when he's charged. If it's not a match, I hand over the gun pronto. If it is, well, then I have a decision to make. But I'm not letting this young man go to prison for the rest of his life or be executed for a crime he didn't commit. And I'm betting you won't either."

"That's flirting with disbarment."

"It is once he's charged. It's flat-out sleeping with it, and jail, too."

"When did Steinmark tell you about the gun?"

"He called me from Charlotte last night."

"From his own phone?"

"No, from an untraceable phone. He's not that dumb. And if you see him again don't let on I told you about this. He has enough to worry about."

"I wouldn't dare." I felt like I had stepped on a pressure-release-armed land mine, can't stand there forever but can't step off, either, or you'll be blown into oblivion. That made two of us now, Sullivan and me, between the rock and the hard place he spoke of.

"You'd have never known this if I hadn't told you," he said.

"Yeah, it's good to know and good not to know. But if by some stroke of luck I do run up on that pistol, then I'll have a decision to make of my own. Won't I?"

"You have to admit I'm giving you an advantage you didn't have before. Now you can work on connecting your suspect with the gun. What would you have done not knowing it?"

"What I've been doing all along, working and acquiring a suspect. And I'm not going to jail for anybody. True, I think Steinmark is innocent, but so am I."

"I'm counting on you not to tell anybody, Wray."

"I won't, unless I'm put in a box."

"I'm willing to push the edge a little. I need all the friendly resources I can get."

"This thing falls apart, you'll be in somebody's crosshairs."

"Long as I'm being thought of. Does your suspect know he's a suspect?"

"I'm not sure."

"No problem, just stay in touch. And don't keep me waiting too long."

"Hey, this is free, don't push."

Sullivan's cell phone rang. "Yeah, Tracy. Yeah. Yeah, lord. I understand. Well, we tried. Okay. No, just come on back now, we'll try something else." He clicked off. "Another round lost. Come on, I'd better get back."

We started through the almost-park to the car.

"I don't know," Sullivan said, "life is a mystery sometimes, like wondering what's on a dog's mind when he looks at you. Know what I mean?"

"I used to wonder about that, too, until I figured it out. It's not that mysterious."

"Enlighten me, bright boy."

"He's wondering how it is we can stand up and walk on only two legs, without falling over."

We both laughed.

"Smart-ass, he said. "An answer for everything."

22

It was three p.m. and I was back at Ames' apartment, had showered and was at the sink in the bathroom with a disposable razor, as usual, when I heard her come in, drop her gear on the counter and the floor, and come back and stand in the doorway.

"If I were somebody special," she said, "I'd have a valet and a limousine to haul around all this *crap*."

"You're Wonder Woman." I was looking into the mirror.

"Yeah, I'm always *wondering* these days about what's next."

"You off now?"

"No, going back." She leaned on the doorjamb, arms crossed. "So tell me about Sullivan."

"Well." I was navigating the razor. "He's a very complicated man with a lot on his mind."

"Good. Tell me about it."

"I don't know what it is. He didn't say."

"Then what's so complicated about it, and how do you know it's a lot? He must have told you something. He's John's Lawyer, isn't he?"

"And I'm on Carol's payroll."

"Are you shooting straight with me here?"

"Of course. Look, he knows less than we do, I'm sure of it. And you seem awfully edgy." I looked over at her. "Please don't so anything now. Not now."

"Wray, I sitting on a bombshell. This is killing me. I can live or die based on what I do here. My head's on the block and I'm waiting for the ax to fall, and you're asking me to wait. Is that fair?"

"No, it isn't. And if we didn't know and trust one another you'd be perfectly justified in breaking it now. But we have a joint venture here, Ames, and not just you and I but Gil Russo, too, and Steinmark, himself. If this story cracks now, everybody will shut down and lock away from the world. I'll be fired. Lawyers will take over and nobody will make a move or say a word. We'll be stuck with what we have so far, which isn't enough, and Steinmark will likely take the fall. But mostly, the most important reason here in this whole thing, T.J. Semieux, herself, might be denied the justice she and her family deserve. The cops aren't making much progress. That much I got from Sullivan. Of course, you never know what they're really up to." I resumed shaving.

"I know what's going to happen," she said. "I, as a reporter and an idiot, for which I'm duly being canned, and can now understand and appreciate, by the way, am going to follow up by doing something else stupid. I'm going to demonstrate a high degree of patience and bide my time, like a damn crow on a fence, while someone else walks in and steals from me the hottest story of the day, a life-saving elixir I refuse to accept because of my unwavering loyalty and sense of ethics. I'll be exposed for the fool I am and be stoned out of the profession. I'll be lucky to get a job as a weather forecaster in a hick town with no weather. Tell me I'm wrong."

"You're going to be a national treasure and the object of a bidding war." I rinsed my face and toweled off. "Learn anything today? How about the medical examiner?"

She took a deep breath and let it out, calming herself. "I called Jacksonville. They won't comment and they won't see me. Somebody must have told them I was a nobody."

I went to her and squeezed her shoulders.

"It's going to work out, Ames. You're going to get whatever story there is, believe me. It won't end when Steinmark is arrested, it'll only start there. You've got Russo holding for you, and you've got me, your best friend in the world. Ain't you lucky? Between the three of us you know more than anybody, including the police. Except for the killer, of course. The killer knows everything."

"But motive, Wray, *motive*."

"Actually, to be technical about it, you don't need motive to prove guilt, just evidence."

She followed me down the hall to the front.

"As long as Jacqui is not a police suspect, or publicly mentioned as such, we've got time to work," I said.

"You have time to work. And quit using time and work in the same sentence around me."

"You haven't mentioned Jacqui to any of your co-workers, have you?"

"No, hell no. Think I'm nuts?"

"Bernie?"

"No. What's this? You know better."

"Just being cautious. And I do appreciate and thank you for your patience under pressure."

"Oh, thank you. I'll put that in the bank and make a car payment with it. A couple more thank yous and I can make a down payment on a house. The rest I'll put in mutual funds."

"You're a trooper."

"I'm an idiot."

"You want to have dinner together somewhere tonight? Wind down, loosen up?"

"No, I've got to stay downtown in case something comes in."

"Like what?"

"Like the tide or something. Who the hell knows. Certainly not an arrest, not my luck. I'll wind down and loosen up when a Mack truck runs over me."

"I've got some calls to make. Am I going to be in your way here? I can go somewhere, use my cell."

"No, stay here. I'm leaving shortly, after I shower and change."

"Can I watch? You know, for old time's sake?" I grinned wide. "Just a joke."

"Your life is a standup routine. Get an agent."

I liked that.

"Sorry, babe." I hugged her, patting her on the back. "Can I ask you something?"

"Sure."

"Do you know Leeza Gibbons?"

"She's married anyway, fool. Who're you going to be calling?" She walked out onto the balcony and looked out at the water. Lot of water-looking these days.

I went to the fridge and rooted around. "I'm going to finish calling the numbers I got from Jacqui's office. Got anything to go with this lettuce, besides cold air?"

"Yeah, water. Going with us to the funeral?"

"Too fattening. Yeah, guess so. I met her parents. Least I can do is pay my respects." And see who shows up. "So where are they going to bury her? Her father said her old home place, then in Thibodaux."

"In Thibodaux. They decided to go ahead now, so they can plan the campus around the site. They're moving Buddy's remains there now."

"See, you're a wealth of current information. It'll be a bigger draw than Gator Bite, I'm sure."

Ames came back in.

"Please call me and let me know something on these calls you make. I'm not getting enough from you."

"I will."

I might.

23

I waited until I heard Ames start the shower, then spread out the notes on the coffee table and punched my cell, a Louisiana area code. A woman's voice no older than twenty answered with a hello but no name.

"Good afternoon. My name is Larrick. Wray Larrick. I received a message on my voice mail to call this number, but there was no name left with it, and no caller I.D. Might it be you who called?" I had no idea how to use the message and caller I.D. thingies.

"No, sir, not me. And you said your name was what?"

"Wray Larrick. Maybe your parents called me. Could that be it?"

"No, sir, they didn't call you." She was friendly enough, but said it as if she'd heard it all before. "What's the nature of your call?"

"Beats me. I'm returning the call to find out myself. If I do, I'll let you know, but only if it's not confidential."

She snickered, like the whole thing was routine but kind of cute.

"Would you like to leave a message?" she said.

"I'd like to. Do you happen to know anyone I could leave one with, who might need one right now?"

"I'm sorry." She restrained a laugh. "Who're you with?"

"No one. I'm alone right now. I have a license to operate a phone alone."

She laughed, unable to keep it in. "I'm sorry. You're probably trying to reach my roommate. Right?"

"I don't know who I'm trying to reach if nobody tells me. Do either of you have a name?"

"I'm Jennifer. I'm not suppose to give hers out, unless I know what it's about. Not trying to be smart or anything. She gets all kinds of calls."

"I'm in the real estate business, Jennifer, here in Virginia." Lying about where I was, of course. "Somebody called me here—it was a young woman's voice—and left your number, so, apparently, it was important enough to her. I'm just trying to make the connection."

"Oh, I see, spending the money already." Said it too soon.

"Beg your pardon."

"Nothing. I'll tell her you called. Her name is Connie."

"Thanks. And her last name?"

There was a hesitation. "McCann."

"Connie McCann. The name sounds kind of familiar, but I'm sure I've never met her. Is she in the real estate business, or looking to move here, you know of?"

There was a slow "Nooo," like I might be pulling her leg. "You sure you aren't some reporter or coach or something?"

"Report or coach what?"

"Tell me this is for real, you really don't know who you're calling."

"Swear it on my mother's grave and she's not even dead yet. So if you ever meet her, don't tell her I did it."

Jennifer laughed again. She was having an awful lot of fun with this. Kids just love funny stuff.

"Well, you're different anyway. Don't know much about basketball, though, do you?"

"I tune in at March Madness. I'm a Duke fan. Duke football, too. Other than that, when I dribble, I have to wipe it up with a towel."

"Ha, ha, funny. Connie happens to be one of the top basketball players in the world, and if you're a reporter or a coach, or an agent, she won't talk to you. You'll have to go through channels and call our coach here."

"So this is a college. Well, I'm not a reporter or a coach or agent, and I'm not looking to get bogged down in any channels. She called me, I didn't call her. But out of curiosity, who does she play for?"

"Southeastern Tech."

"Think I heard of it. You play, too?"

"Yes, but you wouldn't know my name."

"You said it was Jennifer. But you can't go by me, I don't even know what my middle initial stands for."

"I'll tell her you called, Mr. Larrick. Is there anything else?"

"No, I don't think so. I appreciate it. Oh, yeah," I said, as if almost forgetting. "I knew there was something when you said Southeastern. That's where the Semieux girl is from, Louisiana. Right? The basketball player who was killed."

"Yes."

"Did you all know her?"

"Not personally. Wish I did. We played against her."

"That was a real tragedy, wasn't it?"

"That's an understatement."

"From what I understand, it'll take a miracle to fill her shoes, according to experts."

"Yes, it will."

I could hear her voice slowing down, maybe a caution light going off in her head.

"Who would be your guess? To replace her, I mean? Since you know the sport and I don't, who would you pick? I understand from the news everybody wants to play for that coach of hers, Van Autt, I think her name is."

Her reaction was a fraction of a second too long. She was already alert and deftly parried my inquiry.

"I don't know. I'll give Connie your message. I have to go."

"Don't let me hold you up. Please tell her I returned her call, and she can call me back any time, day or night." I gave her my number and thanked her, then clicked off.

Not only was Connie McCann's number in Jacqui's notes, in print, not cursive, but I would bet she had called McCann and made contact. And why not? If you're going to kill your protégé, the best player in the world, for whatever reason, you had better replace her with the next best player you can get or you're in professional trouble.

But, too, no phone call would ever show up on the *Storms'* bill when I got the copy I asked for from Carol. Nobody would be that stupid, certainly not Jacqui. She had the arrogance to walk through a minefield and dare it to blow up on her—it's just a minefield—but she was not stupid.

I punched in another number on my cell, this one obviously in Jacqui's handwriting, the letters TST followed by the number with a Philadelphia area code. Maybe something to do with Dennis White. Voice mail, female. TRISEROTECH LABORATORY. Damned recordings. People too trifling to answer the phones any more. Spend half their time BSing on the phone but won't answer one. They'll have to go when I take over. I punched zero to avoid War And Peace in numbers.

A live woman answered. *Yeh*!

"Triserotech. May I help direct you?"

"Yes, thank you. Maybe you can. My name is Larrick and I received a message to call this number, but there was no name with it." Lying again. "Would you happen to know if anyone there called me? Wray Larrick? Wray with a W?"

"No, I don't have a message for anyone with that name. Are you a physician?"

"No. What kind of work do you do there?"

"We do blood work, including testing for blood-borne pathogens and the like. Are you a medical supply salesman? You have to book an appointment."

"Oh, okay, I get it now. No, nothing like that. I'm just a patient." Lying even deeper. "Maybe my doctor had someone call me or something from there."

"Well, I don't think so, not from here. We don't talk with patients directly. We don't even know who they are. You might want to check with your physician."

"When you say blood-borne pathogens, do you mean diseases? Keep in mind, you're talking to a guy who never took chemistry but took freshman biology three times."

"Yes, we test for things like leukemia, hepatitis, H.I.V.—."

Holy Jeeze. A multitude of images flashed in my mind, memory chips from the videos I had been looking at the last few days.

"Let me ask you this," I said, now with keener interest. "Could I send you a blood sample and have it analyzed?"

"Not unless you're a licensed physician or some medical authority with a need to know. Either way, a physician has to sign off on it."

"Could my doctor have my blood tested and keep any positive results from me?"

"We don't know the identity of anyone whose blood is tested, but the prescribing physician is required by law to report the identity of any patient with a highly contagious health or life-threatening disease to the public health authorities. The patient's name is not made public, though. His privacy is protected, ordinarily. We're required, ourselves, in a case like that, to report the test results, with the code number and the physician's identity, to public health so they can track and monitor it."

"So it's illegal, actually, to keep positive results of these tests secret?"

"From authorities I mentioned and the patient, it sure is. You're not thinking about doing it, are you?"

"Oh, no, not me. I've got enough problems.

"Tell me this," I said further, "am I correct in assuming it's illegal also for you folks, or any doctor for that matter, to tell anyone else besides the patient and the requisite authorities about someone's positive test results?"

"I'm not certain of the illegality of it, but it's definitely unethical."

"How big are you folks? I mean, how many people work for you? I might want to apply for a job."

"Doing what? You never took chemistry and took freshman biology three times."

"Got me there. It's hard for a guy without an education. But I'm working on it."

"Sure. It's a matter I'm not at liberty to discuss. You might contact our human resources office. Is there anything else I can help you with, Mr. Larrick?"

"Just one. Who's the person there to talk to if I needed to get something done without the world knowing it?"

"Nobody here would violate your privacy, Mr. Larrick, as long as it wasn't illegal. But the person you'd probably want to speak with is our director, Doctor Gaylord Hesslar, M.D. He has an email address, if you'd like to have it. He's not available right now."

What in hell would I do with an email address? I was thinking.

"That would be great." I wrote it down for use in the next life. "Are you in Philadelphia?"

"That's correct."

"I thanked her and got off the phone."

Holy jeeze, a motive.

I grabbed randomly at one of the video disks in my plastic bag and inserted it into the player and watched it very briefly with fascination. Then another disk. Then still another. Oh, yes, I think so.

I heard the shower stop down the hall—what do they do in there all that time? I extracted the disk and put them all back into the bag, then called Carol Gambrell at her office. "I've got to talk with you there. It's important."

"Can't do it by phone?"

"No, there's something you need to see."

There was a pause. "Okay, I'll be here just after six."

I went back to the bedroom to dress.

"Any luck?" Ames said from across the hall.

"Naw, can't reach anybody."

She came over to the doorway, combing her hair and spoke, a little more relaxed now. "Look, maybe you're right. Maybe I should loosen up and wind down a bit. Jacqui and Carol are taking a bunch of people out to dinner and dancing tonight, the Harbor Light Dock on the canal, here at the beach. It's kind of a little get-together for the team, friends of T.J.'s, that sort of thing. I'm covering it anyway, might as well make it pleasurable, too. Anybody can come. Bernie and I will knock off downtown at eight-thirty or nine. Why don't I meet you there?"

"I think I can manage. You sure you can contain yourself around her?"

"Yeah, I got it under control. I've been talking to her today. I've got to quit worrying my ass off like a Type A anyway and just let things roll at their own pace. To hell with it. You know?"

"Yeah. Smart thinking. I'll be there."

24

I inserted the first disk into the player in Carol Gambrell's office and turned to pace, with the remote in one hand and the index finger of the other stabbing gently into the air for emphasis.

"I *knew* there was something about these recordings that was bothering me, and I just couldn't put my finger on it. Until now. Watch this and tell me what you see."

Carol stared at the screen from behind her desk, fingers flexing like a spider on a mirror. "The thing we saw before," she said after a moment but studying harder.

"Fatigue." I was now pointing at the screen and moving to it. "Look at the other women. The game's over, they're at the podium. They've already caught their breath. They're relaxed, even starting to dry off."

"Okay." She was still looking but not seeing.

"But not Toni Jean Semieux. She's still huffing and puffing and sweating like a pig but trying to hide it. See? It's like she can't catch her breath. In every case the deep breaths, licking of the lips, the hands on the hips to free up the lungs, and the profusion or perspiration, difficulty in sustaining a smile. Dead tired, during the game and after."

"Wray, she just played her heart out the whole game."

"And the others didn't?"

Carol stopped flexing her fingers and leaned forward. "Let's see some more."

I forwarded the disks one at a time to selected points, as previously. After several minutes, I stopped it.

"And this is the video of the earlier part of the tour," I said. "It gets worse in the later games. This fatigue started showing up, in fact, toward the end of her last season of college play. Something you probably wouldn't notice unless you're looking for it, or you're the coach." I turned off the video player, walked back over and sat across from her.

"Of course, you realize the potential implication here," I said.

"You're suggesting T.J. was ill and Jacqui killed her for the insurance money, and to keep the ball rolling."

"Or bouncing." Pun intended. "What means more to Jacqui than anything in the world, her basketball career or T.J. Semieux? Close call? Maybe, I doubt it. If she had to spend the rest of her life with just one of them, which would it be? Think about it."

"You don't kill someone, Wray, just because she gets ill. If, in fact, she was."

"I don't and you don't. But somebody did, and if you've got a better idea about who or why, I want to hear it. If you're right about who else it might be, you don't owe me a dime. You keep telling me crap like this and I keep showing you how it's possible."

"There's no evidence she was ill, and her performance was tops. Anybody can get tired."

"I'm certain Jacqui was looking for a replacement for T.J. before the murder."

"Oh, really?"

"You know the name Connie McCann?"

Carol's eye stretched wide open, as if surprised I would know the name.

"Yes, why?"

"I think Jacqui contacted her. McCann's phone number was in Jacqui's notes, in her desk. I checked it out."

"That's illegal." She spoke too quickly.

(185)

"So is murder. If you don't mind killing someone, a phone call isn't going to bother you."

Carol frowned. She reached over to the opposite side of her desk for the copy of the phone bill printout I had requested but had not yet seen. She thumbed through it.

I gave her the area code in Louisiana.

"But I'm sure you won't find it there," I said.

"I know it." She was irritated.

I produced the sheet of paper from my bag with McCann's number, from Jacqui's desk, and placed it gently on her desk. She glanced at it and ran her fingers along the extended list. Then she stopped, held her finger in place and looked up, pained and disappointed.

And I was surprised.

I reached over and eased the list from her hand and looked at it. A match.

"The call was made seven weeks before the murder," I said, "says right here. From Jacqui's office, before the tour even started. I'm surprised at her stupidity. I can see maybe leaving stuff like a phone number lying around in a locked desk, but not on a company phone bill. I gave her credit for being more intelligent. I'll have to tighten my credit requirements."

Carol's look was a world away. Tears began sneaking into her eyes.

I did not say anything for a moment, just got up with the phone bill and went to the window, my back turned, anything to give her time to recompose. And to see if Jacqui had made a call to Triserotech Laboratory. It was not on the bill. Another irregularity. How odd. A call that is clearly illegal shows up, and one which might have been perfectly legal does not. But I did not know how all these things worked either.

"Would you be recruiting McCann if T.J. were still alive?"

"No." Carol dabbed at her eyes with a tissue.

"Should Jacqui have been contacting her?"

"No. This conversation is still between us at this point. Is that understood?"

"Yes. And that goes for you, too. Please don't make any arbitrary decision to call things off without checking with me. We're far from proving anything here."

"It's a violation of league rules," Carol said of the phone call.

"And McCann's a top prospect?"

"There are others, but next to Fiaroli she's the top player in the world now."

"Fiaroli?"

"From Italy, the Rome franchise."

"And the league has a draft?"

"She'll go first in it."

"And you want her?"

"Of course. We'll certainly try to get her to replace T.J."

"Could you have legally recruited her if T.J. was still alive and playing?"

"No. We bought off the other teams for the right to sign T.J. It wasn't a shoo-in just because she played for Jacqui. Everybody started from scratch. The deal was, in addition to the buy-out price, we paid the *Sparks* and the *Surf*, the other teams involved, each gets an additional choice before us next year, no matter how we finish the season. The lowest-winning teams get the first picks."

"Well, then, why might Jacqui even entertain a thought of recruiting McCann if she can't legally do it, especially since it's so highly unlikely you'd get her anyway? There has to be a qualifier of some kind. Otherwise, what's the point?"

"The qualifier is," she said, stumbling over her words, then quickly righting herself, "if T.J., for whatever reason, doesn't begin the regular season and doesn't play any during the year, the deal's off, we just don't get our money back from the *Sparks* and the *Surf*. If she so much as shows up on the sideline in uniform, or plays for even one second, the deal sticks."

"And you lose the bid on the top choice next year, including McCann."

"Yes."

"So if T.J. was going to have a problem finishing, or maybe even starting the season, for whatever—sickness, what all—then it would be important for her not to show up for the regular season, so you'd have a shot at getting McCann."

"It would appear that way."

"And she sure won't show up. Will she?"

25

After meeting with Carol, I sat in my car in the parking lot of the *Storms*' office building on New Center Drive and called Gil Russo at his home in Philadelphia.

"I think I've found the motive. But I think I'm going to need some help."

"What's the motive?" Russo said.

"I think she might have been ill with something serious and was killed before anyone knew it, except the killer." I explained what I had discussed with Carol, watching the videos, spotting the fatigue.

"You've got a keen eye, friend. Sure you're not from another world?"

"I've been accused of it by licensed professionals more competent that yourself."

Russo laughed and coughed. "What can I do?"

"Triserotech Laboratory. Ever hear of it?"

"No."

"It's right in your backyard."

"Must be a new outfit."

"They do blood analysis, detect diseases, that kind of thing. Run by a Doctor Gaylord Hesslar, M.D." I accented the name. "That's all I know. But I think there's a connection between it and Jacqui Van Autt, maybe through Dennis White. But I just can't walk into their office and say it, you know. Or to her, either. If there is a connection, it might involve something illegal."

"Yeah, I'll see what I can find."

"And I don't want to tip my hat by going to the police or medical examiner. I know the medical examiner here, like in most places, will keep a blood sample from autopsy victims for several years, especially in these cases, so they'll verify that for sure later, when they know they have cause"

"Sure they don't suspect that already?"

"I'm not sure what they suspect. I haven't had any contact with them. I just know they haven't comeback to any *Storms* people yet, so I'm assuming they don't suspect Jacqui or any of them."

"They will."

"What about you? Anything you can share right now?"

"I'm working on it. But this is a different world. Things are done differently. But the Triserotech thing I should have something on pretty quickly. I'll call you back on it."

"Appreciate anything you can do."

"How's your buddy, Dalton, holding up?"

"A little antsy right now, understandably, but she's holding."

"Larrick, whatever happens, don't let her go with this thing too soon, like we agreed on, with my end of it. I know she's a pro and she's good, and I respect that, but when I go to people it's a high-risk thing for them. They depend on my confidentiality and word to keep them alive. You understand that. Integrity is everything. *My integrity.*"

"Yes, and don't worry, you can trust her. We'll keep a lid on. And I'll call you before either of us says a word publicly or to the police and run it by you, whatever it is, so you can vet out what might be dangerous to somebody."

"Good. I'll depend on that."

"Understood."

"There's going to be a huge-ass funeral in Thibodaux for that girl, I hear." Russo said.

"I suspect so. I'm going with the *Storms* people."

"I'm flying down, myself. We can talk there."

Whoa, what was this?

"You sure that's a good idea?" I was stung with the likelihood of police from numerous jurisdictions around the country, at least Louisiana and North Carolina, and maybe the F.B.I., seeing the man who was probably the best-known organized crime reporter in America, North or South, at the funeral of a national, even world renown, athlete he did not know personally. I could visualize the cops' heads snapping around, trying to make the connection and closing in on anybody related to the case. Of course, I could not tell Russo his business.

"I'm not going to the church or the graveside itself," he said. "I'll stay in my car, nearby, incognito. I just want to see who shows up. Besides, I'm due for another trip to Louisiana at company expense. I usually go twice a year, the Super Bowl, and again in the spring. I've got an old buddy at the Times-Picayune in New Orleans. Mostly, I go to eat the food. Man can't find something good to eat in Louisiana deserves to starve to death. Know what I mean? Don't worry, I won't blow it."

"Yeah. You're not coughing as much, it seems. Sounds good."

"New medication. Give it a chance. Stay in touch, see you later."

If Toni Jean Semieux had been ill before her death, Jacqui Van Autt would have been the first to know, maybe even before Semieux, herself. Hide the motive, like in a diary or something.

But John Steinmark should have known, too. In his own way, he was even closer to Semieux and should have noticed any nuance of physical change, as athletes do. He and she were not close together the last few months, for sure, but it was not likely they were totally estranged. He'd said they were talking again. Except for the month-long tour, they saw one another right up to the end, maybe not frequently or intimately, but closely enough so that he should have noticed if she were ill. People who know one another notice things. He would have seen her play on cable and noticed the fatigue. If I could see it, the man who loved and worshiped her should have too.

So talk to him? Not that easy. That's all Loo Sullivan would need, as Steinmark's lawyer, is to get wind of a potential motive pointing away from his client and he would call the cops so fast he would be cited for speeding on the telephone. And though I was precariously close, if not over the line, when I might be guilty of failing to turn over evidence of a crime to authorities, I would hold out and keep working the case. Let the cops work theirs. The slightest mention of a possible illness with Semieux would set off lights and foghorns all over the case and the harbor of Wilmington, and who knew how that might end. Too risky.

A question central to all this was now evolving. If, in fact, John Steinmark knew or suspected T.J. Semieux was ill, why had he not told anyone after the murder? It would be the smart thing to do, could take the heat off himself by introducing an alternative motive and help lead to the real killer. It would be stupid not to mention it. So why not? If he knows, who is he protecting? What is he protecting? Certainly not himself. Or could it be he was so imperceptive he never noticed she was ill, or did not think her illness or condition was related to her death? That was just as likely. The alternative might be that he and Jacqui both knew and conspired to keep it a secret, which does not make much sense because she is supposedly framing him for murder, whether or not he knows it, and he has not spoken out in his own defense. If he faked the frame job, himself, purposely sloppy as I had earlier considered, to make it appear someone was trying to stick him with the murder, then Jacqui would have to be awfully nervous now, maybe even to the point of being erratic and doing something stupid, or something *else* stupid, wondering what in hell Steinmark was trying to accomplish. But she was not. She was cool and focused, like the cold-blooded black widow I believed her to be. No, Steinmark does not know she was ill, and neither do the police. But, hell, with this bunch you could not be sure of a damn thing, what with all the lying and conning going on.

Enough theorizing. I was on her tail and should not get sidetracked, just keep plodding along. With luck there would be enough to blow the case wide open in her face and, when I did and the dust settled, I would be the one standing there with the hammer in my hand looking at the cold-blooded bitch nailed to a cross upside down.

I called Ken Enright and caught him home on the couch, apparently with a bag of Cheese Doodles, from the sound of it, watching *wrasslin'* on TV. What in hell did these boneheads do before cable?

"You still on the job?" I said.

"Yeah, I got one of my people watching the coach's condo now. And Steinmark's, too, like you said. What's up?"

I looked at the phone. He has "people" now. "Why the coach's?"

"I got two guys, like you said. I needed something for the other one to do. You don't want both of them on the same job, believe me."

"I want you to stay away from her place, meaning don't be seen there. But I want you to watch her everywhere she goes, but also don't be seen doing that either. Okay? It's important your buddies there not be recognized or act suspicious. So don't get too close. I'll pay you extra for the mileage. I'm particularly interested in who she sees and talks to when she's not on the basketball court."

"Not a problem."

"I don't want you getting the idea coach Van Autt is a suspect here. She's not. You've been around the team and her home and you haven't noticed the police bothering her. Have you?"

"Well, no, I—." He reacted like I had thrown him a curve, which I had.

"The whole purpose of watching her is to protect her more than anything else. Somebody has already killed Semieux and we don't want anyone else hurt. That's really why the *Storms* hired me."

"Yeah, I know, I figured that." He was also lying and maybe a little confused.

"So make sure the NASCAR Brothers don't go around town running their mouths about this."

"Oh, don't worry, they won't. That's cute, NASCAR Brothers. I'll tell 'em that."

"And don't be seen or go anywhere near her when not working, unless she's actually being assaulted. In that case, you protect her. That goes without saying."

"Yeah, yeah, okay. I got it."

I don't know. Get a voyeur to watch someone.

There was a silent moment and I sensed something from Enright's end because of the halting way in which he had spoken.

"Is there something else you'd like to say?"

"Uh, well, yeah, I was going to tell you. I might as well tell you now. Hope it don't cause any problems. You're paying the bills and I'm just doing what you're paying me for. I don't want to get caught in the middle of anything."

"That's right, I am paying the bills. But you don't have to defend yourself if you're doing what I'm paying you for. What is it?"

"Well, when Eddie was in the parking lot this morning watching coach Van Autt's place, Miss Dalton drove up and went to him and told him y'all were working together. We didn't even know how she knew who Eddie was."

"That was when?"

"Around eight o'clock, Eddie said. She told him there'd be some paint and wallpaper guys there shortly to do some work on the coach's place, and the coach wouldn't be there. And she wanted Eddie to go in there when they were working and pretend to be the maintenance man and just look around, see if he could find anything."

"Like what?" I was already angry.

"She just said anything, like firearms, you know, bullets, hardware, containers, chemicals, fuels, hoses, I think she said. Gas cans and hoses, dirty towels or rags with oil or fuel smells on them. Store receipts related to any of the stuff, that kind of thing. I guess she thinks the coach has something to do with the murder." Enright's way of letting me know he was not stupid.

"And did he go in?"

"Yeah, he went in."

I cringed. "Damn."

"Well, I know, and I told them just to look, not go in, but she did say y'all were working together. Of course, I kind of figured something was fishy when Eddie told me, because she gave him fifty bucks and told him not to say anything to me or you, she'd tell you herself."

"Doesn't make a damn who told you what, it's illegal to enter someone's home like that. Did he take anything out of her place?"

"Well, yes and no, depending on how you look at it."

"What in hell does that mean?"

"Well, he did eat a turkey sandwich on rye and a diet Pepsi when he was in there."

"Son of a bitch." I was not hearing Enright's further explanation and apology. "Did he see anything in there?"

"Nope. He didn't really look anyway, except the trash and clothes hamper and kitchen cabinets. Didn't want to snoop too much."

And the refrigerator.

"Right, real honorable of him. Did he call Miss Dalton back?"

"Yeah, even asked her to go out with him. Eddie's like that. Of course, you don't have to worry, a woman like her ain't going out with a man like him. If he gets any more hair growing out of his ears and nose, he'll look like a Chia Pet." He thought that was funny and set him apart from the other clowns. "They're good ol' boys, just need a little guidance."

I was steaming mad and tried for damage control. "Listen to me very closely. Your friend has committed a felony, illegal entry, which could lead right back to you. From now on you don't use them or anybody else, just yourself, when you have time, and only when I say so. And you tell them to keep their mouths shut forever, unless I ask them otherwise. Understand? If they don't, I've got the paint contractors as witnesses to a felony. And I will get statements from those painters, and nail Eddie's ass to a cross." Whoever he was.

"Loud and clear, boss man. I'm sorry it happened, but I guarantee they won't say a word to anybody."

"Is anybody out there at her place now?"

"Ricky is."

"Tell him to leave."

"Gotcha."

No you don't got me, either, you idiot. "I'll call you later."

I dialed Ames. Her phone was off. Must have been on the air or interviewing someone. I would damn sure let her hold it later.

26

I stopped at Ames' to change and freshen up, then went back to the canal, to the Harbor Light Pier, just before nine. The canal was lit up everywhere, yachts coming in for the night, houses, restaurants, streets, strands of lights and lamps around the piers on both sides of the canal, and traffic moving back and forth across the bridges nearby to and from the beach. Families and the older crowd were leaving the restaurants now and the sundowners were taking over. Those in their thirties and forties relaxed with dinner, drinks and casual conversation in the waterfront ambiance. Those in their twenties jockeyed for tables with the best vantage points for seeing and attracting attention to themselves, and making enough noise to insure it.

The *Storms* occupied the far-end half of the dock protruding out into the canal and for about thirty yards along the shoreline. Portable partitions were set up as a quasi-boundary for the semi-private affair. Plain clothes security, less Ken Enright and company, thankfully, manned their stations. The partitions were covered with posters of the *Storms* players and team regalia and, particularly, that relating to the late Ms. Semieux. Tables long and short were set up with white cloths, flowers and candles. A dance area was marked off. Garland decorated the four-foot-high lifelines around the dock. A beach music combo was setting up. Guests were beginning to arrive, most casually dressed, a few still in business attire, and groups formed to chat. Cajun style food was being prepared on site, almost ready, and drinks were being passed out. The smell of steak and seafood, fresh-baked breads, salt air, perfume and cologne wafted in the light prevailing breeze coming off the water, a very welcomed relief on a warm night.

I did not stray too far from my summer wardrobe of navy golf shirt with monogram, tucked in, putty-colored khakis with braided leather belt, topsiders—no socks—a regular preppy archeological exhibit. I wore my watch—matching leather band—and for the first time a new cologne my daughter gave me for Christmas which she said was wonderful, a babe magnet of dubious promise.

I saw Jacqui talking with the setup people. She seemed focused, as if nothing more important was on her mind. Some people could compartmentalize with no more difficulty than brushing teeth. She looked good, of course. What else? Light slacks, pastel blouse, hair shiny and tied back, action-ready, mouth accented with just the right, subtle lipstick and the figure which held a man's eyes like Crazy Glue and evoked more images and angles than a box of Animal Crackers fighting a card of Bobbi Pins. If ever there was a point-seven without being a perfect point-seven, she was it. What a damn shame for a woman so attractive, who would surely go to waste behind bars for a lifetime in unflattering prison garb, or be strapped to a gurney with a dozen belts and a needle in her arm, if I had anything to do with it. Of course, there are times when it would be nice to be wrong.

I took a mixed whiskey from a bartender and picked up a cup of steamed baby shrimp appetizers. Nothing like arriving early, a barbarian, which is to say *on time*, but I did not feel guilty. I wondered how many guests were cruising the street or hiding around the corner now, waiting for the right time to make their entrances. That better be quick or the baby shrimp would be gone. I leaned on a piling by the water and indulged my snack, occasionally waving at or speaking to someone, including Ethel Palmer, whose smile said she wished she had never met me so she would not have to like me.

Jacqui caught a glimpse of me, first staring a moment, then a big smile, not a trace of guilt in it, waving, not like we were old friends, which we weren't, but more like we somehow shared the same old joke. Maybe the mouse teasing the cat.

The music started with a warm up and the serving line opened, buffet. A few dance lovers jumped onto the floor and the dining-oriented went to the food. I would wait, I hated lines, would rather not eat than stand in one. I was always intrigued by the way people acted around food, including myself at times. Always competitive, no matter how abundant the food. No matter how civilized, how sophisticated one was on the surface, just beneath lay the rage of a killer if you got between one and one's chow. If I had to, I would put A-1 Sauce on my damn ice cubes and pretend they were steak before I would stand in a line.

Within minutes I was on my second drink and another helping of somebody's babies. I spotted Ames and Bernie coming through the partition. Bernie took a plate and got in line. Ames saw me and held up a finger for me to wait while she grabbed a drink from the bar. I was steamed more than the shrimp and lobster.

"How long you been here?" she said, coming over. "God, it's a hot one." She faced the water and pulled at her blouse in a fanning motion. "Here, get in," she said to the breeze.

I remained silent a moment, just looking at her, which was a tip-off.

"What? What's the matter?" she said.

"Gee, I wonder what it could be?"

She looked at me but could not hold the look.

"That skanky bastard. I gave him fifty bucks to keep his stupid mouth shut. And don't look at me like some Richard head, either."

"You paid him fifty bucks to commit a felony on my watch and hide it from me. You crazy?"

"I paid him fifty bucks to try and find something you haven't found yet, so don't get huffy with me." She looked over her shoulder and smiled at someone she knew passing by.

"You sent him in there for incriminating evidence in a murder investigation and he came out with a turkey on rye."

"So I feed my help."

"You're supposed to be cooperating with me, Ames. I'm the paid investigator here."

"And I'm still a paid reporter doing a job. I'm sick of sitting on the sheriff's front steps, getting calluses on my rear end. You think I'm supposed to stop working just because you're on the case? You think I'd hide something from you if I found it? Of course not. But I can't stand by, either, primping and doing thirty-second spots because no new information is coming in, waiting for you to maybe find something and spoon feed it to me while I ride jobless into the sunset. No way. I'm part of this too. We're partners here, don't forget. I'm just doing my part."

"What'd you expect to find? And why get this Eddie guy to do it? Why not yourself? You think Jacqui is stupid enough to keep evidence lying around for felons like you and Eddie to find?"

"Cute. Cut the bullshit. If he were caught going in there, I would deny I ever met him."

"Start getting reckless doing stuff like this and you could be in jail with her walking around laughing at you."

"It's the risk you take to survive." She took a stiff belt from her drink. "Whatever it takes." She fanned her blouse again.

We both leaned on the piling, looking out over the canal, our faces close together.

"Look, I was going to tell you, really," she said. "I just felt so useless. I just wanted to do my part, make a contribution, be something besides a pretty face and a fine ass for people to look at. Think I don't know what people are thinking and saying when they see me on the air? Even Bernie pans my rear and legs every chance he gets. Helps ratings, he says. He should have a ball with the infant who replaces me.

"There is something else, the reason I sent Eddie in there. I didn't tell you earlier because I didn't want you involved or implicated, in case something went wrong. Let somebody else take the fall. Bonehead's probably been in jail half his life anyway."

"Whatever you sent him in there for, it was illegal."

"Maybe. Just listen, you be the judge." She took a cautious look around. "The day before T.J. was murdered, I was with Jacqui this particular night, met her at the gym after work. We grabbed some Chinese, went to her place—."

"You assaulted and kidnapped a Chinese person?" The booze was kicking in.

She stopped. "You want to move forward and learn something, or what?"

I waved her on and nibbled the shrimp.

"So we flick on the TV to watch the news. She hits the shower. I go in the kitchen for the wine. I'm looking for the bottle opener in the cabinet drawer at the counter. There's a piece of paper, a receipt, in fact, on top of the microwave. It's partially covered by the bread basket she keeps her mail in. My eyes only glance at it because I'm looking for the opener and it's right in front of my face. And I think it's like when your eyes take a picture of something and stores it in the back of your mind somewhere and you just don't think about it consciously at the time, but it's there. You know? And I didn't think about it. I'd completely forgotten about it, didn't give it the slightest thought. Until this morning.

"It stunned me out of my sleep," she said. "I jumped out of bed. You were on the beach somewhere. I knew Jacqui would be at work and the painters would be at her place. And that one of the *idiots* would be in the parking lot. So I paid him to look around, just in case the receipt was still there, or anything else."

"Is this a cliffhanger?"

"You don't want to know what the receipt was for?"

"If you don't tell me, I'll die."

"A gas can. In fact, two of them. From SuperMart."

Indeed, that was interesting.

"It's not illegal to buy a gas can from SuperMart. I've done it. I'll bet I can go there and buy one right now without a permit."

"Gas cans purchased just before the murder, maybe earlier. I didn't think the receipt would still be there. We could look. It should have fingerprints. The wallpaper people are there tomorrow."

"We? Does she have or use a gas can, you know of? In the trunk of her car maybe?"

"No, I don't think so. I think I would have seen it at some point this last year I've known her. But these were ones obviously purchased here, in Wilmington, and before the murder. And even though I've thought all along she couldn't have killed T.J. because, mainly, I mean, well, maybe you're right, maybe she does have something to do with it. Maybe not directly, but maybe indirectly. Maybe her cousin, Dennis White, is using her in some way. I mean, she buys gas cans and then mysterious gas cans start showing up all over the place. Maybe she bought a truckload of them. You're not going to say there can't be a connection, that she just collects gas can receipts."

"One gas can receipt makes you change your mind?" I knew she was unaware of the motive I was working with, the one of illness. "You're no longer bothered there's no motive?"

"Like you said, it's the evidence that's important. Maybe we'll never know the motive."

"You sure the receipt said 'gas can' or 'cans'?"

"Yes, positive."

"So you're saying?"

"I think somebody needs to get in her place and take a good look around. Maybe her car too."

"The only thing Eddie found was the refrigerator. It's all illegal."

"I didn't say steal anything. Just to know it's there so the police will know. Since I'm supposed to be a friend of hers, and I use the term with license here, I could tell them I saw something while I was there with her, all perfectly legal. They could get a warrant. Think they wouldn't jump on it?"

"Did you touch the receipt?"

"No."

"You've been in her place a couple times since the murder. Right?"

"Once."

"Notice the receipt then?"

"No, I didn't think about it until this morning, like I said. Doesn't mean it's not there. Even if that *idiot* didn't see it."

"Here comes Bernie. We can talk about it later. If I get buzzed, you drive home."

"I'm starving. You coming?"

"Shortly."

More people were pouring in. The noise of talk and music rose. The combo was now interspersing beach music with Cajun, and it had a nice effect.

So that is the second stupid thing Jacqui had done, I was now thinking. First allowing a rule-violating, even illegal, phone call to Connie McCann show up on her bill, then this, if Ames' vision is correct, a receipt in plain view in her home for anyone to see for items which might have been used in a murder, among other serious felonies. How stupid could one very intelligent person be? Split the question. Why is it the police seemed not to have the slightest suspicion of, or interest in, Jacqui? Why have they not stumbled on or been given something to cause them to focus on her? Now, in the other cell, why is good old Wray bumping into stuff at every turn? It's not because the cops are dumb. They're not. All things considered, they're more able to solve a crime—any crime—than anyone on the face of the earth. Yet, here in their own backyard, nothing. 'Yet' being the operative word. Was it the scientific stuff, evidence testing and the lab work and the waiting that was making it slow for them? I bet things would move a hell of a lot faster for them if I turned over to them what I had on the human side.

But they would get there without my help, and I did not want that to happen. It was not just the ego and the challenge of it, or even the nobility of bringing the victim's killer to justice. The quarter-million-dollar reward money, the bonus negotiated with Carol Gambrell, and the other hundred grand from Jacqui, herself, was a great motivator too. I would have to confront Jacqui real soon with what I had and go for broke, force her hand and see if she would fold, then, win or lose, let the police take it all and run with it. I would have earned the bonus at that point, if she were indicted.

But not now. After the funeral. First I needed to insure Ames did not do anything stupid or illegal again. I would have to share more with her and hope she did not go to the airwaves with it, trying to save her own career. I would talk with her later. Share with her or not, either way was a risk, as she was more impatient now.

"I hate lines, too." Bernie was in shorts, sandals, and Hawaiian shirt, which seemed to be his own signature dress code. "Baby shrimp. I didn't see that. Where is it?" He set his plate atop a piling and picked up his food.

"They're sleeping now. Don't wake them."

"Booze is good, though. Must be spending a fortune on this gig."

"Anything coming in downtown?"

"Naw. Same old same old. What about you? Or can I ask?"

"Not a whole lot." Maybe a lie, depending on how you looked at it.

"Don't wish him any bad luck if he's innocent, but I wish they'd arrest Steinmark so I'd have something to do."

"You're an old softy. Ames said you're having a great time shooting her rear end though."

"Who wouldn't? The world needs to see more of this woman, head to toe. People see, people like. It can't hurt. A drop-dead face with a wake-up body might create demand. If it helps, I'll get credit for it, too. She's my connection and I need the work as bad as she does."

"You know many of these people?" I nodded at the crowd.

"Know several of them to one degree or another. Only a couple of them personally. You've got your mayors here from Wilmington and the beach, there and there. A couple council members and commissioners. Lots of courthouse people here, I notice, and chamber of commerce types. A couple big shots from the university."

"Some small get together. Why the accent on community leader types?" I was thinking out loud.

"You mean, other than the fact they like schmoozing and free stuff? Jacqui's idea. They're lobbying Carol." He nodded to where Carol was in the center of a small group. She was in a custom-made navy pantsuit with gold accent epaulets and solid gold earrings, from the looks of them.

An admiral. Admiral Canary.

"For what?" I said.

"They want her to move the franchise here. This area is booming, too damn much, as a matter of fact. The university needs a law school and a football team, and a place to play. And Wilmington needs a major sports complex. Maybe not today but in another eight-to-ten years. They figure if they can get the *Storms* away from Charlotte, and they succeed and draw in another pro franchise of some kind to go along with it, they can make it happen. They're even talking a major NASCAR track up off I-40."

"I-40 is already a NASCAR track. Rockingham's not far away, up 74. Right?"

"I hear that, yeah, but that track is closed now. But the real problem is, I hear, too," he said, leaning in, "and don't tell anybody I said this—I have to get along with these people, bread and butter, you know. But Carol and Jacqui are butting heads over this thing. Serious disagreement. Jacqui wants to make the move here, to Wilmington—she likes it here—and Carol doesn't, likes it just fine in Charlotte where the market is bigger. Said it'd take thirty million dollars, at least, to buy out the Charlotte deal and make the move here."

I was stunned once again. Keep listening, keep learning. A twenty-five-million-dollar life insurance value collected on the death of T.J. Semieux would go a long way in offsetting any expense needed to make that move, Jacqui's move. First there was no motive, now they're falling out of trees like ripe fruit. Take your pick.

"How'd you know this?"

"Something else I want you to keep to yourself. Ethel Palmer told me."

"Why would she tell you?"

Bernie grinned real big, like a rake.

I immediately looked over at Ethel Palmer sitting at a table with several others, picturing the connection.

"You and Ethel?" I grinned back at him. "You devil, you. A married woman, too."

"I'm single and her husband is not interested any more. She thinks he's got a younger girlfriend, so why not. She's here, he's there. She's a nice gal, smart too. And don't let her age fool you. Very athletic, tennis player, was a gymnast when she was a kid. And you can tell."

"Nothing like networking. I'm sold." I wished I could run into Mary Jane Hathaway.

And thank you, Bernie. You have no idea the value of the information you just gave me, I was thinking.

"Is Ames—Morgan—aware of this little moving deal dilemma between Carol and Jacqui?" I said.

"I'm not sure."

"Why would somebody want to move a franchise away from a major market like Charlotte to a small place like Wilmington? What's the advantage suppose to be? It would seem like financial suicide."

"Carol would like to get out of the business. She jumped into it too fast. It's costing a lot more than she figured, business plan shot to hell. If she could unload the franchise to a bigger market, where she could get her money back, she'd sell in a heartbeat. But if she sells to Wilmington, she'll take a big-ass loss."

"So the buyer for *here* could pick up the franchise for a fraction of its worth, if she'd sell it to them."

"Right. Then maybe re-sell it later at a huge profit, when it's maybe successful, because it'll never make the big bucks here, not for a few years anyway. Until then, you'd have to eat the losses. Carol doesn't like eating losses, she was raised on a better diet, something like that."

"And especially since T.J. Semieux won't be playing. When she went, so did the big draw. Kid played a hell of a game of ball."

"Exactly," Bernie said. "They'd have to find another big draw somewhere, and she'd have to have that special something T.J. had, and that's not likely."

Jacqui is one step ahead of you there, buddyro.

"So would Jacqui want to eat the losses and risk failing?" I said. "It can't be just because she likes the beach. There has to be something in it to override the stupidly of it."

"That's the sixty-four-thousand-dollar question." Bernie gulped down a bite and licked his fingers. "But without T.J. it's going to be a tough time, even in Charlotte. It'll be tougher on the other teams. They don't, or didn't, have any T.J.s. Maybe Jacqui figures if she's going to lose anyway, why not do it at the beach."

No, it had to have been in the works long before Semieux was murdered. It is likely there is a short-term profit for Jacqui and a long-term advantage built into any such deal. What else would be the motivator? Let's see, local business people, with Jacqui's help, buy out Carol for a fraction of the team's current Charlotte value, so they dream, move it to Wilmington—without T.J., it loses either way—Jacqui is given a large piece of the ownership action for her part, and without Carol she's the top dog, she runs the show. She then builds the franchise by recruiting flashy, attractive players and winning lots of games, which she is capable of doing. Makes no difference where you are based, you can play anywhere by traveling, so you can go where the crowds are. By doing so she re-increases the franchise's value and creates options to either stay in Wilmington and grow with it, or to move immediately to a more lucrative market. Either way, she can't lose, it's always OPM, other people's money. Beautiful. Maybe that's why she murdered T.J., to de-value the franchise, scare the hell out of Carol so she would want out, then show her the way.

Most people would not think like that if the plan actually required killing another human being. But if you came from a family in which your father and uncles were mobsters who lived and died violently, your cousin, with whom you are very close, still is a mobster hiding his birth name and identity from the public while he cooks the books for the mob right on, and tries to rip off three million dollars from your protégé with your blessing, then you are more likely to be one of those who do think along this line. And if said protégé is sick with a performance-threatening, maybe even terminal, illness, well, then, it makes this likelihood a whole lot easier to accept.

Bernie gulped down the last of his food and drink. "Guess I better get my gear," he said.

"Gear for what?"

"We're shooting a piece for the late report. You'll see."

"Inside information, of course." I grinned.

"Of course. I have my sources. Film at eleven."

"You've got a nerve is what you've got." Big laugh.

I went to the serving line, which was now tolerable, and got a little dinner to go with another drink. I took the empty chair Ames was saving for me next to her. I was used to the kind of attention she was getting from people who approached her, especially the men, a certain amount of celebrity and a whole lot of beauty and sex appeal.

"Bernie said you're doing a report here."

"Yes." She spoke close to my ear, out of range of the others at the table. "Carol is dedicating a statue of T.J." She nodded to the entrance where two security people were moving aside one of the partition units to make room for the other two men who were carrying the plastic-wrapped sculpture.

The men placed the statue in the little area near the head tables, next to a microphone, leaving the plastic taped over it, creating a buzz of curiosity.

For the next thirty minutes Ames and I ate and talked with those at our table. She signed several autographs for people bumping me around to get to her. For their children, of course. I hit the bar at least once more and was now feeling the warm buzz hitting my brain. I looked at my glass and pushed it aside. Too much to think about for much of this.

Ames left the table to join Bernie, who was ready with the camera just a few feet to the side of the mic and the covered statue.

Within a couple minutes Carol stood before the mic and turned it on. A spotlight shown on her, her gold glaring, her flaxen hair ruffling in the breeze. The music eased off and all became quiet.

"This won't take long," Carol said. "First of all, I want to thank you all for coming. And please stay until all the food and drink and music are gone.

"I want to give special thanks to Mayors Tennery and Carpenter, from Wilmington and Wrightsville Beach, respectively, for joining us, along with their fellow council members, and to commissioners Lockhart and Pennaman from New Hanover County, and their colleagues. And to Jane Berg and Don Macklin of the Chamber of Commerce, as well as Doctors Wycoff and Haislette of the university, and the distinguished folks from Carolina and Kure Beaches. And to the others of you, too, who were gracious enough to take time out from your busy lives to join us in celebrating, in this small, humble way, the memory of our incredible and beloved Toni Jean Semieux."

No problem for me. You never have a problem drawing people out for free food. You could have it scheduled in a hurricane, standing room only, with the waves washing over the sides, and people would fight the waves for the trough.

"I won't dwell on the tragedy," Carol said. "T.J. wouldn't want it that way. Instead, I mention only the positive. We are here, at this place, because T.J. loved it, the beach and the water. We're eating this food because this is the food she liked and would want to share with you. And we're listening to this music because this is the music she loved. And we're informal and casual because that's the way she preferred things.

"As some of you know," she continued, "there are four main entrances to the new facility in Charlotte. The south side entrance is ours. We've been long thinking about how best to accent our entrance and lobby. Since we're a new team in a new league, we can't line it with huge trophy cases full of victorious awards." She smiled. "That'll come later."

"Hear, hear!" someone shouted, and cheers and applause erupted.

"Well, we can go ahead and order the trophy cases," she said. "But because of our recent unfortunate loss, that decision came quickly and easily." She nodded to the two men attending the statue, who began unveiling it. "We commissioned a leading sculptor to produce a life-size likeness of Toni Jean to be placed in the center of our lobby for all to see and admire. It was a rush order but I think you'll be impressed by this quick mock-up model. We want people to know who we are and where we come from, how we got this far and why we're going even farther.

"This dream that we're beginning to live now never would have occurred were it not for the dreams and efforts of our great coach, Jacqueline Van Autt, and of Toni Jean Semieux, herself."

"Hear, hear!" the same voice proclaimed, and more cheers and applause.

The statue was unveiled to oohs and ahs and a brief standing ovation.

The model statue was in a bronze color, on a three-foot-high foundation. In the rendering she as in uniform, standing casually, one foot slightly behind the other, as if about to step forward. In the crook of her right arm was a basketball held against her hip, in the left a teddy bear held loosely at her side at arm's length. Her face was level and strong, the look of a warrior of good who had triumphed over evil and now knew peace.

"We want people to know that embodied in this beautiful young woman," Carol said, pointing at the statue, "were the scars of the worst struggles, the courage of the greatest challenges, and the rewards of the greatest victories. That no matter our stations in life, no matter our accomplishments, no matter what we do as individuals, our greatest achievements are accomplished in concert with, and on behalf of—and because of—others, as members of a team. This is how Toni Jean survived. This is how we all survive.

"We want most of all for young people to see this likeness of Toni Jean and be inspired by it, to know her story, to know that no matter how difficult or painful life can be, it can get better. This is what we stand for, aside from any business considerations, and it's why Toni Jean established the Buddy Semieux Foundation, which our organization will continue to support."

Another round of applause.

"In the spirit of this purpose," she continued, "this mission and our team's close association with it, we've made another decision, as well. We've changed our name. From now on, our team will be known officially as the *Carolina Tee Jays*. Our mascot will be Buddy the Bear."

One of the players stood facing the audience and held up the new jersey with the number One on it. A brief applause followed, then Carol made a final statement, eyes moistened with tears.

"Toni Jean's jersey will be retired, permanently displayed in our lobby. There will never be another number One jersey on our team. An empty chair will be placed on the sideline with us at every game we play as a reminder for us and our fans of her ever-present spirit. We do this for you, Toni Jean. And wherever you are—and I know it's in the best of all places—we love you, we miss you, and we'll never forget you. Not ever."

Another, longer, standing ovation and many watery eyes. I felt the emotion, myself. The booze, of course.

Carol left the mic. Ames was speaking into the camera for the upcoming news spot.

I looked at Jacqui, now rising from the head table to join Carol and Ames before the camera. Huge tears, heavy as glycerin, flowed down Jacqui's face.

Life is full of little surprises.

And a few curves.

27

It was after midnight when I got in from the pier party. I had showered and was sitting on the sofa, having just watched again Ames' spot of Carol's statue dedication, when Ames walked in, haggard from another long day, put down her gear and kicked off her shoes.

"Well, at least you had something to report," I said. "You don't have to feel guilty about taking their money today."

"They can go to hell." She was not at all angry. "I don't feel guilty anyway.

"You know, in retrospect," she said, "I should've had an agent negotiate all this for me from the get go, like people were telling me to do. But, no, I didn't need one, I was so tickled to get this great big career break, so grateful to have it I just signed my ass away and they gladly accepted it. I was going to work my way up to capitol correspondent. I got this dead-end beat, instead. I could have had a buy-out or severance pay clause or something, but I don't even get cab fare home. It won't happen again, that's for damn sure. Of course, up until now I've enjoyed it."

"Then maybe you should get an agent before doing any interviews on your own."

"That's where I am now." She went into the kitchen and poured a soft drink.

(211)

"You know," I said, "Bernie's been in Ethel Palmer's personal space the last month."

"Did he tell you that? I knew."

"And he didn't tell you what he learned from her?"

"About what?"

"About Carol and Jacqui at odds over moving the team to Wilmington permanently?"

"No." She stopped, surprised. "I mean, I knew a group wanted the team moved here, but I didn't know anything about a disagreement between them over it. I assumed neither one would consider moving here."

"Wrong." I gave her the rundown on what Bernie told me, while she listened in stunned silence. I could tell she was disappointed, even hurt, that Bernie had not confided in her.

Ames put down the glass hard on the counter.

"He's been working closely with me all this time, but he tells *you*. You wait until I see his sorry ass in the morning. What is it with you men." It was not a question.

"Agreed. It was unfair of him to tell me and not you. I'm sorry. But I'm not holding it from you, myself, and there's more."

"Oh, more? Did you clear it with him?"

"He's not privy to this."

"*Wee.*" She put up little Richard Nixon victory signs. "Well, there's one damn thing for sure." She came around and sat in the chair across from me. "All this crap will be over with soon enough, then good-frigging riddance."

"You're acquiring quite a knack for foul language."

"The company I keep." Her expression said she was killing Bernie repeatedly.

She looked at her glass. "Shit, I need something stronger than this." She went to the kitchen for the hard stuff. "Join me in misery?"

"Not tonight. One of us has to remain alert and stupid"

Ames was fetching her drink with unusually loud slamming and footsteps. She came back around and dropped back into the chair.

She threw her head back and ran a hand through her hair a couple times. She let out a big breath and sipped her drink. "More what?"

I told her of the illegal phone calls from Jacqui's office to Connie McCann in Louisiana, about the possibility of T.J. being ill, and of Triserotech Laboratory and my suspicions of a possible connection of these things, which I would be learning more about soon. I told her, too, of Ethel Palmer's seeing Jacqui in her office the night of the murder, when she said she had been home in bed with menstrual cramps. I did not, however, mention John Steinmark's owning the now-missing thirty-two Beretta because, in the event she did go public prematurely, I did not want to jeopardize Loo Sullivan or Steinmark, as I had promised I would not. If the gun was never found, and it likely would not be, it would be a non-factor anyway, and no one, including Ames, would need to know. With all this evidence now beginning to fall like rain, including more than one possible motive, and how the twenty-five-million-dollar insurance payout on T.J. was figuring into it all, a very clear picture was forming as good as any Triple A road map directly to Jacqui's door.

"I've got to push this thing," I said, "make something happen. I'm way past the point where I have to go to the police with what I have. I can't keep putting it off."

"How do you push it?"

"I'm going back to Steinmark first, see if he knew or suspected T.J. might have been ill with anything. Put some pressure on him, see what breaks loose."

'Wouldn't he have told you when you talked with him before?"

"Not necessarily. He might not have known or, if he did, he might not have figured it was a big deal, or related to her murder. And maybe it's not. Or he figured it was none of my damn business. Maybe a reason for keeping it secret. I hope so. But he hasn't been arrested, so he hasn't been frightened yet. It's time he had the crap scared out of him."

"But T.J. wouldn't have told him, Wray. He wouldn't have known if she were ill. They were broken up."

"He could've known something before they broke up. Or she could've confided in him before she was murdered, when they were talking again. Then I'm going to confront Jacqui."

"That ought to be interesting."

"I suppose I ought to wear S.W.A.T. gear when I do it."

"John is in Charlotte now."

"And I need to call Sullivan in the morning and ask him if Steinmark is going to the funeral."

"Why don't you call John? You have his number, don't you?"

"I'd rather go through Sullivan. After all, he is his attorney. It's the right thing. I don't want anybody pissed at me more than they already might be. I've run out of pissed-off-excuse tickets for now. Besides, he's a good man, no reason for me to go around him."

"So when are you going to talk with John?"

"After the funeral, when he gets back to Charlotte. If he goes. I want to look him in the face when I talk with him. But first I want to see if Gil Russo comes up with anything on Triserotech. If there is a possibility of a connection, I can use it to maybe squeeze something out of Steinmark, if he knows anything, even if I have to bluff him.

"This whole thing doesn't make sense from a rational perspective," I said. "Intelligent people like Jacqui make multiple dumb mistakes, and other intelligent people like Steinmark don't cover their rear ends when it seems they should. With two intelligent people who know one another, have a common interest in, and love for, the same person—the victim—then one might assume there is a connection between these two dumb-doing, intelligent people, too. Two intelligent people in the same environment doing something stupid related to the same event. Doesn't make sense, unless the dumbness is for a shared, purposeful reason. Does that make any sense to you?"

"What do you mean about John not covering his rear end?" I did not answer. She took a long draw on her glass, staring out into the bright night and ocean. "Yes, it sure does make sense," she said, almost inaudibly. "And I feel so dumb, myself. You never saw T.J. in your life, yet you look at videos and see fatigue and too much sweat, heavy breathing. I knew and was around her for a year, in the flesh, and never noticed a thing. Bernie hardly knows you and tells you things he's never told me, and I'm his meal ticket. Or was. And now you see a conspiratorial relationship between John and Jacqui, two other people you're hardly acquainted with and, yet again, I never saw a thing. But you're right about that. You're even better than I thought. After all, that's why I recommended you. Isn't it?" She gave a tired smile.

"Is that a good thing or a bad thing?"

Ames slowly got up and smiled back at me. She rubbed a hand gently through my hair, studying my face momentarily, a blank expression now on her own face. "You're doing a terrific job."

"You feel alright?" I said.

"I'm fine." She turned and went down the hall, putting her glass on the counter in route.

"It'll all work, Ames. It's going to be a great story. All yours. You can call it *Foul Shot*."

"I know, Wray. I know," I heard her say from the darkness of the hallway.

28

The next morning Ames had already left and I had just showered after my workout, when my younger brother Jeff called from his law office back home in Hampton.

Jeff had been born two years after the disappearance of my—our—younger sister, probably as a result of it, and I had watched over him almost obsessively as he was growing up. We had formed a close bond and, as far as Jeff was concerned, there was nobody like his brother Wray, which always made me feel good. We favored a lot, he with the edge on looks, and you could tell we were brothers, though he had never excelled in sports. He had wanted to when younger, to be like me if for no other reason, but it just wasn't there. What he excelled in were academics and girls, graduating from William & Mary with honors and making Law Review at UVA, and dating as many girls as he wanted. And he wanted. But it had never gone to his head. I always said Jeff was the luckiest, most spoiled brat in the world to be such a decent human being, with a great wife and kids, a perfect life to boot.

"Well, old boy," Jeff said, "I've got some good news and some bad news."

"Which amounts to bad news. Drop it on me, I'm a damn bombing range, so what else is new."

"I found a way to keep you grandfathered on the pier. I knew I was right on that to begin with. Even though you tried to end run the permit process, I got it worked out with everybody so you don't get arrested. And I showed it to Williams, and he was duly impressed." He was referring to the zoning director with whom I had been having a running battle.

"But?" I said.

"Then he was duly *un*impressed. He knew it was grandfathered all along, he said. But the structure itself is now condemned."

"Condemned? Bullshit. How is that?"

"Degenerated structural integrity, unsafe. You'd have to rebuild the entire pier, tear down the old. The old members are not reparable. And, naturally, the catch is you can't put up any new structures. That would be babying in, not grandfathering."

"Over three hundred years on the point and now they say we can't live a few feet out over the water when there are businesses all over the creek."

"Environmental necessity, careful planning. Reversal of encroachment. When you get home, take a look around, Wray. I mean, really look. You'll notice the population and demands on resources have increased dramatically since John Smith, Gosnold and Newport came this way."

"Sure, but it's okay for working, you can tie up a boat and work it and not have to tear it down, though."

"Exactly."

"Have you talked to dad?"

"Yeah, he's got some guys coming over tomorrow to move the stuff out and disconnect the utility lines. Put some of it in the garage, the rest in the old boat shed. Power company won't touch the electrical because they didn't put it in, so you have to hire somebody, or do it yourself. You know that."

"And the aquarium. Don't let them kill my fish."

"They won't. And you might still have to answer for the illegal wiring, too. Williams didn't hassle you about it, but the power company reported it because it was illegal, even though it's connected to the main house, their boxes."

"And they're perched on the fence watching to make sure somebody burns my ass. It's not like they're losing money. The bill is paid."

"For a guy of your intelligence, you sure are hardheaded about some things. I'll work on it. Don't worry too much."

"You are doing this pro bono, aren't you?" I was kidding

"Pro bono, Sonny Bono. Sure, you're working your case for free, aren't you?"

"Fifteen hundred a day plus, and a big bonus if I get it."

"You ought to be shot. You're worse than a lawyer. Shakespeare had it all wrong, he was really talking about you guys."

"You wish." I laughed, though with some pain at the news he had given me. "Is Tucker there?" I was referring to our older cousin and Jeff's partner.

"Not until after court."

"Tell him I ran into an old fellow down here he played against, a guy named Loo Sullivan. Played tackle at East Carolina. Tucker scored on him once, I think. He'll remember. He knew Terry Widener, too. Tell Terry that Sullivan said hello, if you see him before I do. This Sullivan guy is representing John Steinmark, the guy who's suspected of killing Semieux. He was her boyfriend. You've seen the story, I know."

"Saw it on TV, it's in the paper. I've been watching the story. Making any progress?"

"Yeah, I think so."

"What can you tell me?"

"Nothing, except the suspect didn't do it. And that's between us. Don't need any talk around town there."

"Tell me more."

"Can't."

"Figures. How's Morgan? You two hitting it off?"

"Off and on. Good friends, just business."

"Too bad for you. How's she doing?"

"Not too good, professionally. Her network is dropping her contract. Don't say a word to anyone."

"No problem. Guess that explains my suspicions."

"About what?"

"You can tell there's a lot on her mind. I'm sure you've noticed."

"Like what?"

"Like lately, when you see her on the tube she seems detached, maybe not to the casual observer, but to someone who knows her."

"Hadn't noticed, myself." Right under my nose and I missed it.

"Well, you should, you know her. Unemotional, I guess is what you'd call it, compartmentalized, detached. Whatever."

"Well, she's known for some time she's getting the ax. Maybe it's her way of dealing with it."

"Tell her we said hello, and we're pulling for her. Where are you staying when you get back? At the house?"

"Couple days, maybe. I don't know yet. Look, Jeff, I got to go."

"Keep your head up."

"You mean down, don't you?" I knew well what he meant.

"No, I mean up. They can't shoot you if it's down."

"You still owe me money, sonny buck."

I then called Loo Sullivan at his office. His secretary, Shirley, answered. "And how are you doing?" she said in her long drawl, before connecting me.

I found her voice so infectious I started drawling right along with her, not realizing it.

"I'm fine, Shirley, I guess. You okay? You've got your hands full with that guy, don't you?"

"Yes and yes. I guess you found that out yesterday, huh?"

"Oh, yeah," I said, snapping out of it.

"Well, at least he's for real. What you see is what you get. But he must have been impressed by you 'cause he was in a good mood when he got back here after lunch, and he's usually not.

"Hey," she said, "do me a favor, will you. Your lady friend, Morgan Dalton. Can you get me an autographed picture of her for my niece? She's majoring in journalism up at Chapel Hill, wants to be a big-time correspondent, like Christiane Amanpour or somebody. They all do. She collects these things, walls plastered with them."

"Sure. Can you get me one of Diane Sawyer or Dawna Friesen? Wow."

"I'll bet you wish."

"Not a problem. I'll drop it off. I'll even throw one in of me."

"You don't have to go that far."

We both laughed and she put me through to Sullivan.

"Hope you called to tell me you tossed and turned in your sleep all night, that your conscience is bothering you so much because you haven't told me who your suspect is. That couldn't be it, could it? Because I sure could use some good news right now."

I could visualize him swiveling in his chair, with one big foot up on the desk drawer.

"This is a bad time then. Maybe I should call you back later."

"No, that's okay. What can I do for you?"

"I want to talk with Steinmark again."

"That's not a problem. About what?"

"Nothing in particular. I just want to see if I can glean something from him he might not know he has. I'll think of something to talk about, just scraping the walls."

"Sure. He's coming back here for a couple days right after the funeral. You can talk to him here if you want."

"Rather do it alone."

"Okay, just let me know soon as you do it. Just don't bring up to him, or anybody, what I told you," he said of the missing gun.

"Of course not. He's coming straight back then?"

"Yes. Look, I'm going to lay it on the line to you, Wray. Things are starting to pick up speed around here. The proverbial little birdie has informed me that, short of another way to go between now and then, John will be arrested early next week and charged with the murder, probably no bond, and be bound over to the grand jury the following Monday. That's Monday, week. And if he's bound, he'll be tried and probably convicted. There's not a damn thing pointing to anybody else. So if you're holding any cards, I sure wish you'd show your hand, at least to me, give us some hope here."

He let me think about it.

"I promise you whatever I have, Loo, for what it's worth, I'll let you and the police have it no later than next Thursday night."

"Then why don't you tell me what you've got and I'll hold it until Thursday, in case something happens to you."

"Doesn't work that way."

"Any particular reason why that day?"

"It gives me more time, and it gives you a working day Friday for paperwork and to have the police consider someone else and pull Steinmark out of the D.A.'s sight before the weekend. And I'm working my own case, like I said, but I'll speed up my end, too, because you just asked me, so don't push."

"Okay, fair enough."

"You going to the funeral?"

"No."

"But Steinmark is?"

"Damn right he is. He wouldn't miss it and I insist he go. I'm not going because it would be presumptuous, since I didn't know the girl. And John doesn't need a lawyer on his arm, looking guilty."

"I'll talk to him there, maybe. I just wondered about any hostility he might encounter."

"You could maybe change all that before tomorrow. It'd look worse on him if he didn't go."

I did not take the bait. "Have you said anything to that buddy of yours around the courthouse?" I was alluding to the "little birdie" he mentioned.

Sullivan hesitated a moment.

"I told him or her we met, but I didn't tell him or her you had a suspect, if that's what you're wondering."

"Thanks. Has your proverbial little birdie mentioned anything that's not already public information?"

"You mean, if I give you something, you give me something?"

"Something like that."

I would not give up names or specifics and he knew it, so I said no.

"Okay then," I said, "unless the whole thing collapses before next Thursday night, we'll talk seriously then. Except I'll call you right after I talk with Steinmark, if he has anything worthwhile. Otherwise, I won't."

"I'll hold you to your promise. I hope to hell you're not just blowing smoke here, that you've got what you say, because it looks like now you're the only hope."

End of call. There is plenty to tell, I was thinking, but thanks anyway for putting your client's life on my shoulders.

29

I went to one of the better men's stores at the mall on Oleander Drive and bought a solid dark suit, double-breasted, summer weight, with accessories, to wear to Toni Jean Semieux's funeral the next day. I took the accessories—shoes, socks, belt, shirt, ties—and left the suit for alteration and would pick it up before closing. I dreaded the thought of wearing a coat and tie down there in that heat. It was something I always considered one of the least intelligent things people did, but if I showed up the way I wanted, I would be arrested as a vagrant.

I sat on the bench at the intersection, at the food court, where all the wings in the mall joined, where the older generation collided with the young, where folks talked and watched and basked in the ambiance of lights, noise, smells of food, and the energy and beauty of youth, kind of a cross-generational carnival. I sat there with my slippery bags sliding all over the place, like a man trying to round up a bucket of greasy ball bearings. The mall walkers were out in force with their funny, exaggerated gaits, looking like Ducks Unlimited in a hurry. I was thinking "AFLAC, AFLAC." Some serious enthusiasts, others screaming for attention and lying to themselves. I'm terribly judgmental that way.

I pulled the cell phone out to call Ames, see what she was up to, but it rang me first. It was Gil Russo.

"Quick pick up," Russo said.

"My eagerness to be a part of the Technological Age. It's also the only gizmo I'm able to operate, if you leave out the part about storing numbers in the memory, call waiting, et cetera."

I told him of the whole Carol and Jacqui mess of moving to Wilmington.

"Looks like your hunch was good from the start. What about the police down there?"

"If they have anything, they're holding it close. Not a peep out of them, and they haven't combed back over the *Storms* people yet either. Makes you wonder."

"The *Tee Jays* now, right?"

"Yeah, you heard."

"On the news, your buddy Dalton last night."

"Anything on Triserotech?"

"Purpose of my call." He coughed and cleared his throat. "Founded two years ago. The 'Tri' is for the three partners in the business, Hesslar, his wife and brother-in-law. Innocuous on the part of the latter two, but Herr Hesslar, himself, M.D., Ph.D., is another story. The bad boy of medicine. The last decade he's had numerous run-ins with the licensing boards of three states, Pennsylvania, New York, and New Jersey. Multiple complaints of incompetence and negligence involving more than one case of death and injury. Been in the courtroom so many times he's been accused of having a fetish for sniffing legal briefs. Can't afford malpractice insurance any longer. Medical board here made a deal with him—he could keep his license as long as he never used it to practice in the state again, a Catch-22. So he opens the lab. His doctorate is in microbiology, a shoo-in. Lab business seems to be successful, no problem there.

"But," he continued, "the most interesting thing I found was that he and Dennis White belong to the same handball club. How's that for a fit?"

"Perfect. Now try this: I see Jacqui noticing Semieux is tiring too easily, maybe even Semieux complaining to her of feeling ill. I see them needing to look into it without anyone suspecting anything, because even a hint of it could negatively affect Semieux's bankability, thus the team's as well, and the new league itself. So they keep it a secret. Jacqui takes care of everything. She arranges for a physical exam, maybe, by someone who can be trusted to keep his mouth shut. Or maybe a blood workup, everything off the record, of course. She contacts her very close, brother-like cousin, Dennis White, to make the necessary connection. If it's in the dark, he can find it. In this case, our good doctor, Gaylord Hesslar, fellow handballer. Whatever is done, exam, blood tests, or both, the results are positive. So Semieux becomes a liability alive, but a twenty-five-million-dollar consolation dead. Cut your losses, cash in, keep moving. But pin it on someone else, the perfect scapegoat, the violent ex-boyfriend who won't leave her alone, John Steinmark."

We both remained silent a long moment, obviously sharing the same sick feeling of this scared, abused girl from nowhere being brutally murdered and discarded like another item of salvageable trash, no better than scrap metal at best, and the man who loved her paying for it with his life.

Russo spoke. "Yeah, I think you've got the picture."

"I appreciate your help on this," I said. "If I'm right and she was sick with something, the medical examiner down here should be able verify it once they test. I know the police don't seem to be approaching things from the human side now, probably more forensic. But I suspect any day now they'll find something under the microscope and start busting through people like Sherman went through Georgia."

"Keep me up on anything you run into," he said. "See you tomorrow."

"Let me ask you something." I stopped him from hanging up. "It would be nice if I could talk to Dennis White personally. I'd like to look him in the face, see if the implication of his possible involvement might make him flinch. I can't let him off the hook, no matter who he's involved with or how dangerous they are. It's just not right."

"Too late."

"And why so?"

He let out a deep, labored breath. "Because I'm doing it. I'm meeting with Dennis today."

"Don't let me hold you up, partner. You're sounding better already."

30

The chartered jet left Wilmington at seven-thirty a.m. for the three o'clock funeral in Thibodaux. Ames, with Bernie manning the camera, spent the flight shooting interviews with Carol and Jacqui, the players and others aboard, each in turn reflecting on her relationship with and knowledge of T.J. It was all documentary and archival material to be part of a special shown that evening and for several days to come on the local network station and fed to the cable network, and narrated in conjunction with Ames' anchor.

On arrival in New Orleans, we were met by a fleet of SUVs that carried us to a suburban country club, via a connection by Carol Gambrell, for a sumptuous lunch, most of which went uneaten because of the somber mood. Then we were driven to Thibodaux.

The funeral of Toni Jean Semieux was on one of the hottest days on record and the hottest of the year, so far. I was muggy and sweaty in my new suit and was comforted, if you could call it that, only in knowing the wretched over-weight and ill among us in attendance were, themselves, miserable beyond hope. But it stopped no one from coming.

The neighborhood around the old gray stone Catholic church in town, typically working middle class of older well-kept homes, was flooded with literally hundreds, including dozens from the press, crowding the sidewalks, parking lot and the street within a hundred yards either way. Numerous dignitaries, sports figures and media people, along with fans, jockeyed for seating inside. Many lived in the neighborhood and were there more out of curiosity, people on the porches and in the yards and driveways, sweaty, dirty kids stopping in the middle of play to see what was going on. A select number of the press, including Ames and Bernie, were allowed in the church ahead of time to set up and record the service. If I had not been with the team, I would not have gotten within fifty yards of the place. I had never seen a funeral as large in my life, even one for a veteran with military honors during the Viet Nam War. This was more like the death of a royal. A minor media and public event, a huge event locally.

A group of young girls no older than twelve or thirteen, who had been playing basketball in the churchyard until overwhelmed by the crowd, stood on the sidewalk at the bottom of the front steps of the church, wide-eyed and awe-struck at the *Storms*, now the *Tee Jays* team members arriving.

"That's T.J. in there, ain't it?" one of them said to no one in particular, her eyes wide.

The team member I recognized earlier in the gym as the best jumper stepped over to her and squeezed her shoulder gently. "Yes, it is. Keep your chin up and keep playing." Then she went inside.

The service was closed casket. Pews, upper and lower, were full. People lined the walls and stuffed the vestibule and enveloped the front of the church outside. A huge orchestrated display of brilliantly-colored vegetation adorned the alter area around the casket. Sunlight poured in the stain glass windows. The air conditioning was wide open, and the hand-held paddle fans took up the slack.

There was a single noticeable exception to the white, gray, black, and dark blue attire worn by those present, and that was the bright yellow suit worn by Edna Fortier, sitting in front with her husband, Maurice, and their sons, the bronze casket laid out before them. I had been told it was a Fortier family tradition that the survivor closest to the deceased, usually and in this case the mother, wear yellow to symbolize a ray of sunlight and the spirit of love and warmth brought into the life of the survivors by the deceased and emblematic of the contribution to those qualities by the one wearing it. If there was no female parent or guardian to wear the yellow, the closest male would wear a yellow carnation with a dark suit.

I stood by the wall, near the front, so I could see the faces of the family and those closest to them. Though it might be hard, I would try not to be drawn into the emotion of the moment. I was still on the job, but on occasions I was also a sucker for a choke as much as the next hard head, especially now that I had learned so much about T.J. and had been brought closer again to the long, deeply ingrained memory of my sister and the hurt it had caused everyone and what this was causing now for those here and my identity with it.

One of the last to come through the door was John Steinmark. A hush came over the crowd. He could not have picked a worse time. He might have come earlier and taken a seat so as not to be so noticeable. He could not have planned it this way. Heads turned, some with harsh looks. After all, his face had been plastered all over the news since the murder as the likely and only suspect. With him were two men of equal physical prominence Teammates, a very imposing trio. One I recognized as Bo Hodge, a *Cougars* defensive end, a six-six, two- hundred-eighty-pound block of quartz who, himself, had made news the year before, having been tried on a felony count of aggravated sexual assault on a female, reduced to simple assault and a slap on the wrist. Great choice of friends to bring along to the funeral of a murdered woman. Maybe Sullivan needed to be more involved with his client. He would not have wanted this.

Steinmark looked distressed, his face pale, ghost-like, his friends doing the looking around for him, while he stared straight ahead. They took up position near the front, without resistance, and stood against the wall, hands crossed in front of them. Steinmark gazed over at the casket as if to speak to it with the expectation of maybe it speaking back. Then he bit his lip and looked down, probably to keep from losing it.

Bernie captured the moment.

The murmurs started and all eyes were moving between Steinmark and the Fortiers, as if this might become a double funeral.

The muscles in Maurice's jaw tightened, his head moved around as if he were unable to bare looking at the man he knew in his heart killed his daughter and had the nerve to show up at her burial.

A slender, distinguished-looking man in an expensive tailor-made suit, with gray sides and a balding pate, leaned forward from a pew behind Maurice and gave him a brief, comforting pat on the shoulder. Paul Bonham, I figured.

As the whispers reached a crescendo, the priest entered and all drew quiet.

Bernie's camera rolled.

The priest, Father Gentry, a heavy-set, middle-age man, opened the service with the requisite rites. Then there was a special song from the choir. Then he spoke personally of Toni Jean, as he had known her since she arrived into the Fortier family. There was another song from the choir, a prayer, then the eulogies were given.

Maurice related to the congregation, as he had to me on my earlier visit, the story of the blue ribbon won on May Day and the effect it had on Toni Jean, of it being the beginning of so many other great life-changing things, and of the family's eventual mixed feelings of sadness, emptiness and happiness when she left for Ivy Ridge. And of her doing so well there and of growing happier every year. He thanked Carol Gambrell and Jacqui Van Autt and their organization for their honor to Toni Jean and Buddy, the re-naming of the team, for the statue and the mascot.

Then Maurice's mood turned bitter. He pulled from his breast pocket and help up the tickets he and his family would never use to see Toni Jean in the Olympics. He spoke of her first professional game they never would witness, of the continued happiness she never would know, the marriage, the children, the family she never would have.

"But sadder than these things," Maurice said, "worse than any of it is the terrible, shameless and evil way she was taken from us. And I believe that, just as surely as I'm standing here, so is the one who took her."

Steinmark and his buddies were clearly stunned by the remark, though it was not completely unexpected. But his demeanor was now more of rising to the challenge than of cowering. He held his head high and looked straight at Maurice. So did his buddies.

Ames looked at the floor. Bernie recorded the moment. It would be dramatic footage, for sure.

"We'll leave judgment to the courts, to God," Maurice said. "But whether or not he ever faces justice with his fellow man on earth"—he turned halfway and pointed with a stiff arm to the Crucifix—"he will face justice from this man's father." He left the podium and returned to his seat. Bernie's camera was still rolling.

After an uneasy moment of recomposing among the congregation, Jacqui took the podium for the team. She was less emotional, more controlled.

"Several years ago," she said, "an old friend of mine who coaches basketball in New Orleans called me. He'd gotten back from a summer basketball camp. He told me, 'Jacqui, there's a young girl down here. Very young. But you must see her. And if you don't do it soon, it may be too late, because a lot of people are going to be seeing her.'

"Well, I considered it. Along with a hundred other things and girls. But I must admit it didn't move me. So a month later he called again. 'Listen, are you going to see this girl, or what?' So I figured, to shut him up, I'd visit him and his wife on Labor Day weekend, then as a side trip I'd go meet the girl, if he still insisted and she were amenable.

"Well, he made the arrangement for us to go down and meet *the girl* and her family." She put up little quotation marks. "There was this very nice family there, nice parents, two nice boys. Typical All-American family, so far. Then this shy, skinny, cute but scraggly-looking girl walks in the room and I'm thinking, *I came here for this?*"

Laughter broke out in the church, releasing some of the pressure. Even Maurice managed to crack a little.

"The whole time we're in the living room having tea and enjoying the company of these nice people this young girl is sitting there and not saying a word. She wouldn't talk, she'd just say, 'Yes, ma'am, no ma'am,' or shake her head. So to break the ice, I say to her, 'I understand you shoot some mean hoops. Let's go out back.'

"Well, folks, let me tell you something. When that ball went into her hands, she came alive like nothing I'd ever seen in a girl that age, and explosive energy and savvy. I knew right then that girl wasn't going anywhere but to Ivy Ridge."

More laughter.

"I spent every minute I could with her over the next four years, traveling back and forth, whenever my schedule allowed, to the point, I believe, that the Fortier family must have thought I was some kind of northern fungus invading the South."

Louder laughter.

"And, of course, the rest is history.

"But that's not all there was to this girl. In fact, there was much more. This girl had a history, this girl had a story. This girl grew to have a mission in life and a reason for being here, a mission and a reason that touched all of us who knew her. I don't have to tell you all because you knew her, you were her friends and neighbors and fellow parishioners.

"Toni Jean had been under a lot of stress in the last months of her life. There had been the pressure of the season and the championship tournament. Six-and-seven-day-practice weeks, the traveling. Final exams and graduation. The endless awards and ceremonies, personal appearances. The European tour. The growing number of business decisions to make for the first time in her life. The Olympics to prepare for, and the upcoming pro season. Her life was relentless, with little time for rest, and it was showing on her, and I was beginning to be concerned for her.

"I stopped by her apartment one night," she said, "the first week we were back from Europe, to look in on her, just a few days before we lost her. She asked me if I'd take a look at something she'd been writing, something she wanted to say that could be engraved and mounted in the main entrance of the Buddy Semieux Center here in Thibodaux, when it's finished. Something that would capture the spirit and purpose of the place. I said sure, let's see it. It's entitled *Forever Into A Sunrise*, and I'd like to share it with you.

"*There is no past but memory, and no present, for the moment we sense it, it is gone. There is only the future, wherein all life resides, and how promising it is. One need only reach and pluck from its vines its wondrous fruits...There is no oldness, no defeat, no hopelessness in this life but that the mind and soul allows it. There is only life to live and unlimited possibilities...There are no scars, only stamps of our travels. Just when life seems to wound and deny, it offers healing and boundless opportunity...There are no failures, only steps into time, an endless stream of days of soaring hope moistened by morning dew and of flight forever into a sunrise. And one is awe-struck on this journey both by the world lit up around one and within, for, as we discover, we are not only created but are a part of that which creates and nurtures and frees. We're the very stuff of life, and our life is either diminished or enhanced in the living of it...Fear not life, nor time, nor station, today is yours, now gone, and tomorrow your creation. Lift up your wounded but able wings and take flight in the warm air of the new day and fear not painful memory. Pain is never a burden too heavy, and there is always a sunrise.*'

"She asked me, 'Well, what do you think, coach?' and I said, 'I think it's perfect, babe.'"

Jacqui glanced at the casket and smiled. "Thank you for being a part of my life, Toni Jean. Thank you for needing me and for giving me more than I could ever give you. Thank you for your dedication and your loyalty, for your sweat and your sacrifice. Thank you for the crying and the laughing you shared with me, and for the funny moments and the breath-taking excitement. For the champion spirit. Most of all, thank you for your love and friendship and the happiness you brought into my life and the lives of those who knew and loved you. The world was a better place because you were in it, and it will be less because you are gone. Goodbye, Toni Jean. I will miss you."

There was hardly a dry eye among the women and numerous of the men. Steinmark's face was crimson, his eyes welling with huge tears.

I had a lump in my throat, having been drawn in by the message and away from the messenger.

Jacqui left the podium and returned to her seat, eyes dry as a pile of bones on a desert floor.

I left the service with the crowd, bothered by something, like a mental pulling on the coat sleeves, an incompleteness maybe, or something I should have noticed but did not. Something I had already seen but had forgotten, whatever, but something about an otherwise perfect service that was not perfect. I get these things sometimes. It would come to me, it always did. But it could also have been something as mundane as forgetting to pack my dental floss. Something else to worry about.

31

The graveside was located outside town in an arbor of trees, on the far back quarter of what would be the campus, where Maurice had taken me on my previous visit. Buddy Semieux's fresh, re-interred grave lay only a few feet from Toni Jean's. Vehicles jammed the grass and dirt road that meandered through the property. Mourners migrated in the heat to the graveside, several men removing their coats. A sign of intelligent life, far as I was concerned. I removed my own and stood off under a thin curtain of moss hanging from an old oak and swatted at the flying insects, which had no respect, whatsoever, for the ceremony here.

Steinmark and his two buddies stood across the grave from the Fortiers, their presence obviously discomforting to some.

The media was heavy but kept a respectable distance. Ames and Bernie, who, himself, wore a black suit with peaked lapels and looked like a parrot head who got drunk and woke up on Wall Street in somebody else's clothes, was just a few yards away, near the road. Ames spoke softly into the mic while the camera rolled.

Ames noticed me staring. She cut and walked over, leaving Bernie behind a moment.

"God, it's hot." She fanned her blouse and joined me under the tree.

"What'd you think of the service?" I said.

"Notice who John brought with him?"

"Yeah, Bo Hodge, Mister Role Model. Surprised you recognized him."

"How stupid. No wonder he's a suspect. Where's Sullivan in all this?"

"My thoughts exactly. I'm going to rattle his cage when I get back," I said of Steinmark.

"You need to leave him alone." There was a trace of authority in her voice.

"You his lawyer now or something?"

"Jacqui." She looked over at the crowd, by the grave. "Wray, I think it's time you went to the police about her. I'll go with you."

"I'll bet. Hold your horses."

"I'm serious, Wray. It'll tie right in with the documentary. I can break it right before air time, late news hour. Maximum exposure for both of us. You've got more than enough to put them all on her. They can put the heat on, you can't."

"I told you, I don't want to shut things down yet. He's going back to Wilmington tonight. I'll see him tomorrow. Then I'll confront Jacqui, lay everything out. I don't want you there yet. I've got some things to do first."

"Who told you he's going back to Wilmington? Are those Neanderthals going back with him?"

"Sullivan told me. I haven't talked to Steinmark. I'll call him right after this."

"So when are we talking about a story here, a break?"

"Soon. Real soon."

She started to leave. "Don't do anything without me," she said. "We're partners, partner."

"Say anything to Bernie?" Which meant she likely had something very special in mind for him at the right time.

"Oh." She turned back to me. "Captain Crile is here. The sheriff's detective. You see him?"

"I don't know what he looks like."

"Right there." She pointed a short finger at a tall, bony man in a dark suit in back of the crowd at the grave. Next to him was another man, younger, shorter, stocky, similarly dressed in a decent suit that looked like a uniform. Cop chic. Each had a bulge under his coat, in back. They're working, too.

"Who's his partner?" I said.

"Glenn Thomas, a sergeant."

"Must be awfully important to have two ranking officers down here."

"So talk to them."

"I don't need these guys asking me anything now, because I don't want to have to flat-out lie to them."

"Well, then, you'd better disappear because they're asking questions all over the place, and they asked me about you. And they've talked to Carol, too."

"Say anything to them?"

"Of course not. Think I'm going to hand over my story?"

"How about Carol?"

"How would I know? I doubt it. See you later." She went back to Bernie.

My cell vibrated. It was Gil Russo.

"Looks like you could use a little relief," Russo said.

"Damn bugs. Where are you?"

"Over your right shoulder, sixty yards down the road. Black Navigator, dark windows. Air conditioning."

"Any flies?"

"None."

"Save me a seat, I'm on my way." I eased off down the road, my coat over my arm. I noticed detectives Crile and Thomas watching me.

"I see a guy of your stature goes first class," I said of the Lincoln. "Your paper pay for this?"

"No such luck. Belongs to my buddy at the Picayune." Russo was dressed casually in traveling attire, with a small portable oxygen tank on the floorboard at the ready. He was holding binoculars and took another quick peek.

"Your friend Dalton sure is everything in person she appears to be on the tube. She's getting more attention than the deceased." He lowered the binoculars.

"Makes you wonder why they'd can her." I said.

"No reflection on her personally, I'm sure. Damn, that's a good-looking woman. They weren't lying when they said it would be a big turnout."

"See anything interesting?"

"Not really. I was halfway expecting, or maybe hoping, to see Carmine Philyaw show up."

"Would that tell you anything?"

"Not necessarily. But if he showed up with anyone else, and I recognized them, it might. There's no reason for this funeral to be mobbed up, actually. These are straight-up people. I'm just nosing around, getting out of the office."

"So tell me about your Dennis White lunch."

"Forget Dennis White. He's dead."

"You're kidding."

"He never showed."

"Jeeze."

"I called his office from the restaurant. Got a recording saying the office was closed for the day. I got the news last night. Dennis' secretary had the morning off yesterday and went to work after lunch and found him dead in the office. Two bullet holes, one in the chest, the other in the left ear. Been dead since the morning, apparently."

I absorbed the news. Too fast a circle for me to move in.

"So he won't be eating his dessert then." I said.

"He made some dumb moves. First, he draws attention by giving back the Semieux money, which was likely mixed with some of their money in a deal of some kind, getting outsiders involved, then compounds that, probably, by talking to me and letting people find out.

"And Docter Hesslar won't talk to me, not that I expected him too," he said.

"So that dead-ends Triserotech for me. No pun intended. I wonder if Jacqui's been told."

"Don't know, too soon to tell. Police are holding things tight."

"So the message for you was, yes, they were involved with White in Semieux's money, and for you to stay the hell out of their business."

"Hard to say, but likely as not."

"Are you staying out of it?"

"Their business *is* my business."

"Do you sleep well?"

"Like a baby, when I'm not gasping for breath."

"Amazing."

"But I'll be losing a few winks knowing I might be partly responsible for Dennis being killed. He was a crook, but only to mostly greedy people who could well afford to lose the money, and he didn't deserve to die."

"That's your opinion. How could they know he was meeting with you?"

"If they did know. Like I said, I was putting feelers out on the street. People add two and two. Who knows, maybe his secretary ratted him out. She might've known he was meeting me. She was conveniently off work when he was killed. Nobody will ever know."

"I'm sorry if I'm getting you in any trouble here."

"No sorrys necessary. You don't get me into anything I don't want into, and I'm not in any trouble. But I don't want to sit on this thing too long, either. I hope you can appreciate that. Dennis' murder pushes thing up, far as I'm concerned. Along these lines, what else can you tell me?"

"You're way ahead of me. But I'll call you in a day or two, let you know how it's going." I opened the door to get out.

"Look," Russo said, "if Dennis was killed because of the Semieux business—and that's as likely as not—and the wise guys are in a killing mood, well, it's something to think about, you know. They won't hit me, but you don't have any immunity here, you aren't shit to these people. You get close, you never know. I wouldn't feel right if I didn't at least mention it. There's always some risk, like I said, about people dealing with me. You see what can happen. Don't come to Philly looking around. Call me if you need anything. I mean that, Larrick."

"I already did call you. Appreciate your help. You'll hear from me. Your medication seems to be working for you."

I walked back up the dusty road to the gravesite.

People were now leaving, the service over, and were stopping to talk in small groups.

I stopped by the roadside to offer condolences to the Fortiers, who thanked me for coming. I wanted to talk with Maurice to see what, if anything, the police might have told him, but it wasn't the time and place. Instead, I looked at the grave, at the last of the mourners leaving, then walked over and sat under the tent alone, close to the coffin.

The aroma of dozens of flower sprays filled the air. It reminded me of spring at home on Larrick Point, when all the smells cultivated by my mother's work exploded and filled the senses and made pleasurable the simple act of walking in and out of the house into the yard. A portrait of Toni Jean Semieux sat atop the coffin, her brilliant white teeth and big brown eyes pulling in the looker, and I felt a peculiar closeness, even a kinship with her.

"You got a tough break, young lady," I said out loud to no one but her.

"She sure did," a man's voice said behind me.

I looked back.

"I'm Paul Bonham." He extended his hand.

"I know." I shook it.

"And you're Wray Larrick, I'm told."

"So far. But all this here makes you wonder about the finiteness of it all." I motioned around the place.

Bonham looked older up close, his side hair slightly curly, probably once brushy, his eyes blue-gray, his demeanor one seemingly of caution and intelligence marked by the adopted—adopted because nobody did it naturally—aristocratic affectation of holding the fingers of one hand just inside the side coat pocket, while the thumb stood guard outside, kind of Prince Charles-like. The look on his face, though signaling need, said he is never too friendly with strangers, except when politicking, because it might turn out later he does not like you, or you are guilty of something, so why bother, a condition acquired through prosecutorial work dealing with the worst of humanity. His accent was south Louisiana for sure, distinctively tidewater, and not a lot unlike that of my own origins, but his with a thin layer of local edge shaved off for wider appeal. First impression anyway.

"Yes, it does." He came around and sat down. He left a vacant chair between us, careful to honor the sanctity of personal space, mostly his own. He was silent a moment, then spoke.

"I remember the first Sunday they brought her to church. In fact, my firm handled the adoption for Maurice and Edna. She'd come a long way since then for something like this to happen. Damn crying shame is what it is."

We were both gazing at the coffin.

"I agree. What can I do for you?" I suspected I already knew.

Bonham unbuttoned his coat and leaned in, elbows on his knees, like a good ol' boy. I could picture him sitting on the porch of a country store, looking out of place but whittling on a stick, cultivating the locals for votes. "How's your investigation coming along?"

"I think it's coming along just fine."

"Anything you can tell me? In confidence, of course."

"I can tell you John Steinmark didn't kill this woman."

"Then you're the only person saying that, besides his attorney. But I'm inclined to agree with you, from what I hear of the evidence. Of course, I can't say that around Maurice. His mind is set. Have you told the police this, or offered an alternative?"

"You mean, have I talked with them and told them, among other things, about the three million dollars and how you went to the mob to get it back, and how Carmine Philyaw was dispatched to take care of business? No, not yet."

Bonham's face reddened. He drew a deep breath. "I see you're a man who likes to get to the point."

"The last time I danced around something it was a Mexican hat and I was drunk."

"Actually, I didn't know who was dispatched. How did you learn this, if you don't mind me asking?"

"I didn't get here by falling off a hayride truck."

"Maurice didn't tell you that. He didn't know. But I understand. I won't ask you for your sources."

"You just did."

"Look," Bonham said, "you're not a stupid man. You have to know what I'm getting at."

"Sure."

"A number of things—." Suddenly, as if the thought just occurred to him, he said, "By the way, you're not wired for sound, are you?"

"Too high tech for me."

"What with the whole mess it could cause for everybody. Even though I did nothing illegal, still, there's the taint of impropriety it could create in the wrong hands. I'm planning a run for governor in the next election, myself, and I don't need something like this around me, no matter how noble the cause, and neither does the state. We've had our share of scandals. I'm sure you read the papers. I need the confidence of knowing this won't jump up and bite me down the road. Nothing illegal. I'd never ask anyone to consider anything improper—."

"Don't worry about it." I cut him off. "You've got my vote."

Bonham absorbed that a moment. "I appreciate that. Of course, I know if you're put in a corner—."

"I won't be. The money and how you got it back has nothing to do with this woman's murder. If anybody hears it, it won't be from me. What you did was a good thing. As far as I'm concerned it's nobody's business. Case closed."

Bonham nodded gratefully and let out a sigh of relief, but very subtle, the way lawyers do in a courtroom when they think you do not know what they are thinking or feeling, how just under the surface they're exploding with excitement. "Thank you. I appreciate it."

"And Dennis White won't tell anybody, either." I was having fun with it. "He's dead now, murdered."

Bonham hesitated, taking it in. "Now that *is* something I wouldn't know about."

"I'm not suggesting you would. You can catch it on the news tonight or tomorrow."

"There's something else I need to mention. You asked Maurice if I showed an interest in Toni Jean's property down in Gator Bite. The answer is no."

"That, too, has nothing to do with the murder, so I'm no longer interested in knowing. But I believe you."

"The police will probably talk with you before you leave. Just thought I'd tell you, in case you might not have expected it."

"They talk to you?"

"Not exactly. Last night I was at Maurice's when they came by. Captain Crile and a Sergeant Thomas, I think his name was. They're out here, by the road there." He nodded over his shoulder. "Your name came up, routine."

"Did they say anything that might interest me?"

"Probably nothing you don't already know, a truckload of evidence against Steinmark, way too much in my opinion. Gas cans found on his property, matching mud from the crime scene in his vehicle, the locker key and the bullets. Her rejection of him and his hanging on. Too much evidence lying around for somebody as smart as he's supposed to be. Of course, as a former prosecutor, myself, I've seen some awfully intelligent people do some equally stupid things. Still, that much evidence, so obviously convenient, sends up red flags. I don't think the police are convinced he killed Toni Jean, but I know the prosecutor must be doing cartwheels."

"What locker key and bullets?" I was hearing that the first time.

"The initial search, they found a bus station locker key on a ring in his closet, in Charlotte. The key fit a locker at the bus station in Wilmington, wherein they found a partial box of thirty-two caliber bullets, the identical kind used to kill Toni Jean."

"Thanks for telling me."

"Well, I guess I'd better get out of the way and let these people do their job." He was speaking of the workers waiting to cover the grave.

We both stood.

"Listen," he said, "the Fortiers and all of us appreciate everything you and Ms. Gambrell and her organization are doing on this case.

And I think you're onto something about Steinmark being too obvious a suspect. Good luck with it.

"I'm going to give you my card," he said. "My private numbers are on it. Call me anytime if there's anything I can do for you. I mean it, Mr. Larrick."

"Don't act surprised, or like you don't know me, if I do some time."

"I won't. And thank you for the other thing, too."

We shook hands and he left. Not a bad guy, I was thinking.

I walked slowly from under the tent, remaining in the shade of the trees. I dialed John Steinmark, who was already back on the highway with his buddies and heading for the airport. The press had swarmed him after the service when on his way to the rental car and he had B-lined it. He said he would see me the next morning at his place at the beach, at eleven-thirty, after his meeting with Sullivan, as long as Sullivan agreed to it.

What I really needed to know from Steinmark was why he would lose the gun and leave the bullets lying around in a locker for the cops to find, unless it was all part of the whole frame-up thing and he did not know beans. But I could not ask him because I promised Sullivan not to tip my hand about the gun. Unless Sullivan agreed to it. I punched his number.

"Did everything go alright there?" he said.

"If looks could kill. But he did good and nobody confronted him but the press. I don't think he said anything. He got out too fast."

"Did he show emotion?"

"At the church he sure did."

"Well, that's a positive. If it hits the air it'll help."

"Let me ask you something. Were you aware of any bullets the police found in a locker John had at the Wilmington bus station? Thirty-twos?"

"What? Bullets? Hell, no. What damn bullets?"

I filled him in.

"Son of a bitch," he said. "That's news to me. It's certainly not public information, unless the police are telling every goddamn body but me, and that's what it looks like. Son of a bitch."

"Don't feel bad, I wasn't suppose to know, either. I think they were just trying to be nice and cooperate with the Fortiers."

"The bullets are not his, can't be. He'd have told me about that. Why would he tell me the other thing, about the gun, and leave out the bullets? No way. The same son of a bitch who took his car and put that shit in it is the same son of a bitch who put any bullets there. Got to be."

"Whoever it was, he was close enough to him to get into his apartment in Charlotte and plant the key. If that's what happened."

"Makes you friggin' wonder. Son of a bitch. Does this information fit your idea of your suspect?"

Fishing again.

"I'll know in a couple days, but I'm sure we can count on it. I just have to make it fit right."

"Uh-huh. Well, John probably doesn't even know, himself. Don't bring it up to him. I'll talk with him about it."

"Good enough." I clicked off.

I walked toward the road where the team was preparing to leave.

Bernie was still shooting everything in sight. Ames had closed up shop. She stepped out to head me off. "What were you doing at the grave? What were you talking to Paul Bonham about?"

"What would he be talking about at her funeral?"

"He wasn't praying. He already did that. He walked over there specifically to see you alone, Wray."

"He just asked about the investigation, is all."

"You didn't say anything, did you?"

"Of course not."

"Good, because he's a politician, and you tell him something and he'll be mugging for the cameras and stealing my show."

"Is this what it is, Ames, your show?"

"You know what I mean. For a reporter I've been pretty damn cooperative and patient, still am, with your and Carol's pleas for confidentiality here. That cuts against the grain of what I'm supposed to do. Ask any one of these others out here to sit on this and see how far you get. So I think it's okay to share something with me without your feeling I'm intruding.

"And, by the way," she said, who were you with in that black car?"

"Gil Russo."

"What? Gil Russo? And you didn't tell me, or invite me over? How could you not?"

"He didn't want anybody knowing he was here."

"I could have met him, at least, and that would be somebody else important I know, somebody I could call sometime."

"Well, he's gone now. But if it's any consolation, he said you looked even better in person. He had binoculars."

"He tells you all this, but he won't tell me."

"Well, at least he said you looked good in person. He never said that about me."

"Oh, shut the hell up. Let's go."

"After you."

As we got into the car, I saw Captain Crile and Sergeant Thomas looking at me again. But they had not bothered to approach me. Good. I guess.

32

The team's charter flight arrived back at Wilmington late in the evening, just after ten.

I went straight to Ames' place at the beach. I had a brief workout on the hard sand near the water, where I could see well enough, then showered and went to bed.

Ames and Bernie went straight downtown after landing, to their studio to file the final report for the documentary-in-progress on the life and athletic career of T.J. Semieux, to begin airing the following day.

I woke up at two-thirty a.m. restless and unable to sleep any longer. I put on long, thin cotton workout trousers from my karate gi, with draw string at the waist, and went into the kitchen. I flicked on the light and microwaved a cup of leftover coffee and took it to the balcony. Light from a near-full moon was half-strength over the water, because of cloudiness, but bright enough for a couple of die-hard lovers to walk the surf line arm-in-arm.

Within seconds my cell phone rang on the counter inside.

"Join me down here." It was Ames. "Bring a glass or a cup."

"Where are you?" I walked back out onto the balcony.

"My favorite place, about forty-five degrees down to your right. Right in that little valley on the dune. See? Other side of the footbridge."

I looked and saw a gray-like figure that must be her.

"What are you doing down there this time of night? I thought you were maybe asleep."

"Naw, tried it. Put some shoes on and bring a folding chair. It's not the pier, but it's beautiful out here. Great place to whine with your wine."

"How about the ice cubes?"

"Got'em."

I put on my running shoes and a shirt, left unbuttoned. I took the flashlight from my ditty bag, for navigating through the sand spurs, like it would do some good or something.

We sometimes did that when living on the pier together at Larrick Point, one waking up the other to share a particularly intoxicating night, maybe a cool breeze coming in after a hot day, or a galaxy of lights from the sky and the multitude of ships in the James River channel and the port of Norfolk, the quietness of water at times, or of the refreshing coolness of the fall. Invariably, it was followed by passionate love-making. This was not likely to happen now. That half of these beautiful moments was gone.

"*Ow. Damn*". I was working my way through saw grass and sand spurs, finally making it and sitting and picking out the spurs from my ankles. "What in the devil are you doing in the middle of this mess?"

"Found it the first night I was here. Even the scavengers with their little metal detectors don't walk through here. What better place for a woman alone on the beach at night? Nobody will sneak up on me, that's for sure." She was wearing outback attire, including ankle-high boots, big shorts, epaulets.

"Not if he's got any damn sense, he won't, which excludes me."

Ames giggled, sipping her drink. "You're so cute when you're in pain. I miss that."

"Great, you miss seeing me suffer pain. You're buzzed up already. Aren't you? How long you been out here?"

"A while." She pulled the dripping bottle from the ice bucket and handed it to me and I filled my glass first with ice, then the cold whiskey.

"Pretty hard stuff. Isn't it?" I said.

She was fingering her glass at her lips. "I want somebody else drunk and miserable besides me."

"Is it a requirement for your torturous and unorthodox hospitality here?"

"Yes, it is." She was licking her bottom lip now.

"Self-pity time."

"Yes, it is."

"I take it things aren't going too well in the job search."

"No, they're not. But it could change."

"It's too soon, Ames. The world doesn't work that fast."

"Doesn't seem to work at all in my case."

"Give it time."

"I put in for a job at New Air News Network, in Atlanta or D.C. It's a big reach. Bigger than my present little-dick gig, so it's a jump."

"You want to be a NANNie?"

"That's right. Why not shoot for the top, long as you're failing anyway. Might as well have vision, at least."

"You'll do fine, Ames. Quit worrying. People look at you and they want you."

"You think so? You think I'm really worthy of success in this business? I mean, when you look at me, Wray, do you honestly see me like you do the others who're up there at the top? She ran her hands through her hair. "Really?"

"Yes, I do."

"Another drink?" She reached for the bucket.

"Sure, misery loves company." Now I was holding two drinks.

I watched her a long moment, drinking at her sorrows, and sensed in her a desperation weighing on her like an anchor pulling her under. "This story will be a bombshell for you, Ames. It'll be your ticket."

"Or maybe just a bomb. And speaking of the bombshell story in question, we've got to move on this thing, move it up." Her speech was beginning to slur now. She leaned over and tapped my knee. "I've got a deadline, you know. I'm out of here at the end of the month, and I need a place to go." She leaned back into her chair. "I wished to hell I was working deadlines again. Boy, do I miss those days."

"The world moves very quickly with the initial buzz. Have another drink and slow it down."

"There's no reason not to go with it now, Wray. Timing is everything in this business, and the time is always *now*."

"Cleaver newsy expression, but your timing is not the only thing involved here."

"Toni Jean is gone, dead and buried, Wray. Life goes on for the survivors. John's being framed and he could pay for it with his life, while the bitch who's responsible for it all is walking around free, and you've got enough on her already to have her arrested. That's why you came here. You've done your job. Now let me do mine, for Christ's sake."

"Maybe."

"Well, what are you going to do, and when are you going to do it? We have to take the focus off John. He's going to be indicted in days and you know it. We can't let that happen."

"Look." I leaned toward her. "I want you to listen to me. I'm going to the police before the grand jury meets and give them everything I have, for what it's worth. It might delay the indictment, maybe even stop it altogether. But I need a few more days to rattle the trees, see what else might fall out. After the police have what I give them, I won't be needed any more, and I'm not ready to quit. I'm staying to the end.

"I'm seeing Steinmark," I said, "then I'm going to Jacqui, lay it all out, see what happens."

"What about Russo?"

"He's still with us." I did not bother to mention he was also getting antsy.

"I don't want to be scooped on this damn thing, Wray, not in my own backyard. That I couldn't take. I don't want to leave here that way."

"You won't be scooped."

"I insist on being with you when you confront Jacqui."

"I don't know, we'll see."

"You know, I think it's strange the police haven't even bothered to talk to you yet."

"They will."

"Wonder why they haven't?"

"They must be making a lot of progress, more than I originally figured, otherwise they'd be desperate for any crumbs they could get. If I talk to them now, it'll say to the world they're not on the right track already. Bad image."

"But they're focusing on John, Wray. It hasn't even occurred to them Jacqui's the one. That's where you—*we*—come in. That I'm going to relish."

"When the time is right."

She moved her glass back and forth along her lower lip, studying my face through blurry eyes. "Whatever you say."

"Now, how do we get out of this damn sand trap?"

33

Before my meeting with Steinmark, I stopped into the SuperMart store at the corner of College and Carolina Beach Roads, a commercial neighborhood called Monkey Junction by locals because for many years a private zoo open to the public has been located in the immediate area. I asked for the store manager, a man named Ron Graczak, a lanky man of about thirty-five, with dark features, well-dressed but, apparently, a hands-on type with the tie loose and sleeves rolled up. I could tell by the way he was built and moved that he had played some kind of ball before.

"Baseball. Triple-A, Pirates, till my shoulder went out."

I gave him my card and told him why I was there.

"We re-use the video disks, record over them after a few days, if we don't need them for evidence of some kind, like shoplifting."

"Has Captain Crile or Sergeant Thomas talked with you?" I wanted it to sound like I knew them personally, like we were old buddies who worked cases together.

"Sergeant Thomas, yes, from the sheriff's office, called and asked me to save any videos we rolled, up until the time of the murder, until they had a chance to look at them."

"They look at them yet? Take any of them? I haven't had a chance to talk with them the last couple days."

"No, not yet."

"Well, they will. I'd like to see them if I could. Not take any of them or anything, just sit back here somewhere, out of the way, and look at them, see who bought gas cans, maybe."

"We sell a lot of cans this time of year," Graczak said. "I don't mind that, but not today. I'll have our security manager, George Ruhler, give you a call and set it up. Unless the sheriff picks them up first. Then you'll have to double date to the movies with them."

"I'd appreciate it."

"Anything to help out. Just call and remind me tomorrow if you don't hear from us."

"I will. Can I buy a big bag of that popcorn you folks sell for a dollar, to eat while I'm watching?"

"Of course, anything to make a sale and keep our customers happy."

It was now eleven a.m. On the way back to the beach, I called Steinmark to tell him I was on my way, but there was no answer so I left a message. When I arrived there at eleven-thirty, a new car was in the driveway, apparently bought or rented because the police had his impounded.

I knocked on the door and got no answer. No sounds from inside. I walked around to the beach side, see if Steinmark was working out or taking a walk in the sea of people on the beach. No Steinmark. I went back and sat in my car. Backed out, you son of a gun. What are you hiding?

I called Loo Sullivan.

"I haven't seen him," Sullivan said. "He didn't come in and he didn't call. I don't know, must have been in an accident or something or he would have been here. I'm sure he's in a rough state of mind, but he better get his ass in here. Could be sleeping hard. You see him, you tell him that."

'Well, a car is here. Did his buddies come back with him, you know of?"

"He said he was coming back alone, didn't say anything about any buddies. I don't chase my clients, they chase me. This is no damn time for him to start falling apart. We've got too much to do between now and next week."

"You don't think he's doing an O.J., do you? Riding up and down the highway with a pistol and a big bag of money, wondering which way is up or out?"

"If he is, he'd better find another damn lawyer."

"I'll call you."

The murder of Dennis White had not made the national news, as I had expected. The fact he was a dubiously reputable attorney who was murdered execution style in a town with an active organized crime family and it had not made headlines, at least there—which would not put it in the news food chain spotlight immediately for the ride up—suggested maybe Russo was the only one, besides the police, certainly, who knew the guy was a mob associate. Russo had said it was not something everyone knew. But it surely would find its way out soon enough. People have a fascination for these things. I was happy Russo was holding up his end of the agreement.

But did Jacqui know? Had someone in Philadelphia, White's secretary maybe, or an old friend or distant relative from the neighborhood who might know her and White's relationship and past, told her?

I called Carol Gambrell. "Is Jacqui around today?"

"She was in earlier. She'll be back later. What's up?"

"She seem okay?"

"Sure, considering. Why?"

"I need to talk to her. Then I need to talk to you."

"Anything new to tell me?"

"Yes."

"What is it?"

"I think it's time to cash in."

There was a pause.

"Then cash away," she said. "I'm listening."

"I'll have more to tell you after I talk to Jacqui."

"Do you really think this whole thing is going directly at her?" There was defeat in her voice.

"I'm afraid it is."

"I still disagree with you."

"But I've probably done as much as I can without police powers."

"That means I'll have to tell them everything. My lawyers didn't offer much alternative either."

"Not necessarily everything. We'll discuss that. Have the police, Crile or Thomas, been back to you?"

"No, not since the funeral yesterday."

"They will be. The second wave will start any time now. They'll comb back over everybody's stories, rake the place clean, unless they're closing in from a different route."

"You don't talk to them, you understand, Wray. You report to me."

"We already covered that. I report to you, until I report to them."

"Jacqui has a practice at four at the gym. You can see her there afterward. I'll tell her. Then you call me. Better come by, I'll wait for you."

"Don't say anything to her. I'll call her myself."

"Wray?"

"Yeah?"

There was another, longer, pause and I could sense the tension from her.

"I want to ask you a question," she said, "and no matter what you think of it, I want you to promise me you'll never repeat it to anyone, ever. No matter what your answer."

"Sure." What the hell, only a question.

"What would it take for you to drop everything and just walk away and never say anything to anyone about what you've found, or think you've found, and let me take care of everything here?"

My jaw dropped. A very sobering question I might have appreciated on one of those rare occasions when I was hung over, since it was so sobering.

"Just say how much." Her voice was about to break. She could not see me moving my head slowly at her pathetic desperation.

"I'm sorry, Carol, I can't do that. It's too late."

She sobbed into the phone and I thought I might sob with her. Well, maybe not sob, exactly.

"I want to find T.J.'s murderer." Her voice was now squeaky. "But I swear to God, I want so much for it not to be Jacqui." She sniffled and broke down.

"I know. And I'm sorry."

"I'm sorry." She caught her breath.

"That's okay, I understand."

I called Jacqui's office numbers at the university gymnasium and on New Center Drive and left messages on her voice mail for her to call me, it was important. Then I called Ames. "Meet me for lunch," I said.

"I don't eat lunch, you know that."

"You did alright at the party the other night, on the pier."

"That was supper and I just picked."

"You can watch me eat. We'll have a nice mid-day drink. Where are you?"

"Just getting back into town on Seventeen from Jacksonville."

"Medical examiner?"

"Yes."

"Struck out?"

"Yes. You got telepathic powers?"

"No, I just know cops and M.E.s."

"Where to meet?"

"Little place up here at the beach where the second bridge is. Right next to the *Wings* store. Something '*Grill*.' Little parking lot across the street from it on the canal. I'll go in and get us a table, if I can."

"I know it. Be there in fifteen minutes."

It was a neat, clean little place, a white building with royal blue awning covering part of the patio, where tables were set up and diners languished watching the traffic and boats going by. I was lucky to get it at this hour. Normally, reservations would be required to hold a spot, I was told.

I got a small table in the corner, outside, and ordered a small sandwich to go with the small table, and a diet soft drink, and started eating.

Ames arrived shortly and ordered white wine. She kept her sunglasses on, partly for the sun, partly not to be recognized and bothered. Local celebrity, you know.

"I thought if I went there in person, I might get something," she said. "This isn't like politics, where somebody is always dying to leak something to you for the vicarious thrill of it."

"The medical examiner, himself?"

"Yes."

"But he hit on you."

"Of course. He can drop off the earth, far as I'm concerned."

"He's human, you're super human. Go easy on him."

"That's a nine-mile-run sandwich you're eating."

"Twelve. It's got mayonnaise. I'll pay it back a mile at a time."

"How'd it go with John?"

"It didn't. He didn't show."

"When were you there?"

"Eleven-thirty. His car is in the driveway, but he's not home. I guess it's his car. And I guess he's not home."

"Well, maybe he was on the beach. Let's go back there."

"Let's? I'll call him later. He didn't show for Sullivan, either."

"Really?"

"Nope."

"Doesn't sound right. What about Jacqui? When do you see her?" She took a sip of wine.

"When she returns my call, I'll know."

"I'll go with you."

"It's not a good idea. It's easier for her to say something without another witness around. If she says anything at all."

"So why'd you call me here?"

"I didn't want to sit here alone and have people think I was an awkward geek."

"Funny. I could be downtown where the action is.

"Last night," she said, "when we left the airport, Carol and Jacqui went back to the office with Bernie. On the way home later, just before I crossed the drawbridge here, Jacqui passed me. She didn't know it was me, or if she did, she didn't show it, or wave or anything. When she got to her place, at the turn-off there, she went right on by me and turned off right here, instead." She indicated the end of the bridge across from us, where the road splits left and right, implying a direction toward Steinmark's. "You don't think they have a thing going, do you?"

"You've known them longer than I have. If they do, how could you miss it? What time was it?"

"I don't know, twelve, twelve-thirty, give or take."

"Could've been anything. They do know one another, you know."

"Yeah, she just likes to ride by his house, like an adolescent. Maybe she put a valentine on his door and knocked and ran like hell."

"You didn't mention it last night."

"You saw how I was last night. Actually, this morning. Besides, you're probably right. It's no big deal. Even if they're screwing one another, it's none of our business. It's just that it's so macabre at a time like this, if it's true. So vulgar. How could John be so stupid, so uncouth. She killed the woman he loved, for Christ's sake."

"I wouldn't read a whole lot into it if I were you." But I would certainly try.

"He'll stupid himself right onto death row, the fool, if somebody doesn't stop him."

My mouth was full of sandwich now. "Umh."

"Anyway," Ames said, "It'll all be over in a flash and I can leave this bad memory and maybe find a real job. Fame calls."

I swallowed and took a sip from my glass, and wiped my mouth with a napkin. "I have an uncontrollable urge to floss."

"Not here, please."

"I'll do it on the road."

"And steer with your knees."

"Of course."

"And look like an idiot in a yo-yo contest."

We were silent a moment. I was pondering the thought of Jacqui driving to Steinmark's place at midnight, just hours after the funeral, trying to juxtapose the picture, consider the possible reasons. Maybe I should take my own advice and not read too much into it.

"Something sticking in my craw," I said.

"What's that?" Ames said, sipping, gazing around.

"If I knew that, it wouldn't be sticking there. Last night I had a weird dream."

"All your dreams are weird."

"I was marooned on a deserted island without my library card."

"Well, you certainly couldn't check out any books."

"It always means something when I remember a dream so well. Something close by, something happens soon. A tapping on my head."

"That'd be woodpeckers."

"I see your sense of humor is returning. I guess that's a good sign all is well."

"I'm a happy person," she said.

"Yesterday at the funeral. That's what it is."

"What *what* is?"

"What it is that's bothering me. I remember coming out of the church feeling very strongly that I'd either seen something or missed something. I don't know."

"Well, if you don't keep the woodpeckers off your head, it's going to get even harder for you."

I grinned, my tongue in my cheek. "You're not ridiculing me, are you?"

"Don't be silly. I've got to get back to work." She stood and gulped down her remaining wine. "Call me in a little bit. We need to stay in frequent touch here on out."

I nodded, my hands together, wiping my mouth. "Don't leave me here like a geek. People will hate me because I have a table all to myself in this busy place."

"Nobody ever looked better as a geek. And I'm sure you can attract company."

She left anyway.

34

I stopped by Steinmark's again, but he still was not there. I decided to kill some time, drive around and look at the property until Jacqui or Steinmark called, if either bothered. I crossed the two bridges back out of the beach and took a sharp left along the canal on Airlie Road, passing the restaurants and dining piers, including the one where the party had been held, and through the shaded boulevard of large homes set back deeply on the lots.

I turned left at the light, onto Oleander, and crossed Bradley Creek with its numerous yachts and schooners tied in and condos lining the creek sides. The tide was low and the smell of the creek and salt marsh was strong, what some inlanders found offensive and what smelled as sweet as sugar to me, like home.

I stopped at the Exxon station on the corner at the next light for a cup of coffee to go, then continued along Greenville Loop through the busy two-lane-only residential area, first of older homes, and more than one treacherous curve in Masonboro and Myrtle Grove. The area only a few years ago was mostly woods and stable, permanent residents, but was now over-developed with nice, expensive properties with little or no yards sporting catchy names alluding to *points, ships, buccaneers, pirates, coves, bays*, and *channels*, and people who would be gone tomorrow. But most of the trees remained, so that was a good thing. At least somebody was thinking.

Altogether, cramped but not a bad place, a homey appeal, something to consider now that I would not be living on the pier at *Larrick Point* any longer—*Oops*, another '*point*.' Maybe a second home for getaways, since it was a great, still-quaint area. Sure, why not move in and help crowd up the place, like an environmental idiot, my daughter would say to me.

I came out of Myrtle Grove at Monkey Junction, where the SuperMart was, and went left down Carolina Beach Road, a four-lane with an island in the middle. It was several miles of residential-commercial zoning, old oaks, crepe myrtle, magnolia and palmettos, and grass fighting with the sand for dominance. Most of it was older and, though growing, there remained still a considerable amount undeveloped. But I could see developers' saliva all over it like a giant foamy frosting. I passed the turn-off to New French Fort, on the left, where Toni Jean had been murdered, and crossed the bridge at Snow's Cut into Carolina Beach at Federal Point. The town hall, a one-story brick complex with flag poles out front, was on the right, and condominiums crowded the point itself, on the left.

The boulevard was four tight lanes of mostly older weather-beaten buildings housing real estate offices, shops, restaurants, tiny convenience stores and take-out eateries, including two popular fast food outlets, rental houses and condos again, small mom-and-pop motels, and a billion T-shirt vendors and people. Mid-beach, a block from the boardwalk, was a passenger boat operation selling rides on the inland waterway and beach. At the end, Carolina Beach faded into Kure Beach, with less retail but a large seafood restaurant, and more residential and resort property, old and new, which thinned out as the road narrowed to two lanes at Fort Fisher. Here ocean fronts and private, multi-colored, cedar-shingled homes in little niches were the run. A fenced-in compound on the right held a number of single-family dwellings for military personnel. Up ahead, on the right, was the Confederate War Museum, as this area had been the site of a Civil War battle involving blockade runners. Numerous hills and bunkers guarded the area from the beach to the swamp and river behind it. There was a picnic area under the trees across the road from the museum, on the beach. The current and surf were too strong, no swimming allowed.

I passed through. Maybe I would stop at the museum on the way out. A little way down the winding road, I pulled into the parking lot of the state aquarium and research station, a multi-level complex of glass and tanks and walkways, exhibits and shops.

Before getting out, my phone rang. It was Jacqui.

"You called, said it was important," she said.

"I still owe you a drink."

"Yes, you do, but it's okay. What do you suggest?"

"After practice, somewhere private, where we can talk."

"Gee, I don't know, Wray. I don't see how I can do it today. So much work. Not putting you off, really."

"This is work."

"About the case? About Toni Jean?"

"Yes, among others."

"Why don't you see Carol first, then we can talk maybe tomorrow, lunch somewhere. My place, even my treat."

"We might not have a chance to talk again after today."

"Sounds so ominous. Is it important, or just routine?"

"More important than you think right now. You asked me to keep you informed. That's what I'm trying to do."

There was a pause. Lot of those around here.

"You're right, I did," she said. "My office at the gym, at six-thirty."

"Great. I'll bring a bottle of wine and ice."

"Not necessary."

"I owe you a drink, and you'll want one."

I rode out of the beach wondering why wine was figuring so much into what I was doing these days. Maybe it was age. *Nah.* But I would have to buy something different for the occasion, maybe one of those red wines with the stupid names that cost twice the price of a half gallon of my usual and didn't taste as good, just a classier-looking label, like something you find on one of those tiny bistro tables with a block of stinking cheese, purchased by some grinning dilettante with a two-digit I.Q. trying to impress his date, like maybe he learned it all in the south of France, the Bordeaux, you know. After all, if you're going to accuse a good-looking woman of cold-blooded murder, and show her what you have pointing to its likelihood, something that could put her pretty fanny away forever, well, why not spring for something special, show a little class, a little respect, soften the blow. Sure, twelve bucks a bottle, tops. I bought two. If Jacqui went nuts on me early on, I could finish it off, myself. If she did not finish me off first, also something to think about.

I then called Ken Enright.

"I'm at the gym," Enright said. "They're drifting in for practice now."

"After practice, when they're all gone, I want you to stick around if you can. I've got a meeting with the coach in her office. Once she and I go in there, you're on my clock and I want you to stay out in the hallway, the lobby area. Don't let anyone interrupt us. Not too near, but close enough to see anyone who might try to get to her. And don't say anything to anyone about it. Your presence will be unknown. Okay?"

"Gotcha, you devil, you." He giggled.

"It's not that."

"*Awwh*. Sure it's not."

"It's not."

"Whatever."

Actually, it was to insure a witness was around, in case she shot old Wray, but Enright did not need to know everything.

I called Carol again. "I'm meeting Jacqui after practice at the gym," I said. "I want to understand you haven't discussed with her anything we talked about."

"You understand correctly."

"I could be in there for an hour or more. Are you going to be in your office?"

"I won't leave until I hear from you. And I expect to hear from you right after."

"Soon as I leave her. Has she received any calls that have been upsetting to her, you know of?"

"That's the second time you've alluded to that. What is it?"

"I'll tell you later." I did not know if she was yet aware of Dennis White's death.

"Not to my knowledge. She seems okay, under the circumstances."

"Yeah, I'm sure she's crying rivers underneath. Why didn't you tell me you two were having a disagreement over moving the team here?" I could hear her thinking on the other end.

"Who told you this? It's not germane to your work for me."

"Everything is germane to me."

"Has nothing to do with Toni Jean. Just a different approach to planning. Jacqui has every right to disagree with me on strategy. She is corporate vice-president, you know. I'd like to know who, in his or her own mind, elevated this to a major conflict."

"I saw it on my own." Lying, of course.

"I'll be here when you get here." She hung up abruptly.

I left the aquarium parking lot and headed back toward town. A while later, passing through Kure Beach, I got another call, this one from Ethel Palmer, and she sounded upset. I pulled into another parking lot, this one at the big seafood restaurant. At this hour, between meals, it was almost vacant.

"What can I do for you, Lady Palmer?"

"A couple things, maybe. I'd like to ask you something, then I'd like to tell you something, if you don't already know."

"Shoot." I cringed at the bad choice of the word.

"I just got the third degree from Carol. Wanted to know if I said anything to you about a conflict, or trouble, she might be having with Jacqui."

"Okay."

"And I never said anything about it."

"That's right, you didn't. But there is a conflict."

"Well, yes, there has been some tension along those lines, but only a few people in this office know about it, and how you came about it is a puzzle."

"I came by it through my own efforts, like any investigator." Lying again. "And I never implicated you. And I won't. I'll clarify that with Carol."

"I'd appreciate that. Wray, I've known this woman since she was a child. We're very close. Our families are close. I love her like my own. Her confidence and respect are very important to me. I don't want that being undermined."

"Understood. If I see anybody undermining it, I'll let you know."

I was going to have some fun with this. Might get something out of it. But I would not rat out Bernie, either.

"You're thinking maybe it was Bernie, aren't you?" I could hear her suck in her breath.

"What? Bernie? Morgan's Bernie? What makes you mention him?"

"Because you two are having an affair."

"My god. Where have you gotten such an idea? Did he say that?"

"Why would he say it? He didn't have to. I saw it in your eyes, and I saw it in his. The other night on the pier. Ethel, if two people are attracted to one another the way you two are, they'll connect very quickly before they lose the chance. You both looked at one another with lust in your eyes the whole time, but you never connected. That's because it wasn't necessary, because you were already connecting. Bernie didn't say a thing. But your secret is safe with me."

Ethel exhaled a noticeable breath. "Morgan said you could see through walls, have a sixth sense. I guess she was right."

"Not really. Just open your senses and let it all come in, *'Become one with it,'*" as the saying goes.

"It's true, we're seeing one another. No one's supposed to know that, and I'd like to keep it that way."

"Of course."

"I like Bernie. He's very special. He's come along in my life at a time when I've needed someone. It's a wonderful friendship. I just don't want it ruined. I hope you understand and respect that."

"Yes, I do, Ethel. And don't worry."

"Thank you, Wray. You'll never know how much I appreciate your discretion."

"And what was it you wanted to tell me?"

"Yes. Morgan said you had her look over a list of prospective buyers for New French Fort, and that she told you she didn't recognize any of the names on it."

"That's right."

"Well, that's not exactly true."

"I'm listening."

"I figured you might find out later on your own, so I thought I'd go ahead and tell you before you did, so you wouldn't think anybody had anything to hide. And don't blame Morgan or Carol."

"Like what?"

"My daughter and son-in-law's names are on that list. Morgan knew that. She said she didn't tell you because she didn't want to cause any of us any scrutiny or possible trouble, since we obviously wouldn't have had anything to do with T.J.'s murder. Bryan and Lila Barnette. Bryan is a sales manager with a security company. His company is opening an office here in Wilmington, in the fall. In fact, he and his boss were here in town the last couple days looking at office space."

"So what makes them different from other potential buyers, other than their connection to you?"

"Well, that's just it, nothing, really. But Morgan knows, through me, that Bryan can be a problematic person."

"How so?"

"Well." She seemed a little reluctant. "This, too, is just between us, I hope."

"Long as it doesn't figure materially in the case."

"Good enough. The man's no good. He's a womanizer, a skirt chaser. You've heard the expression about screwing a snake if you could hold its head. That's him. Sleeps with anything and everything. Breaks Lila's heart, but she loves him. Her father and I have tried to reason with her, we all have, but she won't listen. Who knows what he could bring home."

"Classic case. So what?"

"Afraid so. A couple things, if they were known, might cause some unwanted attention or complications, especially for Lila, and I don't want that to happen. She's too fragile already."

"What kind of things."

"Like Bryan trying to hit on T.J., for one."

"Oh, really?" My ears perked up.

"Yes, twice. That I know of. Right before the team left for Europe, Lila and Bryan were down here with the kids one weekend. He watched the team practice one night, then approached T.J. afterward, in the parking lot, and asked her to go out with him."

"Who told you?"

"She did. We agreed not to tell Lila. What good would it do?"

"What was T.J.'s reaction to Bryan?"

"Told him to go to hell."

"Good for her."

"Then he hit on her again when they got back from Europe, at a restaurant out at the beach, that place right up from the Harbor Light, by the bridge. She and a couple of girls on the team were in the lounge one night and he was there, alone, of course, without Lila, as usual."

"And she told you again?"

"Yes, and again we didn't tell Lila. But that night I remember him being very moody when he got in. It wasn't until T.J. told me the next morning that I knew why he was probably moody."

"She told him to go to hell again?"

"She told him more than that. She told him if he came around her one more time she'd refer his request to her boyfriend."

"Did that stop him?"

"Oh, yeah. He didn't want to tangle with John Steinmark. Who would?"

"Big comprende there."

"But he didn't like it. He's a good-looking man and he's not used to rejection."

"Are you saying you think he could have killed her?"

"No, I'm saying the opposite. I'm saying he's a no-good rat and nothing but trouble, but he's not violent. He's never laid a hand on Lila in anger."

"You're certain?"

"Absolutely. But I wish he'd disappear. What makes it so difficult for Lila is that the kids love him so much. He's great with them."

"Well." I was considering all this. "It's not like he killed T.J. if he was home with you folks when it happened. The rest of his life is of no concern to me. He was home, wasn't he?"

"That's the other thing, the problematic part of it. He was and he wasn't. I wasn't exactly truthful with you before, Wray. Before I went to bed that night, Bryan got up and went out, said he couldn't sleep, was going down to the drug store. I don't know what time he got back. I was asleep by then, so was Lila."

"You know, the police should have known about this right away."

"I suppose you're right."

"But if it's any comfort to you, I don't think your no-good son-in-law killed anybody."

"I don't either, and we and Carol don't need any complications from it. I'm just doing damage control, I hope."

"I know, but it's not our call, it's the police's. Does Carol know about this?"

"She knows how Bryan is, but she doesn't know about this, I don't believe. You think I should tell the police?"

"No, I'll do it, but not now. Could be one or more of the team players mentioned it already, maybe the girls she was with at the beach when he hit on her. I'll take care of it for you. Part of my job as the investigator here."

"Bryan hasn't been questioned, to my knowledge."

"Where's Bryan now?"

"Went back to Charlotte this morning."

"Don't say anything to him. I might want to talk with him."

"I won't."

"It might not ever have to be known, if things work out right."

"That would be nice."

"Do you know if he ever hit on Jacqui?"

"She said he did, but it didn't do any good. I told you he hits on every woman he sees. I think it's a sickness with him."

"So she didn't take him up on it, you know of?"

"Said she didn't, but you'd have to ask her. I don't think Jacqui would mess with a married man, quite frankly. Besides, with her looks and reputation she calls the shots, get any man she wants."

"I understand that, too. I appreciate your confiding in me, Ethel."

"Don't say anything to Morgan, she meant well. I just felt I had to tell you. I didn't want it to come back and bite me on the butt later."

"My, my, if it did, it sure would be lucky. Wouldn't it?"

Ethel laughed, somewhat relieved.

I hung up.

Still too many monkey wrenches in this operation. Way too many. I sat there in the parking lot wondering if maybe Jacqui might be involved with this Bryan Barnette character somehow.

No. She was too smart to be involved with a flakey, transparent jerk like him. Perhaps. Unless she was using him.

35

I bought the wine and glasses at SuperMart, the purveyor of fine wines, of course, the ice at a convenience store, and got to the gym as practice was over. I told Enright to stay away from the door, don't eavesdrop. "I've got some money for you, too, when I'm finished here, bring us up to date."

"You sure are sly, you lucky man," he said.

"I told you it wasn't that."

"And I heard you, boss man." He gave a silly wink, not believing a word.

Jacqui was already in her office. The door was open and she was in the tiny bathroom in the corner, brushing her hair and freshening up, when I knocked and walked in.

"Wray, how are you?" There was just a tinge of caution in her voice. "Be right with you."

"Take your time." I closed the door and set the stuff on the table and opened the wine. "With or without ice?"

"Without." She turned off the light and closed the bathroom door behind her.

I poured and raised my glass for a toast.

"Here's to the success of the *Carolina Storms—Tee Jays*, sorry—and to the late and great Toni Jean Semieux. She must have been a hell of a kid."

(270)

"Here, here." She was still cautious.

We did not touch glasses, but sipped and small-talked a long, uneasy moment, searching one another's eyes for the meaning of all this.

Finally, I put down my glass. "You know why I'm here, don't you?"

She fingered her glass back and forth along the rim, looking at it, then back at me.

"You owed me a drink and you're paying up now. But you came to me. I'm listening."

"I'll make my thesis statement up front. I think you killed Toni Jean Semieux, or had it done, and I think you're trying to frame John Steinmark for it. And I'll tell you what leads me to believe that."

Jacqui's face flushed and her jaw looked like it would disengage.

"Well, I really must admit I wasn't expecting this."

"Remember, this is what I was hired for."

"Not for this, you weren't. You zeroed in on me the day you got here. Didn't you?"

"Yes, I did. Kinda. But you made it so easy to do."

"You're damned right you did. But if you notice the police haven't, because they're smarter than you. You made up your mind I killed Toni Jean because my period didn't coincide with everyone else's around here. Think I don't know what you've been doing? I resent that. You'll be damn lucky if I don't sue you right off the planet. Far as I'm concerned, you're fired."

"And if Carol agrees with you, I will be, because you don't have the authority by yourself. But I don't think she will. And you'd better listen to what I have to say before making idle threats about law suits. You'll probably be filing them from behind bars."

"Damn you." She stood and put the glass down hard on the desk, spilling wine.

"That shit costs twelve dollars a bottle," I said. "The ice cubes were a buck and a half."

"You son of a bitch."

I remained seated.

"I'll tell you what." I spoke calmly, turning my glass back and forth in my hand slowly. "You can listen to what I have to say and maybe benefit from it, have something to take to your lawyer, because you're damn sure going to need one, or you can keep bitching and threatening, and I'll leave and go downtown to the sheriff's office now and you won't know Richard until they slap the cuffs on your rear end and charge you with murder, and your lawyer begs for discovery. It's your call. I really don't give a rat's ass. The only reason I'm here is you're one of the principals who hired me, and I'm a fair guy, just reporting in." All lies, of course.

"You're a pompous asshole, is what you are."

That was more like it.

"Just part-time. The rest of the week I'm a wise-ass." I took a gulp. "So what's it going to be?"

She composed herself as best she could, pulled her hair back and sat down. "You're right. You're right, it was my idea to hire you. My mistake, too. I didn't kill Toni Jean and nothing you or anyone else can say could ever prove I did. So go ahead and let's hear this crap you've come up with. Then you can go back to where the hell you came from."

I wiped off her glass and refilled it. "Here." I slid it over to her. "I didn't come here to beat you up. And I didn't say I could actually prove it. That's the D.A.'s job. And who knows, maybe you won't be charged."

She tapped her fingers and reluctantly took the glass, more to show me she wasn't afraid of me and my monumental bullshit. The way she was breathing, she might have taken anger management classes.

"You're right. The first thing I did was become suspicious of you because the menstrual cycles didn't jibe, junk science as it is. It was just a place to start. And it doesn't prove anything, it just made me think you were lying. And you have a problem with lying. You told me you were home the entire night the murder occurred, because of cramping, and that was a flat-out lie. I'm willing to bet you told the police the same thing."

Her eyebrow arched and her jaw began moving on the hinge again.

"I have a reliable eye witness who puts you in your office, in the conference room on New Center Drive, after ten p.m., alive, well, and looking at scouting videos, just shortly before the murder. Talent, ostensibly, to replace that of the intended deceased. But your car wasn't in the lot."

I did not want to ask her how late she was in her office or where her car was. It would not make any difference what she said. If she were totally innocent, she would blurt it out in her own defense. Otherwise, move on.

"Who?" She leaned over. "Who saw me?"

"Later, not now. I also know about Dennis White. I know that, through you, he tried to tap the resources of Ivy Ridge University and failed. And with your help, also, he got his hands on three million dollars of T.J. Semieux's bonus money to invest with his mob buddies, and almost got away with it, until a certain person down south paid you a visit in this very office." I stabbed my finger at the floor. "He threatened you to get it back. That, too, you lied to me about, telling me some shady characters approached Ms. Semieux with an investment, a motel deal, and you advised against it. All bullshit. And I don't think you mentioned that to the police, either. I guess I'm a special guy."

Jacqui's eyes were wide open, staring straight ahead through me, dumbstruck.

I got up and began pacing, one hand in my pocket, my drink in the other.

"I know, too, you and Dennis White are cousins, and that your original name was DiLuca. I know about that."

Jacqui blinked, clearly startled. "How do you know that? Nobody knows that."

"And I know he's dead, murdered."

She did not seem shocked at this, but I thought I could see her eyes moisten just a little, a faint glaze. So she already knew. But she is very good at dealing with death. Nothing new.

"I know you called Connie McCann at her college, a clear violation of your own league rules, maybe even of the law itself."

"That's a damn lie." She jumped up again.

"From this phone," I said. "It's on your phone bill."

"I've never called her. I never made any illegal call on this phone. What the hell's going on here?"

"Then argue with the phone company. You had full access to Toni Jean's property, including her keys. She had keys to John Steinmark's property, including his car."

"You're crazy as hell."

"Am I? You're not having a fight with Carol over moving the team to Wilmington for your own selfish reasons? A move that so conveniently costs just about the amount of Ms. Semieux's insurance payoff? A move that would devalue the team's worth, until after Carol sells out to her partners, who then cut you in?"

The emotion left her voice and went to her eyes.

"Who's telling you all this?"

She was buckling. I continued pacing slowly around the office. This has a profound effect on the accused in any situation. Here you are, casual, blasé about the whole thing, like it was just another day at the beach, completely safe and immune yourself, while your subject is accused of something that could take away her life, that could kill her deader than hell. It made the accused envious and angry, and prone to err. I needed to rattle her tree, see if it bore fruit, even if some of what I was saying was only suggestive, even outright bluff, maybe even lies. I would relish teasing her with it.

"But I can't see what the motive would be." I threw up an empty hand. "All anybody knows is that she was killed and a sloppy effort was made to make it look like Steinmark did it. Hell, most people think he did it. And you're the last person anyone would even suspect. Except, of course, dumb old me. A son of a bitch, a pompous asshole like me has got to be different and go suspect you, of all people. How stupid of me. I mean, I had no idea on earth what it could possibly be that would make Ms. Semieux worth more to you dead than alive" I looked at her and gave a little smile and sipped the wine.

Jacqui's eyes were locked on me like gun sights, following me as I moved about the office, hanging on my every word and seething with animosity. She slowly sat back down. She was still interested.

"So I kept looking," I said. "I mean, what are the odds of finding a motive like that, a motive in addition to the other stuff here? Worse than the lottery maybe?" I stopped and set my glass on the table.

"But I knew I had one thing going for me. I had my won-loss record. Almost perfect. Of all the cases I ever studied, ever investigated, ever been involved in, the only one in my life I've never solved—not yet anyway—is the disappearance of a little girl many years ago. That one still escapes me, and it is the most important one. But for all the rest of them, I've always found the motive and solved the case. No brag, just fact. All of them. *Every. Single. One.*" I stared into her eyes and pierced the air with a finger to drive home the point. I was on a roll.

"So I kept plugging away. And my persistence paid off. It came to me like a gift from heaven, like an epiphany, you might say. There it was." I stepped over to her desk, just outside her personal space. "And you know what it was?"

Frozen, still glaring at me, now more fearful than angry, she hesitated. "I haven't the slightest idea. But I know it's bullshit."

"She was ill." I said it matter-of-factly. "And weak and going down fast."

Jacqui looked away. Her eyes went unfocused, her body began deflating.

"That's right. I know about Triserotech. And that stinking quack butcher, Doctor Gaylord Hesslar. Didn't take much with him."

I stepped back over to get my glass. I topped it off, sat back down and drank, and let my last remark hang in the air.

Jacqui leaned on her desktop, face in her hands, her head moving negatively. "Everything is going to come apart now," she said. "Damn. Damn you for coming here."

I knew at this point she would either clam up, tell me to drop dead, then call her lawyer, or run like a sieve. Either way, she would take steps to purge herself of any evidence, including the original notes from her desk and the receipt for the gas cans Ames had seen in her condo, if she were aware she still had it, and any evidence she might have pointing to her guilt, which would deprive the police of it and weaken any case they might establish against her, so it was risky. I hoped she would not challenge me and pick up the phone and call Doctor Hesslar to find I was lying. After all, I had no real evidence connecting her directly to the murder. What I had was circumstantial, even if I could call it that, pointing perhaps to Jacqui's less-than-honorable dealings with shady characters, one Dennis White, already dead and useless, and all of it together not strong enough to get a conviction for jay walking in a real courtroom. However, in the hands of the police it could make her life a living hell. I banked on her being smart enough to realize that. She needed to confide in someone. Going to the police would be stupid as a first choice. Going to a lawyer would accomplish the same thing, like, "Hey, I've got a lawyer. Catch me if you can." But attempting to co-opt old Wray might not seem so bad in comparison.

The tree was still shaking. I was just waiting for the fruit to fall.

36

And Jacqui started talking.

"From the very beginning," she said, "I knew it was a bad idea to hire a private investigator. Something told me not to do it. But Morgan insisted it would be good from a public relations point of view. And with her in the media, already friendly and covering us, she could insure the best possible outcome. So Carol and I agreed. That's all it was supposed to be. We didn't know you or anything about you. We just figured you for another gumshoe, I think the expression is. But in all fairness to Morgan, she did say you had an uncanny ability to pull things out of the air sometimes. We just weren't listening to that part of it, and we did want T.J.'s murderer caught. And we didn't have anything to hide about that.

"Of course," she said, "as you well know now, that, too, is not exactly true, especially on my part. Carol has nothing to do with what I'm about to tell you. She's not aware of it."

She looked me in the eyes across the desk. "I didn't kill Toni Jean, Wray. And I don't know who did. And your accusing me of it is the most hurtful thing anyone has ever said to me in my life." She took a drink.

I said nothing to this, just sipped and gave a show-me-the-proof look.

"This could cause a lot of harm if it got out. And I don't see any reason why it has to, but I'm in a corner. I see I have no choice but to tell you and risk it."

I still said nothing, showed no sympathy.

"John has H.I.V. And he infected T.J. with it. The only difference is hers was aggressive, because of her immune system, and his isn't, and we never told her at first that he had it. I could've killed him. How stupid, how reckless of him. And selfish.

"Last fall he came to me," she said, "told me he had it and was worried he might have infected T.J. with it. Said she was starting to tire easily when they were together, nothing real dramatic, but just a little drop in her energy level he noticed. Frankly, I never noticed, myself, not then anyway. But I arranged, through Dennis, to have her blood tested, discreetly, of course. If something like this got out it would destroy both their careers. Nothing could be gained by that."

"Triserotech."

"Yes. I drew a blood sample from her myself. But I didn't tell her the real reason, or the results. I couldn't. So I lied to her and told her everything was fine, just needed some vitamins. She had enough on her mind without having to worry about this."

"So she went without treatment because you didn't tell her."

"No. She got the best available, under the circumstances. She just didn't know at the time it was for H.I.V. But she didn't want anyone knowing she was taking anything. And I kept her away from the team physician.

"It was a couple months later I told her. She was very upset with both of us, understandably. That's when she broke up with John."

"And began avoiding you when she could."

"Yes, sort of. But then, just before she was killed, things were okay again. She started seeing John again, and hanging out with me more, like old times. She made me promise not to say anything about her illness, not even to Maurice and Edna. They still don't know. Well, they'll get an autopsy report. It was moving on her rapidly and she needed to earn as much money as she could for the foundation before everything ended. That meant more to her than anything. And her playing wasn't dangerous to anyone else, the physician said. Doctor Hesslar.

"John has his father to take care of," she said. "He needs as many paychecks as he can get before somebody finds out and his career ends, probably after his team physical, I think in October."

"What about the three million dollars Dennis White had?"

"I didn't want anyone to know that I screwed up. I had no idea what kind of people Dennis might be involved with, not until some goon threatened me to get the money back."

"Who was the goon, his name?"

"I don't know, and I don't want to know. I just know I don't ever want to see his face again."

Good. And you won't learn it from me.

"Maybe in a way it was a good thing. We got her money back."

"You tried to open the Ivy Ridge vault for your cousin, Dennis White, before Semieux got her bonus. You don't admit a pattern evolving there?"

"No, I don't. I've made some bad business decisions with Dennis. I admit it. But I also said I'm a coach, not a business agent."

"So what's the scam on moving the team to Wilmington?"

"*Scam?* What do you mean, *scam?* A group of investors are interested in buying the team and moving it here. And if they do, I want to make sure I go with it."

"Then why is it a conflict with Carol?"

"The conflict, if you can call it that, is that I'm looking at the franchise's success over the long run. Carol is looking at the shorter picture. She wants her money back yesterday."

"So Carol knows nothing of Semieux having H.I.V.?"

"No, she doesn't. And I wish there was a way you didn't have to—."

I was already saying no with my head.

"Great. You don't realize the kind of problem this will cause."

My cell phone vibrated. It was Ames. "Are you with Jacqui now?" Her voice was a whisper.

"Yes."

"Listen to me, and listen very carefully. Watch yourself. I'm out here at the beach now, at John's house. The police are here. Wray, John is dead. He's been shot, murdered."

My eyes locked on Jacqui and I fought to divert them from giving away my alarm.

"Are you okay?" Ames said.

"Uh, yes. What about it?"

"The police came out with a warrant to do another search and found him."

"How'd you know?"

"Scanner. I told you nobody scoops me again. Shit's happening fast. How long you going to be there?"

"I'll call you, we'll get together. I'm kind of busy now."

"You watch your back. I don't want anything happening to you. I couldn't live with myself."

"I don't know why not, you've been doing it for years."

"Smart aleck. You be careful." She hung up.

I feigned a pleasurable response to something personal and put away my phone and looked back at Jacqui. My wish was to reach over and grab her head and smash it through her desk. In fact, I was struggling to control my breathing , acting calm with difficulty.

"You were at Steinmark's last night," I said.

"Are you actually following me?"

"Somebody saw you."

"You are following me, aren't you?"

I did not answer that. My own jaw was sliding around on its hinge.

"Yes, I did go by and see him. I told him at the funeral I had some personal things of T.J.'s I knew she'd want him to have, and I took them there in a box. So what?" She seemed resigned now and not so much agitated.

"So where is Steinmark now?" I studied her eyes for lying. I was not going to get anything from her emotions. The only thing she divulged there was anger and hostility.

"Call and ask him. How would I know?"

"Is there anything else you'd like to tell me?"

"Yes. I'd like to tell you to take your cheap wine and get the hell out of my office."

That hurt. Slay me but not my wine.

"Thank you. You know where he is, don't you? He's dead. The police are all over the scene now, and they're going to be all over you next. You said you could kill him. Apparently you did."

"Oh." Her mouth fell open, she put a hand over it. "You're serious. Oh, no, don't tell me. Oh, God. Oh, John."

"Nice try. Tell it to the cops." I got up and went to the door, careful to watch my back.

Jacqui stammered for words.

"I didn't—I—I didn't—."

I closed the door behind me. Let her mumble herself to death. I motioned to Enright, who was at the end of the hall, a short distance away. I handed him a wad of bills, more than I had agreed to pay him.

"This squares us," I said. "Appreciate your help. You did a good job, except for the turkey sandwich caper. I'll be in touch if I need you again."

"Mucho grassy-ass, boss man, anytime." He winked.

"Go check on the coach. She's not feeling well. Then you can leave."

I started for the front door. As I opened it, I heard Jacqui scream at Enright, "Get out of here, you fat, stupid pervert."

Office grenade.

37

I jumped in my car and called Carol. "I'm on my way." I pulled out of the lot from the gym.

Then I called Ames. "You too busy to talk?"

"Not really, at this moment. What's up? Have you seen Jacqui?"

"Yes. Anything you can tell me?"

"Nothing else, so far. We're outside the tape and they're not talking, as usual."

"Ask Bernie if he has a copy of the funeral video I can look at."

"Of course he does. He keeps a copy of everything he shoots. Hold on, he's right here. Talk to me before you hang up."

"We're going to be hanging out here for a while," Bernie said. "It may be morning before I can get it to you. It's home."

"Good enough. If it's easier for you, drop it off at Carol's office for me on the way to work. Have Ethel hold it for me. I'll get it back to you in good shape tomorrow."

"There're two disks of the funeral, itself. Five if you count the pre-and post-service footage, the documentary stuff."

"I just need the part of the church service, itself, especially inside."

"Will do."

"By the way, Ethel knows I'm aware of your relationship with her. I told her you didn't say a thing, I just guessed it, in case she brings it up. Wish you hadn't told me."

"Thanks for the warning. Here's Morgan."

"Have you seen or talked to Sullivan?" I said to her.

"He's out here now, talking to Captain Crile, just got here."

"Tell him I'll call him later, for what it's worth. Don't say a word."

"Wray, it's time to run with this thing."

"Not until I've talked to the police."

"When, damn it? The bodies are piling up here and we're like idiots waiting for directions across the street."

"Soon. There are some things you don't know about yet. You don't want to jump off with half the story, do you? Just report what you see there now. Don't mention Jacqui, don't you dare."

"Things I don't know about? What the hell's going on here, *partner*?"

"We'll talk soon as I've seen Carol, right before I see the police."

"You've been holding out."

"No, I haven't. It's something I've just learned. Hold your britches."

"Well, it better be damn good, because I'm going out of here in a blaze of glory, come hell or high water. You hear me, Wray?"

"I'll call you in a little while. It's worth waiting for, believe me."

That ought to hold her, I figured. You had to lie to your grandmother to function around here.

Jacqui, somehow, must have been worried about Steinmark spilling the beans to the police about his and Semieux's H.I.V. infection and their cover up of it, something that would open up to authorities the very possibility of an alternative suspect with something to gain by the murder, namely her. Why else would she kill the number one and only chump, the one she chose to take the fall for killing Semieux. But, still, who would she think they might suspect of killing Steinmark, himself, if not someone close to them both? Ethel Palmer's son-in-law, Bryan Barnette maybe? Was he close enough for double murder? Was he somehow involved in all this? Had Jacqui engaged him, flipped him to do the dirty work? Or just used him to take the fall for killing them both? After all, according to Ethel, he had made numerous passes at Semieux, who had threatened to tell Steinmark. Had Semieux told Steinmark, who had, in turn, threatened Barnette maybe? Had Barnette acted preemptively to such a threat? Had Jacqui killed Semieux, but Barnette killed Steinmark? A case might be made against him if he had no air-tight alibi. Better talk to him.

This case was still getting wider when it was suppose to be getting narrower. Concentrate on the local sources at hand first, talk to Carol, the police, look at security videos at SuperMart, the funeral videos of Bernie's, then see Barnette, if needed, I figured. If I could beat the cops to him.

I called Loo Sullivan, who would still be at the murder scene.

"She's out by the street, she can't hear us," Sullivan said of Ames.

"The thing we talked about. Have you told the police yet?"

"Just a minute." He stepped out of hearing range of the others on the scene. "No, I haven't. I'd like to keep it that way for a while. Even dead, he's still my client and he's not guilty, and I'd like to protect his name. Let me be the one who decides when, if it's okay, for the time being."

"Fine by me. Just checking with you."

"Wray, I need to ask you something straight out."

"Go ahead."

"You didn't know and hold anything that might have prevented this, did you?"

"Not a thing, Loo, and I never guessed this would happen."

"I just needed to hear it."

"That's okay. I'll give you a call tomorrow. Might have a client referral for you."

"Now you're talking."

Now let's go tell the boss.

38

When I entered her office, Carol Gambrell was limp at her desk and looked like the weight of a hundred years pulled at her eyes. I did not tell her of Steinmark's missing thirty-two pistol, or of Ethel's and Bernie's ongoing affair, but did tell her Ethel never mentioned her conflict with Jacqui over moving the team. Noble me. I filled her in on the rest and she, understandably, was devastated.

"My god, how could this have happened." It was not a question. "In a million years I wouldn't have believed this. I feel so—so foolish, so guilty. So stupid."

"You're going to have to understand, too, the police are going to know about the H.I.V. they both had, if they don't already. And with Steinmark dead, too, anybody with an interest of any kind in Semieux's death or estate, her contract, her *anything*, more than before, is automatically a suspect until ruled out. That means the police will be coming back to you, as well. Especially you. Though you had the personal alibi, they could figure you hired somebody. Just saying."

"That's what I'm afraid of."

"And you and Jacqui, and Bryan Barnette, are going to be under a microscope."

"Worse than that," she said, "is the feeling of betrayal. I never would have believed this of Jacqui. Anybody before her. And she was careless enough to leave a receipt for gas cans lying around her house? Isn't there a possibility someone could've planted the receipt on her, like the cans on John?"

"I don't know who it would be, or for what reason, unless it's you."

"Oh, God, don't say that."

"It would have to be someone with an interest in both their deaths. And nobody qualifies like Jacqui. She was hiding the H.I.V. problem in collusion with Steinmark. Sure, she loved T.J., in her own way, but she's also a very practical person and a winner. Cut your losses, move on. She comes from a family of mobsters, and her loving cousin, Dennis White, was still mobbed up, as the saying goes, until he was killed two days ago, almost certainly for this business with Jacqui and Semieux. It's not so big a stretch to see her doing this. It's her very cold-blooded value system.

"Steinmark was rolling over for the police to save his own hide. Hell, he was facing death, he had to, and she had to kill him for it. He might even have begun to suspect her of killing Semieux. Now that we know how it all got started, it leads only to one conclusion and one person. We just don't have any hard evidence. The police will search her property. Maybe they'll find something. I'm sure, though, the receipt's disappeared. If it hasn't, it will. Probably being burned right about now." I checked my watch.

"But, Wray, as you say, there's no real hard proof against her. So my dilemma is how do I treat her situation with the team, her contract, if she's not charged with anything?" She stopped. "Why am I asking you? I'm the one who has to deal with that. No PRing this thing away. I'll need to talk with my lawyers." She looked up at me as if she might have committed a sin. "Am I seeming too cold and business-like talking like this?"

"No, not at all. But I'm not finished either. I've got a couple more stops to make. Who knows, maybe something will turn up on the SuperMart security videos."

"Wray, what I asked you on the phone earlier about dropping everything and leaving. I didn't mean turn your back and let a murderer get away. I really believed it impossible of Jacqui and didn't want to cause her any problems. You understand that."

"It's not a problem with me."

"And as you promised, you won't mention it to anyone?"

"Mention what? But it's time we turned over what we have to the police. Jacqui needs to be stopped. Who knows what else, or *who* else, she might have on her mind." Certainly me, I figured. And that was not a stretch, either. "If the police focus on her, it's a lot less likely she'll be able to kill again, if she's leaning that way. She won't have the opportunity, makes it safer for everybody. Besides, it's illegal for us to withhold this."

"Yes. Yes, I see that. I just wish I had a crystal ball so I could see how all this is going to turn out. When I think of all that's gone into this, all the people who'll be hurt, the hope and opportunity—oh, God. I don't want to even think about it anymore today.

"I'm going home and sleep." She got up slowly from the gorilla's lap. "You do what you have to do with the police for both of us. Cooperate fully with them on my behalf. I'll be here tomorrow if they need to see me."

We went down to the parking lot together and stopped at Carol's car. There were no reporters to worry about, now that the funeral was over. They would be at Steinmark's place and downtown at the sheriff's.

"You know," Carol said, "I'm still finding it awfully hard to accept Jacqui's being involved in all this, in spite of what she kept from me. Other than the legality or the ethical consideration, I see her as doing it from a humane perspective, to help Toni Jean, to protect her and help the foundation. Can't see how it all went wrong. I don't know, maybe it's fatigue on my part.

"Anyway, thank you." She patted my arm. "Talk with me tomorrow." She got in her car and drove away.

Captain Crile and Sergeant Thomas had left for the night when I called downtown, but the detective lieutenant in charge of the night shift, who was also on the case, took my verbal statement when I got there. I promised to deliver a written copy in a day or two. I could tell by the lieutenant's reaction, his mannerisms and speech, and more by what he did not say or do, that most of what I was telling him was news to them, that Jacqui had not been a suspect. But she sure would be now.

On my way back to Ames' place at the beach, I considered Carol's suggestion of the possibility of someone planting the gas cans on Steinmark and the receipt for them on Jacqui. Again, why be dumb enough to keep such a receipt? You either discard something incriminating like that immediately, or put it where it can be found by authorities, but not on yourself. Of course—lot of 'of courses' here—Jacqui was arrogant enough to spit in the eye of convention and dare it to catch her. Had she been involved with yet another person, a third party maybe, who turned the tables on her at the last minute? Had Steinmark, himself, for whatever reason, killed Semieux and planted the receipt on Jacqui? *Naah*, too far out. But who in hell really knew? The way this bunch here acted anything was possible. Maybe the police could find it. But now that they knew what I knew, except for Steinmark's owning the thirty-two pistol, the pressure would be enormous on everyone in the murder environment, starting right now.

39

Ames was in the kitchen fixing a drink when I got in, just after midnight. Her perfume indicated she was planning to go out, not to bed. She had showered, her hair up, and was in the blue terry cloth bathrobe.

"You didn't call." Something akin to a frown on her face. "I was expecting you to call. I've been waiting."

"I'm tired of talking on the phone to people," I said, pulling off my shirt. "I've got phone ear. My cabbage leaves hurt, and the receiver is growing to the side of my head. All it needs is watering to take root. Besides, I prefer personal visits, keeps my fans happy. Like an autograph?"

She did not share my humor at this. Her look said, *"No, but I'd like to smack your fucking head sideways.* "You've talked to the police then."

"Just now, yeah."

She let out a breath of what seemed to be relief and her mood instantly began changing for the better. She glanced up at the ceiling as if it were heaven. "Great. Finally, the *story*. What'd the police say?"

"*He* said 'Thanks.'"

She handed me her glass. "Here, drink this. I've got to get out of here." She moved frantically to get herself dressed and as camera-ready as possible on short notice.

"What's the hurry?"

"Quite frankly, I'd like to be there when they bring her in. Right on camera." She reached for the phone. "Bernie? Wake up, meet me downtown at the sheriff's office, pronto. They're bringing in the killer any time now. That's right, the killer, damn it. Move it. And not a word to anybody." She hung up.

"And what if they don't bring her in until tomorrow sometime?"

"Then I'll be there. Won't I?"

"You'll fall asleep and be arrested as a homeless vagrant."

"Good, I'll be on the inside, maybe in the same cell with her, up close and personal."

"They won't necessarily arrest her or bring her in. They'll probably surprise her with a search warrant for her place and her two offices, and interview her there first."

Ames stopped abruptly. "You're right. I didn't think about that. God, I'd hate to be in the wrong place again." She redialed the phone. "Bernie? Go on downtown and wait for me. Shoot what comes in, if anything. I'm going out to another location, in case they go there first. Call me if anything turns up there. Ditto me. Keep the line open with me. Yes, damn it, I told you. Now move. And don't say a word, this is ours." She headed for the bathroom mirror.

I took off my shoes and casually took the drink down the hall after her. I leaned on the doorway and watched her doing her hair and makeup in record time. "There's possibly a third person involved we don't know about yet," I said.

"Third person? Like who?"

"I don't know, maybe Bryan Barnette."

"Bryan Barnette? Ethel Palmer's son-in-law, Bryan Barnette? Bull, he's not involved in this. Stay focused, Wray, like you always say, and let it happen."

"Why would she plant gas cans all over Steinmark so nobody could miss them, then implicate herself by keeping the purchase receipt for them so nobody could miss that either? Doesn't make sense."

"Why does she kill anybody in the first place? She's wacko, that's why. How I could've spent so much time with her this past year and not seen something is beyond me. I'm disappointed in myself for that. I just couldn't think in criminal ways, I guess. It'll never happen again, believe me.

"You know where I'll be," she said. She brushed by me and went up the hall. "Give me a call after you've looked at the disks. Might be something I can use. Maybe we can have lunch, if I can get a break."

"You don't eat lunch."

"You know." She stopped a second. "Maybe I'll break my own rule just this once and treat myself. I deserve it." She grabbed her gear bags and stepped back to me and patted my neck and squeezed gently. "I knew you could do it, Wray. I told them you could do it."

"Then you have a crystal ball."

"And you're going to get credit for it. The whole world is going to know Wray Larrick."

"I'd prefer not."

"Oh, bullshit, Wray. You'll relish the attention like I will. You'll pick your cases, set your fees high."

"I do that now. Don't mention my name, please. I insist."

"Later." She opened the door. "Keep your phone on and *call*." She closed the door behind her.

I held my drink and looked at the closed door a long moment as a multitude of indecipherable stimuli—tiny little messages—exploded in my brain like an electrical storm. Fatigue, probably, concerns about Ames blasting my name over the airwaves, something many would like, but not me. I did not relish at all the idea of being identified wherever I went for the next two years or more. It was bad for the element of surprise, something often important in my investigations, something I had done quite well so far without—the attention, I mean—not to mention the possibility—okay, I'll mention it anyway—of someone taking a shot at me because he knows who I am and what he suspects I might be up to. I could be shot for nothing because some guilty person sees and recognizes me around and gets paranoid. Not good. Not good at all.

I went out on the balcony and called Gil Russo.

"Christ, you ever do anything in the friggin' day time, besides go to funerals?" It was not unfriendly.
"Yeah, I like to wake up people who work the night shift."
"I believe it. What you got?"
"You heard about Steinmark, of course."
"Yeah, too bad. Van Autt again?"
"Afraid so. I just talked to the police, gave them what I had. Didn't mention your name, though."
"Good."
"They'll search her place today, for sure. Might be on their way there now, for all I know."
"Keep me out of it. I want my readers to know I have information. I just don't want them knowing where I get it."
"Sure."
"No go on anything else with Triserotech and Hesslar, either," he said. "I tried again, clammed right up."
"Yeah."
"Your girl's going with the story right now?"
"She's on her way to shadow the police, as we speak. Soon as they move, she'll be on the air with it."
"Then I'll run with it tomorrow."
"It's possible there's a third party involved here," I said.
"Uh-oh, the plot thickens. Any names?"
"Not yet. Male, a relative of one of the team's key employees. That's all I can say now. Don't mention it. I'll tell you after he's been grilled, unless it pops up on the screen first, which is likely now that Ames—Morgan—is out of the gate and running."
"Yeah, she's a real thoroughbred, too. She'll do great in this business if she hangs in, a natural. Too bad for you, though, huh?" He almost chuckled but wheezed instead.
"I hear that. She was pissed I didn't introduce you at the funeral."
"She ain't the only one."
I appreciated that.
"Look, thanks for your help on this thing. And I'm sorry about your boy, Dennis White."

"You're welcome, so am I. It's not your doing. Dennis was a half-honest crook who never took money from undeserving people who couldn't afford it. Until now. Maybe that's what got him killed, acting out of character. He never hurt a soul. But it was his game and he knew the rules."

"I hear that, too. Stay in touch."

"Long as I can, if you'll quit calling me at all hours of the night." He managed a weak laugh. "Anytime, Larrick." He hung up.

40

I got up at six the next morning, took a swim in the ocean and exercised a while, then showered and dressed by eight. Ames was still out, probably half asleep and still hanging on, but nothing was on the news, so I knew the police had not yet moved on Jacqui. I called Ames, who was posted in the parking lot at Jacqui's condo.

"She hasn't come out yet," Ames said. "And no sign of the police. Wonder what's keeping them?"

"Takes time to get a warrant. How're you holding up?"

"I'm holding okay. It's cloudy, so it helps, no sun in my eyes. The vultures are drifting in downtown, Bernie says. Somebody tipped somebody else that he was there, so, naturally, everybody figures it must be something. They just don't know where the hell I am, which confuses them and makes it just fine with me. Where are you?"

"Still at your place."

"Why don't you watch one of her offices for me, in case they go there first."

I looked at the phone.

"Thanks, but I'm not that bored. I have something I can do already. Maybe I could fetch you a snack and run it down, maybe get a pat on the head for it. Remember the expression about being nice to folks on the way up, you'll meet them coming down?"

"Then how about throwing my trench coat in your car, the light blue one in my bedroom closet. The rain is coming in about noon, I hear. Drop it off later, pretty please. I'm just down the street here, a mile. You go right by it."

"I know where it is. I'll drop it off shortly, on the way out."

I dropped off Ames' trench coat at Jacqui's parking lot. I pulled up beside her car, rolled down the window, and handed it over.

Ames' adrenaline was kicking in. She was in her car.

"She's not due at the gym until ten," she said of Jacqui. "I called Ethel. Bernie's following Crile around. He's conferring with one of the judges now, getting the search warrant, I guess. He'll call me when Crile and his people leave, tail them and let me know where they're going, so I can be Johnnie-on-the-damn-spot. What are you going to be doing?"

"I'll serve the refreshments."

"Smartass." She backed up a bit.

"Right now I'm going to look at Bernie's videos," I said.

"Good luck." She said it like she did not expect me to have any.

"Bryan Barnette ever hit on you?"

"Is this dumb question time? What do you think? Get off Barnette, he's nothing."

Sounded like an order to me, not a dismissive remark.

"Yeah, well, you're a big TV star, so you're probably right."

She grinned big. "Tune in and watch me work."

"Yes, here you go." Ethel Palmer handed me the disks. "Use this one over here, if you like." She pointed to the cubicle adjacent her desk area. "And, Wray, thanks for talking to Carol. She told me you covered for me."

"It's okay. Can you do me a favor? I need your son-in-law's phone numbers. He hasn't done anything, I know, but he might be able to help somehow."

"Sure." She wrote them down for me. "Can you talk to him without Lila knowing it? I'd appreciate it."

"Of course, long as he doesn't tell her himself."

I sensed the way Ethel was acting, especially how she kept looking at the door as if expecting Jacqui or the police, or both, to come through it at any second, that she already knew from Carol that Jacqui was under scrutiny for the murder of Semieux. Carol had to talk to somebody. Who better than Ethel? It was as if Ethel wished to burst loose and say something, like, *Hell, no, no way*, but she did not, she just looked at the door.

I walked around to the cubicle, sat at the desk, and inserted the first of two disks I had covering the Semieux funeral service, both at the church and the cemetery. I leaned back in the chair with the remote, sideway to the desk, elbow on it, hand under my chin, already feeling I would not see anything significant. These feelings I had did not always render something material, but they ate at me until I eliminated them, kind of like Chinese water torture, anything to stop the nagging drops on my forehead. Other times they produced something important. I punched the play button and watched from the eye of Bernie's camera.

I figured to run the whole disk through first for a general view, not look for anything in particular, and see what might pop up. Then I would study short sections of it by pausing or repeating each section and scrutinizing for detail. This is what I normally did when fortunate enough to have videos to work with, which was almost never. Don't look for anything, let it look for me first.

Except when resting, Bernie had held the camera the whole time. He had shot the outside before he and Ames moved inside the church, where they were stationed on the left wall, near the front opposite me, as I was on the right wall, also standing, trying not to be a seat hog. He had panned the inside numerous times as the church filled, focusing intermittently on persons and groups from various distances and angles. Most of the footage would never be used, but it would be there if anyone wanted or needed it.

Ames made a couple whispery comments into the mic, on camera. When the doors were shut and the service started, she remained silent but alert, all eyes, while Bernie continued rolling.

Everything went as I remembered it, nothing unusual or different. In fact, the air conditioning in the office here was making me sleepy. Then, after a while—*wait a minute*. I snapped to. What was that? "Rewind this thing," I mumbled. I sat up straight and ran the video back about thirty seconds of recorded time, then re-started it. Bo Hodge, one of Steinmark's two buddies, had a scowl on his face, like he was ready for a fight. At a funeral, no less. What an idiot. Not a bright guy anyway. Probably nobody noticed.

I ran it forward a minute or two further and caught Ames sleeping on the job. "Huh." I pushed the pause button and leaned back in the chair. That's odd, I thought, and sat there wondering about it. It was the point in the service when Maurice Fortier was addressing the congregation and was alluding to the murderer being among them, talking about Steinmark but not by name. *"And I believe that just as I'm standing here, so is the one who took her… "* he had said. At that point Bernie's camera was taking it all in. And as Maurice spoke those words every person in the church looked directly at John Steinmark, then back at Maurice. Then back and forth between the two of them, like crows on a fence. Everyone, that is, except one person—Ames, just a few feet ahead of Bernie. She looked directly at the floor, head tilted down, and remained that way until Maurice left the podium.

How odd. Why would she do that? As a reporter, her eyes should be taking in everything, not avoiding something. Those things must have been what was bothering me.

I ran out the videos. Nothing else. Ames falling down on the job. I would give her a guilt trip about her body language.

41

SuperMart's security director, George Ruhler, had left more than a two-weeks' run of disks to be picked up by the sheriff. I could view them here in the back office security room until then, but only in the presence of a security employee, in this case a young, clean-cut woman who was an off-duty Wilmington police officer in uniform.

"Fine, I appreciate it. I just need to see any footage of the register areas. I'm looking for somebody buying gas cans out to a few days before the murder," I said.

"Some are still frames," she said, "some are motion, depending on the camera and the location. They're marked, so you can pick what you want."

The young policewoman stayed busy watching the monitor for shoplifters.

I looked over the disk labels and picked one, inserted it and settled into the swivel chair for the long run. I could hear the thunder through the roof overhead as the rain was moving in. Within minutes, I felt like my eyes were growing together. I had started first at two days prior to the murder and worked toward it, skipping over most because it did not involve gas cans, except for a couple incidences which I noted. But occasionally the camera captured some bonehead trying to steal something, like a chicken, or a pair of shoes, or a watch, and I looked at it for its informative and comic entertainment value. There are some very stupid people in the world. Some of this stuff was funnier than the Three Stooges or the Little Rascals. I laughed at some of it and wished I had a bag of popcorn.

This went on for over two hours. Then I inserted the disk with which I would hit pay dirt.

It was a motion video, not a still, of the cash register area at the side exit of the store, at the lawn and garden center, with a vantage point of the whole area and everyone who went in and out. Ames had said Jacqui had in her home a gas can receipt from SuperMart, one which she, Ames, tried unsuccessfully to retrieve and, apparently, she was not lying.

The time on the recording was *8:48 p.m.*, the night of the murder. The weather that entire day had been rainy, heavy to light to misty, back and forth. The person who came to the register with the two cans was a female, slightly above average height, dressed in a long raincoat, probably gray or putty-colored, as the video was a bit blurry, a big, floppy, wide-brimmed hat, galoshes, tinted glasses, maybe prescription, not sure. She was wearing gloves and paid with cash. When the clerk offered her the receipt, the woman held open the bag and let her drop it in, presumably so as not to touch it and leave a print. The woman left the store walking right toward the exit where the camera was mounted. And I recognized her.

No one else would like recognize her, as covered up as she was, but I did. No question about it. It was Morgan Ames Dalton. You could dress up a hundred women of similar description, in masks, and put them in a lineup and I could pick her out every time. When you lived and loved with someone the way I had with her, you knew her. I paused the video.

Suddenly, I was nauseous. A sense of vertigo overcame me. I leaned forward, face buried in my hands, breathing deeply.

"Oh, jeeze. Son of a bitch. What have I done?" I said.

The young policewoman looked over at me.

"What's up? See anything?"

I was temporarily speechless.

"Hey, you okay?" she said.

I was biting my lip now, gritting my teeth, trying to hold back the emotion. My eyes glazed with water.

"Hey, you sure you're okay? You feeling alright?" She started to get up.

"I'm fine."

"You're white as a sheet, is what you are, look like you've seen a ghost."

I rubbed my mouth and slowly got up, completely dumbfounded.

Then the anger started creeping in, anger toward myself as much as anyone.

"What a world-class chump." I said it out loud to myself. Not in a million years would I have thought it.

"Hey, what is it? What'd you see?" The young policewoman slid her chair over and looked at the screen, on pause. The picture showed the three registers, two of them open, one with a man, the other a woman, Ames.

"Is that your suspect?" She touched the screen with her finger, pointing to the man.

"No. The other one."

"That's a woman. You're kidding, the woman?"

I ejected the disk and handed it to the officer. "This video is crucial to the T.J. Semieux murder investigation," I said. "Please make sure nothing happens to it, until the sheriff's people pick it up."

"Yeah, they're suppose to come by for it sometime today."

I left SuperMart and walked slowly to my car in the rain, not at all in a hurry or concerned at how wet I was. I did not have the spirit to run just now. I sat in the car, dripping, and called the sheriff's office. I identified myself and asked the deputy who answered to get a message to Captain Crile or Sergeant Thomas.

"Tell them there's a video at SuperMart, at Monkey Junction. The Wilmington officer there is holding it for them, one of the disks they're supposed to be picking up. I just looked at it and I.D.'d who I believe to be the murderer of Toni Jean Semieux and John Steinmark. I'll be in to see them later. There is no further danger to anyone else, I don't believe."

I remained in my car. The rain was now coming down in torrents and I could not have seen my way out of the place safely anyway. Here in the near-darkness, alone in a sea of automobiles, unable to see two feet outside, I felt the strongest sense of shame and embarrassment at being so gullible, so stupid as to let someone use me this way, to commit such horrendously murderous acts under my nose, while I had not a clue, or had not paid attention to it. How my feelings for Ames blinded me, one of the oldest stories in the world.

I had misread her. An understatement. That must have been the other part of her, I was sure, the part she never shared, the part I tried to get close to when we lived together, in order to close the circle and become one with her, but could not, that rare ability some humans have that allows them to commit the cold-blooded slaughter of others, for whatever reasons they elect, that I had mis-guessed as something wonderful and desirable—intriguing—but by which I wished now I had been hurt and disappointed earlier. I had found the center of her heart and there was nothing there.

In this case, she killed for the benefit of her career, no doubt. She was being fired after only two years, her promising career shot down before it took off. She needed a boost, one with punch. She knew the *Storms* people well and had access to their homes. That meant their property, including keys, vehicles, whatever. They trusted her with the particulars of their personal business. She discovered somehow Semieux had H.I.V. and would burn out soon, so it was not like she was stealing the woman's whole career, she was going to die anyway. And who would kill her but John Steinmark? Everybody knew their situation, and nobody was really crazy about him. Who would ever suspect the beautiful reporter—the *correspondent* she was going to be? She was just doing her job. It would not be in her interest for her star subject to die. But you could suspect someone with an insurable interest, in case Steinmark did not have one, like Carol, or, say, Jacqui. Jacqui who handed over Semieux's three million dollars to a mobbed-up Philadelphia lawyer and lied about it, a lawyer they find was her cousin. All the elements of a perfect crime were there. Add a few touches, like gas cans, the receipt, the right investigator—the one you know—throw a little scent on the trail of the hound dog, add a few ingredients to the recipe, and she had the opportunity for salvation in her own hands, the story of the year to break and report—to milk. All she had to do was act on it, and nobody ever accused her of being passive. Who in the world really cared, anyway, about a bunch of dumb jocks and all their money, their repulsive, vulgar wealth. Sure, she liked Toni Jean and Jacqui, and she really felt bad about how Toni Jean had suffered earlier in her life. But so had she, when her father deserted her mother, when her mother drank, and her husband smacked her around, after she left home and married. Somebody had to go, to be sacrificed for the larger good, and nobody else qualified. It was a nasty world, she must have figured in desperation, and she had as much right to survive in it as anyone. Kill Toni Jean, make it look like Jacqui had done it and was framing John, then kill John, too. A package. Put them all away and ride the story into the future. Who knows, maybe one day take over a major network anchor spot. Not such a far reach, just make it happen.

The rain slacked and I took a right out of the SuperMart parking lot toward Myrtle Grove for the shortcut back to the beach.

Why had I not picked up on it earlier? Sure, I had smelled a rat, even before leaving home, when she first called. But it was the wrong rat. Too much chicanery with these people, too many signals, peanut butter in the radar. Obviously, a perfect environment for something sinister. She knew I would come when she asked, because she knew I still cared for her. She first says strictly business, then she is in bed with me. Then she breaks it off altogether, permanently. Hell, it was already off permanently when she took the job and left two years ago. But I forgot that part. And it was her idea to bring me down here so she could direct the outcome of her plot. She knew when she mentioned Jacqui's being home in bed with menstrual cramps, I would jump on it and start asking around and compare cycles, because she knew I had read that study, how my mind worked. That would put me on Jacqui's trail, give the bloodhound a scent, give "Mr. Spooky Crime Analyst," she sometimes called me, a place to start.

But the thing that started the little bells ringing in the back of my head, the thing I paid no attention to when I should have, was Ames' contribution to my interpretation of the notes I copied from Jacqui's desk, the numerals and initials, the cursive and block writing forms, incongruously together on the same papers, some of it clearly Jacqui's hand, some of it maybe not. "Maybe," Ames had said, "and that's in case something Freudian is going on here, those things written in her regular hand are things she might be expected to write about, not be concerned with, but that the entries in block form are somehow alien to the cursive entries, don't belong with them, and she, sub-consciously or something, whatever, separates herself from the block part so as not to be identified or associated with it or reminded of it, of its impropriety or something." That is what she had said, suggested *impropriety*. And it had been an intelligent guess, too intelligent, I could see, intelligent like the firefighter who sets the fire so he can discover it and put it out—be the hero—or the murderer who kidnaps and kills his victim then joins the search, glad to help out. It was a part of her handing me the ball, quarterbacking the play. The block letters were hers.

And the sex. She had initiated our last episode but was emotionally detached and bordering on physically violent the whole time, and I had not given it enough thought. Something had been bothering her and I failed to read it. You think you are smart, then you wake up one day and you're dumb as hell.

The story of the gas cans receipt in Jacqui's place was too convenient and only bordered on reality, but I had let it slip by, too. Another lapse. And the police scanner she bought so she would not be scooped again would likely be found to have been purchased before the murder. That would be easy to track through the serial number and manufacturer. She had it and was listening to it so she would know when someone, most likely she, discovered and reported the murder scene, assuming the dispatcher's radio was used and, apparently, it was. She reported it, then heard it announced over the radio to the patrol units, then arrived late enough not to look like the first to know or be on the scene. The big story would come later for her.

And the reporting of the murders, cold, detached also, for someone who knew the victims. It would take a calculator, I had to admit, to count the things I missed, had flown right by me because they involved her. Anybody else, I would have been right on it. Had I been more alert, maybe Steinmark would be alive. And that, too, was something I would have to carry with me the rest of my life. *Damn her.*

I pulled up at Ames' apartment at the beach. The rain was at a light shower now. Instead of going in, I walked past the building on the sidewalk leading to the footbridge, which crossed the sand dune toward the beach itself. I stepped off the bridge part of the way across it and walked to the right a few yards on top of the dune, to the spot in the little depression, or valley as she called it, and had chosen as her safe and favorite place, where we had sat and drunk whisky the other night. "Found it the first night I was here," she had said. "Even the scavengers with their metal detectors don't walk through here," or words to the effect. I was soaked and stood there and looked down at where Ames' folding chair had been, then, avoiding the sand spurs as best I could, kneeled and began digging.

43

It was well after five p.m. and the rain was coming down hard, only a few diehard body boarders visible in the surf. I finished showering and put on dry clothes. I scoured the apartment for a receipt for Ames' purchase of the police scanner but found none. Figures. So I copied the information off the manufacturer's label, model and serial number, et cetera, so it could be traced to where it was bought, and I put it in the pocket of my trench coat. Then I called Ames.

"Right now I'm at the New Center office, in the hallway," she said. "The police are here. They're searching Jacqui's office, turning the place upside down. They're out at her condo, too, and over at the gym. Hell, she'll probably be arrested by sundown. Already called a lawyer, a guy named Jonah Smoakes, out of Charlotte. Ever hear of him? On his way down now."

"Why don't we have dinner," I said.

She must have looked at the phone.

"This thing is unfolding before my eyes, Wray. I'm working. Listen, I've got to go. I'll be downtown after they finish here, not long now. We can grab a bite and talk tonight, my treat. But it'll be late. And, Wray, thanks for everything. You've done a great job here, not to mention you're going to be three hundred-fifty thousand dollars richer when this blows over."

"Yeah, I'm going to enjoy the hell out of that money. But I really think it would be in your interest to take a break now and talk with me."

"Can't. Look—."

"Doesn't have to be anything fancy, a nice, quiet little place close to your job."

"Wray—?"

"Somewhere we can talk, have a little wine."

"What else but."

"And I can give you all the details of my investigation."

"You're not listening, I have to go."

"Then, for dessert, I'll tell you who really killed those two kids." Throw it out, see how she reacts.

There was a moment of silence. I could feel the tempo of her energy dropping from ballistic speed to a slug's crawl, a jolt of reality that might have made her heart thump hard enough to knock her off balance, maybe the way I felt when I saw her on the video with those damn gas cans.

"You still there?"

"We already know that." She was careful now. "And the police are finding it out right now, as we speak. They're putting things together, thanks to you."

"Jacqui didn't kill anybody, Ames, and you know that."

There was another, shorter, pause and I could visualize her jaw moving on the other end of the line.

"That's a lot of bullshit. I don't know anything of the sort. Listen, I've got to go. We'll talk tonight. You'll get some good press, I promise."

"Stop the story, Ames, it's all wrong."

She hung up.

44

When I finally got downtown the TV station's mobile satellite unit was parked on the street near the front door of the sheriff's office, big antennae on top, flood lights illuminating the area and glistening off wet pavement, generator running and wires going everywhere on the ground. The rain was at a drizzle again, but darker clouds were moving in. Other reporters, print and TV, were setting up, obviously having smelled the story, despite Ames' effort to hide it from them. But Ames, as an insider, had scooped them and was already on the air, clad in trench coat, a headset, a mic in one hand and an umbrella in the other, standing on the sidewalk, hair soaked, and talking into Bernie's tripod-mounted camera with a canopy over it.

I stood off to the side, out of the bright lights.

"..But authorities aren't saying what, if anything, they might've found in their search of coach Van Autt's property," Ames was saying to the world. "Certainly, as far as is known, the murder weapon has not been found and police seem to have little hope that it will be. And Van Autt has not made any statement to authorities that we're aware of.

"Van Autt did, however, when presented with the search warrant earlier today, immediately call Jonah Smoakes, a prominent Charlotte attorney and one of the *Storms*', now *Tee Jays*', legal representatives, though Smoakes, we're told, is a corporate and not a criminal attorney. He arrived at the airport just moments ago, and he and Van Autt are conferring now and are expected to meet with sheriff's detectives and agents of the State Bureau of Investigation regarding the murders. Whether or not she'll answer questions, we don't know that, but they are to meet.

"Ironically, Jim—," Ames continued, "and I say this knowing Jacqueline Van Autt has not been charged with anything, as yet—and we shouldn't make a rush to judgment—but the world which seems to be falling in on her right now is one very much of her own making. Never in a million years would I have believed coach Van Autt capable of anything like the brutal murders of Toni Jean Semieux and John Steinmark, or anybody for that matter. I still don't. I've known this woman for more than a year. I've lived and traveled with her and her team. I've respected her, and she's done so much for the sport of basketball. But on close inspection, it's true, as you mentioned earlier, one has to wonder. It was she, for instance, along with *Tee Jays* president and league co-founder, Carol Phillips Gambrell, who hired Wray Larrick, the private investigator who uncovered the very incriminating-looking evidence against her we're now reporting, and who, by the way, I've been personally associated with a number of years—using my relationship with him here—."

"Yes, and that, too," Jim said, breaking in through the headset, "And that being, among other things, to recap the fact she was—or I shouldn't say fact at this point—*alluded* to have been responsible for Semieux's three million dollars ending up in the hands of an attorney with mob connections, by the way, who, as it turns out, is her own cousin, a man she grew up with, that her family, in fact, has had ties to organized crime going back decades. Very convoluted web of relationships indeed."

"Yes. Dennis White. That and at least one illegal phone call to the top collegiate player in the country, maybe even the world, ostensibly a recruiting call on the sly, prior to the death of Semieux. The twenty-five million-dollars insurance payout and its correlation to the cost of moving the team to Wilmington something *she* wanted very badly, another thing. The fact that she lied to her own investigator, meaning Larrick, concerning her whereabouts on the night of the murder. The fact she hid from everyone, even Semieux herself, and Semieux's own parents, the fact that Toni Jean had H.I.V. and had gotten it from John Steinmark. The whole thing reeks of deception. When you consider all these things and the related matters, as well as the evidence which might still turn up with the police—and remember, they haven't shown their hand yet—you have to admit it paints a very complex, detailed and incriminating picture from which to extricate oneself, if you're Jacqueline Van Autt."

"It does indeed," Jim said. "And I trust you'll keep us apprised of developments as they occur."

"I certainly will, Jim, for our viewers. Reporting live from Wilmington, North Carolina, I'm Channel 8 special assignment correspondent Morgan Dalton."

I watched Ames drop the mic down to her side and let out a deep breath, like she was exhausted, and head for the van. "I'm taking a break, Bernie," she said.

Bernie stayed on watch under the canopy and talked with the other reporters and crews.

I followed Ames inside, apparently unnoticed by her, and closed the door behind me. It was a combination kitchenette-vanity area adjacent a sitting space, with a long counter and mirrors on one side.

Ames was shaking the water off her coat.

"Oh shit." She was startled at seeing me. "Don't do that, you scared the devil out of me." She put down the coat and began towel-drying her hair.

I did not speak at first, just stood there looking at her, my head and open coat dripping wet, hands in the pockets.

"So what's up, Wray?" She was facing the mirrors with the towel. "What are you doing here?"

"I'm working." I moved closer and leaned on the counter. "You know that."

"Well." She switched to a comb. "Not much else to do for you here, huh? Me either for that matter. Brilliant piece of work. Wray Larrick, Super Sleuth, strikes again."

I gave a little grin and took from my pocket a crystal figurine about eight inches tall, something I'd bought a few days earlier as a gift for her condo. I gently pushed it over to her.

"All along I'm watching you struggle for the story that'll save you," I said. "I find myself cheering for you. Then I realize that the whole time the story is really *you*."

"What's that?" She noticed the figurine from the corner of her eye, not stopping.

"Going away present."

"Oh, you leaving now?" She glanced over just a second.

"No, you are. It's a little present I picked up for you at the mall, my equivalent of the Oscar, you might say. Looks kind of like it."

She looked like she might have wanted to stop and respond, but did not, just kept combing and wiping.

"Best Leading Actor in a Double Homicide," I said.

That stopped her. She turned her head slowly. The look on her face told me she now believed the jig was up and the rest would be cat and mouse, because she knew my look, too. She resumed primping.

"You're mad. Go home, Wray. Take the money and run, just cash in and walk away, no complications. It's all over, quit dreaming."

"You know better than that, Ames. You know I'm not going to walk away from this."

"Well, I know there's nothing else for you to do here. I know *that*."

"You killed those two kids."

She turned quickly. "You're crazy as hell."

"You lured Semieux to that construction site and killed her."

Just then the door opened and Bernie stuck his head in.

"Jacqui and her lawyer are almost here, Morgue. Be here any second."

"Be right there." She was still staring at me.

Bernie closed the door.

Ames started her makeup.

"I I.D.'d you buying the gas cans. It's on the video. I can prove it."

"You're insane."

"You planted the receipt in Jacqui's place. It won't have your or Jacqui's prints on it, just the clerk's. Enright's buddy will testify you sent him in there for it."

She glanced over a split second, not too concerned.

"I can track the purchase of the police scanner. I'm certain it was bought before the murder of T.J., not after, like you told me. How else would you have known the police had discovered the murder scene? Nobody told you. All you had to do was tune in and not be the first to arrive there. Who'd suspect?"

Ames was slowing down now, watching me in the mirror as she primped.

"You're the only one in the environment, to my knowledge, who has no alibi," I said. "At least Jacqui was seen in her office prior to the first murder. That's something anyway. Where were you? Nobody gave you any thought. I know I didn't. Nobody asked you much of anything, the local reporter just reporting.

"You had access to their property, their keys, their private lives. You knew about the H.I.V. somehow, probably through Steinmark. That's why you had to kill him, to cover your trail. You had the opportunity and the motive. Walk down the beach from your place to his, shoot him, walk back."

"Motive? Bullshit." She turned to me again. "Jacqui's the only one around here with a motive. You proved that, Wray. *You* did."

"Almost. Couldn't have done it without you."

"I don't know where you get this crazy shit. Compare any phantom motive you could dream up that I might have against Jacqui's and what would you have? Doesn't take a genius to see that picture. A blind man could see it.

"No." She looked herself over in the mirror. "I think you've done a brilliant job, Wray. You're good. Too good to be true, in fact."

She moved closer to me and ran her hand through my wet hair

and down around my neck. "I know you love me," she said. "I even know the moment you fell in love with me. It was that time on your boat, off the point, the time we stayed out for two days, without coming in. Think I don't know that? Know you? And I loved you, too. We've shared some very wonderful times together, Wray. You'll always be very important to me. You helped make me stronger, gave me confidence. You helped me get here, where I am today. You've been—how does it go—part of the winds beneath my wings, you might say. The only question is, with all we have from the past and the rest of our lives in front of us, where do we go from here? What do we do with this moment? What do we make of it? *Hmm?*"

Her look was more seductive than I had ever seen it, but in her eyes this time I saw only a woman I did not know, one who frightened me. I leaned into her, closed my eyes and kissed her gently on the lips. I took her hand into mine and pulled it slowly away from my neck.

"You're a cold-blooded murderer, Ames, and I'm going to help put your beautiful ass away. And that's where we're going from here."

She backed away, surprised. "Go to hell. You have nothing. You can't prove a thing. I haven't *done* a thing."

Bernie knocked on the door, harder this time.

"They're pulling up now, Morgue. Let's go."

"*Coming.*" She put on her coat and grabbed her umbrella and headset.

"Don't go out there, Ames, in front of that camera again, in front of the whole world, and accuse Jacqui of killing those two people. We've both done enough to her. You won't like what'll happen."

"I guess I really don't have a choice, do I? If I don't go, I lose. If I do, I win, because you have nothing anyway, you know that. Tough choice. The police will laugh at you. *Mister Spooky Analyst*. Some lame story that wouldn't hold up in a kangaroo court. No evidence. Stop while you're ahead, don't embarrass yourself." She stopped at the door. "I'll miss you, Wray. I really will. Let's get together again sometime." She closed the door behind her.

I went outside and stood just inside the circle of light, next to Bernie, but outside the canopy a few feet from Ames. The rain was coming down harder now and thunder was rumbling close by, followed by bolts of lightning in the distance. All but the media had left. Jacqui and her attorney were pulling up, double-parked and being dropped off. Reporters and photographers descended on them. Bernie turned to capture the scene.

"...That's Van Autt and her attorney, Jonah Smoakes, who just pulled up," Ames was saying into the camera. "They're getting out of their car now, as you can see, and trying to work their way through the media gauntlet toward where I'm standing, here in the front of the entrance of the Law Enforcement building. I'll see if they might have a comment for us."

Just as Ames took her first step out to intercept Jacqui and Smoakes as they approached, I casually stepped into the light and pulled from my pocket the transparent zip-up plastic bag and held it out and up in front of me, looking straight at her. Inside the bag was another bag. And inside that was the thirty-two caliber Beretta pistol I dug out of the sand dune in the little valley that was her favorite spot. It caught her eye as she was sticking her mic out and saying, "Jacqui?—." And she froze, eyes locked on the bag.

Jacqui and Smoakes slowed, as if to speak to her, but Ames was paralyzed, unable to take her eyes off the pistol.

Bernie looked out from behind the camera. "Morgue?"

Jacqui and Smoakes gave a brief, curious look over their shoulders, and Smoakes seemed perhaps to make a connection, or maybe not. Then they proceeded inside, followed to the door by all others.

"Morgue," Bernie said, not noticing the bag and pistol. "What the hell—I don't know," he said into his mic to Jim.

Ames' mic went slowly to her side. Her umbrella came down. She stood dripping wet like a melting snowman. She looked at me and her whole story came to an end in her blank, catatonic-like expression.

Bernie ran to her. Jim spoke to her, confused.

I put the pistol back in my pocket and called Loo Sullivan, who was at his office.

"Loo? Wray Larrick here. I just found your boy's gun…Yeah…You going to be in your office a while?…The client referral I mentioned…Be right over."

I walked over to Bernie and Ames. Ames was still motionless and dripping wet, like the statue of a pop culture icon in a deserted public square.

"I've got it, Bernie." I put my arm around her shoulder. A sense of great sadness came over me.

"Come on, Ames, let's go. Your day in the sunshine just got rained out. No pun intended of course. I'll buy you a drink. Bernie? We'll talk to you later. I still owe you one."

I took her to my car for the short ride to Sullivan's office, leaving Bernie dumbfounded for the time being as to what was happening.

45

When I walked into the gym at the university late the next morning, practice had just ended and Jacqui was alone on the sideline, a foot up on the bench, writing on a clipboard.

"How about a little one-on-one." I approached her. Some ice breaker.

"Go to hell, Larrick." She didn't bother looking up.

I picked up a basketball and fumbled with it in my hands.

"You didn't make it any easier for me, Jacqui. I had to wade through a minefield of deceit and bullshit to do my job. I'm the one with the right to be pissed off here. So if your feelings got a little hurt, so what. I don't give a rat's ass, and I don't apologize. I just wanted to stop by and tell you that."

She looked at me as if I might be a little too brassy about it.

"Where was your car the night of the murder," I said, "when you were in the office looking at videos?"

"Across the street, behind the diner." She was still writing, not looking at me. "I left it there and walked over after I ate. The police know that, I've already told them."

"Yeah, well, I didn't know. Why didn't you tell me?"

"What difference does it make?"

"You made the call to Connie McCann against league rules."

"Yes, I did, but not the one on the phone bill. My problem, not yours."

"You've got an awfully hard head, you know it? Why didn't your period coincide with everyone else's? It should have, but at the time of the murder everybody shows up but you. I don't understand."

Her expression was sarcastic.

"Okay, it's a female thing," I said. "I'm not suppose to get it."

"And why didn't you catch onto Morgan sooner, so John might still be alive?" she said.

I stopped the ball. "That's a fair criticism and I have no answer for it."

"I'm sorry." She was looking at me now. "I didn't mean that."

"Sure you did, but it's alright."

"No, it's not. She betrayed us all and I'm sorry. I'll never understand."

"Two innocent people were murdered. There's a lot of feeling in the air."

I walked to the center of the court, dribbling the ball. I dropped it and let it bounce in front of me, and stretched my arms up and out. "But let's look at the positive side." I turned to her. "If it might be appropriate. Look at all this." I gestured around the gym. "Maurice and Edna rescued her from the burning, maddening hell she came from," I said of T.J., my voice echoing, "and brought her into a better world and gave her sanity. Then you took over and you made her into a champion. You led her out into the open, into the arena, in front of the greater world outside, and people jumped to their feet by the thousands and cheered her. I can hear them now." I picked up the ball and walked back over to her. "How many people ever experience that in their lives? How many yearn for it, and how many actually experience it?"

I handed her the ball. "You did that. You caused it. I've never done anything like that. I envy you. You create champions the world loves to see, that give hope and dreams to people who have none."

"If this is your attempt at a mutually admirable relationship, it won't work."

I ignored the remark. "All over the world, for years to come, young girls will play this game, unseen and unheard, and some of them lonely and unappreciated, and, yes, some of them brutalized. But they'll hear the distant roar of applause, the cheering for Toni Jean, and they'll seize it for their own, and it'll help them get through their personal hells, mostly because of your work. You're not such a hard-ass, Van Autt, you just need to lighten up."

I turned and walked away, then stopped, turning back. "By the way, I asked Carol, when it comes time to pay the reward—my bonus, you know—to give one hundred thousand of it to the Buddy Semieux Foundation in my sister's name. That's your hundred grand. Since you won't be managing money any longer, I felt safe doing that."

I turned back to the door and winced, realizing I should not have said that past part.

"You mean there's a heart in that carcass of yours?" she said. "You're a noble son of a bitch."

"Thank you." I headed for the door again.

"Wray?"

I cringed but kept going.

"Come see us play," she said.

I grinned in relief and gave a thumbs up back over my shoulder on the way out.

46

At two p.m., wearing tan khakis, topsiders, and a plum pullover shirt, I sat in an interview room on the second floor at the county jail waiting for Ames. It was a small room with a single table in the center and two chairs, one on each side. There was a large window looking into the hallway for the guard to see through. No windows to the outside.

Ames was brought in wearing a light blue jail jumpsuit, hair frazzled, looking worn and sleepless, like a scrub nurse getting off a double shift in a busy O.R. But she was still dazzling, which made it all the worse. A residual fragrance of her perfume remained. Chanel No. 5. Her breath was another matter, maybe Pier No. 7.

The petite female deputy guided her to the chair.

"Remain seated the whole time," the deputy said, "and keep your hands on the table where I can see them. No touching. I'll be just outside. Each of you is subject to search at any time." She closed the door behind her and stood in the hallway looking in.

"Wray." Ames' eyes moved around.

"Ames." It was awkward for a moment. "Sullivan asked me not to come by because I'm a hostile witness."

"I know. He told me I shouldn't talk to you." She looked around. "We're not wired for sound, are we?"

"I don't know. I doubt it."

(318)

"I like the shirt. You always looked good in that color. We're not suppose to talk about the charges."

I did not answer to that, and there was a pause as we sought to find one another's eyes, finally connecting. Her eyes glistened, a look of failure and hopelessness in her expression. "This is a hell of a situation. Isn't it?" she said.

"Yeah. Yeah, it is." I nodded.

"You hate me. Don't you?"

"No, Ames, I don't hate you."

"You pity me, which is just as bad."

"I don't understand you, Ames, is what it is. I thought I did, but I guess I was wrong."

"The grand jury's Monday. There'll be a bail hearing. Sullivan is going to try for bail. It'll be high, but if he can get it, will you help?"

"Bill Gates couldn't bail you out of here."

"I can't stand it in here. I've got to get out."

"It's only your first day, give it a chance."

"Easy for you to say. This is not a frigging day camp."

"You'll never get out of jail."

"You're a truckload of hope. We'll see. You going to testify against me?"

"Yes, I am. That's what a hostile witness does."

"Enthusiastically, no doubt."

"Articulately."

"I don't suppose it would do any good to ask you to reconsider."

"No, it wouldn't."

"But you do love me."

"Apples and oranges."

"Bullshit."

"Fingerprints were found on the gun and the bags. Small fingers, like a woman's. Why didn't you get rid of it after Steinmark? Who else were you going to shoot with it?"

She did not speak to that, but the message in her eyes was as clear as could be, and the feeling chilled me to the bone, not that much would have surprised me at this point. I nodded and gave a faint grin. Chumped again. I placed my hands flat down on the table top and slowly rose from the chair.

"I might have guessed," I said. "I don't know what made me think we had anything to talk about. I apologize for coming here, in event it might have raised your hopes. It won't happen again, I promise you that." I motioned for the deputy.

"Don't leave me here like this." She was trying not to break, a frightened, pathetic look on her face. "Help me. Please."

"If you've got a god, Ames, pray to it. Outside of that, Sullivan is your only chance. And it doesn't look good."

"I don't have anyone else, Wray, you know that. I can't stay here, I'll die here."

"I know. And I'm truly sorry for that."

The deputy opened the door for me.

"Will you be there for me? I mean, you know, if—?"

I stopped for a second, not looking back. "Yes. If you want."

Then I left with a sadness heavy enough to pull me through the concrete floor.

EPILOGUE

Morgan Ames Dalton was convicted of the premeditated murders of Toni Jean Semieux and John Steinmark and was sentenced to death. She was transferred to death row at Central Prison, in Raleigh, to await execution, while her appeals process began. Her attorney, Loomis J. Sullivan Jr., immediately appealed her conviction. Four months later she fired Sullivan and insisted there be no more appeals made on her behalf, death penalty opponents be damned. The state granted her wish and the court reset an execution date, and on August 26, the following year, she was walked into the chamber, strapped to a gurney and, with me among others watching through the little window, smiled at me and was put to death by lethal injection. Her last request was that her remains be cremated, her ashes be delivered to me and that I, if I would be so kind, take them out on my boat off Larrick Point, where the James River meets the Chesapeake Bay and the Atlantic Ocean, and sprinkle them on the water.

I did as she asked.

THE END

ABOUT THE AUTHOR

Native of Hampton Roads, Virginia, specifically Newport News and Hampton, on the lower peninsula. Attended Christopher Newport College of the College of William & Mary, after service in the U.S. Marine Corps, and graduated from Christopher Newport College in Political Science. Lived for years in the Carolinas, South and North. Officially retired from sales and marketing, and involved in small business development. Have a page at www.crimespace.com, and on Facebook(Dan Coleman, Always Something). Have had a Twitter account for years but don't know what to do with it. It might bite me.

Made in the USA
Lexington, KY
22 July 2017